Lake of Gulls

A novel by

Richard A. Gould

The Canadian Publishing Company

www.canadianpublishing.com

National Library of Canada Cataloguing in Publication Data

Gould, Richard, 1953-
    Lake of gulls / Richard Gould.

ISBN 0-9730933-0-7

    I. Title.

PS8563.O846L33 2002   C813'.54   C2002-
902027-1
PR9199.3.G6534L33 2002

The Canadian Publishing Company
C.P.C.
415 Bronson Lake Rd.
Mattawa, Ontario
P0H 1V0, Canada
www.canadianpublishing.com
info@canadianpublishing.com

Cover art and dessign: Richard Gould

The characters and events in this book are fictitious. Any similarity to real persons, living or dead is entirely coincidental and not intended by the author.

Printed and bound in Canada by University of Toronto Press.

Richard Allen Gould has published one previous work of fiction, Red Fox Road (0968035353), which was widely praised by critics and readers. His short stories have appeared in various collections and he has also published one historical non-fiction, Calvin Remembers, a history of the Amable du Fond and Mattawa river area in Ontario.

Gould was born in Toronto, Canada, and studied at York University before leaving for Europe in 1976. He continued his studies at Goethe University, and worked as a writer and broadcast journalist in Frankfurt, Germany. Gould returned to Canada in 1982 and lives on a remote, hundred-acre property in the dark forest of Northern Ontario.

Foreword

In July of 1973 - Friday, the 13th to be exact - 25 to 30 night shift workers at the UOP veneer plant were sent home early. A short while later, one of the two remaining men heard a "whoosh" and was barely able to keep ahead of the flames as he ran for the exit. On his way out, he jammed a piece of wood into the steam whistle causing it to howl in the dark Algonquin forest.

Under a flame-stained sky, Kiosk residents stumbled into the night. For five years, they had fought to keep the homes they had owned since the 1930's and this fire would work against them. The government had decided that this area should be a wilderness park and although the town was only a few kilometres inside the Algonquin Park boundary - a park that is thousands of square kilometres in size - it should be removed.

The characters and organizations in this novel are fictional, but it is in this town that this story takes place. Little of the town remains - a few dusty roads run between clumps of hazel and alder and occasionally, a concrete sidewalk leading to a non-existent front door - but many original residents still live in neighbouring areas. It is not uncommon to see tears when a Kiosk resident talks about the past.

I am grateful for stories told by many Kiosk residents. There are too many to name individually, but some deserve special mention. They are: Rick Bergeron, Claire Ferron, Lorraine Montreuil, Laurie, Sharon and Bruce Maxwell, Thora and Henry Wunsch, Fred and Doris Maxwell, Glenda Heath, Hubert Carruthers, Marilyn Foster, Bruno Lagace, Velma and Walter Beckett, Alan Strike QC., Jack Lockhart, and Dick Tafel QC.

I would also like to thank The Right Honourable Gordon Campbell, (BC), Alice Willems, (Special Assistant to the Minister of Cultural Affairs); Carmen Cross, Terry Dokis, Lawrence McLeod, Vicky Wunsch, Jo Hutchinson, Carole Becket, Isabel Labreche, Constable Todd Proulx, Constable John Kuehni, Sgt. Easton, Colin Sullivan, Jessica Boyle, Knowlton Potter, Denis Chippa (MCTV), Yura Monestime (MCTV), Mike Monahan, Paul Moskal, and Cathy Baril.

Special thanks to Maria Kornacki, Dr. John Kooistra (CEO of Catchfire Press), David Kent (CEO Harper Collins Publishers Ltd.), and Doug and Paul Mackey (Owners, Pastforward Productions). Doug and Paul Mackey will soon release a history of the town of Kiosk.

For Charlotte, Jason, and Chris.

"As long as a people is compelled to obey, and obeys,
it does well:
as soon as it can shake off the yoke, and shakes it off,
it does still better;
for regaining its liberty by the same right as took it away,
either it is justified in resuming it,
or there was not justification for those who took it away."

Jean Jacques Rousseau, 1712 -1778

1. Autumn Last

Patrick ran his fingers through his hair as the dry grass at his feet twisted and bent in the wind. A cool breeze touched his face, carrying the dry, fruity scent of autumn, and a memory of children's voices echoing across the water floated in the distance.

The yard before him was wild and unkempt. Had it not been for the concrete sidewalk leading from the road and ending at nothing, it would have been difficult to tell that this had once been a manicured lawn. He could still picture it - the colourful flower garden with the border of carefully selected rocks; the neat lawn with the picket fence on one side; and the granite outcropping that served as a parking lot for his toy cars. He could smell the sweet tangy aroma of drying grass; he could almost hear the raspy mechanical whir of a hand-pushed lawnmower.

"Excuse me!" The voice came from somewhere behind him. Patrick didn't turn. He had seen the park official earlier, and had hoped to avoid him. He took two steps through the weeds and brittle stalks of grass.

"Sir! Is this your vehicle?"

Again, he ignored the voice. Just go away, he thought. He exhaled unsteadily and looked toward what should have been his house. There was nothing. For a moment, he thought he saw the ghost of the building - a shimmering reminder of what had been - but it disappeared, evaporated like an early morning mist on a sunny day.

The dry grass behind him rustled again. The park official was walking closer. "Sir? Is this your vehicle parked on the road?"

Patrick, a tall man with square shoulders and imposing
build, turned. "Yes," he said, as he looked down at the ground.

"Well, you can't park here, and you have to put your camping permit on the dash." Course weeds clung to the man's brown
uniform pants as he took another step. "You do have a day-pass,
don't you?"

Patrick smiled and shook his head. "I used to live here." He
waved his hand backward toward the house that no longer existed.

"Doesn't matter. You still need to buy a day-pass if you want
to be here."

Patrick's cheeks flushed. The idea that he had to buy a pass
to visit his place of birth seemed unreasonable. "I . . . I'm not going
camping. I . . ."

"You're still in the park."

The cords stood out on Patrick's neck, but his tone was
calm. "Yes, sir."

The park official took off his hat and waved it toward the
car. "As I said, you can't park there either. You'll have to park in the
designated area. I don't have a problem with you snooping around,
but you can't leave your car there."

Snooping? He silently mouthed the word. He closed his
eyes and fought for control. "Yeah, okay," he said.

The warden left and Pat turned. So much of his young life
was tied to this bushy, scraggly field. Just up the street was the
school and not too far away, the house of his girlfriend. A few steps
from where he now stood, his hand would have touched the blue
wooden door that gave entrance to his parent's home. It had been
full of laughter, alive with his mother's Irish accented singing, and
redolent with the smells of a country kitchen.

The house had not burned; there were no charred remains;
it had not collapsed, there was neither a stone, nor a board, nor a
roof shingle left on the ground. It had been erased as if some painter
had decided that it didn't fit in with the background and painted it
out.

It had been a small frame house with three windows facing
Kioshkokwi Lake. His bedroom had been downstairs, across from
the bathroom, and from its windows, he could see the Amable du
Fond River flowing out of the lake. It was a big river, and as a child

he had listened to it surge over the weir and under the bridge. The weir was gone now, making the lake lower, but the water still rushed over the bed of stones on its way to the Mattawa and then the Ottawa Rivers.

On the lake, he saw a canoe, its two occupants working hard against the wind, fighting whitecaps. It wasn't a stormy day, but it did not take much to get Kioshkokwi angry. One minute it was a smooth blue layer of silk, the next it was a turbulent black tempest of cresting, foaming white caps.

Buried beneath the sound of the grasshoppers and crickets, he thought he heard the distant voices of children. They were barely audible, haunting, almost frightening.

He looked down at the dry grass, its rhythmic movement hypnotic. He wanted to escape the ghosts around him - Kenny, Uncle Roy, Andre, Suzette and all the others whose spirits still ran, yelled, and laughed through the yards and streets of the town. The park official had walked away, but in the silence, Patrick was still not alone.

He turned his attention to the Amable du Fond, half expecting to see buildings, fishermen, and children playing, but there was nothing. It was just a desolate expanse of scrub, high grass and creeping alders.

How could it happen? How could an entire town disappear? A school, a post office, a large sawmill, almost a hundred homes - all gone. This was not a ghost town, with vacant houses and empty stores; this was a void. There was nothing except the odd driveway or path leading to a front door that no longer existed. Even the train tracks were gone. How was it possible? He placed his hand over his forehead and then ran it down over his eyes, squeezing them shut.

He remembered the warden telling him he needed to buy a pass to be here! The thought made him angry, and he wanted to protest, but where would he start? Whom would he fight?

He had lost touch with his two best childhood friends and he was on his way to see one of them, Kenny Campbell, but he had no idea what had happened to Suzette Labelle. Suzette had been more than a friend; she had been his first love - the first to cause his cheeks to flush and his heart to beat fast. He remembered her shiny, dark hair, her soft skin, her moist lips and he almost remembered the sensation of kissing her. Stop! he thought. He shouldn't go there. It was part of something else, something lost and gone.

Just as life had been taking shape, Patrick had been removed from the town and, in the years that followed, he hadn't so much as written a letter. All connections had been lost.

Standing here, breathing in the air, sensing the ghosts of this ghost town, he felt something tug at him. He kicked at the ground and watched the dust rise and float off across the yard. It slowly disappeared. Stop, he thought again. It was time to move on.

He slammed the door of the two-year-old Taurus, started the engine, and yanked the gearshift selector into drive. The tires dug into the dirt and made a sound like ripping cardboard.

At the end of the short road, he hit the brakes and turned. He was near the empty field that had once been the school yard, and in the distance, some fencing, which had served as the backstop for a baseball diamond, still remained. He could almost hear the frantic, happy screams of children chasing each other. Pursing his lips, he drove on and then stopped by what should have been Suzette's house. It was another vacant lot. The lacy tops of some asparagus plants bent in the wind - many people had asparagus in their gardens - but nothing else remained to show this had once been the house of his girlfriend.

He closed his eyes and tried to picture her. He could remember her long dark hair and he could almost see her face, but the complete essence of her was difficult to fix. He remembered her smile - her unconditional joy - and he felt a warm sensation spread across his chest.

He drove further, remembering every house. Every once in a while, he glimpsed a ghost walking the dusty road or standing in a yard, but when he looked closer, it drifted and disappeared like the misty shapes on the lake on an autumn morning.

He slowed as he crossed what used to be the train tracks. The rails and ties had been removed and there was nothing left but the broken brown slag and the smell of creosote.

He turned parallel to the lake, stopped and got out. The creosote smell was gone, replaced by the sweet northern aroma of cedar, pine, and water.

A reflection of sunlight caught his attention and he turned to see a couple of Yurts under construction. Each one had a pressure-treated deck, a barbeque pit, and a large black solar panel mounted on a stubby metal post. He looked through a screened window. The units were not yet in use, but were all very modern. They would attract the richer tourists - the people who had chased him and his family out of the town in the first place. And this was only the start.

His first stop in Kiosk had been to the park office, and there, a young female park employee had told him about all the wonderful plans for the future of Kiosk. Office buildings, new campgrounds, comfort stations, flush toilets, new parking lots, there would even be cabins for people to rent. As Pat thought about the enthusiasm of the young woman's explanation, he kicked the wall. The hollow sound echoed across the lake.

He shook his head. The Ministry of Natural Resources, the government agency responsible for maintaining Algonquin Park, was looking for ways to generate revenue. First, it chased out all the residents, saying the park had to be preserved in a wilderness state. Now that everyone was gone, it was building for profit. It was that typical double standard in which the poor had to suffer for the pleasure of the rich.

He returned to his car and drove away. As he rounded the last corner that would take him in the direction of the highway, he hammered the accelerator to the floor. The tires dug into the sand and hopped wildly as the car swerved right and left. He was doing 50 kilometres per hour as the tire chirped on the cold-top surface of Highway 630.

A couple of hours later, approaching Sudbury, Patrick was surprised to see that the area he remembered as a moonscape was now a little more green. The transition was not complete and the huge fields of slag were still visible, but trees and small bushes were evident. A decade ago, this had been an area of bleak bare mining slag.

It was a cruel irony that Kenny Campbell had been moved to this environment. He had been so in love with the forest and the lakes and he had been pulled away from them and placed in an acidic wasteland. Why had he stayed so long? Certainly, in all those years, an opportunity should have presented itself.

Finding Kenny again had been an accident. Patrick had leased his car from the King City dealership in which he worked, but the lease had been handled by Grey Owl Leasing out of Sudbury. He had driven the car for almost two years before Kenny - or 'Ken' as he was calling himself - had spotted his name on the terminating contract.

King City Fine Cars ran their leases though a number of credit companies and they used Grey Owl Leasing only occasionally. The leasing company was small, but willing to handle the difficult credit cases - bankrupts, skips - and, occasionally it offered special rates to dealership employees as a way of encouraging new business.

On the telephone, Ken had called him 'Patty', a name he hadn't heard in decades. Pat had decided to take some time off, visit Ken - it was hard not to think of him as 'Kenny' - and stop at Kiosk on the way. He now wished he had bypassed the town, which had awakened memories he would have preferred to leave dormant.

He zoomed past the Science Centre, drove a few more kilometres, and turned into a suburban subdivision. On Ken's street, he found the house number on a rectangular plastic sign and turned into the driveway. The house was a nondescript bungalow with a postage-stamp lawn and it didn't seem like the kind of place Kenny would choose. The pickup with the rough, metal boat rack was the only thing that was indicative of the outdoorsman that Kenny had once been.

The yard was plain, with a small fence and no landscaping - just a patch of grass. The house was red brick with a cracked, concrete veranda and a dark, shingled roof. White sheer curtains hung in the front window. It was a house like all others on the street, with little individuality.

He stretched, walked to the side door, and rang the bell. Kenny took a few moments to respond. He opened the door from the top of the stairs and then moved back down the hall. "Come in."

Patrick entered cautiously, pulling the door closed behind him. He walked up the half-flight of stairs, through the hallway, and into the living room. Kenny was at the stove in the kitchen. He was wearing white socks, blue jeans, and a blue golf shirt. His clothes were clean, but wrinkled and his hair was thinner, finer, and sun-bleached. He seemed to be in good shape - there was no belly to speak off - but there was something missing, something absent.

Pat looked around the house curiously. The living room was cluttered. There were mismatched canvas chairs, two wooden tables, and outdoors items strewn everywhere. Although the house looked plain from the outside, the inside was decidedly bohemian. It was not the house of a middle-class Canadian family; it almost seemed to be an extention of Kenny's bedroom in Kiosk.

"Can I get you something?" Ken stirred a pot with a wooden spoon.

Pat retreated from his thoughts. "Cold beer would be nice."

"Sure. Gimme a minute. I can't let this stuff stick. Hungry?"

Pat nodded. "I could eat."

Across the hall, he could see into a small bedroom. On the wall was a locked, gun rack containing a couple of .22's, a couple of shotguns, a high-powered rifle with a scope, and a beautiful Winchester 30.30. The Winchester would be the kind of rifle he would expect Kenny to own. Although it didn't have great range, it was a wonderful rifle for walking through dense bush. Ken would not be the sort of hunter who would sit in a blind waiting for a driven animal; he would walk the bush alone. "You do much hunting?"

"Not too much anymore. I only hunt if I'm going to eat what I kill, and there's too much meat on a deer or a moose."

Pat looked at a topographical map pinned to the wall. It was covered in post it notes. "So you live here by yourself?" The question was rhetorical.

Kenny dished out food. "Yup."

A longbow hung from a hook and two canoe paddles were tucked behind a table. On another table was a box of pencils and charcoal and a worn, but closed, sketchpad. "You said you were married, though?"

"Yup. Was." Heavy glass bowls banged together. Kenny walked into the room, moved a bunch of items from a wooden kitchen table, and dropped the bowls of stew. He returned to the kitchen and came back with a coffee mug and a glass of beer.

"You look good, Kenny . . . healthy."

"Yeah, well, there's that."

"So did you and your wife live here?"

"Nope. Not here."

Pat was used to drinking out of the bottle, but he picked up the glass and smiled. "Thanks."

Ken nodded, turned his chair sideways, stretched his feet out, and held his bowl in his hand. "You haven't changed much either," he said, swallowing a mouthful of hot stew.

"I only wish that were true . . . but thanks." Pat laughed and was surprised by the sound of his own voice. It was deep and full, much different from the last time he had talked to Kenny in person. Ken's voice was still soft and quiet by comparison. "A lot has happened in all those years."

"You still haven't cut your hair," Kenny said laughing.

"Yeah, well, I guess some things don't change." Pat looked down at the floor as he ran his hand through the hair, sweeping it behind his ear. The length of his hair was a sensitive issue for him. His ex girlfriend had been constantly after him to conform to current shorter trends, but somehow, this seemed like his last protest. He had conformed in so many ways, and cutting his hair short, would be the final step in a loss of self.

Ken said, "You know, I was really surprised to hear you were selling cars. I mean . . . I had trouble picturing that."

"Well, I have trouble picturing it too, sometimes. It's not a job I'd wish on anybody else, I'll tell ya."

"Whatever happened? I expected to hear that you were a famous musician or something."

"Well, you do what you gotta do, I guess." Pat drank again and looked at Kenny. "So you're a banker. I kinda expected a suit and a pot belly. You've kept in shape."

Ken laughed. "Not from my job. I do a lot of camping and fishing. Every chance I get, I'm out somewhere."

"Yeah, well you always were the 'nature-boy'."

"I suppose." Kenny fidgeted with a pocket knife on the table. "It keeps me sane. I know some great fishing holes. I'd love to show you."

Pat tucked his bottom lip under his top teeth. Although he had already agreed on the phone, he was not that fussy on camping and he had little desire to go back to Kiosk. "Yeah. And I guess you will." He finished his beer, looked at the empty glass, and then looked at Ken. "I'll be right back. I brought a case of beer with me."

"Sit down, sit down. Yours will be warm. I'll get one from the fridge."

"It was a long drive . . . and this time, skip the glass." As Kenny handed him a bottle, Pat continued to speak. "I stopped at Kiosk on the way here."

"Looks different doesn't it?"

"It was hard to tell where the houses had been. I just stood there looking at all these sidewalks going nowhere . . . it bothered me."

"It looks smaller too, don't you think?"

Pat nodded. "Everything we grew up with is gone. The houses, the rec. centre, the school." He took a long drink from his bottle before he continued. "You know, I thought I could hear children playing. I expected to see some kids running through the field, playing baseball. Damn, it was kind of spooky."

"You're not the only one who feels that way. I've talked to a lot of people. They have a Kiosk reunion every year, but it's never held on site. They usually meet in the Mattawa Golf and Country Club because most of them don't like to go back. It feels too weird. I've had a couple of people tell me that they choke up and cry every time they're back in the town."

"How did they clean it up so fast?"

"Well . . . it wasn't that fast."

Pat looked at Kenny sideways. "What're you talking about? Don't you remember? There had to be at least 80 houses . . . and the church . . . the school, the bunk houses, the stores and the mill . . . gee, the mill was huge!"

"Most of the mill burned - only the water tower remained - you know that. Five years ago, there were only five or six families still left and all the other houses were gone. They wanted the place empty."

Pat grunted. "It's bullshit, you know."

"The government never cared about people's homes. They think that people can just move from place to place. I don't think they want the population to be tied to the land. They want everyone to belong to a kind of national, mobile workforce."

"I guess the favours are always given to the people with the most influence. No one gives a shit about the people who pioneered the land."

Ken broke into laughter. "You know what we sound like? We sound like your uncle Roy and our two dads sitting on the porch. I haven't thought about them for years, but I remember listening to them from my room. They were always talking about how they were being ripped off . . . how the government was to blame."

"Well . . . maybe they were right." Pat finished his beer and stood. "I'll be right back." He returned with his own case of beer, ripped it open and handed a few bottles to Ken to put in the fridge. He took one of the cold ones that Ken offered in return.

"Regardless of the politics," continued Pat, "it was pretty disturbing to see Kiosk the way it is. The last time I saw it, it was alive, and today there was nothing. Just dry grass, bits of concrete, and dusty roads. It gave me the creeps."

"Yeah, I guess it would if you saw the change all at once. I've gone back from time to time, so I've seen the changes gradually. Not too long ago, a construction company came in and picked up all the rail lines and the telephone wires. Pretty soon, you won't be able to tell that anyone ever lived there."

"Well, that's what they said they wanted, but it really bugs me to see what they're doing now."

"What's that?"

"Don't you know?" Pat perked up and sat forward on his chair. "They've put up some Yurts."

Ken raised an eyebrow.

"They're sort of half cabin, half tent. They have canvas walls, but they're built on a wooden floor."

Ken nodded.

"You should see them! They've got solar panels, electric outlets . . . everything."

Ken was about to speak, but Pat continued, cutting him off.

"That's not all! I got chatting with the girl in the ranger station and she showed me a draft of the future plan for the park. They hired a couple of architects and drew up a five-year plan. They're gonna put up an office building - a headquarters - for the MNR just where the road comes into town."

"And she told you this?"

"Sure." Pat was surprised by Ken's disbelief. He was surprised that Ken's reaction was the same as his had been. The girl had been so excited by the prospect of growth. "That's not all," he said. "They're putting in a campground where the school ground and our house used to be and they're going to build four replicas of the Ranger Cabin."

"Are you serious?"

"Absolutely. She showed me."

"And where are they going to put the cabins?"

"Three, where they put the yurts - on the old mill site - and one by the river just past the bridge."

Ken scowled. "They won't get away with it. Too many people will protest."

Pat laughed. "Yeah, right! They've already got it started with the yurts. It's supposed to be a wilderness park, but now that everyone's gone, they'll do what they want. They're turning it into a resort for the rich." Pat took another drink.

Ken sank back in his chair. "The bastards waited till the leases were up and then started to build."

"The leases expired a few years ago didn't they?"

"Yup. If anyone had stayed, they would have been forced out. Some of the people with cottages further down the lake had their leases extended to 2017, but the government's still trying to get them out too."

"Yeah? How?"

"Just pestering them . . . coming up with regulations and lots of warnings . . . raising the rent. I know a guy down by Daventry. His rent went from $100 to over $2,000 per year."

Pat shrugged. "I guess if you got the money, you can afford it." He took a long drink of beer. "Someone should do something." The sibilance in his voice was becoming noticeable.

"There's nothing to do; that's why I go fishing." Ken jumped to his feet suddenly and then stopped. He looked unsure of what he was going to do next. The frown he was wearing turned slowly into a grin. "Come on, let's get your stuff. Tomorrow I'll take you to places where the fish are so big, you need steel line to reel 'em in."

Pat rose reluctantly and followed Kenny, beer bottle in hand.

Patrick helped Kenny get the boat off the truck and winced as the muscles strained in his lower back. He walked down the concrete ramp, dropped the canoe in the water, and returned to the truck for more supplies.

They were beside the Ranger Station standing in a large, gravel parking lot, in which many canoeists left their cars and trucks. To the east was a camping area with vehicle access. Each spot had a fire pit with a metal rack, and four yellow stakes in the mowed grass to show the boundaries. Some campsites even had electrical hook-ups. There was a swimming area, picnic area, and even a bathroom with a flush toilet, a sink, and running water.

To get to the Ranger Station it had been necessary to drive through town and Pat had suggested they stop and look at the new cabins. Ken had refused, saying they didn't have time and he drove past without looking right or left.

The ranger station was about a half mile east of the town and it now had the nicest beach in the area. Many years ago, some of the older children had cleared the area when they could no longer dive off the company dock by the mill. They cleaned up the beach, cut the grass and dragged away the deadheads. For many years, the beaches resonated with laughter as children swam and played.

Now it was a provincial park campsite, visited primarily by serious canoeists with expensive gear and top-of-the-line canoes. A short distance away, Pat watched four young men loading their two Kevlar canoes for what looked to be a long trip. Although there were electrical sites for tents and trailers, and a concrete boat launch for the small motor boats, the four canoeists acted as if they were embarking on an expedition into a lost and unmapped wilderness. Their gear was brightly coloured, state-of-the-art, and obviously expensive. One camper played with a digital camera, taking pictures of one of his friends who was installing a nylon cover over the canoe.

Patrick threw Ken's tent, a dirty, faded, blue bundle with old-fashioned, aluminium poles, into the canoe. Ken was obviously not interested in expensive, designer gear and Pat watched as he hefted his backpack, an old canvas affair that had been to some very remote spots, and dropped it into the canoe.

Their food was in another canvas bag, which Pat placed more carefully. They were not allowed to bring glass bottles into the park - even if they were willing to bring them out again - so before leaving Kenny's house, Pat filled two plastic bottles with rum. He didn't want these to get cracked or damaged.

Ken had a season's pass to the park, but it was still necessary to purchase an interior pass. Patrick waited outside with the canoe as Ken went into the station. He did not want to get into another discussion with the enthusiastic woman he had met the other day.

"You going far?" asked one of the young men putting the finishing touches on his canoe He was grinning slightly, his chubby face round like a cherub.

"Nope. Just doing some fishing." Pat lit a small cigar and puffed it a few times.

"Oh, I see," said the young man chuckling and nodding his head.

"Looks like you and your friends are going on quite a trip." Pat's smile curled.

"Two weeks!" The young man's head went up and down like a bobber in the water. "Going down to Brent and all along the Petawawa."

Pat took a drag of his cigar and exhaled. A trip to Brent was a one day journey and these fellows were outfitted as if they were going to circumnavigate the park. "You sure you got enough gear?"

Another of the canoeists caught the sarcasm. He too was heavy-set and his hair was bleached and gelled. "We take gear that's low-impact. We don't want to damage the environment."

Patrick looked at the man and chuckled. "Maybe you damage it just by being there."

Tension hung in the air. The heavyset man was silent for a moment and he looked disdainfully at Pat's canoe. "Look who's talking."

Pat grinned again. "Well, you just have a good trip and don't feed any bears."

After another moment of silence, the canoeist with the camera said, simply, "Yeah. Thanks." Pat walked away.

Ken returned with the numbered, yellow plastic garbage bag, and helped Pat push the canoe further away from the rocky shore. With the weight of the packs and tent, it scraped noisily and Pat could imagine the four young men wincing at the sound. They would probably walk through leach infested mud rather than risk scratching their canoes.

The lake was calm as they paddled toward Wolf's Bay, and Patrick lost himself in the gently rolling surface. He had forgotten how big Kioshkokwi was. It was one thing to see it on a canoe map; it was another to be surrounded by its mass. It was six miles, or ten kilometres, from east to west and in the northwest corner, Wolf's Bay stretched two-and-a-half miles to the north. They were travelling toward Manitou Lake and they would have to cross four miles of water.

The water flowed across Pat's hand near the blade of the paddle and it felt warm and substantive. It was only warm at the surface, he reminded himself. A few feet down, it would be much colder. The lake was rumoured to be bottomless and he remembered hearing about people who drowned and then never surfaced.

As he continued to paddle, he could feel the burn in his shoulder and arm muscles. They still had a long way to go and the stinging pain reminded him how unaccustomed to exercise he had become. Ken wanted to camp on Manitou Lake, but Pat doubted he could make it. He was out of shape.

The sun rose higher in the sky, a breeze played over the lake, and small waves formed. Nothing dangerous, just ripples in the giant surface, but they started to push the bow of the canoe to the south. Pat knew that Ken had to work hard to correct for the wind and he was glad he was not in the stern. "Do you want me to switch sides?"

"No. I'm fine."

Pat continued to paddle, feeling a knot starting to form in his shoulder. "Is there still a beach at Scott's point?" The shore of Kioshkokwi was rocky and bordered by coniferous forest, but there were a few sandy spots. Most of these were covered with dead trees and driftwood, but Scott's point had been kept clean. It was only a

mile away and would be a nice place to camp, but most importantly, since it was so close, if they stopped there he would not have to
tell Ken he didn't have the strength to paddle all the way to
Manitou.

"Still there, but the cabin's gone. Someone burned it . . . or
tore it down. I don't know which."

"Should we have a look?"

"You can't fish from there. It's too shallow."

Pat wasn't interested in fishing. He was sweating with exertion, and he remembered how critical he'd been of the four young
men at the shore. Perhaps a trip to Brent could have been done in
one day, but not by him. Thinking of how much he had weakened
over the years, he turned and looked at Ken. Ken was down on his
knees, relaxed and pulling his paddle through the water as if it
involved no effort. Patrick turned forward. "It's bigger than I
remembered."

"What?"

"The lake. It's bigger than I remember."

"Shouldn't be."

"Why's that?"

"You've gotten bigger. The lake should seem smaller to you
now."

"Maybe if I didn't have to paddle."

"Take a rest if you need to."

"No . . . I'll make it." Patrick laughed self-consciously. "I
guess it's true that some things look smaller. When I look at the forest now, it docsn't seem as big as I remember. I remember the pine
trees towering miles over my head. Now, they look smaller." Ken
didn't reply.

Gull Island was off to their left and Pat studied the rocky
outcroppings painted white with dung. "It looks like the birds on
the island aren't any smaller."

Kenny laughed. "Yeah, or there are more of them." He was
silent for a moment and then he continued, his tone more serious.
"You know what bugs me a little? Some of the cottagers sneak out
there and break eggs in the nests trying to cut back the numbers.
They don't like the idea of bird shit on their porches and their motor
boats. People weren't like that years ago when we lived here."

"Isn't the lake named after the gulls?"

"Yeah, I think Kioshkokwi means Lake of Gulls."

"Would they have to change the name if they killed all the gulls?"

"No more than they have to change the name of the town after they've chased away all the people."

Patrick turned to look at Kenny, who was studying the island. He turned forward again. "Can we switch sides?"

"Sure."

After ten minutes of paddling on the other side, Pat was again tired and he decided he did not want to paddle all the way to Manitou Lake. Not only would it mean another two hours of work, it would mean crossing three long portages. "You know where I used to catch some fish when I was a kid?"

"Where?"

"On that big rock jutting out into the water in Wolf's Bay, across from Scott's point. You remember it?" Ken did not reply and Pat assumed that he was nodding his head. "Let's go there first."

"Only rock bass there now."

"That's okay. It was a nice spot." Pat was silent for a moment and then added, "I need a rest."

"You remember jumpin' off the rock into the water?"

Pat sighed. "Sure do. It was pretty high. We used to dare each other to see who would go off the highest point. Let's have a look." There was no reply, but Pat saw the bow of the canoe move in response to Ken's j-stroke.

At the shore, Pat jumped out, secured the bowline, and held the canoe for Ken. They climbed the rocky shore to the flat plateau above. It was windswept at the end, which meant fewer flies, and there were lots of places to lie in the sun.

This was now one of the 1900 interior camp sites in Algonquin. These spots were located throughout the park and were identified by an orange triangle nailed to a tree. They each had a metal grill for a campfire, an outhouse, and a small clearing for a tent, but they also showed other signs of use. There was little or no underbrush, larger trees were scarred with axe and knife marks, and the ground was grey and dusty rather than dark and organic.

Algonquin was one of the largest parks in Canada, covering

almost 8,000 square kilometres or 5,000 square miles, and since it was only a three-hour drive from Toronto, it was used heavily. The entry points in the south were often so congested that people had to wait in line. Over the years, new land had been appropriated and new camp sites added.

Most of the entry points had large campgrounds with sub-urbanized camping, electrical sites and communal activities, but inside the park, camping was more primitive. The thousand lakes were all linked together by portage trails and it was possible to travel for hundreds of miles. Fifty years ago, only avid campers went into the interior, but now it was overrun. This particular spot must have been popular because, in addition to the usual signs of camping, there were two benches, a handmade picnic table, and clearings for not one, but three tents. It was just far enough away to be isolated, but tame enough to be comfortable for city folk.

Pat walked to the north side and looked down at the water. The rock sloped toward the tip of the point. From where he stood, it was about twenty feet over the water. He had remembered it being higher, but as Ken had said, things looked bigger to a child. "This seems like a good spot to fish. Let's stay here tonight and go on tomorrow morning."

Ken shrugged and made an expression that implied it wouldn't be his choice, but he was okay with it. Pat reached in his shirt and lit a small cigar.

"You shouldn't smoke those things."

"Actually, I'm almost quit."

"No such thing as 'almost quit'."

It was Pat's turn to shrug. He turned and looked east, back toward Kiosk. There was nothing except rolling forest and dark water. He stood silently, drinking in the environment. Images ran through his mind, many of them pleasant, but most unclear. A breeze blew through the needles of a red pine producing a mournful cry and Pat realised that there were no mechanical noises at all. It had been years since he had experienced this sort of quiet.

He took a drag of his cigar, looked at it with distaste, and flicked it out into the lake. The water at the bottom of the rock cliff was catching the sunlight as it rolled up and down. It looked soft and smooth, and the effect of its undulating movement was deeply relaxing. He closed his eyes, breathed in the pine scented air, and sat on the rocky ground as Ken carried the supplies up the hill.

Ken stirred the glowing embers with a stick and watched Pat drink from his bottle of rum. He sometimes enjoyed a cool glass of wine, but he couldn't imagine drinking warm rum out of a plastic bottle. "So what do you think of your old stompin' ground? I can't believe you haven't been back in all these years."

"Brings back a lot of memories."

"For me, it's sanity. I think I'd have gone nuts if I hadn't been able to come back here."

"Yeah, I know what you mean. I'll bet you that lots of people would have liked to come back."

"Maybe after I'm dead, I'll get you to spread my ashes here."

Pat laughed. "Better get someone else. You'll outlive me for sure." His tone became serious. "You know, that was one thing that really bothered my Dad. He wanted to have Uncle Roy buried here, but it wasn't allowed. They buried him in Mattawa for Christ's sake, and Uncle Roy never liked the place. He should have been buried here."

Ken nodded slowly. He grabbed a log, threw it onto the fire and watched as a stream of red sparks floated up into the night sky. "How's your mom and dad doing, anyway?"

Pat was quiet for a while. "My mom's still alive, but the old bastard died six or seven years ago. He was a heavy drinker. I think his liver gave out on him." He looked off into the distance. "I had to go way up north to claim the body."

Ken cocked his head in confusion.

"He used to take off for months at a time. He worked construction jobs all over the place, drifting from town to town. We hardly ever knew where he was. He was often gone for so long that we would think he was never coming back, and then, one day, he would just show up."

"That's too bad."

"Yeah, I remember hating him. I'd tell myself that when he came home the next time, I was going to tell him how I felt, but then he would show up with gifts and all sorts of great stories. I don't know . . . I'd just get caught up in it all. We'd have fun and then he would pack his things and leave." Pat shrugged as if shrugging off the sadness. "He'd say he was going to be home for Christmas, and then he wouldn't show. Months later he would walk back into our lives and we would do the whole thing again." Pat moved his foot back and forth making a level spot in the dirt and then continued. "He always had a new car or a truck. Sometimes he would grab me and tell my mom we were going out to get something, but this would be an excuse. He would let me drive and I felt like such a hot shot driving one of his new machines. We would cruise up and down the main drag. For a while, it would be great, but then slowly his mood would change. He would start to drink and get depressed. He'd slap me and my mom around a little, and then, a couple of days later, he would pack a bag and be gone . . . no explanations, often no goodbyes."

"Did they get divorced?"

"Nope. I don't think she ever considered it. My grandparents were from Belfast and they went through hard times, but they believed in sticking together. They celebrated their fiftieth together and I think my mom wanted to do the same. Booze and cirrhosis put an end to that."

"I don't remember your dad drinking that much . . . maybe he had a couple a' beers on the porch at night, but I don't ever remember seeing him drunk."

"Yeah. That started after we moved to Toronto. No work, no friends, just a bottle of brown."

Ken shook his head. "So, your mom's still okay?"

Pat grunted. "I guess. We don't see much of each other. We had some big fights before the old man died. One day, after another, in a long line of broken promises, I got real mad. I thought she was pissed too and I called him a shit - along with some other names - and I told her she was stupid for defending him. She slapped me hard across the face. You know, Kenny," Pat held his two index fingers an inch apart from each other, "I came this close to slapping her back. It took all my willpower not to hit her. I left home soon after that. She's got a place out in the east end of the city. A lot of her family lives there, so I guess she has people to be with, but we don't talk."

"Sorry to hear that."

"Yeah, well, there's a lot of stuff we can't talk about. Even though my dad's dead, he's still able to come between my mom and me."

Ken remembered Pat's older brother. "What happened to Evan?"

"He got out a long time ago, shortly after we moved to Toronto. He fought with my folks all the time and then took off for British Columbia. We just lost touch. I haven't heard from him in years. I think he phones my mom sometimes, but I don't know . . ." A loon called hauntingly from across the lake, interrupting Pat's words. He shuddered and took another drink. "Enough about me. What about your folks? They still alive?"

Ken looked down. "My dad passed away eight years ago. He worked for the mines and I think the dampness and the dust got to him. Died of lung cancer. One year later, my mom died. She died of pneumonia. Can you believe that? Pneumonia! She wasn't that old. It was like she couldn't live without him. I don't know. They say that happens sometimes."

"I wonder how different things would've been, if everyone hadn't been kicked out of town. My dad wouldn't have taken to drink and your mom would've had other people in the town to support her. It was a good place, Kiosk. People took care of each other."

"It's hard to say."

Pat stretched out on the ground, watching the fire. "You remember old Mr. Frederick?"

Ken mentally pictured the old train-station master, sitting at his typewriter, working on the station log, his dark-rimmed glasses perched high on his nose, and his white hair cut short and neat. Then he remembered him standing on the tracks with arms flailing as he yelled at children who were diving off the bridge. "Yeah, he used to chase us off the bridge all the time."

"Everyone took care of him when he retired, even though he was a cranky old man. People weren't just tossed out."

Ken sat back and stretched his feet out in front of him. "Yeah, but it didn't always happen. You remember Richard Rankin?"

"Sure. He used to take you hunting and fishing. Neat old guy."

"After he retired, he was forced to leave the house he'd lived in all his life."

"Yeah, but that was after that new company took over the mill . . . right near the end. They only thought of the town as a source of employees. Before they took over . . . when the Staniforths still owned it . . . that was when Kiosk was a community."

Ken closed his eyes and pictured the town. It had been an island in the wilderness and the people were a community. He could see the neat houses nestled among the trees and bushes, the gently twisting roads leading through the fields. An image of Richard and Tabby standing by the bridge came to memory and he realised that he hadn't thought of them for years. He could see Tabby with his grey, braided ponytail and his darkened leather jacket and he could see Richard, old and wrinkled, but strong and steady. They were chatting with each other in that carefree manner that exemplified the town. "I wonder whatever happened to Richard and Tabby."

"Don't ask me."

"I've been to their cabins, but there's very little left, just some rotting logs among the trees. I guess after Kiosk fell apart, there was no reason to stick around."

Pat grunted, took another drink of rum, stood, and stumbled into the bush. He returned doing up his fly. "You know . . . it's funny . . . when we were kids, I hated to hear about all that town history stuff. Whenever my uncle and my dad started talking about it, I would tune out. Now, I meet you, after all these years, and we spend most of our time talking about it."

"Yeah, you're right," Ken laughed and threw a stick into the fire. "But, probably if either of us had kids, they would tune us out, too." Ken saw Pat's expression darken and he studied him for a moment. "You never married?"

"Define marriage. I lived with a few women - one for quite a time - but I never went to the city hall and signed a paper."

"And no kids?"

Pat shook his head and shrugged.

Ken assumed that Pat did not want to talk about the lack of children in his life. "I was married," he said. "Married to Mary, but it wasn't too merry." He chuckled at his own weak humour. "I used to work for the Bank of Nova Scotia, but they wanted to move people around, and I refused a transfer to Hamilton. Sudbury was bad enough, but Hamilton!" He emphasised the name as if it were a dirty word. "Mary was angry. She loved southern Ontario and Hamilton was close to Toronto. She wanted me to be a bank manager and that would only happen if I transferred from place to place, but I wanted to stay in the north. She just took off one day. Damn, we were different . . . shouldn't have been together in the first place." Ken poked at the fire with a new stick and broke out into laughter again.

"What's so funny?"

"Just thinking . . . another family, screwed-up by what happened to this town."

Pat laughed, drained the last of the rum and dropped backward. He looked up at the stars. "I guess it always comes back to that."

Ken sighed. "I guess."

"A lot of people have come and gone and there are a lot of ghosts wandering around these woods. I could almost hear them when I walked around town."

"What're you talking about?"

"I thought I heard children playing; I heard voices . . ." Pat's words trailed off. He sat up suddenly, swung around and pointed to the north, just over the top of the forest. "Is that Mattawa?" A glow silhouetted the trees to the north.

"Mattawa's fifty kilometres away and still a small town. That's the aurora."

Slowly the glowing light shifted, growing in some places, diminishing in others. It was not spectacular, just a pale glow, like the last light after a sunset, but its movement was fluid and it drew the attention. It was like lightening in slow motion, almost unworldly. "Shit, I forgot about the northern lights. Haven't seen them in years." He closed his eyes for a moment. "Damn, where I live, you can't even see the stars."

"Some nights the Aurora gets so bright, it's like street lights.

Sometimes it flows through the sky and dances right over your head."

"Yeah, I remember."

They watched the sky silently and then Ken stood and brushed off his jeans. "Well, it's time for me."

"You go ahead. I'm gonna stay here awhile." Pat stretched on the hard packed ground, looking like he intended to sleep by the fire.

Ken slipped into his sleeping bag and closed his eyes. He was tired, but he didn't fall right to sleep. Images of Kiosk, images that had been forgotten for years, danced through his head. Just before he fell asleep, he heard a sound that reminded him of voices of children. It was the wind playing through the pines, but it made him think of the ghosts that Pat had described

Pat felt a little better once they were out on the water, but the morning had been hard. He was stiff and sore and his head pounded. The wind was stronger today, but thankfully, Ken kept the canoe close to the shore. This lengthened the journey but cut down on the work.

It took over an hour to reach Camp One, a lumber camp that had once existed at the end of the lake. Pat had visited it often as a child. It had been the quarters for many of the wood cutters, a busy place, but more importantly to a young child, it was the location of the annual town-picnic. Once every year, the entire town put all of its creative spirit into a weekend of fun, games, and great food, and it was a highlight of the summer.

Camp One was also a great place to see deer. The camp cook was well known for his habit of feeding them and sometimes in the winter, thirty to forty would gather, waiting to be fed. Some even stood on their back legs, like begging dogs, looking for food and attention. "Any deer still hanging around?" Pat asked.

"Nope. Not like the old days, anyway. I think most of them got shot."

Patrick turned to face Ken. "Shot?"

"Hunted."

"There's no hunting in the park, is there?"

"Well . . ." Kenny hesitated. "There are a lot of hunt camps on the park border and some of the deer wander."

"Hell, I can remember hundreds of deer around here. Surely they didn't all wander outside of the park."

"Well . . . there are . . . other things."

Pat exhaled sharply. "What other things?"

"I'd rather not get into it."

Patrick shrugged. The canoe was close to the shore. "Should we go and look at the camp?"

"Nothing to see, really."

"Like the town?"

"Even worse than the town. The camp disappeared long before the last houses."

Patrick remembered the large buildings, the offices, the long row of garages, the piles of logs. When he had seen it as a child, it had all seemed huge. It was hard to imagine that it was completely gone, but then he would never have believed that all the houses would be gone either. He looked into the water and saw a black ABS pipe that had, at one time, carried water from the lake to one of the buildings. It was small evidence that Camp One had ever existed.

In a weedy bay, they reached the start of the portages. The first two were fairly short and separated by a leisurely paddle on the Amable du Fond River, but the third portage was a difficult twelve-hundred metre odyssey over a long hill. Ken wanted to do it in one crossing, so he carried a heavy pack and the canoe, leaving Pat with two packs and the life preservers.

Although Ken had the heaviest load, Pat struggled the most. Each time he looked forward, he would see a little rise in the distance, and assume that the lake was just ahead, but there was always another ridge - more trail. Blood pounded in his neck as sweat soaked his shirt and he had to force himself not to give in and stop. Finally, after a particularly thick area of scrubby brush, they reached the sandy shore.

When Pat had arrived in Northern Ontario, he had noticed the air, the wonderful smell of clean air. Those first breaths were so different from the ones he took in Toronto and it felt as if they were cleaning and purifying his body. This view of Lake Manitou was to the eyes what those first breaths were to his lungs. If Kiosk had been a great disappointment, Manitou made up for it.

It had been a dry summer, the water was low, and as a result, the beach, which was about three hundred metres long, stretched twenty metres back from the water. On the other side of the bay - they could only see a very small portion of the lake - the trees were tall and strong and touched the edge of the rocky shore. There was a sense of purity, of cleanliness and Pat was stirred in a way that he had forgotten. He stopped, oblivious to his heavy load and soaked in the image.

Ken walked ahead and dropped the canoe at the edge of the water. He turned. "Are you coming?"

Pat lurched forward, dropped his pack near the canoe, and wiped the sweat from his face. "I had forgotten this lake."

"What do you mean?"

"It's a . . . so incredible."

"Kiosk's just as nice. It's just tainted by your memory. There're too many ghosts."

Pat felt a chill run down his spine. Ghosts - there was some truth in that. He shuddered. "Yeah, I guess so. But the trees look bigger here." He grinned. "Didn't they log here?"

"They did. If you go inland, you'll see it. They just didn't log around the lake. This was the old Dufond farm, so maybe they bypassed this spot."

"But the Dufonds were gone before we were born."

"True . . . but I think people were . . . intimidated by them . . . even after they were gone."

Pat noticed a hesitation in Ken's voice and he angled his head questioningly. Ken just shrugged. "You seem to get cautious whenever you talk about Indians."

"I have some mixed feelings."

"Like?"

"Nothing I really wanna talk about."

Pat raised his hands, palms forward, in compliance. He dropped to the sandy ground and leaned against a backpack. A hawk or a falcon circled above in a sky that was so deeply blue that it seemed unreal.

"Wanna get out on Manitou?"

"Woah! Slow down! We just got here. Let's stay and have lunch." Patrick leaned over and dug through the food pack. He found the plastic bottle of rum and held it out in salute to the beauty of nature before him.

Later in the day, Ken and Pat found a beautiful campsite on a small island down in the southern crook of Lake Manitou. It was a nice island, a fair distance from shore, which would mean less aggravation from curious bears and raccoons, and since it had only one campsite, it would be quiet. Ken had wanted to travel further into the park, but he could see that Pat was no longer accustomed to the exertion of paddling and he resigned himself to stay here until it was time to leave the park.

It was a great spot from which to do some evening fishing and Ken sat organizing his tackle as Pat rested by the tent. He knew this lake, had fished it all his life, and he knew where there were some deep pools with nearby shallow spots. With his favourite lure, an old silver William's Wobbler, he could land a beautiful meal.

He walked to the beach, which was not very deep but about twenty metres long. It was littered with broken clam shells, indicating that a raccoon was probably somewhere on the island. He lifted a shell, tossed it out of the water, and watched it splash, bounce and slide into the depths.

He looked at the canoe and then the overcast sky, and changed his mind about an evening fish. Manitou was equally dangerous during a storm and the storms came up fast. His mind was full of difficult images and he decided to practice some Qigong. He walked along the shore until it curved back away from the camp, and started some simple stretches.

When he felt his muscles relax, he began some movements. His breathing became regular, deeper, as he felt himself slipping away, and he tried to focus his thoughts on nothing.

Qigong suited him, but not perfectly. Over the years, he had walked many spiritual paths. He had learned a little yoga, meditation, and he had tried prayer, but the regimentation and structure had always gotten in the way. He had been searching for something that didn't come with an entire set of rules, but most religions were either all or nothing.

He had looked into Buddhism, Confucianism, Hinduism, and Islam, but none of these seemed to offer what he was looking for. He still considered himself a Christian, even though he no longer went to church, and because of this, he was excited when he learned of Gnosticism, based on the Nag Hammadi scrolls, but even this group had its regimentation. It seemed that a person had to believe in the whole package or none and he always came away with the feeling that a main piece of the puzzle was missing. There was a power in the universe, something great, but he could not see it in the ceremony and structure of any organized religion.

With Qigong, which was more of a meditation and exercise, he could modify what worked for him and discard the rest. He had hoped that he'd gain an insight into something, but so far, he had been unsuccessful. Some said that the practice of Qigong was only effective in a group, and if that was true, it explained why he still had not found what he sought, but joining a group was definitely out the question. Groups had never worked for him.

With his thoughts firing off in all directions, he tried to focus on nothing, but he was unsuccessful. He kept replaying the image of Pat sleeping in the dirt. Qigong did not work well this way and he tried to force his mind into a deeper meditative state, seeing blackness and energy. Then the image of Kiosk returned . . . the loss of the town. It was annoying, like trying to lift something that was just a tiny bit too heavy, and he felt his anger starting to grow. Anger was really unproductive. His thoughts shifted quickly and he became aware of someone behind him. He turned and saw Pat standing in the trees.

"What was that?" Pat asked.

Ken's breath burst from his lungs. "What was what?"

Pat waved to indicate what Ken had just been doing. "Some kind of martial art? I didn't know you studied karate."

Ken's face flushed. "Not karate . . . it's just an exercise . . . like Tai Chi."

Pat took a puff of a cigar as he leaned against a tree. He suddenly laughed.

"What's so funny?"

"Old people in China do Tai Chi. Somehow the image of

you doing Tai Chi on an island in Algonquin Park is . . . I don't know . . . funny."

Ken walked back toward the camp, forcing Pat to follow. He looked across the water. The waves were rougher and he knew he couldn't take Pat fishing. They would wait until sunset. "Feel like a coffee?"

Pat nodded, sat on the ground and reclined against a large Red Pine. He made no move to assist in the chore. He laughed again. "I guess if there were any old Chinese people living here, they would've been kicked out too."

"Yeah, along with all of us . . . and the Indians."

Pat puffed on his cigar and grimaced. "There it is again."

"What?" Ken was having trouble following Pat's meandering thoughts.

"The Indians . . . You have a funny tone when it comes to the Indians. What's up with that?"

Ken smiled and shook his head.

Pat looked at him curiously. "At least the Indians can fight for land claims; we can't."

"Yeah, I guess we wouldn't get very far if we tried to protest. I mean, who cares if we were thrown out?"

Pat was silent for a moment, deciding which way he should steer the conversation. "Well, maybe we should . . . protest, I mean."

"You think the government's going to let us back into Kiosk?"

"Maybe."

"The problem is that we're not Indians. We were born here! Both of our parents built their own houses here! But we aren't allowed to claim land as our birthright, cause we ain't Indians."

Pat looked uncomfortable. "It's a little different, Ken. At one point, the government promised not to take away any Indian lands and then it did. The Indians were not fairly compensated."

Ken was silent for a moment. "How were you and I ever compensated?"

"Well . . ." Pat was lost for words. "Forget about the Indians for a moment. Just focus on our rights. I think we might have some claim to the land."

"But we never owned the land?"

"So? What does that mean? That the government never gave us a piece of paper? My grandfather lived and worked in Kiosk and he built the house in which my father and I were born. Three generations of James' lived there and then the government came and said, 'sorry, you can't stay any longer'! We all leave and everyone thinks that's okay? I don't think so."

Ken shook the pot of water as if this would make it boil quicker. "Why are you getting so steamed about this? You haven't even been here in years. Why should it bother you?"

"I guess because being here has opened some wounds. It reminds me of what a friggin' waste my life has been." Pat stood and brushed off his pants. "I've done nothing at all." He looked at the lake for a moment. "All these years . . . just gone. Then I come back here to see this beauty, this place, and I see that the government is going to build cabins and new parking lots and laundry rooms and office building. My uncle died trying to find a new job and couldn't even be buried here. My dad left after all the years of work and he died poor, and now, if I don't do something, I'll die and be buried in some anonymous graveyard in Toronto, too." Pat turned and looked at Ken. "I don't even have any kids, for Christsake."

Ken shrugged and answered softly. "Neither do I."

"But why not? Why are we both doing jobs we hate? Why doesn't either of us have a home? A family? "

Ken shook his head. He was about to say that he had a home, but it was unimportant. "The town hired a lawyer. If there had been anything they could have done . . ."

Pat exhaled abruptly through pouted lips. "Lawyers! They only work in the framework provided by the government. If the government says it's not legal, then the lawyers work with that. And anyway, who even cares if it is legal? Maybe this isn't even a matter of what is and isn't legal. Maybe it's a matter of what is and isn't right. Maybe everything was perfectly legal and maybe the government acted within the letter of the law, but it still wasn't right! You can't displace an entire population, an entire town, for the sake of people who want to have a nice place to go camping on the weekend. The government was wrong. They have no respect for home."

Ken looked down at the ground and smiled. A short while ago, Pat had looked so tired. Now he was full of energy. "I guess there's some truth to that. I had to leave the Bank of Nova Scotia because I was unwilling to transfer from place to place. The only way to get a promotion was to move from city to city. They didn't think that an employee should have any connection to any place."

"And it all starts with the government. They're building a mobile work force." He spread his arms to indicate some great notion. "They'd like to have all Canadians living in mobile homes attached to SUV's so that they can pack up and move with the employment market - hordes of families on the Trans-Canada highway, heading for salt mines in the Maritimes after a year-long sojourn at oil fields of Alberta. No more fixed, local schools, but internet classrooms conducted by cell-phone and laptop. If the fisheries get destroyed on one coast, we'll ship 'em all to the other coast. All the land owned by the government; the workforce mobile and ready."

"Okay, okay . . ." interrupted Ken with a chuckle. "I get your point. And what do you suggest we do about it?"

"I don't know." Pat turned and stared off at the water. The surface was rough, grey and dangerous. "Maybe make a big stink in the press . . . maybe do some kind of protest."

Ken looked at Pat. "And what makes you think anybody would care?"

"Because the damned government threw us out. That's why!"

Ken put instant coffee into the two plastic cups. "That may be, but all that was long ago. What good would a protest do now? It won't change anything."

"It might. The Indians are winning land claims."

"Now you're being ridiculous. They'll never give us the land back . . . ever!"

"You shouldn't be so sure. But even if they don't, at least they'll have to admit that they took it away wrongfully . . . and, even if they don't do that, other people will know and it might not happen so easily again in the future."

Ken handed Pat his coffee and as Pat was about to continue, he held up his hand in protest. "Let me think about it, will ya?"

A dark expression drifted over his features and disappeared.

On the final day of their trip, they journeyed out onto the water in the early morning before breaking camp. It seemed only fitting to catch breakfast before returning to Kiosk. The sun rose slowly, a soft, red orb shimmered through the morning mist, and Pat closed his eyes, feeling the air roll across his face like a silky fabric. The incredible quiet was broken only by the hollow sound of the water gurgling along the sides of the canoe and soft thump of Pat's paddle, which occasionally touched the gunnels. The smell of cedar and pine drifted through the fog that lay like a blanket on the water.

Ken's reel whirred as line played out, and Pat was disappointed. It would be the last fish they would catch on this trip and he would have liked to catch it. Off in the distance, hidden in the mist, a loon called and splashed, and then a duck flew overhead, the sound of its beating wings filling the air.

Within fifteen minutes, they were back on the shore, breaking sticks and feeding a fire. They had a beautiful lake trout and as it sizzled, the fog began to burn away from the water. It covered the lake like a cloud, but it was only a metre thick, and Pat stood tall, looking over its top. It was like looking out the window of a jet, high above the clouds, and seeing the clouds roll off endlessly in the distance. But the trees on the far shore poked through the clouds, looking vastly out of place. Tree tops that poked through the flat layer of clouds? There were so many visions here that could not be found elsewhere.

The coffee, the fire, and the fish filled the air. Pat lit another cigar, took a puff and then stubbed it out in the dirt.

"Why do you smoke those vile things? You obviously don't like them."

Pat poured some sugar and creamer into his cup. "I quit smoking a while back and I have the occasional cigar to help with the cravings. You're right, though, they are vile - especially out here. They taste better in the city."

After breakfast, they packed their gear and pushed the canoe out onto the water. The fog was now just a wisp of mist swirling over the lake. It took most of the day to return and back at the ranger station, Pat helped Ken load the truck, but again he avoided going into the ministry station, choosing to tie the canoe to the truck racks.

They drove through the town slowly, talking about buildings and people, and then they swung around to the cabins on the old mill site. Ken shook his head, but did not comment. He turned and drove until he reached the bridge at the west end of town.

They parked and walked along the overgrown gravel road toward what had once been Ken's home. At a large stand of pink double roses, Ken stopped and took in the fragrance. "I remember these from when I was a kid."

Pat chuckled briefly. "Funny that the houses, the school and the church should disappear, but a bunch of roses should survive."

At the bottom of the road, they reached Kenny's yard. There was little to show where the house had once stood. Tag alders and clumps of wild raspberries covered most of the area, but littered among the growth were tar shingles and some bent and twisted pieces of metal.

Ken picked up a small piece of galvanized metal. He turned it slowly in his fingers and then said suddenly: "Come on, let's get out of here. There's something I want to show you." He walked away quickly forcing Pat, still tired from the long paddle, to follow.

A couple of kilometres north of the town, Ken turned off the highway onto a gravel road. The truck bounced, as its tires were forced over rocks and ruts in the unmaintained road.

"Hey, slow down. You're gonna lose the canoe!" Ken had been in a hurry since he left the town and he was going much too fast for the condition of the road.

"I've got a hunt camp up here that I want you to see. I use this place in the fall. It's rustic, but I think you'll like it."

After a long trip through the bush, they reached a small clearing and a path. The clearing was large enough to park a few vehicles but the path was only wide enough for an all-terrain-vehicle, or ATV. Ken stopped the truck and jumped out.

"Maybe we should be getting back," said Pat hesitantly. He remembered that Ken's short trips often meant hours of tramping though the bush.

"No, no, come on. It's a short distance, really." Ken had not been too talkative since they had left Kiosk and he walked away quickly. Pat groaned as he followed, looking back at the unlocked truck. It was hard for him to leave a vehicle without locking the doors. It was something he would never do in the city.

The bush was thick and although the sky was clear, the air was heavy and damp. A sweet spicy smell reminded him of the swamps and bogs around Kiosk. After a short walk, they reached a rustic cabin. The wood was dark and untreated and the windows were small and covered with boards. Ken fished out a key and removed a huge padlock from the solid, wood door.

Inside, a musty quality filled the air. Ken unlatched a wooden window cover from inside and went outside to remove it. Light streamed into the dark cabin illuminating the dust in a golden band. Some basic wood furniture sat between shelves of supplies and although Spartan, the place was fairly neat. "You were talking about living in Kiosk. This place is just out of the park boundary and I spend many weekends here."

Pat picked up a coal oil lamp, feeling the oily film that covered the base. "I guess it's quiet."

"Come here and look at this." A large topographical map was pinned to the wall. It too, was dark and frayed. "We're here." Ken pointed with his finger to a pushpin in the map. "And just a short distance along this trail is Lauder Lake. There's hunting trails all through these woods." Pat nodded as Ken walked out the door. "Come here, there's something else I want to show you."

Behind the cabin was a locked lean-to. Ken removed the lock and pulled open the heavy door. Inside a light-blue, Suzuki four-wheel-drive ATV sat ready for use. An old Sportspal canoe hung from the rafters and Patrick could see that it could be lowered onto the metal rack of the ATV. "Does it run?" he asked referring to the ATV.

"Sure." Ken swung a loose board and retrieved the machine's key. He placed it in the ignition switch, adjusted the choke, and after only two attempts, started the Suzuki. "Do you know how to drive one?"

"I had a friend who used to race these in a little town north of King City. I drove his lots of times. Can I?"

"Sure! Go ahead."

Pat sat on the machine and toed the gearshift lever into first gear. With a little shot of gas, the machine lurched out of the shed.

"Follow the trail. It will take you to Lauder Lake."

"That's in the park, isn't it?"

"Yeah, the park border is only a short distance away. Only half of the lake was in the park when we were kids, but they moved the park border to take it all.

Pat pushed the throttle and drove the old machine through the forest toward the lake. He liked the feeling of power, but he also liked the feeling of being alone in the forest. Since he had arrived in Kiosk, he had always been with Ken. Now, he was off on his own. It felt good.

The trail was well used, but on both sides, the forest was thick. This was all second growth and if there was a park boundary, he couldn't see it. All of the forest had been cut. The trail widened a little and by the tire ruts, appeared to have been used by cars and trucks. A wider trail turned off to the right, but he passed this and continued on toward Lauder.

As he approached the lake, he saw that trees were larger, older, and he decelerated. Logging companies were not allowed to cut right to the shore of a lake and this fooled campers into believing that they were camping in old growth forest, when in truth, there was only a small circle of old growth around the lakes.

At the shore, Pat found a tiny, hand-made dock. He remembered the Lake. He had fished in it with Kenny many years ago, but then there had been no road access. It had to be reached by two portages from Kioshkokwi Lake

He turned the ATV around and followed another trail to a small cottage. Like Kenny's cabin, the windows and doors were heavily boarded, but there were signs of recent occupation. He was surprised because he had assumed the only cottages left in the park were the ones given to the Staniforths before the mill fire.

Shutting off the machine, he walked to the shore and looked at the lake. A small floating dock had been left in the water and he could picture a family relaxing on lawn chairs as the sun sparkled off the jewelled surface of the lake.

In the distance, barely audible, he heard the sound of children's voices. He looked right and left, but could see no one on the lake. Ghosts again? He felt the hair on his neck bristle. There was a sensation that someone was off in the bushes watching him.

The wind moaned as it blew through the needles of a tall white pine. The laughter was gone. Pat jumped on the Suzuki, started it, and spun its tires on the needle-covered ground as he turned back toward Ken's Cabin.

He backed the machine into the lean-to as Ken walked toward him. "It runs good," he said, turning off the key.

"Not bad."

"Why didn't we come here instead of going camping?"

"The fishing in Lauder isn't as good as it used to be. I thought you'd like Manitou better." Ken worked the lock back into place.

"You've got this place well outfitted."

"I've got a couple of caches around the area too."

"Oh?"

"You know, Richard showed me how to do that. I find a nice spot, dig a hole, bury a stove, an axe, a tarp and some pots and fishing gear and then I cover it with a piece of tin and some dead branches. You're not supposed to do that, but no one ever finds the stuff."

"So nothing ever gets stolen?"

Kenny laughed. "Oh, one or two times I found some of the stuff used - it was not put back the way I had put it there - but so far, nobody's taken anything."

"But you've got this place pretty well locked up."

"Well, you don't want to tempt people. This is all out in the open."

Pat shook his head. "So, someone found one of your caches, used the stuff, and then put it back?"

"Yep."

"I remember that mom and dad never locked their house. They would even go away for a whole day and leave the place unlocked. You wouldn't do that in the city."

They walked back into the cabin. "If you ever want to use this place to get away, feel free."

"Thanks." Pat looked at the trees in the distance. They still seemed gloomy and the sense that someone was just out of sight, watching him, stuck in his mind. "But I doubt I'll be back soon. This place is a long way from my life."

A light breeze tugged at Kenny Campbell's jacket as he stood on the shore of Kioshkokwi Lake and looked up the path that climbed through the trees. The sky was a rich blue, beams of light danced across the uneven forest floor, and sunlight sparkled on the new maple and birch leaves. It was unusually warm for May, but there were still no blackflies or mosquitoes, and since school was closed for the day, it was a perfect time to do some exploring.

He was looking for a new location for a camp. He already had a few, but most were on the town side of the lake and none on the south shore. Whenever he could, he would visit one of his camps, spend a night or two, and enjoy complete freedom. He'd bury a cache - an old axe, some fishing line, some pots and pans, and some nails - so he could return whenever he wanted. Richard Rankin, one of the old-timers, had taught him this.

His mom would be angry if she knew he had crossed the lake alone. She didn't mind him camping overnight, but she feared the lake. "You're not even twelve years old!" she would say. This was typical parent-talk that made no sense. He was old enough. Some of the men had started driving logs down the rivers and across the lakes at thirteen. Sitting in a canoe, even during a storm, was safe compared to driving a log down a fast river. He was a good canoeist, an excellent swimmer, and canoes didn't sink.

The canoe drummed and banged against the rocky shore as its stern bobbed in the water. The hollow sounds echoed back from the hills. Kenny turned and pulled the boat onto dry land. He could see across to Gull Island, but the north shore was small. This was a big lake, with lots of little bays, and Kenny had explored them all. He knew all the creeks that led to all the hidden marshes and beaver ponds, and all the trails and paths that led through the bush. He had quite a few camps.

Sometime soon, the blackflies - small, biting flies about half the size of mosquitoes - would arrive. Then, exploring would be less fun. Kenny never abandoned the outdoors because of the flies, but he knew enough to stay away from the wind-sheltered, damp areas. He knew that if he were stuck in a bad place on a wind-still day in early June, the flies would eat him alive.

Kenny found a small white object on the ground. It was long and narrow and shaped like a tooth. The Indians had travelled through this area; maybe this was some kind of artefact. He rotated it in his fingers. Naw, he thought. It was just a piece of shiny, white rock, a crystal. He slipped it in his pocket and started up the path.

The breeze blew through the tops of the trees rustling the leaves. They moved first on his right, then on his left, and then way up the path. It was a pleasant sound, soft, gentle, inviting.

Although the incline was steep, he walked quickly, struggling up the stony path. It was sandy, but on the steeper sections, erosion had exposed lengths of stone making it look like a dried riverbed. The rocks ground and rolled under his feet.

At the top of the hill, the land flattened. Many years ago, this had been a pine forest, but now it was open to the sky. As he walked into the clearing, a warm breeze reached him and he felt the heat of the sun bore into his skin. He stopped, closed his eyes, and turned his face skyward.

Blackberry and raspberry plants grew in profusion. It was too early for berries, but when they ripened, Kiosk residents would arrive and play the old game: pick-two, eat-one, pick-two, eat-one. He walked between the tall, reddish canes and touched one of the small leaves. The blossoms would be out soon and then, a few weeks later, the berries. He licked his lips . . . raspberry pie, raspberries and ice-cream, wonderful!

The air smelled alive, lush and organic. This normally didn't happen until later in the season, but spring had arrived early. It felt good just to stand here. He took out the crystal, looked at it, tossed it in the air once and caught it.

A loud hissing sound startled him and he whipped his head around. Nothing. The sound repeated. It was loud and threatening and he immediately ducked into the bushes. Prickly thorns scratched his arms as he parted the canes. All was quiet.

A gentle breeze rustled the leaves and a woodpecker's drumming echoed down from the treetops. Slowly he stood, looking in the direction of the last sound, but he saw nothing. Curiosity replaced fear and he crept through the raspberry canes, craning his neck. Seeing nothing, he began to turn away. Again, the noise broke the silence, but this time it was closer, just off to the left. With fear grabbing at the bottom of his stomach, he realised what it was. He whipped his head around and saw a large black bear standing on its two hind legs.

The bear was looking right at him. Its mouth was open, foamy saliva oozing between its jagged teeth, as it swayed back and forth menacingly. Kenny felt an empty, dark fear, but he knew he had to resist the impulse to run. Richard Rankin had told him to stand tall and slowly back away from a bear. This may have been good advice for a grown man, but would an eleven-year-old boy look big to a bear?

Mustering all his courage, and almost standing on the toes of his canvas running shoes, he made himself as tall as he could. The bear hissed, the sound almost guttural, and flexed its claws. Dangerous claws. At the dump, bears opened tin cans with them.

What is it doing here, he wondered. Then he remembered the tall grass. They loved the first spring shoots. He stepped back, keeping his eyes on the glistening black fur. Raspberry canes restricted his movement and he struggled, forcing his way through the thorny branches. He took another step and something moved behind him. His neck muscles strained, but he forced himself not to look, willed himself to keep his eyes on the bear.

The raspberry canes had wrapped around his legs, and seemed to fuse into the fabric of his jeans. He thought about being trapped. Push! Move! His eyes widened. He stopped and tried to breathe. He couldn't let the bear sense his panic. He wanted to look down, to find a way through the canes, but he dared not break eye contact.

Where was the dammed path? He had to get back onto the path. Damn, damn, damn he thought as he tried to force his right leg backward. It wouldn't move. Then he tried his left leg. It moved marginally. He felt as if he were standing in mud to his knees.

"Oh, please, God," he whispered, "let me get out of here. Please, God, I'll be good."

The thought of being ripped apart by a bear was bad enough, but the idea that this patch of raspberries would assist, was somehow worse. Not only would the bear's claws and teeth rip him to pieces, but these thorny bushes would hold him captive. With face red and fists clenched, he moved, inch-by-inch, away from the hissing bear.

"Think, damn it, think," he said to himself quietly. Bears were fast, they could easily outrun a man, but people said that a bear could not run down a hill. A man - or a boy - might escape an attacking bear if he ran down a hill. Kenny clung to this.

He shook his head and gritted his teeth as he moved further away. Once he reached the path, he would turn and run at full speed toward the lake. Maybe he could outrun the bear. He grunted as he moved his one leg back a full step. The sound of the thorny canes rubbing on his legs sounded like tearing cloth. The bear roared. It was so loud that the sound of the rustling leaves and the birdsong disappeared.

He wanted to turn and run, but he was not yet on the path. The bear would easily outrun him in the canes. It roared again and its rank odour assaulted Kenny's nose.

Something was moving behind him, something smaller than the bear. Forget about it! He had to concentrate on the danger in front of him. He had to back away from it, to get away. If the bear charged, he had to be on the path. It was his only chance.

The canes continued to hold him, like an adult who was intent on administering punishment. "Let go!" he grunted between clenched teeth. The sound was louder than he intended and his eyes widened. Would the sound of his voice cause the bear to attack?

A soft growl at his feet drew his attention and, for the first time since he had spotted the bear, he looked away, down at the ground behind him. Two baby bear cubs were at his heels. The bear mother hissed loudly again and Kenny looked up. Drool was dripping from between its yellowed teeth and he imagined the damage these pointed fangs would do to his flesh. "Oh God," he whispered. The bear, the mother, dropped to all fours and only her arched back was visible above the raspberries. It started to move.

Kenny turned and broke through the last of the canes. He stumbled and his mouth opened in a cry. He was about to fall. He flailed his arms and regained his balance, but as he did, he saw the two bear cubs running at his heels. The stupid things were following him.

As the slope increased, so did his speed. His feet moved in wild arcs. Gravel exploded under his running shoes and he was in danger of falling, but he could not slow his flight. The snorts and grunts of the mother filled the forest behind him, and the two cubs still ran at his heels. It seemed as if they too, were afraid of the adult bear.

The foliage blurred past, and he imagined that, at any second, he would crash to the ground, and the bear would leap on his back. He imagined his blood gushing from multiple bite and slash wounds, the pain, the horror, and then, suddenly, the forest moved back into focus. Just as this horrible destiny seemed inevitable, his descent, his flight, became more controlled. He seemed to glide rather than run and some force seemed to stabilize him, keep him level. The feeling of impending doom disappeared. He still had to escape by his own effort, but something was aiding him.

Sticks and branches lashed at his face and the air whipped past his ears like it did when he was riding his bicycle on a hard-packed road. If he reached the shore at this speed, he would flail right past his canoe into the water. The bear might not chase the canoe, but she might chase a lone boy in the water. "Get away from me!" he yelled. "Get away!"

The canoe was just yards away and his running shoes pounded the ground as he tried to decelerate. The shock travelled up through his ankles, through his knees and into his back. Dust swirled and rolled around his feet.

He reached the canoe, grabbed the bow, and, still running, ripped the boat across the shore and into the water. The fibreglass hull screeched as if it were being torn open on the rocks, but Kenny knew it was tough; it had suffered harsher treatment in the rapids.

Standing in the water, he turned and saw the two cubs. They stopped, looked around, bewildered, and then ran back up the hill toward their mother. Dumbfounded, Kenny stepped backward, slipped on some slimy rocks, and fell into the icy-cold water. He gasped and then started to laugh. He laughed until the sound was dry and hollow, and then he stood and listened to the water drip from his jeans. He was safe.

He took two small steps toward the shore, wanting to watch the cubs, but they were gone. He considered sneaking back to watch the mother, but, instead, he climbed awkwardly into the canoe. He looked up the trail, but could neither hear nor see any of the bears. They had disappeared as if they'd never existed.

He kicked off his shoes and watched the cloudy water drain into the bottom of the boat. He paddled a few strokes - just to be careful - and then stretched out. The sunshine was warm. As the dark material of his jeans absorbed the heat, he reached in his pocket and took out the crystal rock. Maybe it was magic, he thought, maybe it had helped me glide down that hill so quickly. He rotated it in his fingers and then slipped it back in his pocket. Slowly, the canoe drifted toward Kiosk and the Amable du Fond River.

He floated aimlessly, like a log from the mill, allowing time to drift. He watched the clouds and dreamed of adventure on the open water. The sun moved across the sky toward Camp One and he realised that it was time to go home. He paddled for a while, feeling the strain of muscle, but even as he pulled his canoe onto the shore near the town, he was still excited.

He decided that if his parents asked him about his day, he wouldn't tell them about the bear. They would overreact, and although it was an exciting story, it would not be worth a loss of freedom. He flipped the canoe into the bushes near the train bridge and walked toward the tracks. His shoes still squished but his pants were almost dry.

He would have liked to visit Pat James, his best friend, but their houses were on opposite sides of the river and it was already late. He stopped and looked at the train bridge. It was a shortcut, but if he crossed it, someone might report him to Mr. Frederick, the old train stationmaster. This would cause problems. He was anxious to tell Pat about the bear, but it would have to wait.

He ran up the embankment and onto the wooden railroad ties. They were sticky and smelled of creosote, but he stepped from tie to tie, allowing his running shoes to tear off the surface of each. He pretended he was high in the air crossing an open bridge and when he found this too easy, he balanced on the one of the rails, pretending he was on a tightrope high over some canyon.

He jumped off dramatically and scrabbled down the far side. On the hill to his left was the snack bar. He knew Pat was often here, but it was time to get home. A car passed and turned onto the crossroad, dragging a plume of dust in its wake.

Kiosk was built on the north shore of Lake Kioshkokwi and was divided roughly in half by the Amable Du Fond River. Houses could be found on both sides, but the school, the church, the bunkhouse, the store and the mill were all on the east side. The train bridge was right near the mouth of the Amable and the car bridge was a few hundred yards downstream. A weir, a type of small dam, was located under this second bridge, and although it was used to control the level of water in the lake, and to help the mill with the incoming logs, its headwater also provided a fun place to fish and swim.

A few weeks ago, floodwaters had broken one of the weir gates, and the townspeople had raised the money for materials and had started fixing the damage themselves. Kenny could hear them hammering and talking in the distance.

He crossed the bridge road and descended the gradual slope toward his house. The air was redolent with the fruity smell of double-roses, a wild rose that blossomed very early, and his thoughts drifted to the sweet taste of freshly picked blueberries and raspberries. Berries were wonderful.

Berry picking was a popular pastime in the area. Twenty-five years ago, the road had been opened to Highway 17, making it easy for tourists to reach Kiosk, and each summer more people arrived to camp and canoe - and to pick berries. Most patches were well picked and people tried to keep their favourite spots secret, but Kenny knew them all.

Before the road had been built, Kiosk had been isolated.

Many of the early settlers had arrived on foot, walking the twelve miles from Fossmill, a lumber mill that burned in 1934, to start a new life in Kiosk. Both Kenny and Pat's grandfathers had worked in Fossmill and Kenny's father still told stories about the hardships they endured.

Kenny walked past a small boxy building, close to the bridge road. It was an older house, but it looked more like a cottage. The newer houses were larger and owned by their residents, but the mill had built these smaller places for the workers and still owned them. There were no mansions in town, but even these small places had nice gardens and lawns, with lilacs and roses and quaint brick paths leading to welcoming front doors.

At the bottom of the dusty road was his house. It too, was small, but his father, Dave Campbell, had built a huge porch across the entire front. He had done this with his own hands and with lumber he had helped cut in the mill. More time was spent out here than in the house, and this evening, like most evenings, a few men sat on chairs and benches, drinking beer and chatting after a day's work.

Kenny's dad was a short man with a wiry build and a thick crop of black hair. He had perpetual stubble. The hair grew down under his collar making him appear like he needed to wash. After a hard day's work, he had a habit of rubbing the back of his neck with his hand and he was doing this as Kenny approached.

"Kenny! You're home, boy," he said. "Supper's almost ready."

Kenny nodded and walked up the stairs onto the porch. Roy James, Pat's uncle, was leaning against a post, and William James, Pat's Dad, was seated in a chair balanced precariously on its back two legs. A third man, dressed a little more 'fine', also sat on the bench.

"This is Mr. McConkey, Kenny," his dad nicked his head toward the third man. "He's one of Patty's uncles. He's visitin' from Toronto."

"Good day, sir." Kenny nodded.

"Nice ta be meeting ya, lad," said McConkey, saluting Kenny with a beer bottle. He had the same accent as Pat's mom, which Pat had explained was Irish.

"Yes sir." He turned to his dad. "Is Pat here?"

"No son," said Pat's uncle, "he's at home. We just brought Frank over to meet your folks . . ." he nodded his head at Mr. McConkey, who smiled, "To show him what life is like away from the dirty city."

Kenny didn't know what to say, and he looked at Roy, waiting. Roy looked like a scarecrow leaning against one of the porch posts. The two brothers did not look much alike. Roy was tall and thin whereas Bill was built like Kenny's dad, stocky, not too tall and very muscular. He had a tangle of brown curly hair on the back of his head, but he was already going bald.

Bill broke the silence. "Pat has some chores to do at home." He grabbed another Old Vienna and opened it with a splotch in the chrome-plated opener that was screwed to one of the porch railings. "We're gonna need some firewood, and its gotta have time to dry over the summer."

Kenny nodded, but didn't speak. He didn't want his father to start harping about firewood. "I'll just go wash up, then." The men were already talking as he walked through the front screen door. It squeaked loudly and then swung shut with a bang.

He took off his shoes - his mother wouldn't let anyone except his dad wear shoes in the house - and walked through the living room to the kitchen. His mother was standing with her back turned, cutting some vegetables on the arborite counter. He washed his hands in the white enamel sink, looked around for a tea-towel, and considered using the skirt around the sink, but changed his mind. His mother was in the kitchen and even though her back was turned, she always seemed to know what he was doing. He flapped his hands on his legs.

Kenny turned and looked at his mother. She was wearing a puffy blue dress with big sleeves and seemed overdressed for a weekday. He wondered if Pat's 'Toronto' uncle was someone important.

"Did you have a nice trip?" she asked, her back still turned.

Kenny froze. Did she know he had been in the canoe? "It was okay," he replied cautiously.

"Did you go for one of your bush walks?"

"Yeah . . . sort of . . . I'm going upstairs now."

"Okay, dear. I'll call you when supper's ready. Do your

homework."

He darted out of the room and ran up the wooden stairs two at a time.

The house was a story and a half with two upstairs bedrooms. His was the smaller one at the front of the house. It had been dry-walled, but the seams had never been finished and the drywall nails still showed like metal studs on the four-by-eight sheets. One day his father would get around to plastering the joints and the nail heads, but until that day came, he could not paint the walls. They had yellowed slightly and the room smelled of heat and dust.

He took off his clothes and draped them over a chair. He stood naked in the room, letting the warm air flow over him, but he double-checked the door to make sure it was closed. He walked over to his dresser, an old four-drawer unit, pulled open the top drawer, and grabbed some underwear. The dry clothing felt good.

As an afterthought, he retrieved his pocket-knife and laid it on his dresser to dry. As he dug into the pockets, he also found the crystal, which he rotated in his fingers. He opened a cigar box on top of his dresser and tossed in the stone.

Outside, he could hear the sound of laughter. Roy, usually the centre of attention, was probably telling jokes. Kenny pulled up the double-hung wood-frame window and breathed in the air. He could not see the people below, but he could hear them just fine.

". . . And as for farming, you can't farm up here. Did you hear about the two thieves who went into farming in Mattawa? One of them stole the cattle and the other one stole the feed." Roy paused for a moment. "Yeah, and they still lost money."

Loud laughter wafted up through the quiet Kiosk air.

"One of the farmers from Kiosk quit farming and moved to the city." Roy said. "When one of his friends found him selling hammers on a street corner, he said: 'Oh, it's not too bad. Every morning I buy a bunch of hammers for three bucks a piece and then I set up here and sell them two for five-bucks. I know it don't sound like much,' the retired farmer said, 'but it sure beats the hell out of farming."

Laughter again filled the air and another beer splotched open. Roy continued talking but his tone was more subdued: "Nope, if they close down the mill, there won't be nothing much for the people around here to do."

Kenny was disappointed. He wanted to hear more jokes, but the conversation had changed. He dropped on his bed and sank deeply as the slat springs twanged.

Pat's uncle's voice drifted in the window. "And I'm telling you, if those bastards have their way, that's what they'll do - close down this whole town."

"I jest don't get it," said Frank McConkey with his Irish accent. "Tis a fine wee place. Why would the government be wantin' to close it down?"

"It's money, Frank! The politicians need to get elected and the people that pay for their campaigns are the same people who want this town shut down."

"But why would anyone want to knacker the town? I don't get it. Who cares bollocks about some little town way up here?"

"This town is in Algonquin Park, and a couple a years ago, with lotsa pressure from down south, the government decides that this park is gonna be a 'wilderness park'. And the reason it's supposed to be a wilderness park, is so rich people from Toronto can come up here and get away from the mess they created down there. That means that there shouldn't be any motors and there shouldn't be any sawmills. They want to come up and have a nice time going boating and birdwatching. They don't wanna be disturbed by . . . by . . . us."

"Roy, the government's gotta protect the country a little. We need to have parks."

There was silence for a moment and then Kenny's dad answered. "Sure, we gotta have parks, but who agreed that our town had to be in one. My father walked here from Fossmill - twelve miles through the bush! He built this house. Why should our lives be thrown out the window to benefit some people in Toronto?" Someone tried to interrupt, but Kenny's dad continued. "What would happen if a group of people decided that one of the suburbs of Toronto should be torn down and turned into a wilderness park? Do you think that everyone would just pack up and leave quietly? No! Course they wouldn't! Well, it's the same thing here. What I see is that the people down south have screwed up their homes and now they want to come here and take over ours for their benefit. The people up here won't put up with it." Kenny could hear the anger in his father's voice, and he was surprised. Pat's uncle Roy was a hot-head, always stirring up trouble, but his dad was usually more reserved.

Frank's Irish accent returned to the conversation. "I jest doubt the government would try to shut down the town. Wouldn't they lose taxes and support from the mill? Only an eejit would try and do such a thing."

"Why would they lose taxes?" Roy asked. "The mill will just build somewhere else and people will work in it. The government will still get its taxes. And, when the mill is gone and the town is gone, that'll leave this whole area open for tourists. See, it comes back to the money. The people in Toronto don't have a decent lake to go to, so they want to take control of this here place so they can come here in the summer. And those people is rich. They pay for the campaigns of the politicians. So what are the politicians gonna do, support the rights of a thousand poor people in the bush, or support the rich people who pay to get them elected?"

"But what about the mill?" asked McConkey. "Tis a big operation. They wouldn't be takin' that layin' down for sure?"

"That's just the thing. The mill's probably in cahoots with the government. Ever since Staniforth sold it, it's been going downhill. The government will probably give them money to build somewheres else. Just this spring the weir gave out and the mill refused to fix it. Now, why is that? The mill uses the weir to control the amount of water in the lake. So, why would they not want to pay to fix it unless they knew they were moving?"

Bill James, Pat's dad, answered quietly: "It's because they use trucks on roads to bring in the logs. They don't need to depend on the lake so much."

"What about the hot pond?"

The hot pond was an area sectioned off the lake used to keep the veneer logs. The level of the lake was important, if it dropped, it would be harder to get the logs into the mill. It remained quiet for a moment and then Roy spoke. "You mark my words. This whole town is gonna disappear before our very eyes."

"I don't think it'll ever go that far," answered Bill. His voice was low and pensive.

"If the mill closes, they may as well close down the town," said his father. "And that's what they're counting on."

There was silence again. Kenny had already heard about the government's proposal to shut down the summer operation of the lumber mill, but he didn't know too much about it. He had never considered the idea of the entire town disappearing. For the last few years, there had been meetings and special committees, but last Christmas, some people became really worried. One of the older men, a man he had always thought was tough as nails, broke down and cried. Everyone had been upset. The provincial government had released some kind of study that said there should be no logging during the summer months because it was disturbing the canoeists - hurting the tourist business. The mill owners said they could not afford to close down for two to three months a year. They threatened to close the doors and if the mill was gone, then the town could go too.

The issue had calmed, but now that summer was coming, it was flaring again. Urbanites in the south always seemed to be complaining about the people in the north. The government had created a Department of the Environment and a new organization called Green Peace had started somewhere in Canada. They were both against the hunters and woodsmen of Northern Ontario. The adults were talking about it all the time, and although he did not understand, it frightened him. Most of his friends had been born here. He had been born here. It was his home; it was his life - he could not imagine living somewhere else.

"I wrote to the Toronto newspapers for support," said Roy, "But I don't know if they will even print the letters. They don't seem to give a damn about what happens to us up here."

Kenny looked at his wall. A large poster of a giant Marlin jumping out of the water hid an unplastered seam in the drywall. He studied the fine fish and wondered where you found creatures like that. He knew how to catch trout and bass, but he had never seen a fish that big.

"I'm telling you," his dad continued, "the government don't care what sort of letters you write. They've got a plan and they're gonna follow it. The people down south with lots of bucks are gonna get their way. They're gonna close down the town and turn it into a park for the birdwatchers."

'Birdwatcher' was the derogatory term that Kiosk residents used to describe the tourists from Toronto. Birdwatchers did not participate in nature; they stood back at a distance and watched it. A real outdoorsman was respected, but a birdwatcher was treated with contempt. People from Southern Ontario who canoed through the park usually brought every comfort they could carry and would be just as happy in a floating cottage. They had no real connection to the wilderness.

Kenny picked up a schoolbook and tried to tune out the conversation. He had a math assignment due, but as soon as he opened the book, he realised that he had no desire to do school work. He was getting average grades and there was no sense overdoing it. He hadn't done homework all year and now that school was almost over, it was kind of late to start.

A fishing magazine caught his attention and he flipped through its pages. He could still hear the men outside talking about the end of the town, and he threw down the magazine, finished dressing, and bounded down the stairs. If he had to listen, he might as well sit outside until supper was ready.

As he put on his damp shoes, he thought about the bear. She had been very impressive and he wished he could tell his dad about her, but he knew it would be unwise. The people in town did not fear wolves, but they were always cautious of bears. Tell them you saw a bear and they would tell you that you couldn't leave town. He would have to save the story for Pat.

After supper, as he walked out the door, he overheard his dad telling his mom something interesting. It seemed like there was going to be some trouble. He listened for a moment and then hurried off. Now he had two things to tell Pat.

Pat threw the last piece of split maple firewood on the row and sat down on a block of wood. He breathed deeply and wiped the sweat off his forehead. Piling wood was a hateful job because, each year, they burned twenty face-cords of hardwood, and every year he had to split and pile every piece in every row.

Normally, they cut the firewood while it was still cold - the bark didn't get full of sand and the cold wood split easier - but it was warm this May and his father had been late. He had been busy with a town protest. Every second time he hit the wood, his axe stuck. He hated it.

He walked to the side door of the house and called to his mother. "Can I have something to drink?"

His mother, Lisa James, with her thick Irish accent, answered that she would bring him something and that he should wait outside. He knew he was dirty and she didn't want him in her kitchen. Although she had been in Canada for at least twenty years, she still said she was Irish and her accent left little doubt about the truth of that statement. She was a short, heavy woman with curly red hair and a wicked temper. His father always said that she would beat you as soon as look at you, and Pat always laughed even though he never quite understood what this meant.

She brought him a drink of something red and sweet and he drank it in one gulp. "Go aisy on that, lad," she said, "you know it don't be growin' on trees."

He looked at the glass. Of course it didn't grow on trees, he thought, it's a glass of juice. "Thanks, mom." He handed her the empty glass. "I think I'll go for a swim." He started to take off his dirty shirt.

"Don't be daft, lad. You'll catch yer death."

"Aw, Mom!" he begged, dragging out the words.

"You be getting outta them darty clothes and wash yarself." She turned and walked into the house still mumbling to herself. "Going swimming in the freezing waters of spring! Tis livin' in a house of lunatics, I am."

Pat knew better than to cross his mother. 'She would beat you, as soon as look at you,' he thought. He took off everything but his Stanfield underpants, brushed off the sawdust and bits of bark, and went into the house.

The bathroom was a small room with a tub, sink and toilet and since the window was small and high, it was fairly dark. He did not feel like taking a bath so he sat on the cold metal tub and ran the water as he washed himself with his hands and a bar of soap. He was in a hurry, so he quickly scrubbed the dirty parts and then splashed water over himself in an attempt to rinse. Water was all over the bathroom floor, but at least he was clean. He wrapped a towel around his waist and walked to his small bedroom.

My Ding-A-Ling was playing on the radio in the kitchen. He could just hear it and he wondered if his mom knew what the words to this Chuck Berry song meant. Wouldn't she be surprised? Usually the North Bay station played only country and western music and Chuck Berry, Rod Stewart, and Santana could only be heard on the American Stations that drifted in and out at night.

An old starburst guitar leaned against the wall and, after he dressed, he strummed it a few times. The strings hurt his fingers because they were far away from the frets and it took a lot of pressure to get them down on the neck, but he liked to play and he had already learned a couple of songs. A guy in school had taught him six chords and with four of them, he could play the song, "On Top of Old Smokey." It was an old-folks song that he would only play for his parents, but when he played it for his friends, he sang the funny version: "On Top of Spaghetti, all covered with cheese. I lost my poor meatball. I'm down on my knees."

He practised the "A" and the "E" chords, because they sounded good, but he had a little trouble with the "D" and the "F". He was getting better and pretty soon he hoped to learn some of the songs he heard on the radio at night. He practised transitions for a while, going from chord to chord and then heard his mother called him. He leaned the guitar carefully against the dresser and walked to the front of the house. Kenny was waiting in anticipation and his mother handed him a jacket as he went out the door.

They walked quickly away from the house. "Come on, we gotta go see something."

Pat stopped suddenly. He did not want to be dragged into the bush and he planted his feet firmly. "I'm not going to look at some stupid, dead porcupine or something."

"No, no! I heard my dad talking. There's gonna be some trouble at Ray Smith's place." Pat continued to walk.

Ray Smith was the new mill manager and he was not well liked in town. The Staniforths had always been good to people, treating them like family, but old man Staniforth had died and now the company had been bought by some corporation. Smith was the latest in a string of mill managers and he was a hard boss.

"What kind of trouble?" Pat asked, now trotting to catch up. "Pat!"

The voice had come from behind and Pat turned to see Suzette Labelle running toward them. She only lived a few houses away, between the school and the Catholic Church, and she must have seen them pass. He told Kenny to wait.

Suzette wasn't like most of the French kids who stuck together in a group. She spent more time with Pat and Kenny than her father liked, and as far as Pat was concerned, that was just fine. She was pretty and he secretly had a crush on her. He often felt awkward when she was around and he might stutter or mix up his words, but it didn't matter.

"Are you going to Smith's house?" Suzy asked.

"Ssshh." Kenny put his finger to his lips.

Suzette huffed and slowed to a walk. "It's no secret." Her dark wavy hair flew out to the sides as she turned her head right and left. Others were walking toward the south end of town where Smith lived.

"What's . . . it all about?" asked Pat, fumbling with his words.

Suzette knew all the French gossip. "Mme. Desjardin made a . . . a . . . a . . . " she stuttered, lost for words. Suddenly they burst forth like water from a dam. "She. . . made a scarecrow and they're going to burn it in iffigy."

Pat knew the word "iffigy" was wrong, but he couldn't think of the right one and he knew what she meant. "They're doing that now?" Suzette nodded. "Come on, let's go!"

In the gloaming light, the town seemed welcoming. Warm yellow flowed out of the doorways and windows and rolled across the grass and the walkways. The sky over the forest to the north glowed in shades of violet and orange. As people gathered at the home of Ray Smith, the frogs chirped, and the birds sang their last songs of the day.

Desjardin dragged her mannequin and her husband carried a wooden pole. She was a weathered woman with wire-brush hair and a face of craggy lines. It was somewhat unwise to burn something so close to the mill - fire was something to fear in a lumber yard - but it was clear that only a fire would satisfy the anger of the people.

"How're ya doin', Kenny?" said an older man as he passed.

"Good, sir." Kenny replied.

Pat shook his head. Kenny was well liked by adults. His love of the forest endeared him to the men who were stuck in the mill. He grabbed him and steered him away from the group.

Mr. Desjardin drove the wooden spike into Smith's lawn. On his second swing, he missed and the mallet swung around in a circle as the stake fell to the ground. People laughed, but Kenny, Pat and Suzette covered their mouths. Children were not supposed to laugh at adults.

"Come on!" Mrs. Desjardin said to her husband. "Get on with it."

Planting his feet firmly, and obviously uncomfortable with such a large audience, Mr. Desjardin continued. The sound of the mallet hitting the wooden spike was loud and it echoed between the buildings and back from the trees, but no one came to the window of the Smith house. Either Ray Smith was frightened and staying away from the windows, or he was not home. Pat suspected the former to be true. He looked at Kenny. "Pretty neat, eh?"

"The guy deserves it!" Kenny said.

"What do you know?" Suzette asked defiantly.

"The guy bosses everyone around. He came here and everyone helped him and now that he's the manager, he shoves everyone around. He wouldn't fix the weir and he even gave the men who fixed it a hard time."

"My dad never said anything bad about him," Suzette replied.

Pat smiled. Suzette's dad would never say anything bad about anyone. Not only was he a quiet man, but he had a bad stutter. It would take him ages to voice a complaint about someone.

Kenny continued. "I'll tell you one real bad thing he did. You know Richard Rankin?" Pat and Suzy nodded. "Well, he just retired and after working for the company for . . . for . . . all his life, he was told to get out of his house."

"What for?" asked Suzette.

"They want the house for somebody else."

"Nooo!" Pat said. He believed it was true, but it sounded so shocking. Kiosk had always been a place where people took care of each other, where everyone helped each other.

"It's true!" Kenny said. "Smith told him to find a new home!"

"So what's he doing?"

"He's moving out of Kiosk." The sadness was evident in Kenny's voice.

"Why doesn't someone talk to the Staniforths?" asked Suzette.

Pat smiled again. Suzette was always trying to help. "My dad says they sold the place and don't have much to say anymore. They're never here, anyway."

"I'll bet you the Staniforths wouldn't treat people like that."

Kenny shrugged. "It doesn't matter. Ray's the boss and he's throwing the man out of his house."

Mrs. Desjardin and Mrs. Ouellette rammed the scarecrow onto the post. It hung, limp and drooping. "Hey, Mr. Smith, come on out and talk wid us." Some people looked at the house expectantly, but there was no movement. Pat thought he saw something, a movement of curtain, but he wasn't sure. "Come on!" taunted Mrs. Desjardin. A few people yelled at the house, but there was still no reaction. Mrs. Desjardin moved beside the mannequin. "Well, Mr. Smith, dis is what we tink of you! You're a limp man!" Many people laughed.

Pat looked at Kenny. "Pretty neat, huh?"

Kenny nodded.

Raymond Gravelle, a tough-as-nails woodcutter, walked forward with a gas can. Everyone was quiet as he doused the mannequin and threw a match. The match spun and then the air thumped loudly as the gasoline caught. The flames licked and flapped in the quiet and then someone shouted, "Burn, you bastard burn!" The crowd erupted in hoots and hollers as the blue light of the burning fuel cast eerie shadows on the grass. Suzette moved away, and Kenny and Pat followed.

Pat looked at another group of children, the French Catholic group. They too had moved further away from the fire. Somehow, it was not proper for children to watch adults behaving in this way. Then he spotted Armand, the young snotnose, waving his fist at

Ray Smith's house. Armand looked young for his age, but he tried to dress and act like an adult. He was spindly and he wore glasses that were too big for his skinny head. He seemed comfortable among the adults, cursing Ray Smith.

"Come on, let's go to the snack bar," Pat said.

"Just a minute," Kenny said.

"No. Let's go." Suzette started to walk away with Pat.

Pat turned and saw that Kenny wanted to stay. Kenny stayed back for a moment, hesitant, and then also decided to leave. He caught up to Pat and Suzette at the bridge.

The noise of the water going over the weir replaced the noise of the crowd and Pat stopped and looked at the slow water on the high side. The men had fixed it, and the water was slowly coming up to its old level. Its gently rolling surface reflected the lights of the town and the mill and contrasted sharply with the noise of surging water under his feet.

"It's a pretty place, isn't it?" Suzette said.

Pat was surprised. Suzette had read his thoughts as she often did. Whenever this happened, he felt this strange sensation in his chest. It was like jumping into the lake. First, there was this shock of cold, but in seconds, it turned into a feeling of warmth and comfort. He nodded.

Kenny idly swung back and forth on one of the winches used to raise the weir. He looked like a kid on a maypole. "The fish will be running soon too."

Pat peered into the dark water as if daring a fish to approach. "I don't see none."

Kenny didn't look at the water. "I gotta tell you guys what happened today."

Pat turned and saw the look of excitement on his friend's face. "What?"

"Well, for starters, I found a magic crystal."

"What?"

"Really!" Kenny began tentatively to describe the encounter with the bear, but his narrative gained momentum as the story developed. His voice sounded as if it would crack when he reached the part about his flight down the hill.

"Man. I would have been scared to death!" Pat said.

"I would have died," added Suzette.

"Once I was down the hill, it was okay," Kenny said, slower. He looked at Pat. "I even thought of going back up."

"Oh yeah! Right!"

"Sure!" Suzette said dubiously, stretching the word out.

"It's true! Once the cubs were back with their mother, there was no more danger. I could've gone back. I would've!"

An old pickup truck drove across the bridge and Kenny stopped talking as it approached.

"Hello, kids!" said Mr. Pelchat out of the window of his truck.

"So where's this crystal?" asked Pat, ignoring Mr. Pelchat.

"It's at home." Kenny waved as Mr. Pelchat drove away toward the mill.

"Well maybe you better keep it on you and find some for us too. There's lots of bears around this year."

"Aw, normally bears don't bother you."

"People get killed, you know."

"Naw. Really, you don't gotta be afraid of bears around here."

"That's easy for you to say," Suzette said, "you practically live in the bush." She looked around tentatively. There was dense bush on the north bank of the river. Bears could easily hide in the undergrowth. "Let's go to the snack bar."

Everyone agreed. They walked along the dusty road and then up the hill to the recreational centre and snack bar. "Did you tell your parents?" Pat asked.

"Yeah, Right! You think I'm nuts?"

"Yup." Pat laughed.

"My mom's afraid of bears," Ken said. "It must be a girl thing."

"Hey!" Suzette protested. She punched Kenny in the arm.

Kenny laughed and ducked in order to avoid a second hit.

A few kids were sitting on the wooden fence that surrounded the rink and Pat, Kenny and Suzette each bought a soda and joined them. They blew the wrappers off the straws, competing to see who could blow the paper wrapper the furthest. No one had heard about the burning of the scarecrow and this became the topic of discussion. Most of the questions were in French, but both Pat and Kenny could understand enough to get by.

Kenny then told a group of kids about his experience with the bear and Pat shook his head. If Kenny didn't want the story to get back to his parents, he shouldn't tell these kids. This was a small town and secrets were hard to keep. As Kenny talked to the crowd, Suzette grabbed Pat's sleeve and caught his attention.

"Do you really think that the mill's going to close?" she asked.

"Oh, I don't know. Everyone's been saying that for years, but nothing ever happens."

"I don't want to move somewhere else. I like it here." Suzette looked at Pat. Her voice was soft, fragile. "Do you want to move?"

Pat took a swig of his pop, looked at the other kids, and shrugged his shoulders. "Maybe. I'd like to learn to play the guitar better and maybe have my own group. That's hard to do in Kiosk."

A look of shock spread across Suzette's face. "But what about your friends?"

"I know . . . but I also want to see something of the world."

"Wouldn't you miss everyone?"

Pat noted something strange in Suzette's tone. Did she like him? he wondered. He was uncertain. "Yeah, that would be tough." He was silent for a moment and then said glibly: "Maybe we can all move away together."

Suzette looked down at the ground. "That would be okay . . . I guess."

"Don't worry about it," he continued. "It's not gonna happen anyway, 'cause they ain't closing up the mill." This didn't bring back Suzette's smile. He tried again. "Ah come on Suzette. No matter what happens, we'll still be friends."

Suzette looked up. "I have something for you," she said suddenly, the smile returning. She reached into the pocket of her windbreaker and took out a compass. "I know you're going camping with Kenny this summer. This will help you not to get lost."

Pat felt awkward. He took the compass and looked at it. It was not new, but it was oil-filled and in really good shape. "Gee . . . that's great . . . I . . . I don't have . . . anything . . ."

"That's okay Pat. I just wanted you to have it. I want you to be able to find your way home." She blushed and looked down at the ground.

Pat felt warmth, a strange, but nice feeling. "Th . . . thanks," he stammered. He didn't know quite what to do. Should he kiss her - no - that was too dangerous. She might laugh at him and there were others standing not too far away. He would get teased forever. He put his arm around her and gave her a half hug. She wrapped her arms around him and he felt suddenly as if he were somewhere else, somewhere distant, but somewhere nice.

Armand Gingras held his wool overcoat tightly closed as he walked along Rue Montcalm toward Julio's, a restaurant in Hull. His knees and calves burned from the frigid February cold.

He would have been more comfortable in jeans and a down-filled winter coat, but he was not yet in that league. The truly rich, the upper echelon, could dress as they pleased, but he was still struggling to the top, a journey made in suits and camelhair overcoats. Unfortunately, he had not come from a family of means and his clothing was off-the-rack from places like Tip Top Tailor and Jack Fraser. Not forever, he told himself.

He vaulted over a salty puddle, careful not to damage his ridiculously delicate leather shoes, and pulled the large brass handle of Julio's front door. Inside, the air was heavy and he strained to see his informant somewhere in the dim light.

Jeannine Dupuis, like so many people who lived in Ottawa, was a political operator and she depended on her contacts to keep her moving through the bureaucracy. She was trading useful information for future considerations with Armand's boss, the Minister of Indian and Northern Affairs, Francine Roussel, and since she worked for another Minister, she couldn't let her identity be known.

He spotted her sitting at the bar drinking a beer while she watched the room. She nodded her head ever so slightly. Her shoulder-length black hair was flawlessly coiffed and the dark jacket and white blouse were expensive, conservative and neat. Had it not been for the scars left by adolescent acne, she would have been stunning.

Armand ordered a beer for himself. "How's everything?

Okay?" He placed his black, leather binder on the bar. He knew that this restaurant was a safe place to meet. It was not on the circuit. Hy's, The Empire Grill, and D'Arcy McGee's Irish Pub - all in Ottawa across the river - were the places people went when people wanted to be spotted. Ottawa was a small town when it came to politics. Everyone knew everyone, and secrets were hard to keep. Even when informants weren't known, a list was made and it was narrowed down and narrowed down until their identity was revealed.

Jeannine nodded and then suggested that they move to a table in the corner. There was always a danger of being overheard.

Armand too had to be cautious. Armand's boss, a Liberal MP and Cabinet Minister, might possibly become the next Prime Minister of Canada and if this happened, Armand imagined that he would be the Chief of Staff in the Prime Minister's Office. This was the most powerful civil position in the country and one that Armand wanted.

It was time for the current Prime Minister, Jean Courchesne, to retire. He was closer to eighty than seventy and if he left now it would be on a high. Unfortunately, Courchesne was keeping everyone guessing, and as soon as anyone in the Liberal Party expressed an interest in the PM's position, it was seen as a display of disloyalty - political suicide.

The race for the leadership of the party was therefore run behind closed doors and the front-running candidate was Paul Matthieu, a Liberal Cabinet Minister of power and money. At one time, Matthieu had been the Minister of Finance, and now he was in Health. While in Finance, he had cut health care spending to show how he could get the budget under control, and now, in Health, he was throwing money back into the beleaguered system. He had been a hero for cutting and a hero for spending. His career had been flawlessly managed, and everyone assumed he was heading for the PM's office. But there was dissention. Matthieu was quick to hire outside consultants and advisors and his own aides were often left to flounder. This made his staff edgy, nervous. Armand suspected that this was the case with Jeannine.

Francine Roussel was the second choice to replace Courchesne and she was a distance behind Matthieu, but gaining. She would be sixty years old soon and if she did not run in the next election, she would be getting close to sixty-five for the following one. Now was the time and Armand was trying to make it happen.

Unfortunately, the race had to be run in secret, away from the public, because as soon as the press made any comment about anyone replacing Courchesne, the PMO - Prime Minister's Office - was quick to spin some negative press for the contender. If Armand did anything public to enhance her chances, the PMO negated the effort.

"So what do you have for me?" he asked settling into the booth.

"Did you tell anyone about our meeting?"

Armand closed his eyes for a moment as if trying to maintain his patience. "Only Madame Roussel, as we agreed." This was a lie. He had not told Roussel and he wouldn't until it became necessary.

Jeannine reached into her purse and took out a piece of paper, which she unfolded and handed to Armand. It was a list of all the companies with which Paul Matthieu had been affiliated. Armand scanned it and shrugged his shoulders. "So? This is public knowledge."

"But if you look at the lists that are officially released, you won't see any mention of the directorship with Imasco. He was there for over two years."

Armand wasn't sure what she was driving at. Imasco was a respectable company and if Matthieu's bio failed to mention that he had been on the board, it was probably just an oversight.

"You've heard of British American Tobacco?"

Armand nodded. BAT had been in the news recently because of some incriminating documents that suggested the tobacco industry was deliberately enhancing the addictive quality of cigarettes and targeting children as the most profitable market. Consumer groups were pressuring the government to take action against BAT.

"Well, you may know that Imasco owns Imperial Tobacco."

Armand nodded again, even though he had not been aware of this.

"But . . ." Jeannine took a deep breath, "what you probably aren't aware of, is that it's a subsidiary of British American

Tobacco."

Armand smiled. This was good news. The Minister of
Health had been a director of a company that was being blamed for
deliberately spiking cigarettes with stronger addictive properties.
"That is interesting. What are they saying in the office?"

"It's a non-issue. No one says a thing. It just doesn't exist."

The waiter arrived and took the order. Jeannine ordered a
julienne salad and Armand ordered veal.

After he left, Armand spoke again. "What is it that you don't
like about Matthieu?" He immediately regretted the question
because he could see from Jeannine's face that he had opened an
uncomfortable door.

She squirmed in her seat and moved the fork and knife on
the tablecloth, arranging them. "It's not that I don't like the man . .
.," she said tentatively. "There are some problems. I don't think he
should be Prime Minister." She shrugged her shoulders. That was
all she was going to say.

Armand steered the conversation away from her motives.
They talked about some of the many foolish people and some of the
more comical situations on the Hill, which was the way they
referred to Parliament Hill. There was no shortage of buffoons to
laugh about in Ottawa. Jeannine picked at her salad.

"So you think he'll retire?" Armand asked referring to the
PM.

"Word is that he's going to go. Everyone thought he would
retire last year, but he wanted to show he could hang in. He's getting tired. He'll go."

"You think Matthieu still thinks he's going to go?"

Jeannine nodded. "I guess for him it's the last shot. He
already said he would not run again if another election is called.
He's sort of backed himself into a corner." She parried her fork in
the air.

Armand wanted to discover this woman's motivation, but he
knew he couldn't ask. If she chose to tell him, fine, but otherwise,
it would remain a mystery. "Is there anything else you can tell me?"

"Not at this minute." She ate a bite of salad and then waved
the fork like a magic wand between them. "You know, you should
check into his days working with the Power Corporation. There

were some pretty ruthless manoeuvres. I'm sure there are some skeletons hanging around there that very few people know about."

Armand studied Jeannine's eyes. Did she know something that she just couldn't talk about, or was this just conjecture? "What sort of skeletons?"

"Just things . . . typical power things." She took another bite of salad and dropped her fork into the bowl to signify she was finished eating.

Armand wiped his lips with the cloth napkin and dropped it onto his plate. He hadn't learned as much as he would have liked, but it was important to keep contacts in key places. "You've been really helpful," he said. "It won't go unnoticed. I promise."

Jeannine stood and slipped out of the restaurant, leaving Armand to pay the bill.

As Armand sat waiting for the waitress to return with his credit card, he thought about British American Tobacco and the Minister of Health. He obviously could not make a public statement about the Minister's involvement, this would be political suicide, but there might be another way to get the information out to the public.

The outside air hit him like a thousand tiny pins. The wind was merciless and after the moist warmth of the restaurant, it felt like it was cutting through the material of his pants. When he saw the cab, he quickly jumped in the back.

When he reached his apartment building, he entered the austere lobby and took the elevator to the sixth floor. It was not a classy building, but he needed to save. One day it would all be different, he thought, one day.

In his apartment, he dropped the sheet of paper listing Matthieu's affiliations on the kitchen table. He looked at it and grinned. Although it did not even hint at a conspiracy, like a piece of string tied around the finger, it would remind him of the negative publicity that was available, and would remind him to sniff around the Power Corporation. Courchesne was going to leave soon and he had to knock down Matthieu before that happened. It was the only way that Francine Roussel would become the first female Liberal Prime Minister and this was the only way that he would become the Chief of Staff in the PMO.

He hung up his coat and poured himself a rum on the rocks. He would have liked a little coke, but he knew there was none in the apartment. Shopping was not one of his strengths.

His wife had left him after six years of marriage. She had had a child from a previous marriage and he had been happy to see them both go. The little girl had been a nuisance and the mother had not been much better. He preferred being alone. It was easier. He also did not like the idea of sharing the wealth that he would one day earn.

He took his drink into the living room, stood silently, listening to the sound of the heating system - a gentle mechanical whirr - and then he flopped into a large leather chair. The rum gently burned as it rolled down his throat.

He studied the floor-to-ceiling bookshelf that lined the south wall. He had designed it himself. The fourth section was on hinges and it hid the entrance to the bedroom. It had been a quirky thing to do, his first rebellion after his wife had left, but it had made sense at the time. It accomplished nothing, it served nothing, but it felt right. He looked at the books, and thought about the bedroom behind. Whom could he trap in this hidden room, he wondered? Fantasies formed in his mind as he drifted off to sleep.

          Suzy Levasseur shifted her position under her boyfriend and looked up at his face. She grimaced. His eyes were closed, his expression was tense, and he had his lower lip between his teeth. He continued to thrust and pump in a slightly frantic, arrhythmic manner. For a moment, she wondered if he wanted to get this over with as much as she did.

She turned her face and watched the converging patterns of shadows move about her ceiling. The wind, which occasionally vibrated the windows in their frames, was moving the clusters of pine needles in front of the street lamp. The contrapuntal movement of light and shade, and the pattern of nature, brought her back to her childhood in Kiosk.

Jean Guy grunted and mumbled something and she gratuitously sighed. Within minutes, it was over and he was up, out of bed, and in the bathroom. Before he returned, she was on her side, one pillow under her head and the other snuggled in front, pretending to be asleep. She heard Jean Guy crawl into bed and was grateful when he ignored her.

Her sleep was restless and disturbed. She dreamt of forests covered in snow. Then the snow disappeared and was replaced with green rustling leaves. There was nothing but endless shades of green and a wind that was so loud that it drowned out all other sounds. Then she smelled smoke and she choked as she sat up in bed.

She was awake in her small bedroom, feeling the cold radiate through the walls. There was no smoke, but the wind was blowing violently outside her little home and branches scraped on the siding. She looked at the soft green digital clock. It was time to get up.

Downstairs Jean Guy continued an argument he had started on the previous day. He spoke in that controlled, even-paced tone that drove her crazy. "I'm not trying to tell you what to do . . . but dis is not a smart idea."

She had taken a job doing stand-up with a news crew and it meant going freelance. Most of the crews worked for themselves, but were kept busy by MCTV, the CBC or Global. She had been working for the station, but if she really wanted to get on-camera, the only way to do this was to get on a crew and freelance, and it was either now or never. She had kept her shoulder-length dark hair neat and her complexion clear, and she was still attractive, but many of the newscasters appearing on the nightly news were good-looking twenty-eight year olds. In the not too far distant future, she would be in her forties.

"Eh, You're jus too damned old," he said.

She closed her eyes, trying to calm the storm that was brewing just below the surface. He often prefaced his sentences with 'Eh,' but it was harsh and sharp, a French Canadian "Hey!" It was one of his many annoying habits. She did not reply and he droned on.

"You gave up a job that's a sure-thing for some part-time work. You get no benefits . . . nothing."

Suzy turned and looked at Jean Guy. He was of average weight, but his poor posture emphasised his pot belly, and he tried to hide his balding head by parting his hair almost at his ear - two more annoying habits. He had just taken a shower and his hair was dry and stringy and threatened to stand straight up as it made its journey up and over the top of his shiny skull. She smiled. "Well, it's done, so live with it." She turned and walked to the front hall, forgetting what she had wanted in the kitchen. "Take care of Michelle, would you? I'll be back by supper." She grabbed a winter coat and stepped out into the frigid morning air.

As she walked to her minivan, she thought about Michelle, her ten-year-old daughter, staying with Jean Guy in the townhouse. It made her uncomfortable. Jean Guy was not a threat, but he wasn't the greatest influence. He certainly wasn't the role model she would have hoped for. She pictured him with his arms outstretched saying: "Eh!" and she shuddered.

She turned the key and the motor protested as it started. It was only a few years old, but already it was having trouble with the Canadian winters. Her tires spun in the unplowed parking lot and she struggled over the hump left on the entrance by the snowplow.

After a full day of work, she dropped the equipment bag on the tech bench and started to put away some patch cords. "It went well, don't you think?" They had just filmed a short on a local farm that had been lambing in February.

Jaro Dack, the cameraman, was a few feet away storing gear in a large metal cabinet. A cigarette dangled from his lips as he spoke. "Not bad . . . but pretty mundane stuff. I doubt it will even make the Toronto news." Jaro, in his mid twenties, had a burning desire to break into the major market. He was normally a happy fellow, smiling with the androgynous good looks of a soap star, but when it came to his career, he was ruthless. The metal door of the cabinet banged shut. "Every time there's a good story, they give it to the crews from Toronto."

"We'll get a chance."

Jaro didn't say anything, but his silence was a commentary on the term 'we'. He walked out of the room leaving Suzy to complete the equipment log.

Although her parents lived just outside Montreal, Suzy had studied journalism at Ryerson in Toronto. While in college, she worked at CJRT, the campus radio station, and she thought that when she graduated, she would walk into a broadcasting job with the CBC. She had been wrong.

She wandered the city and found that, outside the world of college radio, her experience did not account for much. After a short stay as a receptionist in a Brampton radio station, she moved back to Montreal, frustrated and disillusioned. She married Lionel Levasseur, a fellow who worked with her father in Pointe Claire, and Michelle was born a few years later.

Her broadcasting career had been put on hold for a few years. She lived in Pointe Claire and worked at an English language radio station on Green Street in Montreal. On top of her shift, she had two hours of travelling and Lionel expected her to take care of every aspect of raising Michelle.

Lionel became involved in the Parti Québécois and spent most of his free time trying to get Quebec to separate from Canada - or at least drinking with his friends and talking about it. He could not be bothered with doctors' appointments, parent-teacher interviews, or anything else that involved Michelle, and when it came to her work, at an English language radio station, he was abusive.

He wanted Suzy to have more children, but she saw this as multiplying her problems and resisted, secretly taking birth control that he knew nothing about. When Lionel found out, he was enraged.

She turned to her family for support, but her parents were on good terms with Lionel, and they also did not agree with Suzy's one-child family. What was wrong with more children? They had five children, four of whom were still alive to this day. Birth control was a sin. Lionel and her father worked together at the same furniture company and they talked about Suzy at work. The marital problems, they agreed, all stemmed from her job with the English.

Eventually her father lost his job at the furniture company and then he and Lionel stopped being friends. This, she had thought, would make it easier to break ties with Lionel and when she came home one night early to find him in bed with a petite, heavily made-up Francophone girl, she left with Michelle and filed for divorce.

Her parents refused to help her, trying to push her back into her marriage with Lionel and family life disintegrated further. Her dad was drinking heavily at the time, making his stutter worse and her brothers and sisters rarely came back to town. The family drifted apart. When a job in Barrie presented itself, she took Michelle and left Quebec for good.

She also wanted to break into the major market, which in her mind meant Toronto, but she was finding it difficult. Most of her coworkers were surprised to learn that she had been an announcer at CJRT, which was now a big Toronto station, no longer associated with campus radio, but it would take a lot more than this to make television crews take notice of her.

Even in Barrie, she wasn't a superstar. The media was full of complaints. People complained about her age, about her slight French accent and about her kid. The audience wanted young sexy reporters. And single-mom reporters could not easily cover breaking stories; it was difficult for them to get away at a moment's notice.

In the next room, she could hear Jaro talking to Mike, a suave young sound-technician. "We need to get someone else," he said.

Where they talking about her? she wondered. Although Jaro was really only the cameraman who occasionally did some stand-up, he liked to think of himself as a director/producer. She moved closer to the wall and strained to hear.

"She's not that bad," replied Mike.

There was a jumble of noise as two other people started talking, but she heard Jaro saying, "too old," and, "not camera candy." Camera Candy! That was an expression that had evolved around the station. It described sweet young reporters who were more adept at showing breast than reporting a story.

She walked into the room and shook her head when she saw the sheepish expressions on Mike's face. They had been talking about her. "Better get that tape into editing," she said to Jaro.

Jaro looked at her dryly, a styrofoam coffee cup in his hand and blue smoke drifting up from his cigarette.

Suzy stood with her hands on her hips. "Come on, get moving! This is the news, not fiction." Jaro tapped his cigarette in an ashtray, doing his best to ignore her. "If it isn't on time, it ain't worth the tape it's shot on," she added.

Jaro hesitated and then reached a decision. He put down his coffee and walked to the editing room, but he looked back at Suzy with a strange expression. There was something more than defiance in his eyes and Suzy felt cold.

It was minus thirty and a strong wind howled as it blew snow under the front door of Gary Pinneskum's Mattawa home. He rolled off the sofa, crossed the threadbare carpet and kicked an old coat against the door to stop the wind from howling underneath. Particles of snow danced around the jacket, blown by a gust of February wind, and he kicked the door in disgust.

He picked up his water glass from the coffee table and finished the last of his rye. It burned as it went down and he considered making something to eat, but then decided it was too much effort.

In the early winter, he had worked in the bush for Richelieu Logging, but he had been unemployed for the last two months. At first, it had been good to get away from the hard labour - his aging body did not fare well in the bush - but after a few months at home, he found that time dragged. His wife, Pierrette, worked at the nursing home, his children had both moved away, and there was no one to talk to.

A dark wooden clock ticked on the mantelpiece of the phoney fireplace and the sound filled the room. He stood staring at it. The ticking became louder and louder until if filled the room. "Shut up!" he shouted and then he backhanded the clock and sent it flying. It hit the floor, its glass face shattering, but it continued to tick loudly. He looked at it impatiently and walked into the kitchen. It was a mess. Dishes littered the counter top and dirty pots and pans covered the stove. He found a clean looking glass on the counter and poured a large triple of rye. This almost emptied the bottle. He drank half the contents in one gulp.

There had to be a better way to live. He hated Mattawa and this little house in the poorer section of town. He had been raised on the shore of a lake just north of Algonquin Park, but his parents hadn't owned the land. His father was an orphan raised on the

Dufond farm and when he was old enough, he moved into an abandoned logging shanty a few miles away. No one questioned an Indian family living in the middle of nowhere in an abandoned camp, but when his father died, there was nothing left. There was no reserve, no land, no money, nothing to pass on to his children.

Gary had worked in the bush and lived in dozens of places after his parents died. He worked as a guide, a trapper, a wood cutter, and he even tried to start a small business. That was after he had been sent to Toronto by the federal government. They had filled his head with foolish dreams. He would become a leader. It didn't take long for him to realise that he could only do this on the backs of others. If he hated his life before he went to Toronto, he hated it more afterwards.

He pulled up his worn wool socks and walked back to the small living room. On the wall was a large buffalo skull. It had some sage grass in one eye socket and there was a feather hanging from its horn, but it was still missing something. Something was still not right. He took another drink, but this did not help with the answer.

For a while, there had been a fascination with Indian art and he had made dream catchers and religious artefacts, which he sold to the naive tourist from Southern Ontario and the USA, but the process of doing so had forced him to look at the spiritual background of his people. At first, he would slap something together, only interested in its commercial appeal, but lately, he had felt a growing need to get it right, to make something significant.

The buffalo was a symbol of the Plains Indian and there were certainly no Plains Indians in the Mattawa area, but it was still powerful. Who knew where his grandparents came from? They might have been forest, plains or tundra Indians. He assumed his parents were originally Ojibwa and Algonquin, but they could have just as easily been Cree, Huron or Iroquois. They had grown up on Manitou Lake with the Dufonds, an Indian family that took in many orphans.

Old Amable Dufond was an Algonquin from Lake of Two Mountains and he originally moved into the area before the 1850's. By the turn of the century, his two sons ran farms in what was now Algonquin Park. They were small communities containing Scottish and Irish immigrants, young bush workers, and adopted Indians from all over the area. At one point, old Imaqua Dufond, one of the many decedents, spoke of twenty-seven children being raised in the one house. They took in children from Cree villages, Ojibwa villages, and Algonquin villages, anyone who needed a family.

Both his father and his mother had been orphans from different places, but they had grown up on the same farm. He had been told that there had been one table for the girls and one table for the boys - a busy place.

He dropped back onto the sofa and looked around the room. It wasn't busy here. He emptied his glass and felt too lazy to get up for the rest of the bottle.

Armand Gingras shuffled through some papers and noted the tension in the room. Francine Roussel, the Indian and Northern Affairs Minister had called the meeting in her constituency office, a dark old room with high ceilings and heavy walls, and Adrienne Denny, the press secretary, and Bob White, a senior aide, were in attendance. Roussel usually conducted business in the Ministry Office on Slater Street, but the constituency office was more private. Armand dropped a file folder on Roussel's huge oak desk, which looked more like a conference table, and waited for Adrienne Denny to give her report on the recent Liberal meeting at the Constellation Hotel in Toronto.

A group of Paul Matthieu supporters had gathered to voice their support for Matthieu as the next leader of the Liberal Party. This was a daring move, but the spin had been good. Politicians were always concerned about the 'spin' on an issue. Then Jean Courchesne publicly announced that he was not yet ready to retire. Many people, Denny included, felt that Courchesne would retire and that all of the chicanery at the PMO was part of some political agenda, but no one could put a finger on it. At any rate, the Matthieu camp had gone public and so had Courchesne. The non-race for Party Leadership was heating up.

Roussel waited for Denny to finish talking and then looked at Armand frostily. "I thought you said that Courchesne was going to retire?"

"All the intel says he will."

"Well, the intel is wrong."

"Perhaps not," said Denny. "Courchesne doesn't want to appear weak right now. He might be waiting for the appropriate time."

Roussel turned to Denny. "Then why go public? Why not just keep quiet about it?"

"Matthieu forced his hand. Having a public meeting at the Constellation Hotel was a foolish thing to do. The Prime Minister had to respond."

Roussel put a pencil to her lips. "Okay . . . possibly . . . but now the country, the press, sees Matthieu as having Liberal support as a leadership candidate. We're out in left field."

"Minister, I'm still against going public," said Armand. "I think it's unwise."

Bob White interrupted. "I don't know, Armand. Now that Matthieu has gone public, I think we would be in the clear. I think we should tell the press that there is another choice."

Denny shook her head. "No! If we were going to do that, we should've done it first. That was Armand's mistake - advising the Minister not to go public - we should've gone public, but before Matthieu. But, if we do so now, we'll be making two mistakes." She held up two fingers and then folded the first one down. "First, we are responding, following, rather than taking the initiative. And secondly, we would be going public after Courchesne has stated he is not retiring." She pulled her second finger down. "How would that look to the public? No . . . we missed our chance."

Armand placed his hand under his chin, mimicking the pose of Rodin's famous statue. The room was silent, waiting for him to reply. He smiled and looked up. "No, it was no mistake. Matthieu made the mistake. This is a race between contenders behind the scenes. Going public now is foolish. Let me show you something." He pulled out three copies of the Matthieu background and handed them to everyone. Denny took the pages with annoyance, Roussel with caution, and White with curiosity.

He explained the background; dragging out the information for all that it was worth. "Can you imagine," he said finally, "how damaging it would be for the Minister of Health, if the public learned that he had been a director of the company that was found guilty of spiking cigarettes and targeting children for tobacco addiction?"

"Mr. Gingras, surely you don't expect us to release that sort of information to the press!" Roussel only addressed Armand by his last name when she was annoyed with him.

Denny noticed the tone and added, "We may be competing for the PM's office, but it is not acceptable to bring down another Minister!"

Armand smiled patiently. "Of course we wouldn't release the information. We can't publicly damage the career of a Liberal Minister, but we don't have to go out of our way to protect it either." He turned to Denny. "Do you honestly believe that Matthieu would shield The Honourable Francine Roussel from political scandal? If you do, you're too naive to be a press secretary." Denny started to protest, but Armand held up his hand. "The trick here is to get the information out without having it come from this office." He stood and handed everyone a small bio and waited as they scanned the pages. "What you're looking at is the biography of Joe Capputto, an outspoken public activist. He's been fighting for tougher anti-smoking legislation for years and is just the fellow to lead up a task force investigating BAT illegalities."

Bob White grinned. "You're proposing that we set up and help arrange the funding for such a committee."

Armand shrugged. "We have to look out for the interests of the people and if that means supporting a public activist, and if that public activist uncovers some information, well . . ."

Roussel leaned forward. "How can you be sure what he'll find, or if he'll find anything?"

"Does it matter? Either way, we're just acting in the public's interest. The tobacco industry is not popular. The worst that can happen is that we wind up looking like public crusaders."

Denny's brow was furrowed. "What about campaign contributions? You might chase away some much needed money from a future campaign."

"We're not heading the committee, Joe Capputto is. We'll keep an arm's length distance unless we see an advantage in not doing so. Anyway, I don't think BAT contributed to our last campaign and if we don't drop Matthieu in ratings, there won't be much of a campaign to worry about."

Roussel leaned back and thought for a moment. She suddenly sat forward and pointed a pencil at Armand. "Go ahead with this, but you better be right."

Denny raised her hands, palms forward, in a cruciform. "I . . . don't know . . ."

Armand smiled and grabbed his papers. His failure to acknowledge Denny was recognized for the dismissive gesture it was. "Yes, Minister." He stood and left the meeting. Bob White nodded and followed. Denny scrambled to her feet.

Suzy heard Michelle's voice and decided to get out of bed. Jean Guy was still asleep. He had been drinking last night, something she didn't condone when he was alone with Michelle, and when she had come home at two in the morning, he was amorous and gropey. She had spent the evening at a chemical fire and had no interest in romance, but rather than argue, she had submitted - quick, distracted, and disinterested. His sour breath in her face had caused her to turn her head and look out the window.

She stopped at the bedroom door and turned to study him. His wiry hair twisted over the pillow, his skin was sallow and oily, and he snored lightly. The bedroom air was oppressive, like the air in the room of an ill person, and she knew that, tired as she was, she would get no further sleep for today.

Quietly she descended the half-flight of stairs to the kitchen. From here, she could see through the black iron railing into the living room. Her daughter was giggling at the antics of some scantily clad female warriors on a Saturday morning cartoon.

She plugged in the kettle and as she got the glass tea pot and put it on the table, she heard Michelle call to her questioningly. "Yes dear, it's me," she said.

"Okay Mom, I'm just watching cartoons."

Suzy opened the cupboard and heard Michelle sneak up the stairs, put the cereal bowl on the kitchen table, and return to the living room. "I already had breakfast," she called when she was safely back on the sofa. Michelle was not supposed to eat in front of the television.

Suzy smiled. "Okay, dear. I'm going to make something for myself."

Jean Guy came down the stairs and dropped heavily into one of the chairs. "Eh, you were late last night." It was more an accusation than a statement.

Suzy exhaled heavily. They had talked last night, but Jean Guy had only been interested in sex; now he wanted to discuss her work hours. "So?"

"I told you dat dis job would be no good," he continued. "You don't make any more money and now I got to work as a baby-sitter for the brat." He jerked his thumb in the direction of the living room.

Suzy rubbed her eyes. Michelle was watching TV and probably had not heard Jean Guy's comment, but it annoyed her nonetheless. "I'll get someone else, then," she said, doing her best to sound flippant.

Jean Guy grinned. "Wouldn't bother me none. I got better things to do wit my time."

She squeezed her eyes shut. What was she doing? Living with a man that she didn't love - maybe even didn't like - so that she could have a baby sitter? There had to be more to a relationship than this. She drank from her tea. "Well? Who do you want me to call? I have to go into the station and do some editing, so someone's got to stay with Michelle."

"Maudit," said Jean Guy rolling his eyes. "I'll take care of her today, but we have to do something different in de future."

Suzy looked down at Michelle. She seemed to be paying no attention to the discussion, but she still would be disappointed when her mom was gone again for an entire Saturday. It couldn't be helped. "I better get ready." She felt like having a long hot shower before work.

Gary Pinneskum chose the spot for the next hole and fishing line. The frozen surface of the lake was beginning to look like a Texas oil field with all the lines he had set up, but he wanted to make the trip worthwhile and bring home a case of fish.

The ice was thick, but he knew the gas-powered auger would cut through it easily. He pulled the cord a few times and the small gasoline engine burred to life, breaking the deep silence of Kioshkokwi Lake. He gunned the throttle a few times, and listened to the high staccato pulse echo back from the surrounding hills.

The machine dug in and twisted, but he held on tightly. He applied downward pressure and eventually the water bubbled up and turned the granulated particles of ice into a soup of dark blue crystal and water.

He shut off the auger and listened to the silence return. He steeled himself and then, taking a deep breath, he dropped his gloves and scooped out the ice. This helped keep the hole open longer, but the mixture of cold water and ice stung his hands like a swarm of angry hornets. He stood, opened his jacket, and jammed his hands under his armpits. With each new hole, his hands were getting colder and each time it was taking longer for the circulation to return. He was ready for a warm-up break.

His old GMC 4X4 was parked facing the shore. It was an old truck - so old that it had the round headlights that looked like eyes - and he didn't dare take it out on the lake. The ice was thick enough, but pressure cracks made it rough. The truck was running on borrowed time and there was no sense working it harder than necessary.

The carburetted 350 V8 protested, but finally turned over, and after a few moments, Gary felt the heat roll out of the dash. He poured a cup of the lukewarm coffee from his thermos and wrapped his hands around the plastic cup. As he drank, the wind pushed at the cab, moving it slightly, howling around the large mirrors and through the holes in the rusty doors. The late afternoon sun was weak and the cold of the night crept over the land. Night came early at this time of year.

Carved by the sharp winter wind, the rippled surface of Kioshkokwi looked more like a desert than a snow-covered lake. A sudden gust caused ice crystals to dance between the ridges of turquoise and mauve.

Gary climbed out of the truck and walked to each of his holes. There were a few fish, but nothing compared to what he had caught a week ago and he wondered if he was wasting his time. The cold wind snapped at his coat and snuck underneath. It was too cold and the sun had set. He decided to give up and go home. He loaded his gear, threw the fish in the insulated case and began the long drive on Highway 630 and then Highway 17. In just over an hour, he reached the small town of Mattawa.

A few vehicles plowed through the snow on Main Street, but people were staying off the sidewalks. The blackness of evening made the yellow brightness of the stores seem warm and inviting.

Gary parked in front of the jewellery store and ran across to the Algonquin Office. He was not greeted by anyone as he stomped his feet and rubbed his hands together. "Is the meeting still on tonight?" he asked a woman typing at the front desk.

She looked at her watch and then answered. "Yeah, soon. And it's time for me to go home."

Gary walked over to the coffee machine, grabbed a styrofoam cup and poured himself a coffee. It was hot and he wrapped his hands around the cup, absorbing the warmth. "Gonna be many people?"

The woman was cleaning off her desk and she didn't look at Gary. "Don't know. Guess you'll see." Her tone was dismissive.

Gary was accustomed to this treatment. He wasn't popular in the native community; he was an outsider, keeping mostly to himself.

He walked back into the office, a large, mostly unfinished space, and sipped the bitter fluid in his cup. This had once been a hardware store and it had never been remodelled after the band took it over. There was nothing to see, there were no other people, and he walked around looking at the missing ceiling tiles, the exposed wiring, the missing partitions, and the cuts in the industrial grey carpeting. He wished he had a drink.

Slowly people started to arrive and by seven o'clock, there were eight others in the office. He knew three, an old woman named Mary, and Leonard and Thelma from Mattawa, but the others were strangers. Mary introduced him to Billy and Sharon Raconteur. Billy, a thin, short man dressed in blue jeans and cowboy boots, was a native elder from Oka, and he and his wife, Sharon, were here to give a talk on native spiritual issues. A white woman stood by herself smiling. She looked as if she were an artist or an aging hippie with lots of money. She wore a batik dress and lots of clunky jewellery, but her hair was perfectly coiffed. Although she looked out of place, she seemed completely relaxed.

Gary had asked his wife to come, but she declined. She often said that she was more a Mattawa person than a native person, so, now, he sat here alone, not quite sure what to expect. Although Billy was an elder, he was younger than Gary, and this made Gary feel slightly ill-at-ease.

It was dark outside and the cold wind howled and buffeted the building creating drafts that moved the ceiling tiles. The other six people sat quietly in chrome and plastic chairs as Billy walked in a small circle, holding a feather in his hand. He explained that the feather was customary and it would be passed to other people who wanted to speak.

He began his presentation by saying "Bonjo". This, he explained, was not quite the same as "hello", it was more like "how is your life?" Then he talked about his own past and how he had come to be a Tribal Elder. He explained that as a teenager, he had been addicted to drugs and alcohol and had been in trouble with the law. He said he had drifted from place to place without purpose or direction and was in trouble with everyone, the police, the elders, his parents and friends. One day he was asked to help the tribal elders at Oka and he took on the role of keeper of the pipe. He said that listening to the old ways had affected his spiritual mind-set.

On an easel, he wrote the word, heart. He said that this was at the centre of the lives of the people and he talked for a long while about living in the head and in the heart. After a pause, he flipped the page and wrote eight words - one for each person present. "Simplicity, Observation, Patience, Consistent, Endurance, Acceptance, Responsible, Commitment." Taking his time, he explained each one and its importance to his people's way of life.

An hour later, after a short coffee break, Sharon took the feather and began to speak. She transformed as she stood in front of the group. While her husband had been speaking, her expression had remained dour and sullen; now, she smiled and became animated, even excited. She explained that she too had come from a troubled past. Drugs, alcohol, and abuse had all been ingredients in the mix. She talked about a troubled childhood and hinted at physical abuse and withdrawal.

She said that their people had to learn from each other and she made a comical reference to the Migwetch - the moccasin telegraph - that served to spread information among the people, but she warned of the powerful negative side that is always waiting to overcome the positive. She said she had learned from others and had been saved.

Gary was becoming uncomfortable. The elders were talking more about recovering from alcoholism, abuse and drug addition than about Native spirituality. Listening to this reminded him of his own problems with alcohol. He did not want to think of this. Although he did not drink often, when he did, he lost control, never knowing when to stop. He would pass out and then suffer for many hours afterward. He looked around the room and saw that Sharon's words were reaching most of the people in the room and he suddenly realised he was in a world of broken people - of people who felt unconnected, lost. Maybe those were the people who were attracted to these seminars.

Sharon was talking about balance again. She spoke of the four components to balance: the physical, the emotional, the thinking, and the spiritual. It was necessary to be healed in all of these areas. And, in order to be healed, the people had to be flexible. "Flexibility," she repeated for emphasis. The people should look at the trees, strong, powerful, yet flexible in the wind. The people had to be like that. Time is very important. Life is precious. Then she said that she would pass the feather to each of the people present, so they could tell a little about themselves and say what they had learned from the meeting.

Gary suddenly wished he wasn't here. He did not want to talk about himself. He looked at the white woman and saw the relaxed smile on her face. The idea of speaking about herself did not trouble her. He looked at the door. It was a very long way away. The feather was passed to Mary at the opposite end of the room. At least, he consoled himself, he would be one of the last people to speak.

Each person, with the exception of the white woman, talked about their troubled childhood, their disconnected upbringing and their feelings of alienation and loss. It was, as Gary suspected, a room full of broken people struggling to find themselves. When the feather was passed to him, he gave thanks, mumbled that he had learned much, and then hurriedly passed the feather on to the last person in the room.

To end the evening, they all stood in a circle, held hands and said a group prayer of thanks. When it was over, Gary said good-bye and rushed out the door. He knew that the bottle of Canadian Rye, carefully hidden in his workshop, would probably be empty by the end of the night.

"Let Angela take a try," said Jaro. "I want to get her on tape anyway." He busied himself with the equipment as he turned his head to avoid his own cigarette smoke.

Suzy stood holding the microphone cable with her left hand so it would not trail in the dirt and she looked at Jaro questioning-ly. This was a fill story about a spring-time farmer's market. It did not deserve much attention. Why was he wasting their time? Jaro had brought a cute, dark-haired woman named Angela, whom he wanted to get on-camera, but there was more to this than a simple audition.

Angela seemed excited. She was barely out of her teens and she bubbled with anticipation as she took the clip-on microphone from Suzy. With shoulder-length, curly hair, a short skirt, a tight top and lots of makeup, she looked more like an exotic dancer than a television reporter. She fumbled with the clip-on and then smiled sweetly as Mike attached it to her flimsy top. Looking over her shoulder, she checked the background and then asked if she could begin.

She did the stand-up reasonably well, but most of what she said was a copy of the stand-up that Suzy had done. She had a great auditory memory. "Did you like it?" she asked.

"Sure, it was great. You hit the right kind of mood."

She clasped both of Jaro's hands. "Thanks."

"Are we ready to go yet?" Suzy asked.

"Yeah, let's pack up."

They stowed the gear in the back of the Jeep and left Oro

township. Back at the station, they looked at the footage of Suzy's stand-up and then put together the background for the two-minute news clip. It went quickly. After an hour's work, it was mostly done and when Suzy finished her voice-overs, she decided to go home. She didn't like leaving Angela and Jaro together, but there was something she needed to take care of.

The air was dry and clear as she drove. It was a beautiful spring day and she took a longer route along the quiet suburban streets. This gave her a chance to think.

As she approached the parking lot, she saw Jean Guy's car. She walked into the townhouse, found Jean Guy, without a shirt on, drinking beer and watching television. Michelle was nowhere to be seen.

"We have to talk," she said.

A few days later, dressed in a skirt and bra, Suzy stood before the bathroom mirror and studied herself. She looked like the girl next door, she was not stunning, and she did not look like a dynamic reporter. She plucked her eyebrows to thin fine lines, refining her appearance, but she was still not pleased. Her hair was thin and straight, just touching her shoulders. It wasn't sexy.

Michelle walked in and sat on the edge of the tub. Her hair was thick and wavy. "You know, mom," she said, "I'm old enough to stay by myself."

Suzy looked in the mirror and smiled. "Yes, I know you are, but sometimes things can happen. I just feel better."

"But Mrs. Sutton's such a cow." Anne Sutton, the woman who lived in the same townhouse complex and looked after Michelle during the day, was quite strict. She had two young children of her own and Suzy complained that she often felt out of place.

"She's not that bad . . . She's better than Jean Guy."

"At least Jean Guy let me use the telephone."

Suzy paused and looked down at the sink. "Do you wish Jean Guy still lived here?"

Michelle was quiet, weighing her words. "No . . . no." There was a hesitation in her voice. "I'm glad he doesn't live here any-more, but I just wish you'd trust me enough to let me stay home by myself."

Suzy's mind was off in another direction, not really listen-ing to her daughter's plea for more independence. "Did Jean Guy ever . . . do anything . . . bad?"

"Like what?" She smiled coyly. When her mom did not reply, she continued almost laughing. "Aside from drinking beer all the time, leering at my friends, walking around here without a shirt and with his belly hanging out, and burping and farting, he's a per-fect gentleman."

Suzy burst into laughter. "Yeah, that's pretty much how I saw him too. Listen, I'll tell you what, if I know I'm only gonna be out for a short while, I'll let you stay home by yourself, but when I think it might be longer, you have to go to Mrs. Middleton or Mrs. Marcotte. Okay?"

Michelle acquiesced with a shrug. "Next time you get a boyfriend, get a decent one, would you?"

"I don't think I'm going to bother with any boyfriends for a while."

"Maybe, you should let me pick them."

"Yeah, right!"

"No, seriously, mom. I'll bet I could find the perfect guy for you."

"You'd probably pick out some guy with a pierced nose and tattoos who likes to go snowboarding." Michelle did not reply and Suzy looked over at her. She was pouting. "Well, maybe without the pierced nose, but I think we have different taste in men."

"I think the only thing you have to do is, find someone you like."

Suzy pressed her lips together and then took a tissue to wipe of the excess lipstick. "Yeah, yeah, okay, but in the meantime, I gotta get to work." She grabbed her blouse, slipped it on and then headed Michelle out to the van. She was already late and if she did-n't get to the scene on time, Jaro would start shooting without her She had been paying too much attention to her problems with Jean Guy and she knew that Jaro had to be watched.

T he German fellow, who was taking delivery of a used Mercedes, acknowledged Pat James at the showroom door and then led Pat back toward his purchase. He was a finicky, meticulous man, expecting his used-car to be in new-car condition, and he made note of every little scratch and mark ostensibly hoping for a further discount. There was none to be had.

Pat stood stoically listening. He did not like the customer and a few times, he almost lost his temper, but he managed to complete the sale. When the Mercedes left the lot, Pat exhaled heavily, the air escaping him like a tire blowout.

He drove his Ford Taurus along a newly paved, King City street and stopped at a restaurant for lunch. The meal was slow and relaxing but this made him dread his return to work. It was a crystal-clear day and surely, there were better things to do than sell cars.

Outside the restaurant, a light breeze made the air feel like silk as it slid across his skin, but the smell of exhaust and chemicals were still present. He remembered his visit to Kiosk last summer. As soon as he had exited the car, he could smell the freshness of the air.

In the afternoon, he walked the car lot with two different customers. One was a twenty-year-old wearing a Wal-Mart BUM Equipment sweatshirt and 725 jeans. He had arrived in a five-year-old Neon with only 36 payments remaining and he wanted to take a forty-eight thousand dollar BMW for a test-drive. The second customer was a retired fellow who must have said twelve times that he was 'just looking'. His wife was shopping and he was - had he said it before - just looking.

Pat entered both names on the tracking sheet, thinking of ways to avoid calling either of them in the future, and went to his desk to pack up for the night. He felt drained.

By seven o'clock, half of the sales staff was drinking beer or rye in Eric's office. Every Friday and Saturday, it was the same ritual. Although the salespeople were beaten and abused all day, at night, rather than go home, they sat and drank alcohol in one of the sales offices. They told jokes and talked about customers until the sun no longer graced the sky, and then a few went to a bar to drink some more.

Pat usually stayed for one drink, but tonight he was not in the mood. He considered going to the Lion's Head, a bar on the main drag, but suddenly decided he was getting too old for the place.

At home, he opened a bottle of rye whiskey, turned on his big-screen television, and dug through the cupboard for a tin of ravioli. The cola usually gave him a headache, but he didn't like the rye straight. He poured a strong one, drank it quickly and poured another as he heated the ravioli in the microwave.

He felt a little better as he worked on his third drink. This one was half rye and half coke and it was giving him a pleasant buzz. He liked the feeling of numbness and he started to watch an old, black-and-white movie.

He lifted his glass and realised it was empty. As he walked to the kitchen counter, he stumbled. He was almost out of coke and the drink was mostly rye, but it would be his last of the evening.

He returned to the sofa and stared at the television. A string of commercials played and in frustration, he hit the 'off' button. Without the bluish light of the TV, the room darkened. He sat quietly sipping his drink.

When the telephone rang, he immediately assumed it was a customer. His home number was on his business cards and customers thought nothing of bugging him at home. He answered, slurring a little, but trying to sound professional. "Hello. Patrick James here." He listened for a moment, smiled, and sat up. "Kenny! Good to hear from you! This is bizarre! I was just thinking about Kiosk today."

Pat listened for a long while then he sat ramrod straight. "Really! . . . This week! . . . You're gonna do this on Thursday! . . . Gee, I don't know . . . are you sure?" He wiped his forehead with his hand as if this would clear the disbelief. "You're gonna do this!" He shook his head and slumped back in the sofa. "Friday night or Saturday morning? I don't know, I have to work Saturday . . . yeah, sure . . . where?" He listened for a while. "Okay, if I can't reach you, I'll meet you at the Kiosk rapids on Sunday at noon. Why at the rapids?" He nodded, and then he thought about how Eric, the sales manager, would react when he asked for the day off. To hell with it, he thought. Ken was talking as Pat's thoughts returned to the conversation. "Sure . . . Yeah . . . I can stay at your cabin. What do you need?" He wrote down a list of items. "Yeah . . . I'm supposed to work this weekend, but I'll get out of it." He thought about this for a moment and then nodded to himself. "I'll be there."

When he hung up, he thought about the decision he had just made. What was he doing? He hadn't seen Ken in almost a year. Why would he jump to meet him? He fell back and closed his eyes, the alcohol numbing him again. Ah, what the hell, he thought. He wished he had another coke.

Ken drove cautiously into Kiosk, turned right at the end of the highway, and manoeuvred his truck across the wooden bridge. He did not want to be seen just yet and he watched furtively. Luckily, there was no one around.

He drove across the old rail bed, parked, and then walked until he found a suitable hiding place for his canoe and motor. He owned seven canoes, most of them in poor shape - an old Sportspal patched up with tar, a short and heavy fibreglass canoe that was missing a thwart, a plastic job with two broken seats - but they were useful for hiding in the bush. This canoe, however, was his best. It was extremely light and had a flat stern that allowed the attachment of a small motor. He rarely used the motor, which was hard to portage, but on a lake the size of Kiosk, he could be easily run down by an MNR motorboat. Using a combination lock, he chained canoe and motor to a tree and then drove to the vacant lot that had once contained his parent's home.

Vehicles entered Kiosk on Highway 630, the only road in or
out, and usually turned to the left to the MNR station. Very few
people turned right and crossed the bridge. With the exception of
cottagers with special permits and Natives with band cards, people
were not permitted to take motor vehicles into the park. Working on
this side of the bridge, he would likely remain undiscovered for
some time.

Standing in his front yard, he felt strange. Although he often
visited the park, he rarely came here. Some things were familiar
and others were strange, and he had the eerie sensation that something or someone was watching him. He felt the hairs on the back
of his neck bristle and he walked around a group of trees trying to
get away from the feeling.

There were many more trees in the area than there had been
twenty years ago and looking toward the bridge he saw he was
completely hidden. If he built his cabin here, no one would ever see
it and there would be no point. He wasn't really happy about staying here anyway and he jumped in his truck.

Back at the bridge, he looked for a suitable spot. If he built
on the east side of the bridge, he would be spotted before he ever
finished the cabin and the protest would end before it started. He
had to build west of the bridge. On the south side of the road, not
too far from the old pump house, was an area of pines and alders.
He could clear a small area and then, after his cabin was finished,
cut down the alders to make the cabin visible from the bridge. It
was the best spot.

He pulled his truck off the road into the trees and shut off
the motor. The truck engine creaked as it started to cool and a few
birds sang in the distance. He stretched and then unloaded the first
of the 2X4's.

When the pile was on the ground, he walked back to the
bridge. He liked the site. It was hidden, but once he cut the alders,
it would be easily visible. This was necessary, because a protest, of
which no one was aware, was not a protest. To raise media attention he had made a stop on his way to Kiosk. From a shopping mall
in North Bay, he had faxed newspapers and radio and television stations, informing them of what was about to happen. He wrote about
the injustice of moving people against their will and about the dam-

age that had been done to all the people of the town. At the top of each fax, in bold letters, he wrote: "Some of the most tragic events in our history revolve around the forced relocation of a small group of people to satisfy the desires of a large group of people!"

He returned to his truck and unloaded the chains, plastic, Fabrene (a locally manufactured, tightly woven, heavy-grade plastic sheeting), nails and tools of construction. Prior to coming, he had measured and cut the lumber in his backyard and it was now ready to assemble. He even used pressure-treated lumber for the bottom of his shed - although he realised that this was probably unnecessary since the building would likely be destroyed before the lumber ever had a chance to deteriorate.

The building was ten by twelve feet and it would contain a cot, a small cupboard/table unit, a small chemical toilet, and a sink in a stand. The front was ten feet tall and the back, six feet, creating a lean-to roof.

This was going to be a luxurious cabin by Ken's standards. Although it was not lawful to erect permanent structures in the park or on crown land (land that was still the property of the government), he had often erected quick buildings at his buried caches. Within walking distance of the old town of Kiosk, he had five hidden caches buried in the ground and when he felt like staying someplace, he would erect a structure by cutting some poles and stretching some Fabrene. These structures were usually primitive and only served to give shelter from the elements, but they allowed him to move from place to place with relative ease. He took them down as soon as he was done.

Once he had the building materials on the ground, he pulled the truck further out of sight. He had considered moving it to another location, but he decided against this. There were still many bears in the area and it would be safer to keep food in a cooler inside the truck than in his small cabin.

The sun was high, but dew still lay on the grass and he could feel the dampness creeping through his shoes. He stopped for a moment and, closing his eyes, turned his face toward the sun. It was warm and luxurious and it caused colours, from amber to burning red, to dance across his eyelids.

A chickadee called from a popular tree, perhaps marking

territory, and another replied, then a third and a fourth. The song, as thick as cream, floated through the air filling the empty spaces. Far in the distance, Ken could hear a duck quacking near the shore and slowly the tension flowed out of his body.

The lake was a distance away and he thought about how easily sound carried. The sound of him hammering on his building would echo from this lake to the next and then return. It would not take long for the MNR to learn of his presence. Something flew between the sun and his face creating a brief shadow and he flinched. He opened his eyes to see a swallow circling and swooping in the air.

The first job was to clear a small area of hazel, alders and moose maple. With a pair of two-handed clippers, he snipped the stems close to the ground and then gathered up the stalks and piled them at the back of the lot.

His shirt was now wet with sweat and he stood looking at his pile of lumber. He felt like relaxing, but he needed to get to work. The press might show up in hours - if they showed up at all - and he wanted to have his building started. He placed two boards together and held the hammer, but somehow, hammering that first board was an enervating task. Did he really want to start?

Up until this moment, this was just an idea. He could pack his truck and leave, but as soon as he started to nail, he would start a process that might spiral out of his control. So far, his life was a series of canoeing and camping trips spaced out between weeks at work. He was able to come and go with anonymity and he could do as he pleased, but the protest might give him a notoriety that would make camping in the park difficult. He had taken a leave of absence from work, but this protest might drag out and he might lose his job.

He took a deep breath and hammered the first nail. There was no way to hammer quietly and the sound echoed, just as he expected, back from the distance. It returned three times. The first two quick and soft, and the third, a moment later.

He had expected the birds to be startled by the noise, but they continued, uninterrupted, in their song while the raps of his hammering filled the forest, bouncing around like Ping-Pong balls. As he picked up a new nail, he listened; no one was approaching, the world was as calm as it had been.

After he finished the first two walls, he tacked in two-by-fours for angular support, stood them in place and nailed them together. They looked larger than he expected, and he walked a distance away. It felt good to see something standing in the town of Kiosk. It gave him a feeling of accomplishment, but it also gave him a feeling of connection. Something rustled in the trees and he looked over his shoulder - just the wind, no visitors yet.

Although he was hungry, he decided to continue. Even with the alders in the way, the structure was now visible from the bridge and he wanted to have more of the cabin finished before he got into a conflict with the MNR.

As he lifted the heaviest front wall into place, he wondered if it had been wise to start on a Thursday. He had chosen this day so that the press would have a chance to show up before the weekend, but now he had to work by himself until Pat showed up on Friday - if Pat showed up. Much of this work would have been easier for two people working together, but he would have to finish it alone.

A serious concern was the threat of forcible removal. It would be easier to drag away a single protester than a group and there was the danger that the park wardens would simply carry him off the property before the first reporter arrived. He assumed that he had a bit of leeway here - they would not carry him off at the first meeting - but he knew that, eventually, they would try. He had a couple of locks and lengths of chain and if it became necessary, he would chain himself to the frame of his truck. A good set of bolt cutters would get him loose, but it would stall his removal and give the press more time to cover the action.

Timing was important. Once the story was on television, others might speak out. There were lots of ex-residents who were very unhappy with the way they had been treated. A little press coverage might start them talking.

The afternoon had warmed considerably. The dry summer had greatly reduced the number off mosquitoes and blackflies, those pestiferous demons that licked blood like microscopic vampire bats, and only a few horseflies and deerflies remained. There were also a few sandflies in the air.

The wind was a companion. It rustled the poplars. It moved and answered itself much like the echoes of his hammer blows. It carried the fruity smell of a deciduous forest, of organic soil, and of a multitude of wild and cultivated flowers. It wafted through a giant patch of double roses and carried the sweet fruity smell to him. He turned his face to the sky. The sun warmed, the wind cooled, and the moisture lifted from his skin. It was a glorious day.

When the framework was in place, he looked at his watch. It was almost 4:30. Not a single person had visited. It was strange. All day he had been worried that confrontations would develop before he had the building started. Now, he was almost finished and he had not yet seen a soul. He was glad that the MNR had stayed away, but the fact the media had not arrived was troubling. Were they not interested? Was it too far for them to drive?

As September approached, the sun was setting earlier, but it would still stay light until after seven. He would have enough time to finish most of the cabin and by tomorrow morning, it would look complete - if anyone ever bothered to come and see.

Craving a bit of starch, he ate a sandwich, and then returned to work. He pulled the plastic over the roof and began stapling it in place. The wind died and the clearing was heavy with the sound of crickets punctuated by the staccato "thunk" of the stapler.

By the time he had the plastic in place, the ultraviolet light of evening was beginning to wash across the grass. He would not get all of the furniture into the cabin, but he would manage to make it liveable. Since the mosquitoes would be coming soon, he knew he would be glad to be able to work inside.

He had one last chore to do outside that he approached with anticipation. Using a small crosscut saw, he downed the row of alders that stood beside his cabin restricting visibility from the river. The trunks were easy to cut and when he had cleared a twenty-foot swath, he walked back to the bridge to look. It was perfect. He returned and off-loaded the remaining supplies.

As he set up the cot, he heard the soft crunching sound of gravel under tires. In the gloaming light, he looked through the clear plastic window to see the warm yellow headlights of a vehicle coming from the bush. The road that crossed the bridge at one time led to Camp One, which was no longer in existence, but it also led to the Junior Ranger Camp, which was on one of the bays of Kioshkokwi Lake. The Ministry of Natural Resources used this road for access to the interior.

The vehicle slowed as the driver studied the cabin. It almost came to a stop and then accelerated away. Whoever it was, was curious, but not curious enough to get out and ask questions. It would have been fun to talk to someone, but at least, now, someone would talk about this strange structure - and talk in the north was like a bush fire in July, it started with a tiny spark and spread very quickly.

On Saturday morning, Ken woke slowly, sat up and rubbed his eyes. Accustomed to sleeping on the ground without a tent, he found the cot and the cabin luxurious. Birds sang in the trees and the wind rustled the leaves around his cabin.

He walked outside, carefully moving the door on its new hinges, and looked at the clouds. They were high, dark and well defined. They gave the impression that it was possible to see for a very long distance. It would probably rain soon and he turned and looked at his cabin of plastic and wood, happy for the shelter.

There was still no sign of interest in his cabin, and he was surprised. He had half expected to be interrupted during the night, but no one had arrived. He shrugged and went to the truck to dig out some eggs. He felt like devouring a good, hearty breakfast.

Pat hurried into the sales meeting with just minutes to spare. He looked around at the morose beings seated around the table. None of them wanted to be here.

Earlier, he had asked Ivan, one of the salesmen, to switch Saturdays with him, but Ivan had refused. Ivan never took a day off and trading would have meant nothing to him, but he complained that although he was intending to come in, he might need to leave early and he could only do this if he had the day off.

He had then asked Alvin, but Alvin couldn't reach a decision. Alvin suggested that he talk to Eric, the sales manager, first. Alvin was always afraid of doing anything that might anger Eric.

The meeting started and Pat sat quietly through the

harangue of abuse without saying a word. The sales manager rant-
ed about the company long-distance phone bills. "Too much wasted money!" he complained, "And even with all these calls, there
still aren't enough sales. If I find out that someone was making personal calls, their company account is going to be charged and they
might find themselves down-the-road." This was a favourite
expression: "Down-the-road." Cars had to be 'down-the-road' but
unproductive salespeople were going to be 'down-the-road' as well.

With talk of telephones, the meeting turned to prospecting
and a few of the salespeople groaned. "You aren't doing enough . .
. you aren't working hard enough . . . you're all lazy pieces of shit .
. . you're stupid . . . blah, blah, blah." Pat tuned out.

Slowly the meeting drew to an end and the inevitable question was asked. "Who's not coming in tomorrow?" Ivan said that he
had the day off, but would be in and then Alvin said that he would
be in as well. Alvin looked at Pat in anticipation, but Pat had decided to wait till after the meeting.

He watched as people started to file out of the room and
when only Alvin and Eric remained, he walked over and asked quietly if it would be okay if he switched with Alvin for this Saturday
off. Eric looked at him in dismay. "Why didn't you say something
during the meeting?"

"Well, I wanted to talk to you first."

Eric started to gather his papers. "Won't do you any good.
Alvin's already said he's coming in."

Pat shook his head, as if trying to shake out the murky logic.
"I have to go up north and see a friend of mine."

"What's wrong with you James? You making too much
money? You know, we're running a full page ad in today's paper
and that'll bring in a lot of people. You think a couple of fried trout
is worth missing all that business?"

"No sir. I just have to go . . ." His voice trailed off.

Eric packed up his papers and looked away from Pat. "Well,
do what you have to, but remember, we can't afford to keep a lot of
dead wood around here. We're gonna start getting rid of the bottom
guy on the board every month. Someone's gonna find themselves
down-the-road. You know where you are this month?"

Pat winced. He had only two sales. Alvin smiled at Pat's discomfort. "I still have to go . . . in fact, I really need to leave early today."

Eric's face reddened. "Just do what you have to do!"

"Thanks . . . I'll make sure that all my customers are taken care of." Pat rolled out of the room and walked to the showroom. Why could he not stand up to Eric? The man did not warrant respect. When he reached his desk, he remembered something that was at home in a box somewhere. If he could find it, he would take it with him. It was something he had looked a few times since his meeting with Ken in Kiosk.

The drive to Kiosk was four and a half hours and as long as he got out a few hours before closing time, he could still make it to Ken's cabin before day's end. Then he remembered the bush road. It had been almost a year since he was there. It would be difficult to find and he should arrive before it got dark, if possible.

The smell of frying bacon filled the air and Ken smiled. If the hammering had not attracted attention, perhaps the smell of food would. He stood, turning the strips, feeling very content. He knew that it was a temporary thing, the OPP (Ontario Provincial Police) or the MNR, would eventually force him to move, but for now it was his home.

It felt strange to be so open about his camping. He was so used to being discreet. He kept away from people; he covered his tracks, and tried to remain invisible. It was wonderful to build a cabin, to make a fire, to hammer nails, to cook bacon, and not worry about who knew he was there. It was the way things should be.

He placed his bacon on newspaper, then took the pan outside, and poured most of the fat over a log that he would later burn. He broke the eggs into the pan, just as a MNR pickup truck stopped abruptly in front of his cabin. He watched his eggs, grinning widely, and decided not to respond. He would go about his business as if nothing was out of the ordinary.

The park warden, dressed in his uniform of blue pants and sand-coloured shirt, stood with his hands on his hips looking at the cabin. He seemed to be waiting, and when Ken did not react, he took out a pad and pen and wrote down the licence number of Ken's truck. Finally he spoke. "Just what do you think you're doing?"

"Making breakfast. You like some?"

The warden was momentarily stunned by Ken's flippancy. "This is not a camping spot, you can't camp here. And you're not allowed to build any structures in the park."

"No, only the MNR is allowed to do that." Ken turned off the flame and shovelled his eggs onto the plate with the bacon. He started to butter some bread. "This isn't the park," he said in a non-confrontational tone. He saw the anger on the warden's face. "It is not my intention to cause you any grief - I know it may seem strange to you, but this is the place where I was born, where I grew up. This is my home."

The warden relaxed a little, but he kept his arms crossed and his feet firmly planted. "So, you're one of the old Kiosk residents, are you?"

Ken nodded. He had intended to eat outside, but while the warden was present, he decided not to leave the cabin. He still had-n't chained himself to the truck and the wall of the cabin, although only plastic, was still a defence.

"Well, that may be, but you can't stay here. This is Algonquin Park now, and you can't do what you're doing."

"They were forced to sell their homes."

The warden shrugged. "It's still a public park."

"That's what you say. I say this was always my home, and, it still is. I'm staying."

The warden took a step back. "I'm afraid I can't allow that."

Ken took a bite of his bread and spoke with his mouth partially full. "Look, I don't want to make trouble for you, but there is more involved here than you think. This land should have been deeded to my parents. They never should have been forced to move. I intend to make people aware of this." He swallowed, dipped his bread in the bacon and egg mixture on his plate, and took another bite. "Are you sure you don't want some? It's really good."

"Are you telling me you refuse to leave?"

"Yes."

"You're trespassing."

"It's a point of view, isn't it? Since this is my place, since I grew up here and never once agreed to give up my right to this land, I say I have more right to title of the property than you." Ken looked down at the warden's feet. "I would say that you're trespassing, not me."

The warden was silent for a moment. He opened his notebook again and poised his pen over the page. "Your name, Sir?"

"Kenneth Campbell . . . with a 'P'."

He wrote down the name. "Your address?"

"That would be, RR # 2." He paused for a moment to let the warden write and then he continued. "Kiosk . . . Ontario."

The warden looked up and snapped his notebook closed. "Very funny. I'm going to have to ask you to come with me."

"I'm sorry, but I have other plans for today."

"My name is Derrick Mayhew, I'm a Park warden for Algonquin North and I'm placing you under arrest for trespassing and failing to provide proper identification." He reached into a pocket and fished out a small card. "You have the right . . ."

The frivolousness had ended. Ken's tone was sharp and aggressive. "I have the right in the Charter of Rights and Freedoms to freedom of peaceful assembly. This was my birthplace. By many definitions, this is still my property. You do not have authority outside of the park and when you step on this land, you have left the park. This is my place and if you don't leave, I'll charge you with trespassing."

"Mr . . ." he had to look down at his notes. "Campbell . . . with a 'P' . . . you're resisting arrest. If you don't come with me now, you're in for a world of trouble."

"Mr. Park Warden, if you don't leave now, it's you who's gonna be in a world of trouble."

"Are you threatening me?"

"No . . . but I'm also not leaving with you."

The warden shook his head, turned, and climbed into his truck. He picked up a microphone, changed his mind about speaking, and drove back to the bridge.

Ken took another bite of egg and smiled. That had been easier than expected. He wasn't sure if park wardens were considered peace officers, but he was fairly sure that their authority, outside of the park, was very limited. Unfortunately, many of them took their status far too seriously and as a result, the confrontation could have been more aggressive. The wardens were obviously given training and told not to force a situation.

When he finished eating, he took two large plastic containers and his dishes down to the river. He filled the jugs with water and then washed the dishes. For the next little while, he would have to restrict his movements to the area around his cabin. He would not do too much cooking, because washing dishes would be difficult. As he approached his cabin, he saw a tall thin man and a short stocky woman snooping around. "Can I help you?"

"Oh, hi!" said the woman. "Are you the guy who built this?"

"Yep," replied Ken, placing the water in the back of his truck and putting the dishes away.

"We were just at the ranger station and we heard a guy talking about it." She laughed. "He was pretty upset."

"That's the idea. To get some people upset."

"You used to live here?"

"Yep. I was born in a house right here." He pointed over his shoulder.

"Oh yeah? I had a cousin who lived in Kiosk. She was a Desjardin."

Ken nodded. "Silvie?"

"No, Annette."

"There were lots of Desjardins."

The woman nodded. "So whatcha doin' here anyways?"

"I'm just trying to let people know what happened to the families who lived here. It was unfair that they forced everyone to leave their homes."

"Yeah, a lot of people feel that way, eh. My cousin told me this used to be a big town." She looked around at the scraggy fields and stunted trees. "It's hard to imagine, eh."

"It was a big town, a close town, and after the fire . . ."

"Oh yeah, I heard about that. My cousin told me that it was real bad. She said that it was all very suspicious."

"Well, whether it was or it wasn't, they still shouldn't have chased everyone out."

The woman, who never introduced herself, talked on incessantly while her husband stood quietly by her side. Eventually he nudged her and asked, "Shouldn't we get going?"

"Yeah, yeah, in a moment," she replied, anxious to continue talking.

Ken was thinking about all the things he needed to do. He turned to the woman. "Might I ask you a favour?"

"I don't know. What do you want?"

Ken took a five-dollar bill out of his wallet and handed it to the woman. "I need to get the press out here. I sent them all faxes, but so far," he spread his palms to the side to indicate the area around him, "no one has come. Take this money, find a payphone and call as many people as you can. Call the newspaper, the radio station, the television stations, and tell them that there is a nutcase who built a cabin in the old town of Kiosk. Tell them that the park wardens tried to arrest the man, but he refused to go quietly. Build it up a little."

The woman pushed the money back into his hand. "I'll be happy to. Keep your money."

Ken nodded and walked to his truck. He picked up the two padlocks, wrapped a chain around his ankle and locked it in place. "Make sure you tell them that a serious conflict is brewing and tell them that you spoke to me and that I would be willing to do interviews." He wrapped the other end of the chain though a hole in the frame of his truck and locked it in place as well. He turned back to the woman. "Can you do that for me?"

"Sure, mister. What's your name anyway?"

Ken told her and she introduced herself and her husband. By the time she walked away - they had parked on the other side of the bridge - Ken had forgotten their names. He had never been very good with names.

The warden returned to Ken's cabin just before lunch and this time brought reinforcements. Ken grinned. "Good day gentlemen." The second person was older, perhaps in his fifties, and radiated authority. His hair was peppered grey and he had a thick moustache.

"Good day Mr. Campbell. My name's Boart, Michael Boart. I'm a park warden and group leader."

Ken nodded but kept his distance.

Boart waited for a moment and then spoke. "So just what is it that you think you're up to?"

Ken smiled, but didn't answer.

"He thinks he's too smart to answer your questions," said Mayhew, the younger warden.

"No." Ken shook his head, and looked at the younger man. "I just figured that you might be smart enough to tell him why I was here. I don't like repeating myself."

The younger man was about to speak, but Boart interrupted. "Derrick did tell me, Mr. Campbell. I was just trying to make conversation . . . hear your side of things."

Ken sighed. "I grew up here and years ago, the provincial government forced us to move. They forced everyone to move. I don't think they had the right to do that and I've decided to return - and in the process let a few people know what happened to us."

"There are other ways to tell people things. A protest is not the first course of action."

"The town did all that. There were lawyers, citizen committees. This is the way."

"That's all well and good, Mr. Campbell, but now this is a park for the benefit of all of the people."

"That's fine. I don't intend to stop anyone from going camping. I'm not blocking access. I don't want to close the park. I just feel that three generations of my family were here and you can't just take that away."

Boart bit his lip, thinking. "You know that we can't allow you to stay. We just can't."

Ken walked forward, bent, and picked up the chain locked to his ankle. "I hope you thought to bring . . ." He stopped. He was about to say 'bolt cutters', but there was no sense in giving them ideas. ". . . something to cut off my foot, cause otherwise I'm staying here."

Derrick turned away sharply and covered his face with his hand. The older man spoke again. "Just what do you hope to accomplish here?"

Ken lashed out angrily. "I just told you that! I've said enough! This is my property and you're both trespassing. Unless you have something else of importance to discuss, I'm asking you to leave."

"We don't have . . ."

"Just leave!"

Derrick turned and faced Ken. His face was flushed; his fists were clenched. "You goddamned asshole, don't . . ."

Boart grabbed the younger man's arm and spoke softly. "Derrick, get in the truck." He turned to Ken. "So you refuse to leave?" Ken nodded. "And you were already informed that you were being placed under arrest? Derrick read you the caution?"

Ken laughed. "I'm already in chains." He wiggled his ankle causing the chain to rattle.

Boart nodded and returned to the truck. They drove away.

Ken shrugged. It was all too easy. He had expected more, but he also knew it was a long way from over. Now that the second warden had confirmed that Ken would not go quietly, they would probably call the OPP.

For the next few hours, Ken checked the road across the bridge from time to time. He had known park wardens and conservation officers all his life. He had little respect for them. He could easily lose them in the bush and they seemed more like buffoons rather than serious figures of authority. The police, on the other hand, were more threatening. There was an OPP detachment in Mattawa and the police could be here in forty-five minutes.

The first vehicle to cross the bridge was an old GMC Suburban. The body was covered in dents and the paint was scratched and worn. It had obviously seen many narrow bush roads. A blonde woman in her early thirties and an older man with a receding hairline got out and walked straight to Ken.

"Hi! Kenny Campbell?" said the woman thrusting her hand toward him. Ken nodded and shook the hand. "I'm Annette Dupuis," she continued. "You might not remember me but I was born in Kiosk. My dad was Gaetan."

Ken didn't remember a Dupuis. "From Kiosk?"

"Yes. My name used to be Desjardin. You met my cousin earlier today. She called me."

"Oh, yes. She told me about you. Are you Silvie's sister?"

"Silvie was a cousin."

"There were lots of Desjardins." They both said this in unison and then both laughed.

"You should remember my grandmother," Annette continued. "She was a big protester. She was involved in starting the union and she was the one who burned the scarecrow on Smith's front lawn."

Ken laughed. "That was your grandmother? I remember that night."

"Yeah, well, I guess protest runs in the family. That's why we're here. We heard about what you're doing and we came to help." Before Ken could respond, she turned to the man standing next to her. "This is my husband, Tirj. He didn't live in Kiosk, but actually lived in Camp One. His dad and him were staying there when I met him, just before we left. Both our folks moved to Mattawa. The rest is history."

"Yeah, history," said Tirj smiling widely.

Ken looked at the two for a moment and then addressed Annette. "You know why I'm here?"

"Sure, you wanna let people know what bullshit it was that they closed down the town and you wanna get our land back."

Ken winced. "Umm, I don't think there's much chance of us ever getting our land back, but you're right, I do want people to know what happened here . . . and what's going to happen." Ken told them about the five-year-plan and the idea of building replica ranger cabins that would then be rented for profit."

"That's complete and total bullshit!" she said and then she looked at her husband. "Well, we're all for it. Ain't we Tirj?"

Tirj nodded. "All for it."

"So you built a cabin." Annette looked at the structure nodding. "What we thought we would do is, pitch a tent on another lot. My folks lived on the other side of the river, but I don't think anyone would mind if we temporarily used one of their spots. Maybe we'll put it up on the Racine's place."

"That would be great." Ken had figured that the MNR or the OPP would come and he hoped that the press would come, but he had never counted on any of the past town residents. "Sure, that would be great," he repeated.

Pat finally turned onto the 400 Highway at 6:00 P.M.. It was later than he intended, but he had had trouble getting away. It was always difficult leaving work on time.

King City was just north of Toronto, but the two cities had merged together. Southern Ontario was now an urban sprawl of many millions that had spread for hundreds of kilometres and consumed much of the surrounding farmland.

For the last half a century, the population sought its recreation in the north. "I'm going up north for the weekend," was the battle cry of many Torontonians. Every Friday in the summer, armed with boats, suntan lotion and fly dope, they escaped the city in a crawling traffic jam.

The 400 Highway was a six-lane pavement artery flowing north and south. It started in Toronto, snaked its way up north through Barrie and then flowed into Highway 11, a smaller highway that continued straight north for a few hundred kilometres. Northbound on Fridays and southbound on Sundays, these highways were often so packed that vehicles barely moved, and on some occasions, travellers took out lawn chairs and sat on the side of the road waiting for traffic to clear.

It was into this mess of traffic that Patrick drove his car on Friday evening. As he moved north, barely a car length behind the car in front of him, he looked at his speedometer. He was travelling at 45 km/hour.

After a few hours of travel, he pulled off at Webers, a fast-food hamburger restaurant built in an old railway car. There were two-dozen people in line and the acrid smell of fat and burnt meat assaulted his nose, as a young girl took his order. So many people, he thought, like cattle in a feedlot.

Fifteen minutes later, he was sitting outside at a wooden picnic table eating his cheeseburger and fries. The food wasn't as good as he had expected and he washed it down with an overly sweet soft drink. He used the washroom, another decommissioned railway car, and then continued up north.

In the gloaming light, most cars had their lights on and at the top of the first hill, he looked ahead at the line of taillights. They coiled through the countryside like a mean red snake.

Further north, the highway cut through some heavy rock,

and the change in landscape made him feel as if he were moving into the north. In Southern Ontario, rock outcropping was rare, the land was flatter, and the tree cover - what little there was - was mostly deciduous. Northern Ontario had a different flavour. The Canadian Shield broke through the surface exposing the planet's oldest rocks, and the bodies of water were not murky, but cold, clear, clean gems of blue. The forests were mixed, but the windswept silhouette of a giant pine on the shore of a rocky lake was certainly an identifiable northern image. The pines often dominated, leaving the forest floor covered with a soft bed of dried needles and air fragrant and alive. Somehow, this section of Ontario seemed like home, his place.

After the town of Huntsville, the highway narrowed to two-lanes, one in each direction, and the traffic became a solid, a red and white line of lights stretching off toward the horizon. The fatigue of the drive began to overtake him and the oncoming vehicle headlights caused his eyes to burn. He pulled off in a roadside gas-station/restaurant, planning to fill the car with gas and himself with coffee.

When he opened the car door, he was immediately struck by the smell of freshness. The scent of cedar, rich organic earth, pine, dogwood, combined to energize him, and he stretched, placing his hands behind his head and raising his elbows to the cloudy sky above.

An attendant approached, his footfalls curiously loud on the gravel parking lot, and Pat asked him to fill the car with gas. The man nodded and removed the metal nozzle from the pump, the metallic clink curiously loud as well. Even though there was a constant growl of vehicles on the road behind them, sound carried differently in the cool north. Noises were crisper, sharper.

"I'm going in for a moment," he said. The attendant nodded. Inside, he found a few Formica tables with well-worn menus perched beside chrome napkin holders, a long counter with a glass case containing homemade butter tarts and brownies, and a few shelves filled with candies, chocolate bars, maps, souvenirs, bug spray and suntan lotion. There was also a rotating rack full of sunglasses and, in the corner, a refrigeration unit full of soft drinks.

Pat took a Mars bar and ordered a large coffee, double

cream, double sugar. He could smell that the coffee was old and bitter, but he didn't care. He just wanted the stimulant. He paid the
woman, who had hardly said a word, and returned to his car.

With the soft green light of his dash illuminating his coffee
cup, he drove out into the stream of red and white and continued
north. He turned up the heat, sipped his coffee, but felt the fatigue
return. He shook his head trying to force the tiredness from his eyes
and took a big bite of chocolate.

Ken sat, still chained at the ankle, with six people
around a campfire. It was a dark starless evening and there was a
risk of rain, but no one seemed to care as they talked about people
who had once lived in the town. Annette and Tirj had set up their
tent and two of their friends, Simon and Jocelyn, had arrived and
parked their campervan on a third lot. Two older people had arrived
in a new Dodge Pickup, saying they came for a visit, but did not
intend to stay the night. Their names were Joanne and Howard
Scoffield and they too had once lived in Kiosk.

Ken remembered them as a middle-aged couple with young
children and they remembered Ken well. They greeted him warmly, asking about his parents, and were saddened to learn that both
had died.

Simon and Jocelyn had beer, which they generously offered
to everyone. It was against park policy to drink in public and Ken
was concerned that some people might say that this was just a
drunken party, but no one got drunk and the atmosphere remained
very calm. It reminded Ken of his dad's friends sitting on the porch
drinking a beer after a hard-day's work.

They talked about the buildings, the work, and the many
people they remembered. Ken was surprised to learn how many had
died. It seemed that, removed from their environment, the people of
Kiosk had a short life-expectancy. It was odd because he remembered some really old people living in the town.

In the distance, by the bridge, vehicle lights appeared from
time-to-time. It was impossible to tell if they were police vehicles,
MNR vehicles, or just curious onlookers, but Ken was starting to
worry about the other people around the campfire. For him, this

protest made perfect sense, but he didn't want to be responsible for anyone else. He could not imagine how Joanne and Howard Scoffield would react if they were arrested.

Ken saw headlights stop at the bridge and then go out. An interior light came on and then there was blackness again. Finally, he saw the swirling, dancing lights of two flashlights. He tapped Tirj on the shoulder and pointed. Everyone looked and conversation slowed to a stop.

Two women walked into the wash of camp fire light, but stopped a distance away. One spoke cautiously. "Hello? Is one of you the fellow who faxed us about the protest?"

"That would be me," said Ken standing. "And you are?"

"My name's Maggie Perrault and this is Denise, my photographer. We're from the North Bay Nugget." Maggie was dressed formally and it did not look like she would be comfortable sitting on a log by the fire.

"Wonderful," said Ken walking forward. The women moved back a tiny bit and Ken put up his hands. "I was beginning to think that the media was not interested." He stepped forward again, his chain rattling, and held out his hand. Both women looked down. "My name's Ken Campbell."

"Yes, it was on your fax," Maggie looked up from the chains, leaned forward and shook his hand. "We didn't know what to make of it at first. We heard today you had a run-in with the MNR?"

"Not much of a run-in, really. They told me to leave. I said no, and told them to leave. A stand-off."

"Hmm. We wanted to come out and have a look . . . hear what you had to say."

"Well, that's great Maggie." Ken ran his hand through his thin blond hair. "May I call you Maggie?" She nodded. "I have a lot to say, and I have a feeling that the others will have lots to say as well. We'll tell you anything you want to know."

"That's great. So you're all involved in this?" Heads bobbed up and down in affirmation and Maggie flipped open a notebook, "You feel that you shouldn't have been forced to leave the town?" Heads bobbed again. "The first question that comes to mind is: Why now? Why not five years ago, or ten?"

Ken shrugged. "Well . . . almost anything."

A few people chuckled.

"No," said Ken, the mirth evident in his voice, "that's a fair question." He paused. "I've always thought it was wrong that they took away our homes, but there was so much support for a wilderness park that it was difficult to protest. But I think the MNR has started to look for ways to make money. They've been renting cabins for years. In the interior, there's the Highview and the one on Birchcliff Lake, and, of course, right here there's the ranger cabin. They get about fifty dollars a night for the interior ones and $80 for the Kiosk cabin. I guess they've seen the revenue potential so they've decided to expand. Now they're going to build four replicas of the ranger cabin here in Kiosk and they're going to build an MNR office building right across the river." Ken pointed toward the bridge.

"In addition," he continued, "they're going to open two new campgrounds, with concrete convenience centres, and they're going to put in a few parking lots to boot. This will piss off a lot of the former residents. The government told us that our houses couldn't stay because this was a wilderness park. Now that we're all gone, they intend to do all sorts of construction." He watched Maggie writing and he leaned back and shook his head. "But it's not just that . . . or at least that's not all of it.

"This has been brewing under the surface for years, brewing, stewing, but I think what brought it out - for me - was seeing an old friend. I saw how the years had treated him . . . I thought it was just me that was screwed up . . ." He picked up some sticks and threw them into the fire. "but . . . it's hard to explain."

"Every time I came here," said Howard, picking up the conversation. "I felt something was wrong, and after awhile I just didn't come anymore. It's like this deep, empty hole that you don't want to look into." People nodded in agreement. "As you grow older, you see that those things you just accepted as a part of life aren't necessarily the way things were meant to be."

"But aren't you still concerned about the timing? It was only two years ago that the terrorists bombed the World Trade Centre. Since then, the government's been a lot harsher with protesters."

"Then maybe this is a good time," said Ken. "Just because

the government is more powerful, this doesn't mean we have to back off. This has been going on for many years."

Maggie scribbled in her notebook as they talked about the protest starting in 1969, about the softening position of the government in 1972, and about the fire in 1973.

"Yeah, that was a con-job," said Annette.

"I'll say," agreed Joanne Scoffield.

Ken was surprised. He had always heard that the fire was suspicious, but he never repeated it, because it seemed too incredible for most people to believe. He was surprised that these two women were willing to talk about it openly.

"What makes you say that?" asked Denise, the photographer, now fully engrossed in the conversation.

Mrs. Scoffield talked about the fact that ten acres of buildings - six separate buildings - burned in ninety minutes. "Even the night watchman said that the fire swept through the buildings like lightning. Wood burns, but that fire burned like gasoline."

The others talked about the water tower that had been emptied two or three days before the fire; the power and phone lines that went out within minutes of the start of the fire; the staff that had been sent home early; and the line of box-cars that were conveniently parked between the mill and the town. It all seemed suspicious.

"Even the time of the fire was strange," said Howard. "It started at eleven-thirty, which was the perfect time. If it had started during the day, it would have likely spread to the town and run into the forest, and if it had started at four in the morning, it might have caught the town unaware and killed a lot of people. If you were going to start a fire, eleven PM would be the perfect time to do it."

Maggie took a deep breath not daring to make a comment. "So once the mill was gone, there were no more jobs, and the town died?"

"No, it didn't die then." Howard said. "The town could have easily gone on without the mill, but the government used that as an excuse to close it down."

"But with the mill gone, there would have been nothing for the townspeople but welfare."

Annette looked at Maggie as if she were a foreigner. "Oh,

you would think that! All the people out here can only go on welfare."

Maggie's mouth opened but she didn't speak. Howard looked at her and said: "A lot of people think the same. They think the closing of the mill was the disease that killed the town, but in truth, it was a symptom, not a disease. The disease was the government caring less about the people than about something else in their agenda. The disease was big business and big government. They wanted the mill and us gone. It wasn't easy, but first they got the mill, and then, they worked on us. They told us if we didn't leave, we'd lose our houses anyway."

"But there was no work. The mill was the only employer."

"Yes, that's right. The mill was the main employer, but we could have done other things. A new mill was built within a year in Rutherglen, and we fought to keep our homes. We all got together and raised money, we hired a lawyer from North Bay, and we petitioned, we lobbied. We could have started businesses, tourist operations, all kinds of things, but the government kept pushing. If we didn't sell to them, they said, they would take our homes anyway. They wore us down, but it took a long time. For the first couple of years, hardly anyone left, but after three or four, it seemed hopeless. No one cared. It may surprise you to know that some people stayed into the 1990's. There were still people fighting less than ten years ago."

"How do you feel when you come back now?"

Joanne answered, saying that she felt as if they were standing in a field surrounded by ghosts. Ken's head snapped in her direction when she said this because he had recently heard the same thing from Pat.

"Yeah, I know what you mean," Annette said. "I come to Kiosk from time to time, but I drive straight to the Ranger Station; I never look right or left." A few people nodded in agreement. "I remember standing and looking at the spot where my parents' house had been. There was nothing left but a few of the flowering bushes that my mom had planted. Everything was so empty, so hollow, like standing in a cave. All the places that were important to me were gone. All the people were gone. It was like some of them were watching me, mad at me for leaving." Her usually gruff voice became softer. "It was like someone had ripped a part of me away. I started to . . ." Her voice cracked and a tear ran down her cheek, which she desperately tried to hide. Tirj put his arm around her, but she pushed it away, sniffled and forced a smile, making fun of herself.

Maggie looked at the faces around the campfire. They all shared the sense of sadness. "Didn't you get any support?"

"From who?" Howard asked.

Maggie shrugged. "You had a committee, it must have approached people. What about your Member of Parliament?"

When Maggie looked at Ken, he rotated his hands palms up. He had no idea.

"Francine Roussel." Howard said. "She promised support, but never did a thing."

Maggie looked confused. "Isn't she in federal politics?"

"She is now. That should show you what kind of woman she is. She used to be a provincial Conservative and then, when the PC's were losing popularity, she jumped ship and became a federal Liberal."

"I met her once," said Annette, her sadness replaced with anger. "All sugar and sweet, but she was digging the knives in our backs the whole time."

Absorbed in the conversation, Maggie had stopped writing, but she now flipped her notebook open. "Why do you say that?"

Annette stumbled for words and Howard answered. "She came here once. She talked about the provincial government's commitment to the rural, northern communities. She said that it had been our spirit that made the country great in the first place. We were going to get the government's support. Oh yeah, sure, we got it okay." Howard snorted. "Right where the sun don't shine. It wasn't too long after the mill burned that the provincial government told us we could only sell our houses to them, and if we didn't sell to them by 1999, they would take them anyway. Some support."

Maggie scribbled more notes and then looked up. "Were the prices fair?"

"They said they were. They did everything to convince us."

Maggie looked at Howard with an expression that implored him to continue.

"I got about fifteen-thousand for our house. The government said that given the fact that we didn't own the land, that the town was dying, and there was no industry or future, that was an incredibly fair price. And, given these facts, they were right, it was fair. But if the town was not being shut down, and given the fact that we had waterfront property in a gorgeous location, it was robbery."

Maggie looked at Howard and tilted her head to the side. She did not follow what Howard was trying to say.

"Look, if the town had not been destroyed by the provincial government, if it still existed, our half-acre-lot, just down the road from the beach, would be worth a couple of hundred thousand dollars. The provincial government gave us fifteen."

"Yes, but that was a lot of years ago. There has been inflation in that time."

"Okay," said Howard patiently. "My wife and I used that fifteen-thousand to buy a house in Mattawa. Today we could probably sell the place for sixty thousand. That's a long way from two-hundred-thousand."

"Hmmm." Maggie looked like she was about to argue, but stopped. "One final question." She looked at Ken. "What do you hope will happen as a result of your protest?"

Ken broke a stick and threw it into the fire. "My, my, you do ask difficult questions, don't you?"

"Well, you must have thought about it. Do you hope to get the land back?"

Ken looked at the faces around the fire. There was anticipation. "Do I think we'll get the land back? Well . . ." Annette made circling motions with her hands, encouraging him to continue. Could he say what he didn't believe? He was silent for a long while. "No," he said finally, shaking his head. He saw Annette's eyebrows furrow. "Don't get me wrong," he added quickly, "I want the land back, but I'm not stupid. I don't think the government will ever care about a small group of people from the north. They never cared in the past and I don't think that'll change." Howard's face, like many of the others around the fire, showed disappointment.

"So what's the point?"

He answered slowly. "I can't speak for everyone here, but I

can tell you what I want. We live in a country where 'people' are slowly becoming analogous to 'workforce'; where education is not for personal growth, but simply a preparation for employment; and, where 'who you are,' is roughly the same as, 'what you do for a living.' 'Home' means nothing anymore; where you live, where your ancestors lived, this is all somehow unimportant. If you get a good job, you're expected to transfer all over the country. You get promotions based on your willingness to uproot yourself and transplant yourself into new cities. Families are destroyed. Mom and dad live by themselves in one city, and all of their children are married and in different cities. We have all lost our connection to the land, to each other."

No one spoke. Everyone could think of a personal example of what Ken had said. Ken broke the silence with a smile. "Eventually, mom and dad move to a new city, where children aren't allowed, and they put up 'Neighbourhood Watch' signs in childless subdivisions." A few people chuckled.

Ken looked back at the ground and added: "If anything good were to come of this, it would be that we re-evaluate this attitude."

Silence hung over the crowd like an early morning mist. Then Howard spoke. "The leases ended in 1999. The government wanted everyone out before the end of the twentieth century - the end of the millennium - and now, just a few years later, we've all accepted that economic values are more important than roots, land, and family. Those were things that belonged to the past century."

Ken smiled, glad to have Howard's agreement.

"And this just isn't happening here," added Annette, "It's all over the country."

"That's why it was so easy for the government to put the people out of Kiosk," said Howard continuing. "Everyone just accepts that economic considerations are more important than human considerations. What's more important?" he asked, "the needs of a thousand people who feel connected to the land they live on, or the needs of a government trying to establish a provincial park? If we can make even a small group see that what happened here was wrong, that the people of this country are more valuable that the sum of their production capacity, that there is value in having a connection to land, to place and to family, then this protest will be worth something."

Maggie was about to ask a question, but Ken interrupted. "And, if we can stop the government from doing this again, it'll be even better."

Maggie looked at both men and smiled. "So, in ten words or less . . ."

Laughter erupted around the fire.

"Will this be in tomorrow's paper?" Ken asked, smiling.

Maggie didn't answer immediately. "I saw a movie some time ago," she said finally, "about some people being moved against their will. One of the characters said something that stuck in my mind - you wrote about it too. He said that some of the darkest chapters in our history involved the forced relocation of one group of people to satisfy the demands of another."

Ken realised that Maggie had read the fax he had sent. He smiled.

Maggie returned the smile and put her pencil to her forehead. "Will this be in the paper? If I have anything to say about it, it will."

5. The Fire (1973)

Rene Laterriere walked past the brightly lit veneer tables and squeezed down the narrow wooden walkway. It was a beautiful Kiosk evening and he would have preferred to find a job outside in the yard, but he had a report that a dryer motor was noisy, and as duty maintenance mechanic, it was his job to check it out. It was only 9:00 p.m., and normally, he wouldn't inspect the veneer plant until midnight, a couple of hours before quitting, but if he needed parts, it would be easier to locate them now.

The report had surprised him. The Kiosk plant was noisy and it was difficult to carry on a conversation, let alone hear a noisy bearing. Usually, he or one of the other mechanics found these problems long before anyone knew they existed. He looked at the scratchy report. There was no signature and he didn't recognize the writing.

The motor was awkwardly placed and it was necessary to step over running belts to get close. Sawdust and wood chips filled his shoes as he stood, ankle-deep, watching the grey motor spin and vibrate. It seemed fine, but he was so accustomed to old equipment that perhaps his judgement was flawed. He opened his toolbox, took out a metal rod and placed it between the housing and his ear. Beside all the usual humming and rumbling, he could hear a grinding sound, like a hockey player turning on an ice rink. He shrugged his shoulders. Someone had been right; the bearing was failing.

It was a big motor, a GE3250, and he doubted there was a replacement. He took a few measurements, opened a wire-bound notebook, licked the tip of his pencil, and jotted down some numbers. He would have to check the shop stores to see if there were replacement parts. He might be able to replace just the bearings, but he might be forced to replace it with a different motor. At least, if he had to call the chief, it would be early enough.

He put away his metal rod, picked up his toolbox and took a last look at the motor. From just a few feet away, it seemed fine. It was certainly odd that someone had discovered it. He leaned forward and felt the casing. It was hot, but not much hotter than usual. Many motors ran hot in the mill. He shook his head, stepped back over the belts and hit the shutdown switch. The decelerating whine seemed loud, but it quickly disappeared as the drier came to a stop. The noise was normal.

"What's up?" one of the workers shouted over the ambient noise. Although the drier was shut down, there were plenty of other machines grinding and buzzing.

"I'm turning it back on! I just wanted to hear it!" Rene flicked the switch and the motor grinded as it picked up speed. Maybe this is when someone heard the bad bearing.

If he was going to work on it, it would be easier to do so once it cooled. He shut off the power again and the whine dropped in frequency. The worker who had shouted earlier looked back at him. Rene shrugged. "I've gotta replace the bearing! Won't be too long!"

He reached the stores, a large fenced area that contained supplies and spare-parts, and pulled a key from his retractable key ring. Surprisingly, the gate was not locked.

Inside, he could find nothing he needed. He looked at his watch; it was time to call the boss. From the battle-worn desk, he picked up the heavy black phone and dialled the four numbers - all phone numbers in town were only four digits long - that connected him to Andre. He described the problem.

"I think you better call Smith."

Rene didn't want to call Smith. "It's not such a big problem," he said.

"If it's not such a big problem, why are you calling me?"

"I just wondered if you knew where there are any replacement motors?"

"Can't you just replace the bearings?"

"The bearings are built in, so I won't know 'til I tear it down. Anyway, I don't think there are any bearings around."

"Did you check in stores?"

"I'm here now." He looked around. "Seems like a lot of stuff is missing."

"Have a look in the mill. Maybe you can pull a motor from something we're not using . . . until we get a new one."

Rene groaned. He did not like the idea of tearing out two motors. These things were very heavy and usually located in awkward places. "I don't remember any that look like that one."

"Well, if there's none, you'll have to order one."

"If that's the case, we won't be able to get anything until tomorrow. Denis will have to take care of it." This idea appealed to Rene.

"What about running for the rest of the shift?"

"Shouldn't be a problem."

There was a hesitation on the phone. "You say the motor is hot?"

"Well, it's hot, but not really hot . . . at least, I don't think . . ."

Andre interrupted. "You call Ray Smith. It's his decision."

Rene was stunned. This was the second time Andre had suggested this. Why would he call Ray Smith? He was the plant manager; he knew nothing about maintenance. Smith liked to make the workers feel uncomfortable. Rene did not want to phone him at home. "Bu . . . but . . . I . . ."

Andre interrupted again. "Leave it shut down for now. Go have a look for another motor and if you can't find one give Smith a call! Tell him you have a faulty bearing in a drier motor and ask him if he wants to shut down or keep running."

"You think we need to shut down?"

"Let Smith make that decision. He already talked to me today about faulty maintenance."

Rene was suddenly defensive. "Andre, this has nothing to do with faulty maintenance! I checked that motor out as soon as I got the report and it isn't that . . ."

Andre cut him off. "I didn't say it was faulty maintenance, but Smith was saying that he wanted to have more control. You call him."

Rene was nonplussed. "Okay . . . If I can't find another motor, I'll give him a call . . . at home." He placed the phone back in its cradle and stretched. He suddenly wanted to find a motor.

He walked out of the veneer plant and crossed the yard to the mill. It was warm and wind-still and a few people were fishing on the lake. He sighed and wished he could join them. If he found a motor, he would have to sweat and strain to get it back to the veneer plant, and if he didn't find one, he would have to call Smith. Either way, it did not promise to be a great evening. With a sigh, he opened a heavy door, entered the saw mill, and started to inspect the various motors on the low-priority equipment. After many measurements, he finally found a motor that would work. He would have to change the pullies and modify the base plate, but the motor was similar to the one on the drier.

He returned to the veneer plant for some tools and the foreman immediately accosted him. "I need that drier running! The whole floor is piling up!"

Rene looked around. Men and women were standing around doing nothing. He looked back at the foreman helplessly. "I have to change the motor. It's running hot."

"Maudit, tabernacle! Everything's running hot! It's summer for Christ's sake!"

"I found a motor in the mill."

"How long?"

"About an hour . . . maybe two."

The foreman looked at his watch. "Tabernacle! Can't we run it for a while now and get caught up?"

Rene's shoulders dropped. Now he would have to call Smith, and replace the damned motor. "Wait . . . I'll make a call."

He walked back to stores and dialled Smith's number. Smith answered immediately and, in contrast to Andre, was friendly. He seemed concerned about the bearing and suggested that they call off the rest of the shift. This was surprising. He was normally only interested in productivity, not maintenance. Rene looked at his watch. It was still early and the shift didn't end until two in the morning. It seemed unnecessary to cancel the shift because of one noisy motor bearing. "Are you sure? The motor is not really that hot

. . . we could run it for the last few hours of the shift and then work on it tomorrow."

Smith was firm. Safety was important, he said. He patiently explained that the other motor should be installed tonight so it was available for the day-shift tomorrow. The best thing to do was call off the shift and send them home.

"You want me to change those motors tonight?"

Smith didn't argue, but was firm. The foreman should send the shift home, then shut down the plant, and Rene should go home for a midnight supper. Everything should cool down. That was important. He should let things rest and then, after midnight, he should return, pull out the other motor, and install it in the drier.

Rene grimaced. There would be no one around to help him with any heavy lifting, but he dared not argue. He replaced the handset and walked back to the foreman. He told him to have the shift clock out and then shut down for the night. The foreman shrugged his shoulders, turned and walked from table to table. The workers had no problem leaving three hours early. Armand Latulippe, one of the long-time mill employees, was having a retirement party tonight, and if they hurried, they could join in. A few rushed to the exit and the plant began to power down. The noise of whining machinery was eventually replaced by the quieter hum of fluorescent lights.

Rene walked back to the motor, took note of the tools he would need, and then returned to the maintenance stores and locked the gate. An extra hour's rest would probably do the machinery some good. The company had not been updating their equipment regularly and many motors and bearings were in poor condition. He turned off the lights and walked out of the empty building. He would return just after midnight and take his time with the job. If he had to work, he intended to make some good overtime money.

Suzette Labelle sat on the overstuffed sofa and watched the English late show with her older brother Gilles. Her father preferred that they did not watch so much English TV, but he was a quiet man and, other than occasionally shaking his head to show his disapproval, he said little.

The local North Bay station did not play many movies and the box office hits, The French Connection, The Godfather, Fiddler on the Roof, wouldn't get aired for years. Tonight they were playing a war movie, something she normally wouldn't watch, but this one caught her attention. It starred Robert Mitchum and some cute, younger guys, and instead of showing the war as glamorous and heroic, it showed it to be tough and unpleasant. A small group of soldiers was hiding in a French farmhouse that contained a mother and two daughters. The situation was very stressful for the women, and Suzette empathised with the turmoil they felt.

These women refused to leave their farm even though tanks, mine fields, and dirty soldiers surrounded them. One day their papa would return, the daughters said, and they didn't want to abandon their home, their family. Would she want to stay in such a place? She thought about how she would feel - how she would react?

A commercial interrupted the show and Suzette stood and stretched. "I'm getting a pop." she said leaving the room.

"Better not," Gilles laughed, "You'll turn into one of the fatties."

"Shut up!" She pulled on the chrome handle and the heavy refrigerator door popped open. Glass jars tinkled against each other.

"Mama said they were for company."

"I can have one." Ever since a town resident had won a thousand dollars on a bottle-cap contest, papa had been buying a lot of pop. The contest was long over, but no one bothered to tell him, even when he asked if they had won. "No," they would answer, looking at the blank bottle caps, "not this time."

"Get me one too, then."

She had intended on getting a glass for herself, but since Gilles was having a pop, he would want to drink from the bottle. She'd feel foolish drinking from a glass while Gilles drank from the bottle. She opened two bottles and cleaned the top of hers with a dish towel. "Gilles, I . . ." She was interrupted by the loud and mournful howl of the lumber yard whistle. It was usually used to announce shift changes, and she had never heard it this late at night. It continued, on and on. She walked back to the living room and saw Gilles standing. She handed him his pop. "What's up with that?" She gestured toward the mill, the sound.

Gilles shrugged and walked out the front door. A reddish glow illuminated the southern horizon.

"What's going on?" Suzette asked walking behind him.

"Don't know. Maybe it's a test."

A test made no sense. "I'm going back to watch the movie."

"Hang on a minute."

She looked at her brother's furrowed brow, his squinting eyes. He was worried. Other people walked outside into the splash of yellow light from their homes and looked in all directions. She went back inside for a jacket.

Her parents had gone to bed at their usual time of ten o'clock, but her father now appeared at the bedroom door hastily wrapping himself in a worn dressing gown. "What is it?" he asked in French. His tangled black hair stood straight up.

"I don't know papa. Gilles is out front."

Suzette put on a red windbreaker and followed her father onto the concrete sidewalk. They all looked at the sky to the south. The eerie red glow was brighter and the smell of smoke wafted in the air. Her father swore. "Maudit tabernacle!"

"What's wrong, Papa?" she asked.

"I better go see that, me," he said as he walked away.

"Better go get everyone up," Gilles said. "The wind is blowing toward the town. Everything could burn."

Suzette nodded as she looked around. People were outside in pyjamas and nightgowns and Mr. Desjardin stood on the lawn in his boxer shorts. Some people had started walking south, toward the mill, dressed as scantily as they had come out of their houses.

"Hurry up!" her brother admonished.

"I'm going!" She walked back in the house.

Her mother, a short, heavy woman, old for her years, usually had trouble getting out of bed. But at the mention of fire, she became agitated. She walked around her small bedroom, haphazardly moving things, as she tried to dress.

"Gilles thinks you should come outside, Mama."

"What about your brothers and sisters?"

"Denise and Andre are in Mattawa, Mama." Her two oldest siblings were living in the nearest town with a cousin so they could attend school there. There was only a public school in Kiosk and once a child was ready to start high school, they either had to quit, take correspondence courses, or get bussed into Mattawa. "Gilles is outside."

Her mother nodded. "Gather your things, dear."

Suzette left the doorway of her mother's room and walked to her own bedroom. There was not much to gather. She looked at her schoolwork, turned, closed the door, and walked back outside.

Gilles had put on a leather jacket, but was still standing on the front sidewalk. "Maudit! It's getting bigger. I'm going to have a look." He started to walk toward the mill and Suzette followed.

A few steps from their house, the power went off and suddenly a heavy layer of darkness surrounded them. From houses all around, people gasped and started banging about in the dark.

Suzette stood still. Slowly, her eyes adjusted. The pale moon illuminated the path and the red glow of the mill lit up the wispy clouds. Red embers rose high in the sky. Gilles turned toward her, his face foreign in the eerie light. "You better go back and give Mama a hand. We may need to pack."

She was frightened by his expression and she wanted to protest, but she acquiesced. Gilles was suddenly gone and Suzette was left alone on the dirt road. All around her, people were talking in excited voices. The darkness was now dotted with flickering yellow candle light, which emanated from some the houses.

"Is that you?" Pat asked.

Relieved by his voice, she turned quickly. "Yeah. You know what's happening?" she asked.

"No more than anybody else. There's a big fire in the mill . . . a big fire." Pat looked around. "Power's out too."

A loud explosion shook the air and instinctively, Pat and Suzette ducked. Pat put his arm around her shoulder and pulled her close. She smiled as he slowly, and cautiously, removed it. Since she had given him the compass in the spring, she had sensed his affection, but he was hopelessly shy and had trouble admitting that he liked her. He sometimes touched her, tentatively, and a few times had even taken her hand when they went for a walk.

In a small town like Kiosk, where everyone knew everyone else's business, holding hands while walking down the street was like taking out a billboard or a newspaper announcement. Suzette knew it must have taken courage, because the other boys teased each other relentlessly. They would chant: "Na na-nah na-nah naa." That was usually the providence of the very young boys, but the boys of Kiosk were immature. Pat was not like them, however. He was quiet, sincere, and sensitive to the feelings of others.

She thought of her mother banging around in the dark and she felt a pang of guilt. Here she was thinking of herself and Pat, when her mother must be in a panic. "Pat," she said softly, touching his arm, "I gotta get back to my house."

Pat nodded quickly and started to move. "I'll walk you home. I better get back home too."

Suzette wondered if Pat would kiss her in the dark, but when they reached the house, she was disappointed. He walked away quickly saying, "See ya later," and disappeared in the darkness.

Her mother was still in the same state she had been when Suzette left, but she was now ambling through the house. "Suzette!" she cried. "Get the suitcases. We have to pack our things."

In the past, other fires had sprung up in the mill, but never in the middle of the night and even though this somehow seemed urgent, she felt her mother was overreacting. "Mama, they'll get it under control."

Her mother puffed on a cigarette and looked at her knowingly. "Tabernacle!" she swore in French. "And what if they don't? This is no time!"

There was no sense arguing. She went into the back room, tumbled items out of the closet and grabbed two worn, scarred and misshapen suitcases. Normally there were more, but Denise and Andre had some in Mattawa. She carried them to the living room and opened them on the sofa.

Kenny finally decided to get up. There was too much noise downstairs and he could not filter it out. He pulled back the covers, revealing his skinny white legs, and swung his feet onto the floor.

The muffled sound of cupboard doors being banged and drawers being scraped open and closed filled the house. He tried to turn on his light, but there was no power. He pulled on his jeans and quietly descended the stairs. His mother saw him at the bottom in the flickering candlelight. "Kenny, you're up! Good! There's a fire at the mill and your father wants to pack all the important things into cardboard boxes."

"I was gonna let you sleep till it was time to leave," his father said as Kenny walked to the living room, "but since you're up, you go and get what you think you wanna keep and put it in one of these boxes."

"What's up with the fire?"

"You just go up to your room and get whatever you think is important."

This did not make sense to Kenny. If they had been willing to let him sleep, why were they suddenly in such a hurry to get him packing? He did not argue with his father, however, and he turned as his mother handed him a candle.

Up in his room, he could see the red glow of fire on the horizon. The entire sky to the south was lit up like an early sunrise. He looked at his clock. It was just past twelve-thirty. He looked out the window and saw the first licks of flame. It must have been high, because the trees between their house and the mill would obscure a lot of the horizon. He turned and watched his giant shadow move and flicker on the plasterboard wall. He watched for a moment, mesmerized, and then started to pack.

He opened his cigar box, put his pocket-knife in his pocket and then looked through the box. There were a number of treasures, a pair of dice, a bird whistle, a compass and some other collectables - like the magic stone that had saved him from the bear. He taped the box closed and threw it on his bed.

A strange sense of apprehension came over him and he walked back to the window. The fire was definitely big. If it just stuck to the mill, the mill could be rebuilt, but if the fire took off into the bush, they could be in big trouble. Forest fires were deadly. They moved at the speed of a car, sucking the oxygen out of the air and cooking everything in their paths. He thought of all the places he liked to go. The beaver ponds, the hidden lakes, the rocky hills, they would all be destroyed forever by a raging fire. A mill could be rebuilt, but all these places would be lost forever. In his imagination, he could see all the animals running from the flames. The moose, the bear, the mink, the wolves, they would all try to run, but would be surrounded and killed.

There was an area north of Kiosk that had burned many years ago. It was a great place to find blueberries and Kenny had often marvelled at the size of the blackened stumps. What must it have been like before the fire? Now, it was an ugly area of tangled bush and weeds, and if it were not for the blueberries, he would have never gone there. What if the entire forest burned like that?

He put on his sneakers, ran down the stairs, and out the front door. "Kenny, don't go near the fire!" his mother yelled, but he was already trotting up the dark road toward the train bridge. From there he would be able to see how bad the fire really was.

He crested the dusty hill and saw the stark shadows created by the light of the fire. It had not limited itself to one section, but seemed to have spread to the entire mill. The fire was so bright, it was difficult to watch. As he walked up the road toward the train bridge, he noticed the people around him. They ran in every direction shouting and yelling and they drove their vehicles jerkily along the road, grinding gears and over-revving their engines. The air shook with an explosion, which Kenny felt deep inside his body, and the fire roared and whooshed up into the night sky.

"Get out of the way!" a man yelled and Kenny quickly stepped off the road. A truck passed him, its tires growling in the soft gravel and its engine whining.

As he neared the bridge, he could feel the heat. It hadn't spread to the entire mill and it was still a distance away from the bridge, but it looked like it was too big to stop. On this side of the river, there were thirty or forty people, just standing and watching. Some stood in groups and some alone.

Not too far away, he saw Mrs Connolly sitting on the riverbank, her head resting in her hands. She was not even watching the fire. Kenny watched her for a moment, heard her sob, and quickly walked away.

He looked back to the fire and saw, silhouetted against the reddish-orange, the shapes of men frantically running back and forth. They were attempting to put out the fire, but they looked so small in relation to the jagged flames that it was obvious they would lose.

"Looks bad, Kenny." Mr. Callahan said from his side.

"Sure does," Kenny agreed. Mr. Callahan was one of the older men. He had retired from the mill and spent his time gardening and fishing. They would have probably thrown him out as well, but he owned his house. "You think it could spread to the town? Or the forest?"

"Fire has its own mind, boy, but the town's lucky that line of box cars is where they is."

Kenny squinted and raised his hand over his brow to block out some of the bright light that was now high in the sky. A long line of metal boxcars stood on the siding between the mill and the town. The lake was on the other side of the mill, so the only way the fire could get out was to the east, through the giant lumber yard. "I sure hope it don't get out into the forest."

"You, and a lot of other people," said Callahan walking away.

Kenny knew he should go back home and help his parents, but he was a little excited and he wanted to cross the river to see the fire. There was a charge in the air that was hard to ignore.

Pat shoved the soft duffle bag in the car, closed the rear door and stepped back. The car was heavily packed and there was little room.

"You stay here with your Mom," his dad said. "I'm gonna park the car on the highway so we can get to it if we need to." He tugged on the gearshift lever and the car pulled away.

Uncle Roy had already moved his truck and he walked toward the house. "My truck's just up past the sign," he shouted to Pat's Dad. A large sign marked the beginning of the town on Highway 630. Roy walked to Pat's mom. "Well, it looks like they got us out."

"Whaddya mean?"

"The birdwatchers wanted the town closed down and now," he turned and pointed to the mill, "they've done it."

"Tis grand, you startin' rumours, Roy James. Are you tellin' me that somebody started the fire?" There was a tone of incredulity in her voice.

Roy put his foot up on the wooden step and lit a cigarette. "Well Lisa, it's mighty convenient that the night shift gets called off by Smith and then as soon as the place is empty, a fire starts."

She shook her head in disgust. The rumours were starting to spread as quickly as the fire. "That's daft!"

"Well, I'll tell you this. The government was surveying these lots so that people could buy 'em. Your husband would have bought this place for sure and other people would have bought their lots. That would have meant the town was here for good. That would have made it mighty hard for the birdwatchers to get anyone out. Now that the mill has burned, I'll bet you that the government reneges on the deal."

Pat's mom pulled her cardigan tightly around her middle. She hadn't thought of this. She had been looking forward to owning the land on which their house stood. Still, she was sure no one would deliberately burn the mill. "You just don't be causing any trouble. There's enough of that on the horizon." She pointed back to the mill.

Roy turned to Pat. "What do you think, lad? Wanna get a closer look at the mill?"

Pat's mom said nothing. She stamped angrily into the house displaying her anger with Roy and his idea to take Pat closer to the fire. Pat was uncertain of what he should do. His guitar and other belongings were already in the car and there was no point in hanging around the house. His mother did not want him to go, but the fire was the biggest thing to happen in Kiosk for many years. He nodded and Roy led the way.

The huge fire was way beyond control. Sparks, angrily buzzing and dancing, competed with the stars for attention, and translucent bands of flame crept up through the darkness and then detached themselves and drifted before disappearing in the void. At the centre, the upward movement of air was fast and furious and large smouldering pieces from the fire were carried high in the sky before falling into the water with a sisshh. Luckily, the wind fanned the flames out over the lake, because if it had been coming from the opposite direction, the town and the surrounding forest would have been subjected to a rain of fire.

At ground level, the flames, jagged and brilliant, arched and jumped as if alive, and they were so bright that they were difficult to watch. A few of the buildings had already collapsed and a weird grouping of wheels, drives and gears could be seen silhouetted against the bright background of dancing light.

A pumper truck sprayed a pile of lumber off to the side, but the atmosphere and the resigned movement of the crowd made it clear that most people had given up. The mill, the veneer plant, the kilns, the semi-dimension mill, were all gone. There was little left to save. Large groups of people stood or sat a distance from the fire, drawn to the flames like moths to a candle.

"Hey Pat!"

Pat turned and saw Kenny Campbell walking toward him.

"Pretty mean, isn't it?"

Pat nodded and looked past Kenny to the street. Cars and trucks were moving in all directions. It seemed like every vehicle in the town was being driven somewhere. He looked at Kenny and did not know what to say. He turned back and stared at the macabre dance of flame.

A group of boys hustled by and one boy grabbed Pat's sleeve. "Come on!" he said in French. "We're going to get the boats away from the fire." Without even realising what the boy had said, both he and Kenny allowed themselves to be pulled along.

As they passed the bunkhouse, they saw a group of men watering down the buildings on the concrete path. The flames were tall here and the wiggling fiery glow cast strange dancing shadows. The men were covered in sweat and they moved methodically.

"Come on!" one man cried, still full of energy, "if it gets out of here, it will run into the town and into the forest!"

Kenny looked over his shoulder and saw that the bunkhouse would take the fire into the town, just as the man had said, and he started to slow his run, deciding if he should help.

"Get away from here, boy!" another man yelled, anticipating Kenny's intention. "This is too dangerous! Go help your family!" The man wiped a sooty hand across his sweat-soaked face and turned back to the fire.

Kenny hesitated and one of the boys grabbed his shirt and pulled him. "Come on, let's get to the dock."

They ran behind the train station, across the tracks and down to the shore. Despite the bright flames that lit up the sky and reflected off the water, the boathouse was dark. There were a few motorboats inside and some of the boys began to untie their mooring ropes. Without the keys, there was no way to control the powerboats, so they pushed them out toward the centre of the lake and let them drift.

There was less danger on the dock. It seemed safer surrounded by water and boys ran back and forth acting as if they were at a company picnic or a rodeo. They were whooping and hollering.

"Over here!" someone yelled.

"Yahoo!" A boy in a boat turned a discovered ignition key and screamed in delight as the engine roared to life. Instead of using the boat to round up the other boats, he roared off toward the centre of the lake. The wake of the boat washed back and the other boats bobbed and banged into the wooden dock.

Another large explosion rocked the air and bright light spilled across the water. "I'm getting out of here!" someone cried. Pat let go of the rope he was holding, ran outside and stood on the dock. The flames roared up into the sky carrying hot pieces of wood that fell into the water and sisshed.

"Pat!" Kenny yelled. "Give me a hand!" Kenny was untying the ropes of the company tug, which sat off to the side of the boat house.

Pat ran over and worked on another knot. It was difficult and his fingers fuddled uncooperatively. The reflection of the flames rolled on the surface of the water and he looked up while he continued to pull and strain at the knot. He could feel the heat on his face.

An older boy pushed Pat aside and finished the task. The pounding of footsteps on the wooden dock competed with the jubilant shouts as the company tug was slowly pushed away from the mill and the fire. One boy, leaning on the side, fell into the water and everyone screamed and laughed, trying to draw attention to themselves and their ingeniousness, but the fire was just too big and few people saw their actions. The tug would be available for work tomorrow, but there would be little for it to do.

Pat grabbed Kenny's arm. "We better get away from here.

The wind is blowing toward us. This whole dock could burn." The smell of smoke lay heavily over the water.

Kenny looked at the flames. "I was worried it was going to run out into the forest, but it looks like it won't now. It'll stick to the mill. But you're right, it could come this way."

"I've never seen nothing like this."

A large section of roof collapsed and whooshed to the ground. A huge shower of sparks rose into the sky, danced, and swirled in every direction. People on the dock moaned and for a few seconds, the "wow's" and "ahhh's" seemed louder than the crackling of the fire.

"Come on, let's get out of here." Pat led Kenny toward the train station. Most of the other kids left the dock as well, but a few jumped into row boats and pushed them away from shore. "I better get back to where my uncle is. My mom will freak out if she thinks I'm too close to the fire."

They pushed their way through the crowd, back toward the bunkhouse. The section of the mill closest to the bunkhouse had collapsed and the fire was not burning as furiously as it had when they first passed. The men were still working hard to keep the bunkhouse and the surrounding buildings watered down, but they were not as frantic. As the buildings collapsed, the danger of the fire spreading lessened.

"Everyone's here." Kenny said looking at the people.

They stood everywhere; people in nightgowns and pyjamas, people in summer clothing, people in shorts and dress shoes. Many stood with their arms folded, looking lost and isolated. Some of the women and some of the men had wet cheeks and darkened eyes.

Roy grabbed Pat angrily and yelled: "Where the hell did you get to?"

"I went to help get the boats out of the boathouse."

Roy whacked Pat in the back of the head. "Well, don't take off again. That fire is dangerous and I don't want your mother beating me with a frying pan 'cause I didn't look after you!"

Kenny settled in beside Roy and watched the fire. The frenetic activity had started to die down. Some people were still driving around, trying to get valued possessions up to the highway, but most just stood and watched.

A man standing beside Roy spoke in a loud raspy voice. "I guess this proves that Friday the thirteenth is not a good day!"

Many people nodded and some appeared surprised. Some had not realised the date.

"This has nothing to do with bad luck! Luck played no damned role in this."

The man beside Roy flapped his hand as if to say that he didn't want to hear what Roy had to say. He turned, ready to walk away, and then said over his shoulder: "I guess I'll see you in the U.I.C. line-up on Monday."

"That's where we'll all be in the next few days," Roy said as much to himself as in reply. Most of the men would qualify for U.I.C., or unemployment insurance, but the payments would be much less than a person made for an honest week of work. Life would be hard for many of the families in town.

Pat looked up, his eyes tracking a large board that floated high in the sky and then fell toward the lake. It was almost like fireworks. "Will they rebuild it?"

Roy turned back to the fire. "They don't want to, Pat. And, even if they did, it would take a long time. There's ten acres of building there. The whole thing's gonna go and there ain't nothing gonna stop it. It takes a long time to clean that up and rebuild it."

Mr. Hackenbrook, one of the saw blade filers, stepped closer and spoke to Roy. "What makes you think they won't rebuild it?" His yellow hard-hat had turned orange in the light of the glowing fire.

Roy turned to face him. "Are you kidding?! This is the perfect opportunity. They can get everyone to move out of town and no one will resist. The damned government has been trying to get us out of here for over five years. Now, with the mill gone, it'll be easy. No one owns their land yet, the leases will be up in 1999, and if there are no jobs, who would want to stay here."

Mr. Hackenbrook nodded. "I guess so. But the company won't want to go out of business."

"They'll rebuild it somewhere else - somewhere where they won't disturb the birdwatchers. They'll probably get a government grant to build. You mark my words."

Hackenbrook rubbed his beard and nodded. "Pretty suspicious that they called off the evening shift just before the fire. It was mighty convenient that nobody was in the plant."

Roy nodded. "Even more suspicious is that they emptied the water tower a couple a' days ago and then the power just happens to go off so they can't pump from the pump house!" A few people looked at Roy and started to listen. "I wouldn't be surprised if someone didn't torch the place to get rid of it. And before they did, they made damned sure that no-one was gonna put it out either."

Hackenbrook grunted his agreement.

Roy smiled. "If I ever need one of them heart transplants, I hope I get a heart from one of them politicians or businessmen."

Hackenbrook looked confused.

A woman who had been listening stole the punch-line. "Yeah, if you're gonna get a new heart, might as well get one that ain't never been used." She cracked up and Hackenbrook smiled as he nodded.

Pat looked at Kenny and laughed, but Kenny did not. "Your uncle may be right, you know," he said. "They really want to get us out of here and they don't care if we was born here and grew up here!"

"Maybe." He shuffled his feet in the sand and shrugged his shoulders. "Maybe it will be good to move the mill further from the town." He looked down at the ground. "Maybe we all need to get away for a while."

Kenny looked sideways at Pat, tilted his head and frowned. "I don't want to leave here. This is my home."

Pat shrugged his shoulders again and nodded at the fire. "It looks like we won't have much of a choice."

A group of men and women were now talking and the laughter had been replaced by anger. One old man waved his hand dismissively. "This is how things is done," he said. "The same thing that happened in Fossmill! They burned that one too, back in '34."

Fossmill was the mill that had existed before Kiosk. It was a distance to the west along the CNR line, and although smaller, it had once been a thriving town as well. The logging limits were weakening and there had been some money troubles. Then, on a Sunday in 1934, when it was empty, the entire mill burned to the ground. Many of the Fossmill workers walked the railway line, through the bush, to work at Kiosk.

"Ain't no one gives a damn about the people," said the man turning his back and flapping his hands as if he were smacking a dog. "Just use 'em up and then burn 'em out." A few other people walked away from the fire.

Suzette coughed and sat up. Her sheets were dirty from soot. For a second it seemed that she could not breathe, but the sensation passed. It was early and she had slept only a few hours, but she knew she would not go back to sleep. The air in the house was hot, sticky and oppressive and her sheets felt heavy. She listened. No one else was moving about. She dressed, grabbed a couple of slices of bread, and slipped out the front door.

The air smelled strongly of smoke. A patina of grey soot coated everything and, as she walked, she left footprints in the sooty ground. Listlessly chewing on the bread, she walked toward the mill. A plume of smoke still rose from what had once been the semi-dimension mill, the saw mill, and the veneer plant, but the violent swirling flames had disappeared. The scene looked like a charcoal drawing; everything was smudged in shades of grey and black.

Nearer to the collapsed buildings, people stood in small groups. They looked very tired and Suzette guessed that they had been awake all night. Some were wrapped in blankets, but those closer to the buildings seemed to feel the warmth of the fire.

The excitement of the night before had been replaced with lethargy. People moved slowly and looked down at the ground as they spoke. There were no children, just men and women who all seemed to share the same demoralized expression, the same defeated demeanour.

She walked over to Mrs. Richer, a heavy woman, who was sitting alone on a tuft of grass. She didn't know what to say at first and she mumbled in French: "The whole thing burned."

Mrs. Richer shook her head and answered in English. "Oui, it's all gone . . . everyting."

"No one was hurt?"

"No."

"It's good no one got killed."

Mrs. Richer suddenly looked up at her. "The town got killed. The mill will never be built again and all the families here will be forced to move." A tear rolled down her soot stained cheek. "All the friends we had . . . lost . . . forever."

Suzette felt her own throat constrict. She wanted to say something, but she choked and feared she would start to cry. "It will be all right," she said finally as she knelt beside the heavy woman and hugged her shoulders.

"I know, dear. I know." The woman hugged her for a moment and then, gently, but a little impatiently, pushed her away. She took out a cotton handkerchief and wiped her tear-dampened face. From the appearance of the handkerchief, it had performed this task a number of times during the night. "You're young. You got your whole life in front of you. Mr. Richer and me, we lived here all our lives. Our children grew up here and we wanted to be buried here. We don't want to go and live in some apartment some-where."

"But none of the houses burned. You can stay here."

"Everyone knows the government will kick everyone out. The birdwatchers don't want a bunch of town people spoiling their . . . their . . . canoe ride."

Suzette wanted to leave. She did not want to hear about birdwatchers. "I heard that they might rebuild the mill right here. I'm sure it will be all right."

The woman looked down at the ground. "Yeah, yeah, I'm sure it will." There was no conviction in her voice.

Suzette walked toward the bunkhouse. From here, if she had not known that the mill buildings should have towered in front of her, it would have been difficult to tell there had been a fire. The bunkhouse had not been damaged and the fire had stayed on the lake-side of the train tracks. Last night she had heard some men say that the line of boxcars on the siding between the town and the mill had probably saved the town from destruction. Here, the only indi-cations of the fire were the ash on the ground and the smell in the air.

As she crossed the tracks, feet sinking into the gritty brown gravel, her nostrils were assaulted by the acrid odour. It was unpleasant. Very different than being near a hardwood campfire, this contained the smells of burned rubber, tar and plastic, and that mouldy, unhealthy smell of smouldering cardboard. The damp lake air strengthened its attack so that it almost could be tasted on the tongue. She wrinkled her nose and continued to walk beside the box cars.

All the buildings were now just jagged mounds of blackened debris. It was difficult to remember their original locations. Among the rubble, a few metal wheels were silhouetted against the lake, looking like some kind of crazy art display. One wheel turned slowly in the wind - performance art.

She walked past the blistered boxcars, which had been warped by the heat. Two men, their faces covered in soot, sat in an open door of one of the cars and nodded as Suzette passed.

To the right, near the water, a huge pile of sawdust still smouldered. No flames were visible, but grey smoke oozed out into the morning sky. A few men with shovels stood near by, dwarfed by its size of the pile, waiting for any re-emergence of the fire-beast, while others picked through the remains of the mill. The faces of the men were so blackened by soot and expressionless with fatigue that it was difficult to tell who was who.

Suzette looked up at the water tower. Curiously, with all the heat and destruction, it still stood. It looked fragile, but very tall, now that the other buildings were gone. Not too far away, the triple smoke stacks of the power plant also stood alone against the sky, like eerie grave markers of the buildings that had once been.

One night last summer, she had climbed one of the three sections of the tower. Her sister Denise had not believed that she would have the courage and this had spurred her on. One section had been enough, however. It had still been frightening to climb the metal ladder. Parents were always saying that the tower was going to fall over, but obviously, it had been stronger than they imagined.

When she reached the train bridge at the mouth of the Amable River, the smell began to abate. The metal bridge had not been damaged, and looked safe to cross. Looking over her shoulder, she realised that there was little danger of any train arriving this morning. The main line was littered with debris from the fire.

She stopped, looked forward and then backward, not sure

what to do. With a little reluctance, she set out across the bridge toward the far side of town. Mr. Frederick, the stationmaster, always yelled when he saw someone on the bridge, but Mr. Frederick had other things to worry about this morning - the whole town had other things to worry about.

As she approached the middle, she looked uneasily up the tracks. She did not want to get caught. She had never crossed the bridge before. With a couple of cautious steps, she walked to the side and looked down at the water. It was hard to tell how strong the current was since the water rolled under the bridge without wave or bubble, but she knew that at the weir, only a few hundred yards downstream, the water raged and boiled.

Occasionally, during the summer, some of the kids jumped from this bridge into the river below. They usually screamed with excitement as they plopped into the raging water. It was a dangerous jump because partially-submerged pieces of wood often floated unseen.

In her memory, she could hear the joyous screams of the kids as they cannon-balled off the bridge. Although she had never jumped, she had often joined in the excitement from the bank of the river.

The words of Mrs. Richer returned to her, "All the friends we had . . . lost forever." The sounds of joy that rang through her memory were suddenly silent. The laughter disappeared and only the gurgle of flowing water remained. A song came to her. It was a hit song that played on the radio. She could hear the refrain and some of the words. "In a little while from now . . ." Then some more, and then: "Alone again . . . naturally."

At the end of the bridge, she scrabbled down the loose slag and then walked past the old pump-house. The area looked deserted. She pulled on the door and found the building locked. This was strange because it was often left open. She pulled again, but the door would not budge.

She ambled down the short hill and stopped to enjoy the wild roses that lined the road. They were a pleasant break from the acrid smell of smoke. She reached down to one stem but immediately pulled her fingers back from the prickly thorns.

Deciding to return home, she walked toward the car bridge.

Perhaps Pat would be awake and she would find him. Last night, their parents had whisked them away from each other and now she longed for his company. She realised, painfully, that she might lose him for good now.

The water under the bridge roared as it fell over the weir and with its dampness, the smell of the fire returned. An old beat-up Dodge banged across the wood planks and Suzette hugged the metal crank handle of one of the drops to get out of the way. People were in a hurry.

On the other side of the bridge, she climbed the grade that led to the main road and just as she reached the crest, she saw Pat in the backseat of a car. He did not see her, but she waved anyway.

Pat's entire family seemed preoccupied and no one in the car looked right or left. The car accelerated toward Highway 630. Again, the words of Mrs. Richer echoed in her mind, "Friends, lost forever." She ran a few steps toward the car before she realised the futility of this. She stopped and watched. Her body jerked with three ragged short breaths. Pat, don't go, she said to herself as tears formed at the corners of her eyes. She knew he would be coming back, but there was something about the image of the car that burned and left her short of breath.

P at turned south onto Highway 630 and looked at the digital clock in the car. It was 10:00 A.M. In a half hour, he would reach Kiosk. He had been too tired to drive the entire way and last night he had stayed in a motel in Powassan, just south of North Bay.

Highway 630 was a narrow, twisty cold-top highway that wound through some verdant forests. At its start were two single-lane bridges that spanned the waterfalls between Smith and Crooked Chute Lakes, and as he crossed them, Pat could hear the roar of water. The road then twisted around Burbot Lake and cut through the town of Eau Claire, a tiny town with a few houses, a fire hall and general store. Pat guessed that a number of former Kiosk residents lived here.

A few kilometres past the town, the road followed the meandering Amable Du Fond River, which churned white as it crashed over its rocky bed. It snaked right and left as it cut through forests of pine, spruce and mixed hardwoods.

Thirty minutes later, the cold-top ended and Pat decelerated as he rolled over the last hill just at the edge of Kiosk. An MNR truck was parked at the side of the road and people milled around. A park warden studied every passing car. Pat coasted past, turned left, and drove toward the ranger station.

The crowd was obviously there because of Ken's protest and Pat didn't want to wind up in the middle of something he couldn't handle, so he decided to buy a day pass and ask questions first. He passed the tangle of horse grass where the store and the bunkhouse had once stood and coasted past the entrance to the old tennis courts. What was he doing? He hit the steering wheel with the flat of his hands. He should have gone to see Ken, but instead he had driven away from the conflict.

He pulled into the parking lot and walked into the ranger station. The main counter was at the back and there were a few bookshelves with maps, books and postcards, but there was no one in the room. After he had stood for a moment, he cleared his throat loudly.

A young woman in a drab brown uniform walked in from the next room. She was the same person he had met on his first return trip. "What can I do you for?" she said wiping her hands on a towel, not recognizing him.

"I'd like to buy a general-use-pass."

"For the interior, or just a day-pass?"

"A day pass. What's going on up the road?" he asked as he filled out the form.

The woman thought for a moment. "Some people are protesting the fact that the government took away their homes."

"Really?"

"Yeah. There used to be a big town here with lots of houses and schools and everything. It was all leased land and when the mill closed, the government didn't renew the leases. They told everyone that they had to leave."

"Is that so?"

"Some of the people tried to fight, but it didn't work. The deadline was just a couple of years ago. Everyone had to leave by then."

"So why are they protesting now? Is anything changing."

"Not that I know."

Pat looked up quickly. This was the same woman who told him about the five-year-plan. Either she did not connect the two events, or she had been told not to say anything. He suspected the latter. "What about the people with cottages? Did they have to leave too?"

"They've got another fifteen years before their leases expire."

"So the Staniforths have to leave their cottages?"

The woman looked up suspiciously. "Well . . . no. They

actually own the land that their cottages are on."

"Really? But aren't they in the park?"

The woman shrugged.

"So what are these protesters doing?"

"Some of them put up tents. One guy - my parents know him - even put up a little cabin."

"Your parents know him?"

"They used to live here - before I was born."

"Oh, no kidding?" Pat tried to sound conversational and only mildly interested. "So what do you think about this protest?"

"Well . . . I don't know. I guess some people have to find out what happened . . . or something, but it is a wilderness park."

It was clear that this woman did not want to take a stand. He wanted to get more information, but he didn't know how to continue. Did she sympathise with the protesters or the government? Her parents had lived here, but the government was her employer. He decided not to tell her he had been a Kiosk resident and not to remind her that he had already spoken with her before. "So what's going to happen?"

"The Group Leader - that's the senior park warden - called into head office and they said just to leave them alone for a while . . . not to make a big thing out of it . . . but then I heard that more people got involved. I think that they might call the OPP."

Pat felt the hairs on the back of his neck stand. "Why?"

"Well . . . they are trespassing."

"But why call the OPP? Why don't they just move them out themselves?"

"Bad publicity . . . they don't want it." She smiled. "Politics."

"You think they'll do anything soon?"

The woman shrugged and looked up at Pat. Her suspicion had grown. "I'm just a contract worker. They don't tell me much."

"Thanks." Pat took his pass and left the office.

He thought of parking in the regulated parking lot and walking back to the bridge, but it was a long walk and the air was warm and muggy. He remembered the warden giving him a hard time about parking anywhere but in the lot, but he decided to take a chance.

He pulled over near the old driveway to the mill, fifty metres from the bridge, and walked down the slight incline. The warden didn't pay any attention to him until he started to cross the bridge. "Hey! Where do you think you're going?"

Pat felt heat flow through his cheeks. "Nowhere, sir."

"No one's allowed over the bridge."

Off in the distance, Pat could see a greyish building, a couple of tents and a number of vehicles. "What's going on?"

"Some people are staging a protest and no one's allowed in."

Pat saw Kenny moving near the building. He felt suddenly annoyed. "Excuse me, but this is a public park, isn't it?"

The warden eyed him curiously. "Yes, but that is not a camping area. So I can't let you in there."

Pat was torn. He desperately wanted to walk past the warden and cross the bridge, but he didn't have the courage. "I think I may know one of the people there," he said weakly. He pointed. "That fellow, Ken Campbell."

"With a 'P'."

Pat was nonplussed for a moment. "Ahh . . . yes, with a 'P'."

"And what do you want with him?"

Pat hesitated. What could he say? "Well . . . I was . . . hoping to maybe talk some sense into him."

The warden stepped back a bit. "Then maybe you better go talk to him, because if they aren't out of here by sundown, I'm bringing in the OPP." Pat smiled and the warden turned sharply to face him. "What are you laughing about?"

Pat shook his head. "Nothing. I was just thinking about your expression, 'They better get out of town by sundown.' It reminded me of a western."

"Oh . . . I see . . . just tell them that they better be out by sundown."

Pat nodded. A few minutes later, he reached the cabin.

"I was worried you weren't going to make it," said Ken shaking his hand.

"I got away late. I slept in a motel on Highway 11." Pat looked around. "Where did all these other people come from?"

"It's a surprise to me. They just showed up." Joanne and Howard had left, but new people had arrived and Ken explained that most of them were former Kiosk residents who had arrived in a show of support. People weren't being allowed across the car bridge, but some had walked over the old train bridge and two people had crossed the river downstream.

Pat looked around at some of the faces. He knew many of them, but as he walked, he had been so worried about a confrontation with the warden that he had kept his eyes to the ground.

He told Ken what he had learned from the woman at the station and the warden at the bridge. Ken did not seem worried. He did not care about the reaction of the MNR, but he was greatly disappointed in the lack of interest by the media. "All these people showed up spontaneously and they all feel the same way I do - we do - but not a single television crew showed up to cover it. If this had been a native protest, there would have been news crews flying in from BC."

Pat looked at Ken. "Yes, perhaps." He looked down at the ground. "But I guess it takes time to get the media interested."

"Yeah right! If there's a fire, they come three days afterwards and film the ashes." Ken told Pat about the possible article in today's Nugget, but he explained that they needed to get more media attention quickly. "Like you said, they may come out here and break this up tonight - and if they're smart they will. Then there'll be nothing but ashes left to film."

Pat suggested he should stay with Ken, but Ken said that Pat should stay on the periphery of the protest. He would be Ken's contact, supplier and media spokesperson. They made contingency plans agreeing where they should meet if the protest was broken and what supplies Ken would need. Eventually, Ken would be forced to leave this location, but until they had received some media attention, he had no intention of leaving the park.

As they talked, various people came up and introduced themselves. The greetings were all warm and friendly and Pat was surprised by the quick recognition. In some cases, people made him feel as if he had never left. It was difficult to tear himself away when it was time to leave.

Suzette Levasseur walked into the office of the news

director and sat in one of the over-stuffed vinyl chairs. It was her day off, but she had been called in. She dropped her bag to the floor and slouched in the chair. It seemed that she was destined to be replaced by a younger, more attractive face, regardless of the quality of her work, and she was becoming more hostile toward her boss.

Bill Nickeyfortune, a veteran newsman with yellow-brown fingers and teeth to match, looked up and spoke. He had a Scottish accent, which he seemed to milk from time to time. "A story came in on the wire about a protest in the town of Kiosk." He exhaled blue smoke as he pointed to a map of Ontario pinned to the wall. "I've never heard of it, but I understand you were born there." Bill never asked if it was all right to smoke.

Suzy sat forward, "Yes. I was . . ."

Nickeyfortune cut her off. "It turns out that this guy running the protest had faxed us the day before the protest started, but no-one here picked up on it. It ran front page of some stupid North Bay newspaper and they put it out on the wire. Now, we look stupid cause we missed it." He stubbed out his cigarette and handed Suzy a photocopy of the fax. "Here's the letter from this guy. His name's Campbell."

"Kenny Campbell?"

"Yeah, that's it. You know him?"

Suzy looked at the letter. "I used to. A long time ago. I haven't seen him in . . . mmmm . . . twenty years at least."

"But you know the guy?"

Suzy nodded.

"I want you to get up there and interview him. I want you to find out something interesting." He handed her a file folder with some background material and the wire copy. Suzy looked through the pages and Nickeyfortune looked up impatiently. "Jaro's here already, so you better hustle. It's a long drive."

"Sure." She stood and took a step toward the door.

Nickeyfortune lit another cigarette. "Remember, I said 'interesting'. I don't want some crap story that's a rehash of what's on the wires. You know this guy, so get something."

She turned. It sounded like he was looking for something specific. "Like?"

He guffawed. "If I knew that, I would do the story myself. You figure it out." The phone rang and he picked up, dismissing her with a backward wave of his hand.

"Kenny Campbell," she said to herself. "Kenny, bloody, Campbell!" She sat down at her desk, and picked up the phone. She would have to arrange baby-sitting and she would have to talk to Michelle. More broken promises, Michelle would say, but there was nothing she could do about it. Her thoughts drifted back to Kiosk. "Kenny, bloody, Campbell!" she said again.

Michael Boart rolled his moustache in his fingers and watched the people across the river. While he had been guarding the weir-bridge, people had crossed the old train bridge near the mouth of the river. It made him angry.

When he had first met Kenneth Campbell, he had thought he was just a nut. This is how he had portrayed him to the authorities in Pembroke. Based on this assessment, they had advised him to leave the man alone, to not make a big issue out of the protest, to keep the public and the press away. Weekends were busy and OPP cruisers with flashing lights brought unnecessary curiosity.

One way or another, they would hand over the truck's licence number and the man's name on Monday, but with luck, they figured that the whole thing would blow over quietly. It was not working out that way.

"What's going on?" asked a voice behind him.

"Just carry on with your own business!" he snapped as he whipped around to face two young campers. He immediately regretted his tone. "This area is not open to the public." He was about to ask for their permit, but he stopped himself. He pointed back toward the ranger station. "Please move on."

"Yeah, yeah, fine," said one of the campers, but they didn't leave. They stood staring at the people on the other side of the river.

The Jeep's all-terrain tires hummed on the paved surface of Highway 11, as Suzette slouched in the backseat looking through the file folder of notes. Jaro Dack and Mike Strogo were in the front drinking Pepsi and discussing stereo systems. Strogo was a music fanatic. He spent thousands of dollars on speakers and amps for his car and he was describing, in great detail, the incredible wattage and response of his system. Dack seemed only marginally interested.

Normally, for a shoot like this, only a two-person crew was necessary. Mike Strogo shouldn't be here. There just wasn't enough money to send in a three-person crew, but Dack had somehow convinced Strogo to work for next to nothing. Suzy knew that Dack was trying to muscle her out and wanted outside support, but as long as he worked the camera, she didn't care. They might share production and editing duties, but as far as the viewing public was concerned, she was the reporter and he was only the cameraman.

She read through a short history of Kiosk and noted a number of inaccuracies. "When the huge mill burned," the report stated, "the government denied Staniforth permission to rebuild, so he rebuilt a few miles outside of the park." At the time of the fire, Staniforth was not a man, but a company, and the company had sold the mill a number of years before the fire; the new facility in Rutherglen was not a mill but a veneer plant; and, the veneer plant was a lot more than a few miles outside of the park.

The article also stated that in 1969, Staniforth's lease was terminated and the provincial government would only renew it on an annual basis. Given the inaccuracy of the report, she didn't know if this was correct, but if it was, it was strange that Staniforth was able to sell the operation to another company. Why would any company buy another company that was operating on a tenuous one-year lease? Unless they knew some kind of provincial government payout was forthcoming? Was the closure of the town known years before it happened? She made a note to herself.

Another page had some background notes on Kiosk. The population, which seemed wrong, was given as 840, and the Member of Parliament had been a woman named Francine Roussel. Suzy remembered hearing the name - a few of the Kiosk women made a fuss about having a woman as their MPP - but she had been completely uninterested in politics at the time.

The constant drone of the truck's engine was hypnotic and Suzy fought the fatigue that was creeping over her like a blanket.

The air conditioning was running, but in the back, she could feel the heat radiating through the windows. She closed the file folder and looked out the window.

They were beside a clear lake with a rocky shore and she imagined being immersed in its waters. She could feel the water running over her body, evaporating from her skin and she could hear the plopping splashes as bodies plunged playfully into the coolness.

The Jeep lurched suddenly. "Jeesus Christ!" Jaro shouted as he swerved to avoid a Chrysler Minivan that drifted sideways into their lane. The driver of the Chrysler saw the Jeep and lurched back into its own lane and the Jeep swung back and forth before regaining its stability. Suzette looked out the side window and saw that the lake was gone.

She thought again about the sale of the mill. Even if the lease had not expired, there were still problems with the government before the sale. What would entice someone to buy a mill that was probably going to be shut down? Had the government and the mill owners agreed in principle on financial considerations for new construction outside the park? Perhaps the protest of the townspeople came as a surprise. It was something no one had anticipated. The owners and the government thought it was a good idea. Had they assumed that the townspeople would think so too? And then with all that money on the table, perhaps the new owners had become worried. If the mill didn't relocate and eventually lost its lease, there would be huge losses. This would certainly give someone a reason to light a match.

Suzette remembered the night of the fire. The people wandering about in the dark had all complained that it was the end, that it had been planned. Maybe they were right. If nothing else, it might make a good story. It was not a big story - if it had been a big story they would have sent a well-known reporter - but since she knew Kenny Campbell, she could get more out of it than anyone else.

She looked at the back of Jaro's head. His dark curly hair moved against the headrest. It was shinny, perfectly coiffed and this annoyed her somehow. He would be willing to bring her career to an end, in order to make himself attractive in the eyes of some young bimbo. It must be difficult for men to attract mates, she mused.

        Pat climbed the wooden steps to Ruby's, a small general store about 25 kilometres north of Kiosk, and ducked as a mud swallow swooped out of its nest in the eves. He looked up and saw a long row of the funnel shaped cones, pasted between the wall and the roof of the porch. The store was quaint, much like the company-store in Kiosk, and he bought a newspaper, a Pepsi, and a chocolate bar. He walked back to his car to read.

        The sun was strong and a gentle breeze blew across the small parking lot, carrying the smell of gasoline from the old gas pump in the middle of the yard. He took a sip of pop and laid the newspaper on the hood. Right on the front page was a small article about the Kiosk protest. It mentioned Ken's name twice, talked about the history of the town, and went on to criticize the Minister for Northern Affairs, Francine Roussel. Pat did not remember Roussel, but the article stated that she had been the M.P.P. at the time of the Kiosk fire. The writer had focussed much of her attention on Roussel, mentioning her name four times on the front page.

        The newspaper fluttered in the wind and Pat folded it and tossed it into the car. He would read the rest of the article later. He leaned back against the door and ate his chocolate bar as he studied the sky over the town of Eau Claire. It was a big sky, with high clouds and it went on and on for miles and miles in all directions. Eau Claire had maybe ten houses and it had survived for over a hundred years, but Kiosk, with its eighty houses had been doomed to extinction by the provincial government.

        The newspaper article was a good omen. He was angry with what had happened to the town and he was pleased with Ken's idea of protest, but he had doubted that anything would come of it. Perhaps, he thought, he had been wrong.

        Two swallows flew high over a hay field and the wind moved the grass back and forth like waves on a lake. A dragonfly, large and prehistoric, landed on the antennae of his car and then flew away quickly.

        It was time to leave as well. He wanted to get to Ken's cabin near Lauder Lake with the supplies. He was much happier with his position outside the park in a wooden cabin with an ice-box than Ken's position in the middle of controversy with nothing between him and the authorities but some woven plastic. He jumped in the car and drove down the cold-top surface, his tires singing in the heat.

"Slow down! The town's just ahead," Suzy said as she watched the river appear and disappear to the right. She had not been on this road for decades and much of it had changed, but it was still so familiar. The pavement ended and Jaro rode the brakes tearing into the gravel. Suzy pictured the first houses that were just beyond the small ridge and group of bushes ahead.

The beautiful blue of Kioshkokwi Lake came into view, and Suzy sat up in the back seat. "Holy Shit!" The gravel road went on toward the lake for about a hundred metres and then turned right and left. Beyond this "T" was a grassy area littered with cars and trucks.

"Yeah, it looks like there are a lot of people here."

Suzy didn't care about the vehicles, it was the buildings, or lack thereof, that had grabbed her attention. They were gone. Everything was gone. "Tabernacle," she said, swearing in the Québécois lingo of her father. It was a word she had not used for many, many years.

She looked at the Giroux house . . . gone . . . the Bellehumeur house . . . gone. All the houses . . . gone! The lots were dotted with poplar, aspen and shrubs and there was little left to indicate that people had ever lived here.

Mike Strogo turned and looked at Suzette. "So where's this town?"

Suzy did not answer. With eyes wide, she shrugged and shook her head.

Jaro slowed the truck and drove toward the crowd. To the right, was the bridge and beyond it were more people, but traffic seemed to be tied up on the bridge. Jaro pulled onto the grass. "We better do this on foot," he said, opening his door and jumping out.

Suzy and Mike stretched luxuriously before moving away.

Jaro locked the doors. "Shouldn't we get the equipment?" asked Mike.

"Let's have a look first."

A park warden sat on one of the metal winches that had once been used to lower the drops in the weir. It was rusted and looked as if it hadn't been used in years. Attached to the metal frame was a yellow rope that stretched across the road to the fence on the other side of the bridge. It would be possible to walk over the bridge, but only within striking distance of the warden.

"Is this where that protester is?" Jaro pointed across the bridge.

The warden half nodded.

"We're with Global; we're going to cover the story."

"So much for keeping it under wraps," the warden said to himself. He rubbed his ear, scratching a bug bite. "You're not the first ones here." He looked across the bridge. There were many people wandering around. "You can't take your vehicle in, but if you want to walk, go ahead."

Jaro looked at Suzy. "Mike and I will go back for the gear. You scout around and see what's what."

Suzy nodded. She turned in a slow circle, looking at the bridge, the shore, the winches, and the water. She remembered it all so clearly. She remembered sitting here with Pat and Kenny, listening to the river, being frightened of bears, and feeling the warmth of the company of her friends. As she walked across the bridge, she thought of Pat. She couldn't quite fix a picture of his face in her mind, but she could see herself running with him, playing with him, and even kissing him. It was an eerie sensation and she suddenly wondered if he might be here.

She studied the faces of people, looking for Pat or Ken. At the bottom of the hill that had once led to the recreation centre, she saw one man interviewing another. It was Ken Campbell and a ridiculous newsman in a suit. It looked like MCTV had sent a crew here as well, and they were getting the story first. MCTV would have an editing facility in North Bay, so they could finish the story much quicker than her crew, but unless the network picked it up, they might not broadcast into Southern Ontario and she still had a chance to break the story across the province.

She walked closer and looked at Ken. He was fairly tall and he had the wiry build of someone who was much stronger than most people imagined. He ran his fingers through his thin blond hair as he spoke and then looked toward her. He smiled. Had he recognised her? She did not acknowledge him; it would be bad form to interrupt the other interview. She stepped to the side and listened to the MCTV reporter's questions.

An old man stood near her and bumped into her accidentally. "I'm sorry," he said with an odd British-Teutonic accent.

"No problem," she replied as she turned to look at him. He was small, old and frail, about seventy. Although it was a warm summer afternoon, he was wearing dark pants and a long-sleeve shirt. She recognized him and, although she would have never remembered it an hour ago, the name came to her without effort. "Mr. Loeffler?"

"Yes, that's right." He looked at her questioningly.

Suzy introduced herself and explained that she had been one of his students in grade school. He said he remembered her, but she imagined that he was just being polite. Then, he asked her if she had ever read Great Expectations. She remembered the day he had given her the book. "Yes, I did!" Her eyes lit up as she looked at him. "My God! I'm surprised you remembered."

A wry smile crept across the old man's face and he winked. "How could I forget someone who hissed many of my mystery classes?"

Suzy blurted out a laugh as she remembered the line from so many years ago, a line that she remembered verbatim; a line that sounded practised. Mr. Loeffler had been the king of Spoonerisms and no one had ever been sure if they had been deliberate or just the product of a cluttered mind. "Are you part of this protest, Mr. Loeffler?"

"No, not really, I just came to see what was going on. A bit of civil disobedience has always been a positive thing." He turned and looked back at the bridge. "They wouldn't let me cross. I'm not even staying here. I have a trailer at the ranger station, but I had to walk across the train bridge, just to get here . . . an old fellow like me . . . they wouldn't let me cross by the normal bridge."

Suzy thought of Mr. Loeffler walking across the train

bridge. He looked so small. "What would you have done if a train had come?"

Loeffler grinned broadly. "Can you imagine what old Mr. Frederick would say if he had caught me on the bridge?" He cleared his throat. "Actually, the only train likely to come down that line would be a ghost. They took away all the tracks. It's just a cinder path now."

Suzy looked toward the tracks, which were not visible from where she stood, and then back at Loeffler. He too, looked like a ghost. She heard the MCTV reporter asking about Francine Roussel, the MPP, and she suddenly realised that she should not be talking to Loeffler, she should be listening to the interview. She dismissed Loeffler, "Well, you be careful walking back," and then turned toward the interview, still in progress, and paid stricter attention. Mr. Loeffler made another comment, but rather than respond, she merely nodded without taking her eyes off the interview. The old man hesitated for a moment and then walked away.

"So, what's up?" Jaro appeared beside her with the SKF1 Betacam hanging at this side and a tripod in his hands. "Is this the guy you knew?"

"It must be, and it looks like MCTV beat us to the interview."

"Yeah . . . could be a problem too. I was hoping they would let us use their editing room, but if they're covering the story, they probably won't. It might mean driving all the way to Sudbury."

"Sudbury's two hours away. We'll have to rent a private studio."

"That sucks. There's not enough money in this to begin with."

"So why did you bring numbnuts?" Suzy jerked her thumb at Mike.

Jaro looked at Mike and then back at Suzy, the irritation showing on his face. He changed the subject. "Listen, before we decide where to edit, let's get the story first."

Suzy looked at Jaro, closed her eyes and nodded "Yeah, we'll do that first." Her tone displayed that she was equally annoyed.

Mike struggled toward them with two duffle bags full of

equipment. "So, what's up?" Jaro and Suzy looked at him as if this was the most stupid question in the world.

The MCTV cameraman had lowered his camera while the newsman talked casually with the interviewee. Suzy saw that the camera was still running. The team was trying to get some under-the-table footage and this meant that the interview had not gone as well as expected. It was time to break in, but she did not want to reveal to MCTV that she had grown up in the town. It was unlikely that Ken would recognize her, and for the time being, she would keep her identity hidden. "Hi, I'm Susan Levasseur. Are you the fellow who faxed all the stations about the protest?"

Ken looked over at her. "Yes, that would be me."

The MCTV reporter shook Ken's hand, thanked him and then nodded to Suzy. He walked to the cameraman, but feigned interest in some of the equipment. He was listening.

She looked around and relaxed a little. "This is a lot bigger than you indicated in your fax. Did you organize it all?" Suzy knew that the camera wasn't set up, but she was trying to get a feel for the interview before it took place.

"Most of it just happened. I'm glad though. I didn't know there would be this much interest."

"You're Ken Campbell?"

"That's right."

"And you went to school at the school across the river?"

"Correct."

Suzy was hoping Ken would recognize her, but it was foolish to imagine he would. It had been decades, her name was different, and he was seeing her as a reporter, not a possible friend from the past. She looked over her shoulder at the MCTV crew. They were still standing near by, listening.

Jaro mounted the camera on the tripod and Mike did a level check. Microphones were clipped in place, pan shots were made and the interview turned formal.

"And where do you live now, Mr. Campbell."

"Right here."

Suzy smiled. "Yes, of course. Where did you live a few weeks ago?"

"I grew up in Kiosk, and lived here for many years. Just

back there." He pointed in the direction of his parent's house.

Suzy nodded but didn't speak. Prodding him to go on.

After a pause, Ken continued. "My parents were forced out of the area by the government and we eventually moved to Sudbury. My dad hated it there; he missed the town and his friends." As Ken continued to talk, the MCTV crew picked up their gear and walked away. They seemed satisfied that Suzy would not get a more interesting interview. Suzy watched them out of the corner of her eye. She kept the rest of her questions simple and short and Ken started to relax. She was just about to tell him who she was, when she was distracted by a dark-blue Chevy that stopped on the road. It had a missing front hubcap and three antennae on the trunk. A single OPP officer got out.

The park warden who had been blocking the road, walked up from the bridge, no longer interested in restricting traffic. The OPP officer, wearing a flak jacket and a dark-blue uniform, looked back at the warden, who pointed at Ken, and nodded.

"Are you Kenneth Campbell?" The officer asked.

Ken's eyes widened and Suzy was surprised by the fear. Had Ken not expected the police? She watched as he answered calmly, but took a tiny step backward. She looked at Jaro and surreptitiously waved her hand indicating that he should get this all on tape.

The officer looked at the camera, hesitated, and then focussed his attention on Ken. "I understand that you have been told it's against regulations to camp here, but you refuse to leave."

Ken's tone was calm and non-confrontational. He explained that he had lived here all his life and did not accept the authority of the warden. He showed the officer his homemade ankle chain and said that he had no intention of leaving. As he spoke, a large group of people gathered, and to Suzy's amusement, the MCTV crew was desperately trying to set up. Some of the crowd was becoming vocal in their support of Ken, and Suzy could see that the OPP officer was looking right and left, carefully appraising the situation. He asked Ken to put a stop to this foolishness, but when it was obvious that nothing less than force would work, he made a strategic exit. Jaro had it all on tape and MCTV had missed it.

The officer sat in the cruiser, made some notes, used his radio, and then slowly turned the cruiser around. As he drove away, the powerful engine caused the tires to dig into the gravel and this caused the people around Ken to cheer. It was a small victory. People shook Ken's hand and noisily talked with each other. Jaro had filmed it all, the retreating police car, the cheers, and the congratulations. He walked from behind the camera and grabbed Suzy's arm. "Come on! Get his reaction!"

Suzy held the microphone toward Ken and asked a few more quick questions. Ken answered distractedly and a few other people poked their heads into view, shouting, "Right on!"

Jaro grabbed Suzy's arm again. "Come on, let's go. We've got what we need here. Now we need to do a commentary and then feed this down south." Suzy resisted. "Come on!" Jaro looked at his watch and then pointed at the MCTV crew. "Let's get this out first."

Back at the Jeep, Suzy did a stand-up while Mike packed the extra gear in the truck. They could spend another hour getting film, but they had enough to edit a good ninety-second segment and that was all the space they had been allotted. It was time to get to North Bay. With a quick edit, they might be able to get this transferred in time for the late news. Jaro still insisted on having his name listed as producer, but she didn't care. People saw her face on television and as far as the public was concerned, she was the reporter; Jaro was a cameraman.

When the Global story aired on Saturday night, it touched briefly on the protest, mentioned Ken Campbell and some of the residents of Kiosk, but then it focussed on the arrival of the OPP. On video, it appeared as if the angry mob had chased the officer out of town, and the following shot of the spinning tires on the cruiser hinted at a hasty retreat. This caused the phone lines between the North Bay detachment and head office in Orillia to heat up considerably.

Originally, based on the first officer's report, Orillia had decided to take a wait-and-see approach. The OPP were the police force of the province and these people were protesting the provincial government. Intervention by the OPP might be interpreted as the provincial government using strong arm tactics to quell public dissent. However, after the evening-news shot of the officer speed-

ing away from the scene of a crime, Orillia reversed its decision.
They decided to send in an ERT, emergency-response-team, at the
break of dawn on Sunday. The ERT team would not take aggressive
action, but they would remain on the scene and control the environment - and be a visible element in any future media attention.

          With the dew still heavy on the grass and the sun not
yet above the horizon, the North Bay ERT arrived in Kiosk. Ken
had been up late talking to old friends and neighbours and he was
still sleeping as the two vehicles stopped on the road near his cabin.
He woke to the sound of slamming doors and loud voices.
          He scratched at mosquito bites as he watched the police
banging on vehicles and waking everyone they could find. One
officer walked up to his cabin and beat on one of the two-by-four
supports. "Wakey, wakey! It's time to vacate the park."
          "What's going on?" Ken asked as he groaned and rolled off
his bed.
          "We need you people to vacate this area. You're trespassing,
but if you leave now, no charges will be laid. If you refuse to leave,
you'll be arrested."
          Ken's mind switched from idle to high-speed. He walked
toward his door, but remained inside. "This is my house; I have no
intention of leaving."
          "If you do not leave now, you will be placed under arrest."
          "On what charges?"
          "Trespassing for starters. Now move!"
          "How can I be . . ." Ken stopped talking. There was no point
explaining his position to this officer. He wasn't listening anyway.
"Give me a minute to get dressed, would you?"
          "Just get moving."
          Ken watched as the officer moved off toward a tent that was
on the hill where the old recreation centre had been. He stepped
outside and saw people being hurried into their vehicles. Others
were packing their belongings. One police officer was banging a
truncheon on the bumper of a truck. The loud clanging noise
echoed back and forth like the dinner bell at a summer camp. The
protest was going to be ended in a swift sweep and it was beyond

his ability to do much about it.

He looked at his cabin and reached a decision. He grabbed his backpack, hurriedly decided what he should take, and started to throw items inside. Another officer walked up to his cabin. "Let's get a move on here!"

"I'm going, I'm going." Ken's voice was edged with fear. "I'm packing as fast as I can." The officer walked away as Ken finished dressing and put on his boots. He tried to think of everything he should take; the police were moving fast and he had so little time. He rooted through his belongings, dropping some items and shoving others into his pack. When it was full, he opened the door and threw it outside.

People were being forced into action. What had been a quiet Sunday morning was now pandemonium. The young people on the other side of the road were emptying their tent and the old couple in the camper were taking down their awning.

The police were all over the place, walking up and down the road and through the field. They seemed aggressive, but Ken noticed that they weren't paying particular attention to any one person. They were just keeping themselves visible and hurrying everyone into action. This was good, because it gave him a bit of anonymity.

They spent most of their time dealing other campers and Ken realised that they did not to make him the centre of attention. The police were intimidating everyone, but leaving him pretty much alone.

It was time. Feeling very uncomfortable, he unlocked the chain from his ankle and let it slip into the trampled grass. He grabbed his pack, checked to make sure the way was clear, and ran half way up the hill that overlooked his cabin and the field. "Can I have everyone's attention?" Faces turned to him expectantly. "I'm not leaving the park! I will not be moved! The police are wrong and the government is wrong! I'm staying in this park . . . living in this park . . . for as long as it takes for them to admit it!" The police watched him motionlessly, but one officer started to walk up the hill. "Make sure you tell everyone this is wrong! Tell them I'm not leaving!" Ken turned and ran to the top of the hill.

Someone shouted, "Right on!" Other voices joined in. What

had started as a blitzkrieg clearing operation was now bogging down into a cacophony of protest.

Ken stopped at the top of the hill and turned. The officer, who was now half way up, had stopped as well and was looking back at another officer. This younger fellow was already running, but he was also burdened with his flak vest and a big black belt with many pouches. Even though Ken had the pack, he was sure he could easily outrun him.

He turned and ran through the low branches of a group of red pines, aiming for the railroad bed not too far ahead. Keeping low, he darted left and right, but something grabbed him and he spun sideways and fell. He couldn't believe that the cop had been so fast, but as he tried to get to his feet, he saw the officer's legs beyond the pines, a short distance away. His pack must have snagged a branch, he realised, and he rolled back on his feet and continued to run.

He started to pull at the one strap of his backpack, thinking he would drop it, when he came to an area of swamp. He remembered the place, and he knew it was possible to cross without getting too wet. Jumping to the places that contained higher tufts of grass and plants that would not survive underwater, he avoided the soft suction of the boggy ground. He was only three-quarter of the way across when he heard the officer cry out and then he heard the soft splat of a body hitting the very wet ground. He laughed silently, but didn't turn back. Another splat. The officer fell again. "Shit!" said one voice and then another yelled: "Go that way!"

Two or three officers were in pursuit. The grin left Ken's face as he realised that this would not be as easy as he had hoped. He ran to the right, trying to draw those chasing him away from the lake. A group of tag alders were so thick that they acted like a barrier, but he forced his way through. His backpack tugged at his shoulders and he again considered dropping it, but there were some items he needed. He would hold on to it for a while longer.

A hundred yards further, he turned toward the lake. It was crazy, he told himself, but he needed to get to his boat. Water would be the easiest route of escape. He forced his breath under control and worked his way down to the tangle of vegetation near the shore.

On the water's edge, he could see the train bridge. He was close. The loose round stones clunked hollowly under his feet and he struggled toward his boat.

The adrenalin pumping though his veins pushed him to run quickly, but he knew that silence was more important. He couldn't take his time, his tracks would be easy to follow, but any loud sounds might bring out new officers up from the tracks.

The sun had just peaked above the trees, but it would soon move up into bands of clouds that filled the sky. The sunlight cast eerie shadows through the forest making it difficult to see movement. Everything was moving, the leaves, the pines, the dry branches.

He inhaled deeply when he reached the canoe, suddenly aware of his shallow breathing and the need to remain quiet. He undid the chain and, as quietly as possible, removed the covering of sticks and leaves. Normally he would have dragged the canoe into the water, but that would have generated a lot of noise, so he lifted it over his head - as he would on a portage - and then gently placed it in the water. The sound of waves lapping against the hull seemed extremely loud.

He looked back at the train bridge and realised he was in full view. He threw in his pack and jacket and then returned to shore for the motor and the paddle. He picked up the chain and wondered if he should take it. It would be noisy in the canoe, but he could drop it on some material to keep the noise down. 'Should I throw the chain on my pack and jacket,' he thought, 'or should I throw it on my jack and packet?' He grinned. Here he was, about to be arrested and he was playing stupid word games. Last night he had met old Mr. Loeffler and they had talked about old-times. It must have done something to soften his mind.

He draped the chain over his shoulder, and lifted the paddle. A loud snap reverberated in the forest and looking up, he saw an approaching officer. "Shit!" He awkwardly grabbed the motor, pinching his fingers as it turned on its steering arm, and ran to the canoe. He could hear the officer breaking through the bush behind him. He had only seconds.

There was no way to get in gracefully, and he dove for the canoe. His face smacked one of the gunnels, opening a gash on his lip, and the weight of his body caused the boat to dip low enough into the water to hit the rocks below. The hull groaned in protest, but it bobbed up and Ken twisted around frantically trying to use his initial momentum to get away from shore.

The officer was only three feet away and with one jump, he could have easily grabbed the canoe. The blood drained from Ken's face and his body felt weightless and numb. He thrust the paddle furiously in the water, splashing like a kid in a water fight, and with the momentum of his jump, he moved away from shore. The officer got over his momentary hesitation, but still did not jump. Instead, he ran into the water.

Ken was in the middle of the canoe, a difficult place from which to paddle, but he twisted onto his knees as he pulled his paddle through the choppy water. It was going to be close. One good spurt and the police would have him. Then he heard a splash - the slimy rocks offered poor footing for even the most experienced bushman - followed by the sharp inhale as the officer surfaced from the water. He didn't look back but he couldn't imagine the cop trying to swim while wearing a flak jacket. He paddled furiously just in case.

When he was a very safe distance from shore, he turned. Two policemen were now on the shore, but the wet one was turning away. He had had enough. Ken dropped his paddle in the bottom of the boat and attached the motor to the small flat stern. It only took three pulls to get it started and the bubbling growl of the motor drowned out the sound of shouts back in Kiosk.

The officer on the shore shook his finger back and forth at Ken, like a mother admonishing her disobedient child, and Ken grinned and shrugged. "Boys will be boys," he said.

He turned the throttle and powered the canoe back toward the train bridge. There were some deadheads, half-submerged logs that could knock the motor off his boat, but if he was careful, he could get to the bridge in relative safety. Without a boat, the police could do little unless they started firing and he was fairly certain that wouldn't happen   not with so many witnesses.

Near the bridge were a number of logs, but the water was deep and he doubted that any of the police were sure footed enough to run a boom. He ran his boat downstream to a spot between the two bridges and yelled as loud as he could. "Don't let them chase you out!" Only a few people heard him but within a minute, more people appeared in the grass by the bank. Ken raised his right fist high over his head. Blood was running down his lip and dripping onto his shirt. "This is our home! I'm not leaving the park until they admit they took it away wrongfully."

A man on the car bridge was furiously taking snapshots. He was dressed in Khakis and had a vest full of camera accessories. Newspaper man, Ken thought. "It's time to fight back!" He held his fist higher and shook it in the air.

A police car sped across the bridge toward the ranger station and Ken knew where they were headed. The OPP kept a small boat at the ranger station. He had to get out of the river and into the lake quickly. Not only would he be trapped in the river, but even if he got out onto the lake, he didn't want them to follow him. He did not want to lose his motor.

"I'm not leaving!" Ken shouted to the growing crowd on the shore and then he swung the boat around toward the train bridge. Four officers were already on the bridge scurrying back and forth trying to find a way to block Ken's escape. Two were scrabbling down the rocky sides toward the water and two were staying on the top.

He opened the throttle wide, lifting the bow of the canoe out of the water and sped toward the bridge. There was little they could do, he thought and then he saw one climb up on the black metal side of the bridge. Was he going to jump off into the canoe? Ken remembered the kids jumping off the bridge into the water, but a fully loaded cop, wearing shoes, jumping into a canoe? It was unthinkable.

In his few moments of shouting, he had drifted a long way from the train bridge, and going upstream was slower. The cop on the top had dropped his vest and belt and was moving back and forth on the metal bridge as if getting ready to jump.

"Shit! Shit!" Ken clenched his teeth angry with himself for his foolishness. He should have just left.

One of the cops on the shore was dropping equipment and looked like he was getting ready to enter the water. Ken drove the boat over to the right, forcing the cop on the top of the bridge to balance along the railing to the new intersection point. The cop on the other shore stepped out into the water.

The boat was sluggish in the river and Ken throttled down so the bow dropped lower. He grabbed his pack and threw it forward. This would make the boat slower, but more manoeuvrable. He powered up again and began to weave back and forth, drawing nearer and nearer to the bridge. The cop on the top was forced to move right and left and his confidence was fading.

Ten feet from the bridge Ken turned hard left, ran parallel to the bridge for a few seconds and then turned underneath. A body jumped out from the side, just ahead of him, and all he could do, was keep going. The throttle was fully open and he was going straight out toward the lake. He could see the hand in the water, just to the side and it reached for the gunnels, but never made it.

With his heart beating furiously in his chest, he piloted the boat a distance away from the right shore as the river widened into the lake. He curved off to the right, around the point, and away from the town of Kiosk and the ranger station. If his stunt had accomplished one thing, it had gotten some extra pictures into one of the newspapers.

"What kind of shite was that?" Nickeyfortune's Scottish accent sounded more pronounced over the telephone. It was early and the phone call had brought Suzy out of a deep sleep.

"It was a good piece. What're you complaining about?"

"I thought you knew this fellow? Your interview stank. You get this fellow talking about his feelings and the MCTV crew has him talking about Native Land Claim issues. You get him talking about ghosts, and they have him talking about current politicians. The MCTV interview will probably get picked up by the CBC and it looks like MCTV broke the story."

Suzy had seen the news clips in her hotel room and she knew that the MCTV interview was good, but they had more background information and they had access to all the local political information. She knew of the Honourable Francine Roussel, but she didn't make the connection.

"We actually broke the story, though." Global had it at the

top of the hour and MCTV ran it in the local segment a half-hour later.

"Not as far as the public thinks. That half-hour means nothing. You better get back there this morning and get me something more interesting than a ghost story."

Suzy and Mike had planned to go back for a follow-up, but they weren't planning to do another feature. They both wanted to get back to the city, and doing another shoot, edit and transmit might tie them up until tomorrow. "I have my daughter with a baby-sitter. I was hoping to get back today."

There was silence on the phone and Suzy could imagine Nickeyfortune holding his breath and turning red. "Just get the story, and do it fucking properly this time." There was a sharp click as he hung up.

Suzy depressed the button on the phone and called Jaro's room. She told him to get ready quickly. They needed to get back to Kiosk. She would call her daughter later. Perhaps they could finish up early.

As the Jeep neared Kiosk, it was obvious that something had happened. A lot of traffic, including a group of police vehicles, passed them, going the opposite way. In the town, they were greeted by a wooden police barricade blocking the road to the bridge. An officer refused to let them pass, with or without press credentials. Jaro wheeled the vehicle across the dirt and grass and drove to the Ranger Station.

They learned of Ken Campbell's escape and they talked to a number of former Kiosk residents who had moved from the open field around Ken's makeshift cabin, to the organized campground near the ranger station. These people were afraid of defying the police, but they weren't ready to go home just yet. Many seemed to be waiting for a reappearance of Kenny, but Suzy doubted this would happen. They had missed one story this morning, however, and they set up their equipment so they would not miss another.

Suzy did talk to some old friends, there were people here that she had not seen in decades, but her mind was on the story, not on the people. She spent most of her time with the two people she did not like, Jaro and Mike.

As she watched the crowd, she kept looking for Patrick. She

thought she saw him a number of times, but she was never sure. At one point, she asked someone if he was here, but the person she asked could hardly remember Patrick and did not know if he was around.

She wasn't sure why she wanted to find him. Was she interested in possibly re-sparking a relationship? No, she told herself. That wasn't it. She had no time for that sort of thing. Finding Patrick might give her insight into Ken Campbell's protest, she told herself, and that might help the story.

A man with a day-old stubble and dishevelled clothing walked toward one of the nearby camping spots. He spoke briefly with two people and then walked to another couple. He looked very familiar and for a moment, she thought it might be Pat. Was it? She felt a tingling in her fingertips and in her wrists. It crept up her arms and into her chest, but just as she summoned the courage to walk over, the man hurried away.

Jaro was fooling with his cell-phone and complaining about the area. He had tried at least six times and each time it had shown as 'no service', but he tried again.

"I'll be right back," Suzy said.

"Don't be long," said Jaro, turning and trying the phone again.

Suzy walked through the parking lot, following the man who had left, but when she approached the old rail bed, she saw him in his car. He drove away without noticing her.

She stood on the hard path of cinder, listened to the sound, as it seemed to widen and rise in pitch, and watched the plume of dust float into the air behind the receding car. She turned in a circle and looked both ways along the rail line. She remembered walking on the steel rails as a little girl, her dad getting angry, because they were so dangerous. There had been five or six trains per day and a couple of people had been killed on the tracks.

She started walking along the line toward town and eventually reached the spot where the Lucky Dollar had been. This had been 'downtown' for Kiosk. The bunkhouses had been here, the gas pumps, the store and the mill office, and although all the buildings were gone, there was still a set of concrete steps and a concrete path leading into an empty field.

She walked up the steps and along the path, barely visible between the weeds and grass, toward an old stone wall. Neat and square, it was only two feet high, but it had served to separate the mill manager's home from the rest of the town. She passed the wall, crossed the main road and walked up a dusty trail. This took her in the direction of her house.

She hesitated for a moment, not sure if she wanted to go, but then slowly her feet carried her forward. Where Pat's house had stood, there was another sidewalk - barely visible, most of it cracked and the smaller pieces removed - but there was nothing left of the house. The ground was uneven, tufts of weed grew on mounds of earth, and it was difficult to see where the house had once stood.

She continued toward the old school. From a distance, she could see that it too was gone, nothing left but a sandy field and a few scotch pines. Her house should have been just to the right, but a group of bushes and small trees had reclaimed the place of her birth. She felt cheated. There was nothing, not even a sidewalk. If she closed her eyes, she could see it, but the ground was so altered that she couldn't even imagine that it had once stood in this location.

Feeling a profound despair wash over her, tears ran down her cheeks. She had not cried for years, she had decided that tears accomplished nothing, but for a moment, they ran so quickly that they dropped off her cheeks and stained her blouse. She closed her eyes, wiped her face, and sniffled loudly. This was foolish, she told herself. She turned and walked slowly back to the main road.

As she passed what should have been the bunkhouse, she tried to escape the feeling of emptiness. She felt alone, but at the same time felt she was not alone. Her pace quickened and she was glad to reach the parking lot.

Pat drove into Kiosk unshaven and unwashed. With all his planning, he had forgotten that there was no electricity or running water in Ken's cabin. He needed a rechargeable razor and a container of water.

Parked cars and trucks littered the area and the MNR rope

was replaced by a wooden OPP barricade. An officer stood menacingly to the side.

Pat parked in the designated lot near the ranger station. It was packed and he had to park near the old rail line.

People greeted him warmly as he climbed out of his car and he enjoyed notoriety as one of Ken's friends. Within minutes, he was told about Ken's dramatic escape from the protest scene and about the OPP's fumbled attempt to stop the canoe. The story was embellished - there were more officers, closer calls, and more bloody injuries - but it still ended with Ken swearing he would not leave until the government admitted it had been wrong.

He walked down to the camping area and found many of the old residents milling around. Although Pat enjoyed talking, he felt vaguely uncomfortable. He wondered if he had the right to be here. Many of these people still lived in the area, and some of them met annually at the golf course in Mattawa for a reunion. Pat lived near Toronto and felt a little like a Kiosk outsider - like an urban bird-watcher. And to make matters worse, while Ken was being chased through the bush and up the river, he had been sleeping in the cabin.

The day was overcast, muggy and hot and he felt sweat dampening his armpits. The heat reminded him of the black pavement of the dealership, of the heat boring though his suit and into his cotton and polyester shirt, and he remembered that he would return to King City tonight. All the other salespeople would enthusiastically tell him about the fantastic Saturday he had so foolishly missed. They would do their best to make him feel envious. It would be difficult.

He looked again at the barricade and wondered what to do next. He had no way to contact Ken and he certainly wasn't smart enough to track him. Then he remembered. If he had trouble reaching him, he should meet him at the rapids at noon on Sunday. He looked at his watch. He still had time.

He drove a short distance up the highway, pulled off the road, and walked into the scraggly bush near the river. The flow widened at this spot and although the water was fast, there were many stones and rocks above the surface. He was able to cross with relative ease, and once on the other side, he stopped and placed his hands on his hips. He saw nothing.

"I was wondering if you'd remember," said a voice from the high weeds near the river.

Pat peered in the direction of the sound, but saw nothing. Slowly Ken stood and came into view as if he were being raised by an elevator. "I only remembered at the last moment. It's a good place to meet. How did you get here?"

"I took the canoe down into Wolfe's bay, hid, and then used the logging road. Those idiots crossed the lake looking for me and I think they're still floating somewhere out there in the middle."

"So what are you going to do now? Are you heading back home?"

Ken looked at Pat incredulously. "Are you joking? What would be the point in that?"

Pat shrugged. "With the police here, what would be the point in staying?"

"Since we last talked, I thought a lot about what happened here. I want to make this work and that will only happen with some continued media support; and, that will only happen if I stay on in the park."

"I don't know."

Ken studied Pat for a moment. "What don't you know?"

"With the police here, the whole thing changes. Everyone will leave and who's gonna care if you're running around in the bush. All they have to do is just leave you alone and ignore you."

"That's where you come in. You're going to keep people aware of the fact that I'm here in the park."

Pat rubbed his eyes, his nose and then ran his hand over his cheek. "And just how am I going to do that?"

Ken fished out a 35-mm film and handed it to Pat. "This is a start. There was a woman from the Nugget on our first night here."

"Yeah, I read the story in the paper."

"Get this film to her. It has pictures of the lake, some of the protest, and a couple of a new camp I set up. There's even some of the OPP."

"When did you have time to take pictures of the cops?"

"Just a short while ago, on my way here."

Pat looked at Ken curiously. "You took pictures of them?

What are you? Nuts?"

"Those guys sure aren't bushmen. They never knew I was there."

"When did you have time to set up another camp? Didn't you just get kicked out this morning?"

Ken grinned. "Well, actually, I didn't just set it up. And it isn't in Algonquin. It's a place I have hidden near Bear Lake. I fixed it up a bit and took some photos. The pictures are on the roll after the police photos, so it will look like the camp is a new one in the park. I will head back into the park, though."

"So what are you going to do then?"

"I'll take some more pictures . . . maybe even arrange to meet some reporters. Can you bring me some more film tomorrow?"

Pat's eyes widened. "Tomorrow? Tomorrow's Monday."

"Yeah?"

"I have to get back to work."

Ken folded his arms across his chest. "Back to work? You want to leave now?"

"It was hard enough getting the weekend off."

"This is more than just a short vacation - a long-weekend camping trip." Ken saw the discomfort on Pat's face and he grabbed his arm. "When I saw you, I saw, for the first time, what was taken away from us - from all of us. I used to get up and shave, but I never looked in the mirror. You were my mirror. I saw the lack of connection, the sense of being lost. That's why I did this." Pat looked down again and Ken continued, louder. "And it's not just for us. There are other people who feel the same. You saw how many people showed up."

"Yeah, but I don't want to get mixed up with the police. It's not that . . ." Pat's voice trailed off.

"The Indians fight for land that was taken away from them over a hundred years ago, environmentalists fight to protect forests and waterways that don't belong to them, but for some reason, we let the government destroy our town, our homes, our families, and our lives." He gritted his teeth and poked Pat in the shoulder. "And we don't think we have the right to fight back."

"I don't know. It's different."

"No, it's not! It's not different. I've spent my whole life sneaking back into these forests, cautious of the rules, and I'm not going to do it any more. Neither should you."

"But I haven't come back. I don't have the right."

"Come on! You were born here, your parents and your grandparents were born here - or in Fossmill - and you grew up here. This was your home. At least you should have the same rights as a bunch of Indians who say they have a land claim to a piece of land that they, or their parents, have never visited."

Pat looked at Ken wearily. "But there's support for the Natives in the constitution."

Ken snorted in laughter. "The natives make a fuss and people listen; we make a fuss and we're lawbreakers. Pat I'm tired of the whole situation. Do you remember asking me about the deer?"

Pat nodded.

"Well, it's the Indians who shot them all. They come into the park with high-powered rifles and shoot deer and moose out-of-season all the time. I've watched them! They drive their trucks and four-wheelers throughout the park and they fish anytime of the year."

"Ken, they do have native hunting rights."

"That's horseshit! There weren't any Indians living here, but they claim the land and they hunt and they fish. We lived here for three generations, it was taken away from us and we have no rights. We can't even visit unless we pay an entrance fee."

Pat was half following the conversation and half thinking of how he might be able to get a few days off. "I don't want to get involved in something . . ."

Ken put his hand on Pat's forearm. "Please. I need your help here."

Pat looked into Ken's eyes. He didn't often ask for help. "All right, I'll stick around for a few days, but I have to get back soon."

Kenny thanked Pat, told him what to bring to the next meeting and suggested some contingency meeting places. They agreed it would best to meet outside of the park, near the old train trestle, just in case Pat was followed. If the Nugget published the photos, the police would know that someone on the outside was in contact with Ken.

Pat walked back to the highway thinking. He was uncomfortable with Ken's anti-native sentiment. The Natives were a noble people and did not deserve to be slandered even it was just Ken giving vent to his anger - an anger that he had helped to ignite.

Ken had given him a fairly long list of things to do in North Bay and it would be wiser to spend the night in a motel rather than at Ken's cabin, but before leaving, he would drive back to the ranger station. It was possible that the reporter might be there and he could give her the film now, rather than contact her in North Bay.

As he passed the bridge road, he studied the gathered crowd. There were fewer people than earlier so the police had had some success clearing the area. Across the river, a worker was tearing down the cabin that Ken had built.

The ranger station parking lot was full and Pat parked on the road side and walked. He was greeted by many people, he felt a little like a campaigning politician, nodding his head and briefly shaking hands. No one had seen any reporters from the North Bay Nugget, but one woman pointed to the main camping area and said that a news crew was taping interviews.

A female newscaster had just finished taping and she chatted with an older woman while the cameraman took his camera off a tripod. She had fine, dark hair, which fell just past her shoulders and skin as smooth as a marble sculpture, but most captivating was her expression. She blinked often and smiled, hesitatingly, at the corners of her mouth. There was something about that smile that tugged at a memory and he stood motionless, looking but not seeing. Suddenly he realised, and the realisation was loud, forceful, overpowering. He was looking at Suzette Labelle.

He stood silently, barely breathing, waiting for her to finish. Twice, she looked over and there was recognition in her eyes, but she made no attempt to approach him. He felt hurt and he was tempted to turn and leave, but before he could summon the courage, she excused herself and walked toward him. "Patty?" He nodded and held out his hand. As she shook it, he felt her warmth, her softness, but he also felt foolish. He should have pulled her into his arms, given her a hug, a hug that would normally be given to a long-lost friend, but instead he was shaking her hand like a customer at the car dealership. He couldn't break the handshake and he could force no further words from his mouth.

"I thought I recognized you earlier," she said, releasing his hand, "but I wasn't sure."

He felt a moment of disappointment. Her tone was distant, almost cool. "You should have said something," he said quickly, fearing his emotions would show. "I didn't know you were here. You're a newscaster?"

She nodded.

He stammered. "So . . . what do you think of all this?"

"I'm not sure. I'd never guessed it would draw this much attention. Most of them are Kiosk people, but still . . ."

"It is rather surprising. You know it was Kenny who started the whole thing?"

"Yes, I spoke with him yesterday." She jerked her thumb at Jaro. "We interviewed him. It was on the news."

"Oh? I'm sorry, I didn't see it." Pat looked at her, studied her face, the way her hair caught the light, the way her mouth moved to a half-smile and then indecisively straightened as if she was unsure of what she was feeling. For a moment, he lost himself in her soft, pale eyes and then he realised he was staring. He looked away quickly.

There was a moment of silence, a time in which Pat wondered if she too had felt something. "No big deal," she said. Her tone was flippant, unemotional. "It wasn't a very good report anyway."

Pat cleared his throat. "I've been talking to Ken. This isn't over, you know."

"I heard he took off in the bush. He taunted the police and yelled that he wouldn't leave until the government did something about what happened to the people of Kiosk."

"Yeah, I wish I had seen it."

Suzette looked sideways and muttered: "Not as much as I do." She looked over her shoulder. "It would have made great footage."

Pat thought about the roll of film in his pocket. Ken had said to give it to the Nugget, but maybe he could get it developed and give Suzette some of the shots. "What would happen if you had some great still photographs?"

"I'd prefer video, but if it isn't available, we'll put up a still and do a voice-over. Why? Do you have something?"

"I may be able to get you some stills."

"Stuff you took?" Her eyebrows rose, as did the tone of her voice.

Pat was disappointed at Suzette's excitement. She seemed more interested in finding good pictures than she was in meeting her first boyfriend. He said quietly: "No, even better than that."

Suzette's interest heightened. "I'd need them today," she put her on Pat's forearm, "but if you could, that would be great."

The touch was electrifying. A surge of electricity ran through his body and his eyes met hers. She looked away. Had he seen a change in Suzette's expression? He wasn't sure. "I might be able to get them to you today."

"That would be wonderful. Here?"

"Well, actually I'd have to go to North Bay first."

"Is that where you live now?"

"No, I'm still in Toronto - well actually just north of Toronto in King City. I'm going to find a motel in North Bay for the night." Telling her this was somehow exciting and he felt his pulse race.

"We're staying in the King's Head. You could probably get a room there. It's on the highway, right near the mall."

He felt light and dizzy. Suzette telling him where she was staying. Was it an invitation? "You and your husband?" he asked, feeling extremely stupid as the question left his lips.

A quick smirk appeared at the corner of Suzette's mouth and then disappeared. "No. I'm divorced . . . me and the two jokers over there," she jerked her thumb at Jaro, "are staying in North Bay while we cover this story."

"Well, can I call you at the hotel later today?" Patrick held his breath, waiting for an answer.

"Sure. We'll be there after supper - if nothing breaks here. If I'm not there, leave a message at the desk."

Pat reached forward and took her hand, holding it this time rather than shaking it. "It's been really good seeing you again." Her skin was soft and her hand delicate; he could feel warmth and he remembered her touch of so many years ago. "On the first day I was back in Kiosk," he continued, "I drove by your old house and I . . ." He stumbled, unsure of how to continue, what to say.

Suzette studied him for a moment and then took her hand away. "Yes, it is hard, coming back here, seeing all the houses gone."

Jaro walked up. "You sure know a lot of the people here." He was studying Patrick closely.

"What do you think? I grew up here." Her annoyance with the intrusion evident.

"Well, I gotta go," Pat said. He looked at Suzette. "I'll call you later." He turned and walked back to his car.

He closed the door and relaxed in the quiet comfort of the car's interior. He could still hear people chatting, but he was insulated, removed. He pictured Suzette, the softness of her hand, the smoothness of her skin, the warmth of her eyes, and he suddenly felt warm.

He twisted in his seat and saw her talking to some people in the parking lot. She did not look over and seemed to have forgotten he was there. He admonished himself for his feelings. They had drifted worlds apart and they knew nothing about each other. Why would she be even remotely interested in an overweight car salesman from Toronto? But still, there had been that electricity in her touch, and it seemed as if she had also felt it. No, he thought, he was just overreacting - seeing what he wanted to see.

He started the engine and turned on the radio. It was tuned to one of the North Bay FM-rock stations and the newest Tool hit was playing, but it didn't suit his mood. He hit the seek button and wound up with a soft-rock tune. He clicked off the radio as he drove the rough dirt road through the empty town.

Ken skirted back around the edge of the clearing and stopped to peer through the bushes. All the town residents were gone, the tents and trailers had been removed and most of the OPP had left the scene. The few police that remained were watching as some workers tore down Ken's cabin. With fresh film in his camera, he photographed their efforts. They had piled his furniture in the back of his truck, which sat alone and abandoned in the field, but they were throwing the wood in a pile.

It was a shame that he had lost his truck, but eventually he would get it back. If he needed a vehicle in the immediate future, he could always get his ATV at his camp near Lauder Lake, but he decided it would be best to stay off the roads. Algonquin Park was thought by most people to be a wilderness area, but logging continued year after year. The loggers were not allowed to approach the lakes, where canoeists might see them, but they had a network of roads through the entire park. Ken could travel quickly from place to place on these roads, but so could the police and the MNR. He decided he would be wiser to stay on foot where he had the advantage.

His biggest threat would come from a CO, or Conservation Officer. Hired by the MNR to enforce hunting and fishing regulations, they carried side-arms and were comfortable in the bush. The park wardens and OPP might be physically fit and well-trained, but they were not woodsmen. The CO's, on the other hand, would not be afraid to wander far out into the forest without backup. He had evaded CO's in the past, and no CO had ever found one of his caches, but they were still a formidable threat. For now, the OPP were involved and this would create a jurisdictional problem for the CO's, who did not normally operate with the police, and the OPP would be easy to avoid.

His camera whirred, and one of the female officers looked vaguely in his direction. He slowly moved down into the grass - sharp movements were easier to pick up by the eye - and continued to watch. She studied the trees for a moment and not trusting her judgement, returned her attention to the destruction of the building.

Ken had left his heavy pack back at Wolf Lake, so he had little worry of capture, but he was not anxious to run another footrace through the bush. After a few moments, he moved into the cover of heavier foliage and walked back toward the Camp-One logging road.

The road would take him to within a hundred yards of Bear Lake, now called Boulter Lake, and back to his camp. It was safe now, because everyone assumed that he had crossed the lake on his boat. However, when it was known that he was giving someone rolls of film, the MNR would start driving this road. He would leave tracks and a sign of habitation, then circle Kiosk, and spend a few days near his camp on Lauder Lake to the east. They would never find him.

He reached his camp at Wolf lake and sat on a rock that jutted out into the water. The grasshoppers were chirping and his hunger touched him, but he decided that before a meal, he needed a little relaxation.

A few feet from the shore, he stood with his feet slightly apart, and imagined a golden cord holding his body weight through the top of his head. He relaxed and let himself hang from that imaginary cord as his breathing became relaxed and more in-rhythm with the world around him. He allowed his thoughts to drift. The tension slowly dropped out of his face, his shoulders, his arms, his pelvis, his legs and even out of his feet.

Slowly he raised his arms, palms facing outward, and continued to breathe deeply. His weight shifted and he no longer felt the ground beneath his feet. His breathing deepened and his mind became less focussed.

He moved his arms to the sides and then, slowly allowed the meditation to direct his movements. The rotation of the earth, the movement of the water, and the flow of air around him, became connected to him - linked and all part of the same movement.

The surface of the lake, gently rippled by the wind, moved toward him and the weeds near the shore were flattened to a mat of green lines that pulsated rhythmically with his breath. The duck-weed near his feet bobbed up and down with his pulse. The movement made him feel as if he were being carried, weightless, floating, drifting over the lake.

The smell of cedar, pine, earth and water, washed past him and he heard a frog croak softly from the shore. In the distance, chickadees called to each other and poplar leaves rustled in the wind. The trunks of some of the smaller trees moaned and creaked as they were pushed gently back and forth and the wind stroked Ken's arms and face.

His thoughts returned to the protest. It was a good thing that so many people had returned to the town, because this would certainly attract media attention, but he realised that his position was not the leader of the group. His place was out in the forest, near the water and on the land. His home was Kiosk, but it was not the

Kiosk of buildings, it was the Kiosk of nature.

He continued to move, turning in the breeze, but when he became aware of the sensation of hunger, he decided it was time to stop. It was a good time to fish, and fish would be a wonderful supper after an eventful day.

He wished he had a sketch pad. There were so many beautiful images around him and it would be relaxing to put them on paper. Then he realised that it was just nicer to absorb them for himself. He did not need to chronicle them for someone else.

Forty-five minutes later, he made a small fire with very dry wood and cooked his supper. The air was warm and sweet with the smell of fire, fish and water and he foresaw a relaxing evening with a setting sun and the call of the loon.

Patrick sat in the food court of the North Gate Square shopping mall drinking coffee and watching the passing shoppers. It had only taken an hour to have the three sets of prints developed and he had decided to give one to Perrault, as Ken had suggested, another he would keep, and the third he would give to Suzette.

He looked at his watch. Earlier, he had checked into the King's Head motel and he had left a message for Suzette saying he would meet her later. Maggie Perrault was meeting him here, but she was late.

As he watched the people shuffle past carrying plastic bags full of purchases, his mind kept drifting back to Suzette. She had been on his mind when he first came to Kiosk, but he didn't realise how much he wanted to see her.

He remembered a divorced female friend had once told him that she was "touch-poor". At the time, he assumed she was talking about a need for sex, but as he thought about Suzette's touch, he realised what she had probably meant. For a long time, his only relationships with women had been disconnected physical ones. Touch was only something that led to something else. There was no warmth, no electricity. When Suzette touched him, he realised what he had been missing. It was that feeling of being connected to someone, of being aware of what they felt.

"Excuse me. Are you Patrick James?"

Pat looked up somewhat dazed - shaken from his thoughts of Suzette. "Yes." He half stood in an attempt to be polite.

The woman introduced herself and showed Pat her press identification. He felt she was being rather officious, but he shook her hand and asked her to sit. She had a large bundle of papers and she held these in her lap as if they were a shield with which to protect herself from Pat. Without saying a word, he pushed an envelope of pictures across the round table.

Holding her papers with one hand, she used the other to flip through the pictures. The first few shots were of Ken's cabin, and she studied these carefully, but when she reached the pictures of the OPP, she stopped and looked up. "Where did you get these?"

"Ken thought you might be interested."

Her mouth dropped and she put her bundle of papers on the floor beside her chair. "Did he leave the park?"

Pat told Perrault that Ken was still in the park and that he had set up a new cabin. He explained that the negatives proved that the cabin was built after the break-up in Kiosk. He then said that he was going to meet with Ken regularly for a couple of days. As he said this, he thought about his job and the inevitable confrontation, but he had already made up his mind to stay. Meeting Suzette had made that decision much easier.

Perrault started to ask questions about Pat's background, but he put up his hand and stopped her. He asked that she not identify him. His role in the protest was as an assistant to Ken, and he did not want any publicity.

"Can I keep these?" Perrault pointed to the pictures.

"Yes. Do you need the negatives?"

"Yes. That would be really helpful."

Pat handed her the thin see-through envelope with the negatives. Perrault stuffed them away immediately.

"Can I meet him?" she asked.

"I'll have to ask, but it might be possible."

"When can we meet again?"

"Tomorrow?"

"Name the time and place." Perrault was already standing. She was in a hurry now.

***

"What's the point in staying?" Jaro asked. "We don't even have anything from today that they'll air and you want to waste money on another night! I don't get it."

Suzy sat across from Jaro in the Highway 11, Tim Horton's coffee shop. They were back in North Bay. She drank from her coffee to give herself a moment before she answered. It was true that they didn't have any interesting footage, but she suspected that Pat was meeting secretly with Ken and he might have something of value.

She tried to think. Was she stalling because she thought there was a story, or because she wanted to see Pat? No, she didn't want any involvements, she told herself, it was the story. "Look, after I meet with this friend of mine, I'll show you what he's got and you can decide. If we leave right after that, we can be back by late tonight, but if there's something really good here . . ." She exhaled loudly and held her hands out to the side.

"Ah, come on," whined Mike. He was sitting beside Jaro with a bowl of soup and he had tea biscuit crumbs all over the table. "The police have pulled out, they cleaned up the protest, and one guy is going camping. It's not a story anymore."

Suzy looked at Mike disdainfully and then turned back to Jaro. "I'll meet this guy and then we'll see." She looked at her watch. "I better get going."

"Wait, we'll come with you."

"No," she said quickly. "I think I better do this alone. I don't want to spook the guy."

"Just don't take all night."

Suzy nodded and left the coffee shop. Although the motel was just across the street, it was difficult to reach on foot. The area had been designed for vehicles and not pedestrians. It took ten minutes to reach the lobby and she was relieved to find it empty. She had enough time to change and run a brush through her hair.

She dug through her travel bag, looking for clothes that she knew see didn't have. She had the clothes that she wore on-camera, and the clothes that she wore when she relaxed, but she had nothing that seemed right for this meeting. Deciding it was better to be less formal, she pulled on a pair of jeans and a soft cotton blouse and then re-applied some makeup.

In the fluorescent light of the bathroom, she looked at herself and was unhappy with what she saw. Her face was so modelled, so painted, and she wanted to look soft. She was so used to applying makeup that would work for the camera that she had forgotten how to apply it just to look good. Was that her face looking back at her? "Arrrggg!." She cried out in frustration and tossed the eyeliner pencil across the counter. This is too much of a fuss, she thought. She grabbed her key and stormed out her room.

In the lobby, she saw Patrick standing at the front desk. He seemed to sense her arrival and he turned away from the clerk and walked toward her. The stubble and dirt were gone and his shirt had those strange creases that showed it had just come out of a package. It made her smile to think that he too had taken time to get ready for their meeting. He looked very proper, but his hairstyle was out of date. He still wore it long, like he did so many years ago.

"Nice to see you again," he said.

"Yes, I'm glad you could make it." For a moment, they both stood in the lobby looking awkward. "Have you had dinner yet?" Suzy asked suddenly.

"No, I haven't. You?"

Suzy shook her head. "There's a Chinese place next door. Should we go and get a bite?"

With dinner, they had wine and they talked about their lives since they left Kiosk in 1975. Suzy talked about Michelle at length, something she normally wouldn't do when she was having dinner with a man, and she was surprised by Pat's seemingly genuine interest.

She ran her fingers through her hair, trying to keep it straight. She tucked it behind an ear and then she straightened her bangs. She was self-conscious about the way she looked and she felt awkward with her cutlery, with the way she chewed, with everything. She looked at Pat and she felt like a schoolgirl. His face was strong, but his eyes were soft; his voice was deep, but his words were kind; his hands were powerful, but his touch was gentle.

As they talked about her parents, Pat reached over the table and lightly laid his hand on her wrist. She felt the warmth in the touch and for a moment, she did not breathe. She had learned not to show emotion, and she gently removed her hand and picked up her wine glass, but she felt strange.

The one subject they avoided during the meal was the protest and Pat's role in it, but as they finished the wine, Suzy became painfully aware of the time. She could almost sense Jaro and Mike's anger at being kept waiting and when there was a break in the conversation, she asked: "So what about the pictures you were talking about? Can I see them?"

She saw a quick change in Pat's expression. He picked up the envelope that had sat on the table since the beginning of the meal and took out a stack of pictures. He explained the sequence and described the locations.

"I'm sorry, but I don't have the negatives. Kenny asked me to give them to the Nugget."

"So, you were talking to Kenny after the police moved everyone out?"

"Yeah. We arranged to meet at the rapids, just north of town. Kenny's pretty hot about this and he isn't going to quit." Pat told her about their recent camping trip and some of the things they had discussed. He cautiously told her that Kenny resented that natives were being granted land-claims, but the people of Kiosk were completely ignored; that Natives were allowed to hunt in the park with high-powered rifles, while Kiosk residents were denied the right to freely walk on the land on which they were born.

Suzy listened with interest, trying to figure where this story could go. She liked being with Pat, but unless there was a story here, she would have to return to Barrie. The pictures, especially without the negatives, didn't make much of a story. "Is there any chance of Kenny doing an interview with me? On camera?"

"I'm sure Kenny would love to see you, but our next meeting place is hard to get to. I could talk to Kenny and try to arrange something?"

"When are you seeing him next?"

"Tomorrow."

"Can I come with you?"

Patrick paused. "Yeah sure, why not? If you want, we can

drive out together tomorrow. About two o'clock?"

Suzy hesitated. Two o'clock was pretty late. She shrugged. "I guess so. Where's he meeting you?"

"On the trestle . . . by Bear Creek."

As they left the restaurant, Suzy stopped to enjoy the evening air. The sun had set and the parking lot was awash with the glow of sodium vapour lights. Moths and other insects danced in the air.

"It really is nice to see you again," Pat said as he stood facing her, "I mean that, it has been . . . I . . ." He seemed lost for words.

He was close, facing her, and she imagined the softness of his lips. He moved closer and then he wavered forward and backward ever so slightly. She could sense him, feel him, moving closer and just as she was about to fall in his arms, she turned. "Yes. It's been nice for me too." The moment was passed and was gone. She pulled her purse higher on her shoulder. "Listen, I should get back. I have to talk to my camera guy."

"Sure, sure. I'll walk you back."

In the lobby, Suzy stopped when she spotted Jaro and Mike. The two appeared to have been sitting in the lobby for some time and their expression showed their impatience. She briefly introduced Pat, but Pat seemed to be in a hurry. He said hello and then, just as quickly, goodnight. He waved and walked away toward his room without looking back. Suzy dropped into one of the lobby chairs to tried to convince Jaro that she wasn't nuts. She told him about the meeting with Kenny and showed him the photos. "It could be an exclusive."

"Yeah, yeah," Jaro said, the annoyance still evident in his tone. "Well, it's too late to check out now anyway. But we have nothing for a full day's work today. What have we got? A couple of photographs that one of the local newspapers has probably already published?"

"You brought the laptop. We can digitize these, do a quick voice-report and send it down by modem."

Mike looked at her incredulously. "This isn't Zimbabwe! We should be sending video feed."

Suzy looked at him. "But we don't have any useful video, do

we? So let's send what we have and tomorrow, we'll get footage of the leader of the protest evading the police."

They reluctantly agreed and walked to the room Jaro and Mike were sharing. Suzy found a path through the mess of clothes and equipment and picked up the phone. She called Michelle and explained that she needed to stay another day at least. Although Michelle said it was okay, the disappointment was evident in her voice. Suzy hung up the phone and immediately got to work. In less than two hours, they wrote and produced a short update. The footage they shot today would be saved for background stock. After the material was transmitted, it was time to leave.

Jaro and Mike decided to go out to one of the bars, and they hinted that they would rather go alone. Suzy smiled and excused herself. As she walked down the concrete hall, she wondered which room belonged to Patrick. It was best she didn't know, she told herself.

Alone in her room, she studied her face in the mirror. She shook her head slowly. Why had she been so anxious about her appearance? Why had she been so nervous during dinner? What had caused her to act so foolishly? She did not need love in her life. She did not need it and she didn't want it. Shoving all her makeup to the side, she turned on the water and washed her face. The soap stung her eyes and caused them to tear for the second time today. She decided she was tired and over-emotional. It was time to sleep.

7. Smoke & Dreams (1974)

Suzette Labelle struggled to escape her dream. Voices and other sounds reached her, but they were distant, disconnected and then she smelled smoke. In fear, she gasped and forced her eyes open. The room was clear. Light streamed through the window and danced across her frayed, blue bedspread, which was pulled up to her chin. There was no fire.

It had been more than a year and she was still dreaming about it - the pulsating red timbers, the pieces of burning debris floating high in the sky. Life had not been the same since. She now went to school in Mattawa, which was a big adjustment, but even worse was the change in the mood of the town. There was a sense of resignation, like kids playing the last inning in a baseball game that they knew they had lost. The game was played out to the end, but it was done without joy.

The twangy sound of a country and western song drifted between soft conversation in the kitchen and she knew it was time to get up. The house was cold, she could feel it on her nose and see it in the frosty window, and she did not want to pull off the blanket.

Her sister and brother still lived in Mattawa, but there had been no room for her, and the school bus picked her up every day. Even though everyone said it gave her a chance to do her home-work, she hated it. Patrick rode on the same bus, but he usually sat with Kenny, and the bus driver took a fit if the kids moved from seat to seat. It took well over an hour and the ride was so bumpy that it was impossible to do anything but look out the window, which was usually dirty from the outside and foggy from the inside.

The song ended and the announcer spoke for a while. Her father groaned loudly and swore in French. He yelled from the kitchen. "Suzette, the school busses are cancelled."

This was good news. She walked to the bedroom window, the hardwood floor chilling her feet, and saw a layer of fresh snow. It was beautiful. Soft billowy fluffs of white sat on the fence posts, the gate, and the bird feeder. Every twig of every tree branch was decorated with a puffy coat that looked like a cotton-baton blanket. The front-yard spruce sagged, its form altered, and in the distance, pines bent so far that their tips pointed toward the ground as if they had decided to return to the earth from which they had sprung.

In the other room, she could hear her father complaining that it was too early, that the winter would be too long. She watched the snow fall past the window. Even though it was only the beginning of November, the snow awakened thoughts of Christmas, of holidays, of sweet treats and warm drinks shared near the heat of a wood stove.

Adults didn't like the winter, but her father had shot a moose in the fall, so there would be lots of meat, and the wood was cut, so they would have heat. It was time to enjoy the peaceful calm days of winter - especially since school was cancelled for the day.

The sky was grey and gentle flakes of snow continued to fall, but to the north, she could see patches of blue sky. It was going to be a great day. Sunshine, blue skies and great packing snow, which would mean snowmen, sliding and snowball fights. She took off her pyjamas, pulled on pants and a big sweater and walked to the kitchen. Someone had already lit the living room woodstove and although the floor was still cold, the air was warm and redolent with the smell of oiled metal - a smell that may have been unpleasant for some, but a smell that brought back memories of warm cosy evenings for Suzette.

Her Papa sat at the kitchen table dressed in an undershirt and a pair of green work pants. He wanted to drive to Mattawa to look for work, but the snow on the road would make travel difficult. "See outside?" he asked in French.

"It's nice!"

"Harumph. Tires on the truck won't think so . . . not gonna be a good drive."

Suzette's Mama spoke up. "Oh, be quiet, you old grump, they plow that road. Suzette's right, it is pretty." She was frying bacon in a cast iron pan on the electric range. The crack and sizzle was almost as loud as the radio.

Mr. Labelle grunted again.

Suzette sat at the table, and thought about her father working in Mattawa. Her eyebrows furrowed. "Papa, couldn't you get a job at the mill in Rutherglen?" The veneer plant had been relocated in Rutherglen about 30 miles away. This was the only place her papa could work that would allow them to remain in Kiosk. Mattawa was just too far away.

"I got my name in there, me," he answered, "but they can't take everybody. I gotta look udder places too."

"Would you drive to Mattawa every day if you got a job there?"

"Not in weather like dis."

Suzette looked down at the table. "But I don't want to move to Mattawa, Papa."

"Suzette, we don't always have a choice. Anyway, it don't look good for de house. The government wants to take the land away." He turned his head sharply to the side and exhaled loudly. "Maybe we can't stay."

Suzette's Mama turned quickly and shook her head. This was meant for Papa's eyes only, but Suzette caught it as well. Papa waved his hand dismissively.

Mrs. Labelle drained some of the fat into a metal bowl and broke some eggs into the pan. They sished and spat furiously as they hit the grease. She pushed them together and then lit a cigarette.

"I'm not hungry. Can I go outside?"

"You need some breakfast for school."

"There is no school."

"Oh, yeah, that's right." Mrs. Labelle said tapping herself on the forehead and shaking her head. "Eat some toast. Then you can go outside."

Suzette dropped some bread into the toaster and went to find some warm clothes.

Patrick lay on his bed listening to the scratchy sound of his radio. Elton John's latest hit, "Bennie and the Jets", was playing and although he liked the song, it was not as good as last year's hit, 'Goodbye Yellow Brick Road'. He could play some of Elton John's early songs, 'Your Song' and 'Burn Down the Mission', but he had no desire to learn 'Bennie and the Jets'. It was too commercial.

Much of the music on the radio was not playable. Suzette loved the Gilbert O Sullivan song, Alone Again (Naturally), and he had learned to play the acoustic lead from the middle, but had not learned all the chords. Sometimes he played it for her, but it was not exactly his taste. Most of the kids his age liked the commercial junk, but he liked the harder rock. He really liked 'China Grove' by the Doobie Brothers, but there was no way he could play that, and the same was true of 'Smoke on the Water' by Deep Purple. Either the songs were full of instrumentation, or they were so electric, that he had no chance of imitating them on his small guitar. He yearned to play an electric guitar, but Emile Chayer, the only kid in town with an electric guitar, wouldn't let anyone touch it. It was a shame really, because Emile, a few years older, wasted his talent on country-and-western music.

When the song was over, Pat turned off the radio, picked up his Starburst, and started to play. He had learned to play a really old song called "House of the Rising Sun" and although he only knew the words to the first verse, he was getting pretty good and finger picking his way through the chords.

He sang quietly because he didn't want anyone to overhear. ". . . and it's been . . . the ruin . . . of many a poor boy . . . and Mama . . . I know I'm one . . ." There was a brief knock at the front door and his mom answered. It was Kenny.

Pat rested the guitar against the wall and the cold air next to the plasterboard chilled the back of his fingers. He wondered briefly if the cold might be bad for the guitar and then he walked to the front door.

"Come on, Pat, we're goin' sliding." Kenny was really bubbly and seemed impatient to start having a good time.

The unused logging road behind the school twisted steeply through the trees. It was a perfect place to go sliding. As Pat pulled his wooden toboggan up the beginning of the incline, Suzette rushed past on a two-rail sled. Her smile was ear to ear on her rosy face. "Hey Patty!" she cried as she passed. Pat waved and waited for her. Kenny rolled his eyes and continued up the hill.

"Isn't it great?" she said running toward him.

"Yeah, great to get out of school!"

She looked down at his toboggan. "Come on; let's ride down on your toboggan together."

As they ascended, they stayed to the right, but walked beside each other rather than single-file. At the top, they saw Kenny, who had still not gone down the hill. He was looking at some red pines off to the side.

"Whatcha lookin' at?" asked Pat.

"Ah, just some birds. Look at the one, upside down on the trunk."

"Yeah, neat," said Pat impatiently. "Now come on! We'll race you to the bottom."

Kenny turned just in time to get hit in the face by a snowball. Rene, one of the French boys, had been aiming at the back of Kenny's head, but Kenny turned at the perfect time. Rene was laughing furiously when Kenny ran over and wrestled him to the ground. A spontaneous snowball fight broke out with everyone laughing, screaming and running. Suzette got hit directly in the forehead, the snow sticking to her eyelashes and raining down into the collar of her coat, and Pat began to act as her defender. Temporary alliances were created, and then broken, and the sound of cheers and shouts echoed through the forest. The snow on the ground dampened the cacophony, but it reverberated through the trees and across the hills.

The battle ended when two boys used toboggans to take flight down the hill and two others followed in pursuit. The rest of the kids broke off and dropped to the ground, exhausted. Pat lay on his back looking up at the patch of blue sky between the treetops and Suzette appeared. "Come on, let's go for a ride."

When Suzette sat in front of him on the toboggan, Pat did

not know where to put his hands. She seemed to be teasing him, pressing against him, and he took his hands from her shoulders and wrapped his arms around her stomach as they started their descent. It was an awkward position.

The toboggan was difficult to control and a few times, it seemed as if they would curve off into the trees, but somehow they continued down the road, snow flying up in their faces. Any thoughts of romance were quickly replaced with excitement as Suzette screamed through the corners. Near the bottom, the grade increased and they really started to travel. Patrick, thinking they were going too fast, deliberately fell to the side, pulling Suzette with him, and they both tumbled loosely through the snow, laughing and screaming.

Suzette landed on top of Patrick and smiling, with snow on her face, she leaned down and kissed him. Patrick laughed, and pushed her off, afraid that some of the other kids might see. He and Suzette had grown close, but he was easily embarrassed. He jumped to his feet, brushed off the snow, and looked left and right to see who was watching. He sighed; they were alone. As he turned back to Suzette, a big splotch of snow hit him in the chest. She screamed in delight and scrabbled away. Other kids were drawn by her cries and within minutes, the snowball fight that had ended at the top of the hill, continued here at the bottom. Snow flew in all directions and now the school and the house of Mr. Loeffler, one of the local teachers, could be used for cover.

Kenny jumped behind a snowbank and tried to dig out a little fort as he fired balls over the top. "Pat! Suzette! Over here!" he called.

Pat jumped over the bank and started to dig as Suzette and Kenny fired snow balls in all directions. The other children, realising the danger of allowing these three to become entrenched in a fort, attacked and using their bodies as battering rams, destroyed the snow bank.

Pat tackled Jean, one of the French boys, and washed his face with snow, but as soon as anyone hit the ground, they were attacked from all sides. Pat jumped up laughing. He tried to run, but his jacket was getting damp and movement was difficult as the heavy fabric acted like a blanket.

He tackled another boy who was hitting him with ball after ball and on the ground the boy yelled, "Truce!" This seemed to be just the impetus that was needed and the word "truce" echoed around the bottom of the hill.

Panting for breath, Pat fell on his back and looked up at the clouds. Light flakes of snow melted on his face and caused little drops of water to roll across his cheeks toward his ears. Someone tugged at his sleeve and he looked at Kenny kneeling beside him. "Come on, let's go for another slide."

Some of the kids wandered off, but Pat, Kenny and Suzette decided to ascend the hill for another run. Walking up, they could feel that the snow was changing. It was wetter. The slide was much slower and nowhere near as exciting. At the bottom, they looked back at the logging road, wondering what to do next. Patrick, who could feel the dampness of his coat, was grateful when Mr. Loeffler asked if they wanted to come in for a cup of hot chocolate. Because the schools in Mattawa were closed, the Kiosk school had closed as well, and Mr. Loeffler had nothing to do.

Kenny wondered if he should go home. Pat and Suzette were huddling close to each other and he didn't want to get in the way.

Mr. Loeffler looked at him and seemed to read his thoughts. "Come on Kenneth, surely you have a moment to spend with your old teacher." Although his name and his appearance were definitely German, Mr. Loeffler spoke with a slight British accent. Somewhere in his forties, he had sharp features and long hair, which he often swept backward with his fingers, and he made jokes that few people understood. He was a lover of language and he could recite poetry and long verses of prose, but he also loved the bush and spent a lot of time fishing and walking in the forest. Now that Kenny, Pat and Suzette were going to school in Mattawa, they thought of Mr. Loeffler as one of their favourite teachers.

"So I guess you have hissed my mystery classes?"

Kenny looked at Patrick, confused. Patrick smiled and whispered: "Missed his history classes." Kenny nodded, but his expression remained confused. Patrick often got the jokes, but even he was uncertain if they were intentional or if Mr. Loeffler was just misspeaking.

Suzette hung her coat on the crowded coat rack and the boys tented theirs on the floor. They did an intricate dance, trying to avoid the puddles on the floor and they made their way to the kitchen. The house was warm and smelled slightly of oil, with which Mr. Loeffler heated in the winter, but it was very clean. Although there were books everywhere, there did not seem to be any dust, any staleness.

"Are you glad to have the day off?" Kenny asked as Loeffler poured milk into a pot on the stove."

"I'd be happier if these old bones of mine would allow me to go sliding down that hill." He pointed in the direction of the logging road. "But it's nice to have a bit of a diversion from the everyday."

"We had a giant snowball fight outside and it was lots of fun."

"Yes, a gentle snowfall is ever so much nicer than roaring pain."

Kenny felt confused, but Pat and Suzette both smiled. Pat leaned over to Ken and whispered again. "Pouring rain."

"I wish we were still going to school here," said Suzette, "I sure don't like the bus ride all the way to Mattawa."

"Well, maybe when that fine North Bay solicitor wins the case, we can find a way to build another school right here in town."

"I'd like that," replied Kenny. Suzette nodded as well.

Kenny suddenly looked down at the ground. It was difficult to go anywhere without the discussion turning to fight for land rights in the town.

"What's wrong, Kenneth?" Mr. Loeffler was the only person alive who called Kenny, 'Kenneth', except perhaps his mother when she was angry. "Don't you think he can win?"

"Well . . . it's just that it doesn't look too good. Most people want us to leave and since the majority rules, it looks like we'll have to."

"Don't take so much for granted. Who said that it has to be done by majority rule?"

Kenneth looked confused again and Pat jumped in the conversation. "Well, that's how it works, doesn't it?"

Mr. Loeffler's voice changed and he pointed his index finger in the air, commanding attention. "Unless it were unanimously agreed upon, where would be the obligation of the minority to submit to the choice of the majority? How have a hundred men who wish for a master, the right to vote on behalf of ten who don't?"

Patrick tilted his head sideways. "Sorry?"

"Hang on a minute." Loeffler turned down the heat on the milk and walked to the living room. He returned with a little blue book, which he handed to Patrick. "It's called 'The Social Contract', written by a man named Rousseau. Try to read some of it. We often take much for granted."

Pat opened the book and thumbed through it. At first glance, he saw it contained some hard words, like 'sovereignty' and 'inalienable'. He placed it back on the table.

"Take it! It's a gift."

"Thanks." He shrugged.

"It may be difficult at first," Mr. Loeffler said, reading Pat's thoughts, "but give it a try. There are some interesting ideas. Rousseau was one of the men who inspired the French Revolution."

Suzette smiled at Pat and then turned to Mr. Loeffler. "Pat reads a lot."

"Good, you should all read a lot. You may live way out in the country, but books allow you all to be world travellers."

Kenny laughed. "My dad hates books. He says they wreck good ideas."

"Your dad is a very practical man and he learns by listening to other people. The Indians had an entire culture based on oral tradition. It's how they passed on their knowledge. And you know, listening to people is valuable." He winked at Kenny who was looking at him.

"I listened to you in class."

Mr. Loeffler laughed, his eyes narrowing to slits and creating a carving of wrinkles around his eyes. "I know you did. You were all good students. And what about you Kenneth, what have you decided to do with your life?"

"I'm not sure really. I'd like to do something that can be done outdoors. I don't think I would do well working in an office."

"Hmmm." Loeffler stood and stirred in the chocolate powder and then poured the hot liquid into four mismatched mugs. "I think I have something for you too." He brought the cups to the table and disappeared back into the living room. Patrick sipped his drink and quickly moved his head backward. It was too hot to drink. Suzette and Kenny sat quietly looking at the blue book on the table.

Loeffler returned with two books. He handed one to Kenny. "This is a wonderful book written by a man who decided to live alone in the woods. He celebrated nature and being an individual. It's called Walden, and at the end, there's also a piece on civil disobedience. I know you'll like it." He turned and handed Suzette the second book. "This one's for you, it's one of my favourites; it's by Charles Dickens, a truly wonderful writer."

Suzette took her book and held it in her hand. It was certainly the biggest and it was a nicely bound hardcover. "Thank you very much."

"Yeah, thanks," added Kenny. "You don't expect a book report or something?"

Mr. Loeffler laughed heartily and took a big drink of his hot chocolate. He didn't seem bothered by the heat. "No, no, no. But if Patrick is right and the town is doomed, I want to feel that I have given you something that may be of help in years to come." A knock at the door caused Mr. Loeffler to turn his head. There was urgency to the knock that could not be mistaken. He walked to the door and opened it.

It was Evan, Pat's older brother. He looked worried. "Is Pat here?"

Loeffler opened the door wider so that the kitchen table could be seen. "Yes. He and his friends came in for some hot chocolate."

"Well, he's gotta come home right away. There's been an accident. It's Uncle Roy."

Pat pushed the heavy chrome chair across the linoleum, gulped his hot chocolate and hurried to the front. "What happened?"

"Just come home. Mom will tell you."

"What kind of accident?"

"A car accident." Evan was already walking away from the house.

Pat pulled on his boots. "Thanks for the chocolate Mr. Loeffler," he paused a moment. ". . . and for the book." Suzette brought it from the kitchen and handed it to him. Patrick pulled on his coat as he went out the door and trotted after his brother.

"We better go too," said Suzette. She walked back to the kitchen. She and Kenny finished their drinks while standing. "Thank you so much."

Mr. Loeffler nodded. "I just hope it's nothing too serious."

"Me too." Suzette looked at the floor.

"I'm sure it will be fine. Pat's a strong boy. You'll see."

"I guess."

"Thanks, Mr. Loeffler." Kenny raised his book and shook it twice.

"Sure, Kenneth. And when you've read it, see if you can discover who was fighting liars." Suzette and Kenny looked at each other. "Or lighting fires," Loeffler added with a smile.

Suzette put her hand on the doorknob and stopped. She suddenly realised the truth: Mr. Loeffler was doing it deliberately.

The door was difficult to open. Mr. Loeffler's house, like many in the town, did not have a functioning lock and only a temperamental doorknob kept the place secure. She wriggled the loose handle and finally walked out into the fresh cold air. "Do you think we should go to Pat's place?"

"Naw, we better not. They probably don't want kids hanging around."

"Yeah, maybe." Suzette turned and walked toward her house leaving Kenny on the road alone.

Kenny passed Patrick's house. The curtains were drawn and he could not see in the windows, but there was a feeling of sadness, a sense of darkness that lay over the house. It made him quicken his pace as he walked.

Snow blew sideways in the cool air and the sunshine had disappeared. He could feel the cold working its way between his fingers. It was in his toes, and when he closed his eyes, it turned the inside of his eyelids a bright red.

Just past the highway 630 turn-off, the road descended to

the bridge and crossed the Amable du Fond. Kenny could see two men, Richard Rankin and Tabby, an old Indian who travelled the bush with Richard, relaxing by a weir gate.

Richard once worked pulling the logs out of the hot-pond. This was normally the job of three or four men, but Richard had always worked alone. He jumped around on the floating docks, his sleeves rolled to mid forearm, and hooked the logs with a long pole. He manipulated them onto the chain that pulled them up two stories into the mill and often had to fight to keep them in place. At the age of sixty, he outworked any two men at the mill.

He had been married, but his wife was long gone - Kenny had never known her - and now he lived alone in a small shack out in the bush a few miles north of Kiosk. The company owned many of the houses in the town, including Richard Rankin's old house, and when people were no longer working for the company, they were forced to leave. Richard loved the area, had no interest in moving to North Bay or Mattawa, and took up residence in a shanty on Wolf Lake. It didn't matter that he did not own it. It was empty, and it was near his friend's house.

Tabby and his family had lived in another shack on the Wolf Lake for years. Most people knew him as Charlie - or Cheech - Pinneskum, but Richard always called him Tabby. In one of his many treks through the bush, Kenny had visited them on Wolf lake and had learned that Tabby was a short form of Tabobandung, which was Tabby's real name. It meant, "He Who Sees Far." It was a name that few people knew, or even cared about, but it was special to Kenny.

Tabby was in town more often now that Richard had moved out to Wolf Lake. Earlier, he had little to do with the people of Kiosk. He picked up some supplies and occasionally met a tourist, but he usually kept to himself. Although there was no serious racial tension between the Indians and the loggers, there was not a great deal of integration, but Tabby and Richard shared a love for the bush that transcended race and heritage.

As Kenny approached, Richard said hello. Tabby had his back turned and did not look around. It was as if he had known that Kenny was there all the time and did not need to use his eyes to have it confirmed.

"Hi!" Kenny said, tucking his toboggan behind him, suddenly feeling foolish with this childish toy.

"School's not open today?"

"Nope. Too much snow for the busses."

"Wonder what they would have done twenty years ago? This is nothing compared to the snowfalls we used to get." Tabby nodded in agreement.

Kenny didn't know what to say. He wasn't even born twenty years ago and he couldn't comment on the snowfalls. "Did you hear about what happened to Mr. James?"

"No, what happened, son?"

"I don't know for sure, but he was in some sort of accident. He was out on the highway looking for a job."

Richard shook his head. "Well, I guess if they stopped the school busses, people shoulda realised it was dangerous on the roads. Everyone goes too fast now; they don't pay attention to the weather. How is he?"

"I don't know. I was hoping you might've heard something. I just know he was in an accident."

"No, they don't tell me much of anything." Richard looked down at the ground and shook his head. "Too bad, really . . . people's gotta travel all over the place lookin' for work. Why can't we just be left alone? This wouldn't have happened if he hadn't been lookin' for work someplace else."

This hadn't occurred to Kenny, but so much was tied to the way the people were being treated by the government - even the way that Richard had been tossed out of his house after all those years. "Yeah, I guess it wouldn't have."

Tabby bent and took something from the pack at his feet. His grey, braided ponytail fell forward. He stood and turned toward the west.

"Are you doing some hunting today?"

"No, we're going down to the Nipissing River. Be gone for a couple of days."

Kenny twisted slightly and his toboggan bumped into his heels. He grinned sheepishly. The Nipissing River was a long way into Algonquin Park. It was a four-day canoe-trip for most people, but Richard and Tabby would walk there and back in three days.

They would be in no hurry and they would travel easily through the bush. Richard had caches, small buried supplies, hidden every-where and if there was a blizzard, he would stop and make a sleigh. If it got really cold, he would stop and build a shelter. The purpose of the journey was not 'getting there', but enjoying the journey itself. Kenny suddenly wished he could join them, but he would have school tomorrow and his mom would never let him.

Tabby picked up his pack and swung it on his back. Snow was gathering on the peppered grey hair.

"We're just going to the Lucky Dollar and the Post Office," said Richard.

Tabby nodded and walked away. Richard followed. Kenny pulled his toboggan across the bridge, still feeling slightly silly.

At home, his father was sitting at the chrome and arborite kitchen table eating toast and drinking coffee. "Did you have fun, son?"

Kenny nodded, peeling off his coat and mitts and placing them near the wood stove in the next room. "There was some prob-lem with Pat's uncle."

"Oh?"

Kenny told him that there had been an accident, but he did-n't know the details. Dave Campbell put down his coffee and walked to the black phone on the wall. He dialled the four numbers that would put him touch with the James family. "Hi Lisa, it's Dave. Kenny just told me that there was some problem with Roy."

Kenny watched as his father's expression changed from curious to distressed. He could hear the sound of Pat's mother, but could not hear the words.

His father spoke again. "Oh God Lisa, I'm so sorry. I just can't believe it!" He dropped into a chair. "I know, I know. How's Bill takin' it?" He nodded his head. "Will they bring him to North Bay or Mattawa?" He nodded again. "I know, I know . . . let me know when you have more details."

Slowly his father hung up the phone. Kenny looked at him expectantly, but instead of telling him what he had heard on the phone, he called his wife.

Joanne Campbell entered the room wiping her hands on her apron. "What is it?" she asked.

"Roy James was killed in a crash on 630." Highway 630 was the access road to Kiosk. "He was hit by a logging truck."

"Oh, gosh, no." Joanne sat heavily in one of the kitchen chairs. She looked over at Kenny, who stood quietly leaning against the kitchen doorframe. "When did this happen?"

"This morning. He was goin' out lookin' for work."

"Crazy fool. He shouldn't have gone out today. They closed the schools. The roads are bad."

"Just cause the damned school busses don't run, don't mean that a fellow can stay home. Good jobs ain't easy to find."

"I know, I know, but to go out on a day like this if he didn't have to."

"What if he already had the job? Could he call in and say it was too slippery? You don't keep a job that way."

"I guess that's the problem living out here, it's a long ways to anywhere. Where are they gonna bury him?"

"Actually, they won't bury him at all. They'll put him in cold storage until the spring." Dave Campbell thought for a moment. "And then they can't bury him here, that's for sure. Ain't no white men buried at Kiosk. They'll probably bury him in Mattawa."

Kenny saw his mom look at her husband and put her finger to her lips.

"Don't shush me. The boy's gotta know what's going on. They don't bury people in town cause the government won't let us. We've lived here for forty years, but we ain't allowed to bury our dead. It's not right. The only person ever buried here is some Indian out by the Ranger's cabin and he wasn't even really buried there. It stinks."

"Why are you gettin' so mad?"

Dave rubbed the back of his neck as if he was trying to scrape off the hair that grew so thickly under his collar. "Ah, I don't know. It just bugs me. People die, but Roy really loved this place . . . really fought to stay . . . and now he's out for good. It's not right, that's all."

Kenny looked at his mom and then his dad. "I'm going upstairs. Is that okay?"

His mom looked at him. "Sure Kenny, I'll call you when I've made something to eat. You want a cup of tea or something?"

"Naw, I'm okay." Kenny turned, tramped up the stairs, flopped down on his bed, and looked at the poster of the giant marlin. One corner was hanging down and had been for some time judging by the accumulation of dust on the shiny fold. There was no sense putting it right, they were probably going to be forced to leave the town anyway . . . no sense in putting anything right.

K en crept across the flat sandy ground, beside what had once been the recreation centre. He had his camera ready - he wanted some new shots of the police - and as he reached the edge of the hill, he crawled through the damp grass. He felt foolish, over-reactive, but he didn't want to get caught.

His truck, its pickup box loaded with items from the cabin, was at the bottom of the hill beside a pile of lumber. There was nothing else in view. He studied the area with a pair of small binoculars. There were no police officers, no park wardens, no people at all. Was this a trap?

He studied the small pile of rocks near to the group of alders. They looked untouched. His key hadn't been discovered. Slowly, he backed away and then circled the hill.

In a crouch, he ran to the pile of rocks and listened. A few birds sang in the trees, but there were no human noises whatsoever. He was safe.

Quietly moving the rocks, he found his key and then stood slowly with its metal coolness pressing into his palm. From this angle, he could see across the bridge. The warden, the older fellow with the moustache, was standing with his hands on his hips watching the bridge road. He was near the fork, and was not looking in this direction.

Ken pulled the driver's door-handle and cringed when the mechanism creaked. He looked through the glass. The warden was still not looking this way.

He climbed in without being seen. It all seemed too easy and his suspicion grew as he was about to insert the key. Was there a trap he was missing? He placed the key on the seat, climbed back out and crept around to the back of the truck. There was no chain, no noisemakers, nothing to attract attention. Then he snuck around to the passenger side and froze. Boards with protruding nails had been placed in front of, and behind, the front and rear tires. He wouldn't have gotten far with two flats. Quietly, he removed them, and pushed them away from the tires.

Feeling triumphant, he crept back to the driver's side and took a picture of the truck with the driver's door open. Then, leaning on the fender, he took another few pictures of the warden near the bridge.

It was time to leave. Giddy, he jumped in and started the motor. It took two tries, but as soon as it caught, Ken ran up the rpm's and threw the truck into gear. He looked over at the warden who was now half walking and half running toward the bridge. With one hand on the wheel and the other on his camera, he took a picture. The tires dug into the soft damp earth and then spun on the wet grass as the truck tore out of the field and fishtailed onto the sandy Camp-One road.

He accelerated recklessly up the hill toward the old train sheds and almost ran off the road when he was unable to see a curve because of a sudden drop. The truck groaned as it bottomed out on a washed out section of rock and then slid sideways as it brushed against some small alders. Just up ahead, he knew he would have to stop. A gate barred entrance to the park, just past the point where the road crossed the rail-line, and although it wasn't locked, it was chained. The plastic and tin grill of his truck would likely not do well against the heavy pipes and chain of the gate.

He skidded to a stop, tires digging into the gravel, and ran to unchain the gate. He could hear the MNR truck accelerating and with the chain released, he jumped back inside and rammed the gate out of the way. In his rear - view mirror, he watched as the gate swung shut again and he grinned. The warden would be greeted by a closing gate.

Branches slapped the windshield and twanged against his antennae as he tore down the centre of the road. If he met someone coming the opposite way, there would be no way to avoid a collision and unfortunately, there were logging trucks using this road. The road gradually dropped and curved to the left and its sandy shoulders still pulled at the tires. He loosened his grip on the wheel and glanced backward.

The warden was still following. He had misjudged the man. The warden was a good driver and would not be easy to outrun.

He swung through the turn and splashed through some deep puddles. The bottom of the truck scraped the ground and water splashed high on both sides. Steam rose from under the hood.

He remembered that the wardens had radios in their trucks. If the warden radioed anyone ahead, Ken would be trapped. It was unlikely, but if it happened, there would be little he could do about it. He watched the road ahead more attentively.

Rounding a corner too fast, the truck rose and dropped as it hit some corduroy. The rear wheels bounced violently and started to break the truck into a fishtail. With a quick movement, he corrected, but too far. The truck swung violently in the opposite direction and he yanked the wheel again. This time the truck did not respond. He was sliding sideways at the mercy of momentum. He held on, waited for the truck to come to a stop, and hoped it was not in among the trees. He lurched abruptly, stopped and then looked out the side window to see the other truck bearing down on him.

Panic caused his hands to tingle and numbly, he threw the gearshift lever into reverse. The tires dug into the gravel as they hopped backward across the road. Steering in the opposite direction, he threw the transmission back into drive and punched his foot to the floor. The engine growled and the truck shook like an old washing machine, but he didn't move. "Shit!" He had backed up too far! He let go of the gas, the truck rolled back and then he punched it again. The wheels grabbed and the truck lurched forward, swinging down the road.

For a split second, he glanced in the rear-view and saw that the MNR truck was close, but he also saw that his truck had thrown a cloud of dust in the air. This might slow the warden, but not as much as he needed. He had underestimated him and he couldn't do this again. He leaned forward, gripped the wheel with both hands, and drove.

He approached a steep hill that was rough and rutted. Much of the gravel had been washed away and only rocks remained. As the truck climbed, the back wheels danced wildly, violently rocking the pickup box from side to side. Wheels ground against the wheel wells, springs stretched to their fullest, and items flew out of the pickup box and bounced onto the road. The truck felt as if it were coming apart, but then with a final bounce, it reached the top where there was smoother and flatter ground.

He had to decide where to stop - where to turn off. Some of these roads crisscrossed the park and led to towns and cities on the opposite side, but many were also dead-ends. Ken had walked them, but he had never driven on them - since he did not have an Indian Band Card and he was not a logger, he was not allowed to operate a motor vehicle in the park - and the roads looked different at high speeds.

He passed the road to Bear Lake and skidded around the sharp turn at the bottom of Wolf's Bay. The road twisted toward the defunct Camp One, but it was not familiar and he had to work hard to keep the high-speed truck under control. The sound of scraping metal filled the cab as branches ripped across the paint and into the metal.

He sped along a straight stretch, but decelerated at the end, looking in his rear-view. He saw nothing. Relieved, he exhaled loudly and then, just at his truck reached the curve, the grill of the MNR truck came into view far back on the straight. The warden wasn't giving up. He swore and he punched the accelerator.

With his knuckles white, he bounced past a few side roads, trying not to hit any trees. He reached a fork and swerved down the left branch, when he realised it was the wrong way. This was the road to the ranger camp. Dust swirled and wheels hopped and accelerated in reverse.

When he reached the beginning of the fork, he had an idea. Instead of spinning his tires down the correct road, he drove away slowly. He crept over a small hill and descended to a point where he could no longer see the road behind him. Driving on the left side of the road, where there was more grass and less dust, he gradually accelerated as he distanced himself from the fork.

It had been a difficult manoeuvre because every impulse was pushing him to drive recklessly, but he hoped the warden would see the dust on the left fork and follow that road thinking Ken was trapped at the ranger camp. The warden would reach the ranger camp and realise that he had taken the wrong route and then the chase would resume, but Ken would have some more space. There were no straight stretches of road for a while and he had no way of knowing if the trick had worked, but he decided to do something similar ahead.

Not too far past Camp One, the road crossed a bridge at the bottom of Kioshkokwi Lake and then branched in many directions. The main road went south toward the Nipissing River, but a large branch swung west toward Manitou Lake.

He slowed just before the branch to Manitou and then accelerated hard around the corner. His tires dug into the soft road and rooster tails of sand sprayed up behind the truck. He slowed the truck and then reversed gently, back to the main road. He turned and continued south. The two deep ruts were easily visible and anyone following would assume he was on his way to Manitou.

Two miles further, he found the dead-end road he wanted. It led to an area across the lake from the town and it was a perfect spot to hide his truck. Unfortunately, it would be a long walk back to the trestle.

Dr. John Mulhouse sat stoically in the studio chair and waited for the camera to click on. Even though it was late summer and unseasonably warm, he had worn a grey wool suit and his shirt was buttoned up to the neck beneath his blue and grey striped tie. The studio air-conditioning was on, but it could do little to combat the heat from the lights that shone from every angle.

The large red light on the camera winked on and he heard the announcer's voice. "Dr. Mulhouse, you said earlier that you agreed the provincial government had been involved in deception regarding the closure of the town of Kiosk. Are you saying that someone in the government was involved in arson?"

The question surprised him slightly, because he had never talked about the burning of the mill. "No, no, not arson - at least, I'm not aware of the government's involvement; I wasn't in Kiosk in 1973 when the mill burned - but the government definitely misrepresented itself to the people of the town before, and after, the fire."

"How did they do that, Dr. Mulhouse?"

Mulhouse looked at the camera as if it were a body of students. "People often confuse the terms, ecologist, environmentalist, conservationist, and preservationist. For example, they call someone an ecologist, when they mean, environmentalist. A conservationist is someone who wants to make use of our resources, but at the same time, conserve them for future use. A preservationist is someone who wants to preserve them in natural form and not use them. The conservationist is saving resources for human use; the preservationist is saving them from human use.

"The Provincial Government told the people of Kiosk that the park was to be left in a natural and unspoiled form so that it would be available for future generations. It was to be," he made imaginary quotation marks in the air with his fingers, "a wilderness park. The townspeople in Kiosk talked about multi-use and sustainable development, in keeping with conservationist thinking. So we had the provincial government basically promoting a preservationist park and the town people promoting a conservationist park."

"And how did the government deceive the people of the town?" asked the announcer.

"The provincial government implied it was promoting a preservationist park, but in truth it really was setting up a conservationist park. For the last twenty-five years, logging has continued, visitors are allowed to fish, the ministry has rented cabins to tourists, and natives have been allowed to hunt."

"But surely, natives cannot be denied the right to their traditional hunting areas."

"I'm not debating that, but the important point here is that if some hunt, others log, and others fish, there is no reason to deny people who were born in an area to live in that area. You cannot take away someone's home because you are going to keep a park in pristine condition, but then make exceptions for loggers, native groups and tourists."

"But what about the tourists? Wouldn't it be disheartening to canoe through the park and come upon a town with stores, churches and schools?"

"Yes, I suppose it would be and this was the concern of the government: Image. They wanted the image of a pristine park and the people of Kiosk damaged that image. Then it becomes a question of what is more important, the rights of people who were born in an area to protect their homes, or the rights of a government wishing to create an image.

"Ken Campbell sent a fax with the following paragraph written at the top, 'We live in a country where people are analogous to workforce; where who you are, is roughly the same as, what you do for a living. Home means nothing anymore; where you live, where your ancestors lived, this is somehow unimportant. The people of Kiosk were all victims of this type of thinking and their loss has been great.' I believe that, given the development of the park, the people of Kiosk should not have been denied their homes, their birthplaces, because of the desire for a Hollywood image of a natural park."

"So you believe that the residents of Kiosk were misled about the provincial government's intentions and were unjustly removed?"

"Yes. The provincial government deliberately deceived the residents because it only sees people as commodities. It knew that Algonquin Park would be logged, and hunted, yet it still forced the residents to leave, telling them that ecological multi-use could not be permitted. It was blatant deception and it goes to the heart of a serious problem in this country: A failure to acknowledge the basic rights of its citizens. And the really frightening part is that Madame Roussel, the Provincial Member of Parliament at the time, is now the Federal Minister of Indian and Northern Affairs. "

"Thank you for your time, Dr. Mulhouse."

"Thank you."

The red light on the camera extinguished and disappointment spread across Dr. Mulhouse's face. He felt he had been cut off just as he was getting to the core of the problem. He was ushered off the stage and a crew of technicians started to move things around for the next shoot. Mulhouse left the set and walked out the door.

       A group of reporters sat in the Indian and Northern Affairs Canada Office and listened to the Minister's response to allegations made by the recently elected National Chief of the Assembly of First Nations. It was routine posturing. The Chief had been stating for weeks that he was not in the federal camp and the INAC Minister was running a public relations campaign extolling the virtues of her department. The press conference was dull and uneventful and only lower-echelon reporters were in attendance. "Minister," said a female reporter holding up her hand. "Do you have any comment about the allegations that you were personally involved in the forced relocation of the people in the Northern Ontarian town of Kiosk?"

       There was a momentary shift in the room. No one spoke and the hum of electronic equipment became the dominant sound. Heads turned to the woman who had asked the question and then back to Roussel. Cameras clicked.

       Roussel was stunned. Her press advisor had warned her of the story - told her that her name had been mentioned in conjunction with the protest in Kiosk - but the term forced-relocation was harsh. "No one was forcibly relocated. Some people were on leased land and their leases expired. This is park land that was being preserved for the good of all the people of the province."

       "How do you respond to the allegation that the provincial government was duplicitous in its dealings with the people of the town and may have even been partially responsible for the mill fire that brought about the death of the town?"

       Roussel's jaw dropped, but she regained composure. She made a quick mental note to find the name of this reporter. She needed to be censored for her arrogance. "Your question does not even warrant comment." Her anger built and she was unable to let it go. "This is the federal Ministry of Indian and Northern Affairs. You'd better address your question to someone in the provincial government."

       "But weren't you the Provincial Member of Parliament, for

the Conservative Party, at the time of the mill fire?" The reporter placed special emphasis on the term, 'Conservative Party'. Roussel now belonged to the federal Liberal party. "The town was in your riding, and wouldn't you . . ."

She glared at the reporter and interrupted her question. "To even suggest that any government in Canada - Liberal or Conservative - would be involved in arson is libellous." Roussel's face darkened. Bob White touched her on the arm and then pointed at his watch. She understood the cue. "Now, if you'll excuse me, I'm expected at a meeting."

"Yes." continued the reporter, undaunted, "but as Minister of Indian and Northern Affairs, isn't it your responsibility to deal with fairness and equity for all the people of northern regions." Roussel stopped near the door and the reporter continued. "It has been suggested that aboriginals in the region receive preferential treatment, but people born in the area, are lied to and treated summarily."

Roussel spun. "I'm sure that few people think aboriginals are given any unwarranted special treatment." She forced herself to smile. Cameras clicked, electronic flashes exploded, and television lights illuminated the room. "Thank you all for your time. One of my aides will provide you with a release outlining the new Aboriginal Education Strategy." She turned to the reporter with the insolent questions. "I suggest you read it and get your facts straight." She walked out of the conference room.

Roussel stopped in the front office, out of breath, and waited for White. She didn't like this office, it was modern, utilitarian and not very private, but the House was not in session until October and she rarely visited her constituency office in the summer. White walked in followed by another aide and she threw the remaining information packages on a small credenza. "Jeesus Christ! Is everybody incompetent in this office?" No one looked up.

Roussel walked to her office door and turned to the young female aide at the reception desk. "Get Armand Gingras! Tell him to get over here. And get Denny in here now!" She walked in. "I'm going to have some words with that bitch!"

"What the hell was that all about?" White asked as he followed her.

Roussel ignored the question and told White to close the door.

By the time Armand arrived, Adrienne Denny was leaving. Armand nodded in greeting and noted Denny's appearance. She looked whipped, tail between her legs and all. It was obvious she wouldn't last much longer. She was making too many mistakes.

Armand had tried to apprise himself of the situation, but the information had been sketchy. He knew about the press coverage from Kiosk, his old hometown; he knew about the surprise questions at the Minister's press meeting in the hall; and he knew Roussel was angry. He had deliberately arrived late enough so that the brunt of her anger would have been spent on Denny.

As was his custom, he walked into her office unannounced. Roussel looked up over her reading glasses and then looked down. "Take a seat," she ordered.

Bob White was seated to the side and Armand took the seat across the desk. The inquisition-seat, he thought.

"It's bad enough," she said, still looking at some papers on her desk, "to be caught off guard by the press, but I really do not need to have my office linked to the Provincial Conservatives." She took off her glasses and rubbed the bridge of her nose. "God, the people I'm forced to work with . . ." She looked over at Armand. "Do you know what's going on there?"

"I heard about the protest and I caught the television interview with Campbell."

"You were born in the town, weren't you?" He nodded. "Were you aware of all this pent-up anger?"

"To be honest, not really. I was only twelve or thirteen when my parents left. I know there was a big labour strike and, later, some of the people tried to fight the termination of the land leases, but I was pretty young."

"So what do these people want?"

"It's not clear. I don't even know if it's a real protest. My feeling is that it is just one or two people making some noise and a bunch of other people coming to hear them. It seems to all revolve around this Kenneth Campbell. He went to the park, built a house and said he wants his land back. Because he was there, some of the other town residents showed up."

"But if other people showed up, it shows he has support." Bob White added.

"You know how these things go. It turns into something like a party. That's a pretty depressed area, there's not much to do. There's something going on at the provincial park and everyone goes to have a look. It's something to do. It's a pretty drab area unless you're a blackfly or a mosquito. I remember that much from my childhood."

"So why is the press making such a big deal out of it?"

"Two reasons: The press said Campbell made some negative comments about the Indians, and that created controversy; and Campbell made a fool of the police and that gives him a folk-hero appeal."

"And three!" Roussel added testily, "they neatly tied a Federal Minister to a fiasco in a Provincial park."

Armand looked at her without speaking.

"The CBC interviewed some doctor of something or other," White said, "and he tied the Minister directly to the Kiosk protest. If I know the CBC, they'll rebroadcast the interview a couple of times today."

Armand had not seen the interview in question and made a mental note to get a copy of it as soon as possible.

"If he's making anti-native statements," said White, "won't the native organizations take care of his public image?"

"Probably," Roussel said. "They'll slice him up faster than the leader of the Reform Party - sorry, the Alliance party - at a pow-wow."

White laughed. "It probably should have been the CRAP party."

"Umm, I don't think so." Armand said in response to Roussel's comment. "They would have already said something and they're staying out of it. I think they'll keep quiet. You see, he didn't really say anything anti-native."

"A minute ago, you said he did."

"Well, actually, Minister, I said that the press said he made some anti-native comments. I listened to the two interviews that

aired. What Campbell said was that the Natives were allowed to
make claims on their traditional homes, but the people of Northern
Ontario were not. He said that Natives were allowcd to hunt and
fish, using modern techniques, in the park, but the people who were
born in Kiosk were forced out of their homes. And he touched on
the fact that Natives had free access to the land that rightfully
belonged to the people of Kiosk. I don't think that any Indian group
wants to get into a discussion about Indians hunting and fishing,
off-season, with high-powered rifles and ATV's, in Ontario's
favourite park."

"They fish with high-powered rifles?" White said and then
laughed.

"You know what I mean."

Roussel didn't laugh. "Where is this Campbell fellow now?"

"He's still at large."

"But he's cut off from the press."

"The cops swept the area on Sunday morning, but Campbell
got pictures out to someone later in the day. Global had copies and
there are others on the wires. So a newspaper and a television crew
had access to him."

"And what are the OPP doing to apprehend this fellow?"

"I have some contacts and I'll try and find out, but my guess
is that they'll do nothing for a while."

"After they've been made to look like fools?"

"They can contain the area, keep a low profile and hope the
wholc thing blows over, or they can go in on-mass and attract every
reporter from Ottawa to Toronto."

"You're right, of course." Roussel looked at him closely.

Armand smiled with satisfaction. "You know, it's hard to
imagine that Kenny Campbell is doing this. He was such a quiet
boy when I knew him."

"You knew him?" Roussel sat forward on her chair.

"He's a little older than me, but yes, I remember him. He
was one of those outdoors types - quiet, always off in the bush, fishing, canoeing or camping. He certainly didn't seem like the type of
person who would taunt the police for the sake of media attention."

"You know these people. I want you to get up there and
look around."

Armand's eyes widened. "There's no point in me going up there. There's nothing I can do up in Kiosk." Armand had no desire ever to see the place again.

"This is very bad timing and I don't want this to spin out of control. This ties the Ministry of Northern Affairs to the Provincial Conservatives and that could seriously compromise our shot at the federal leadership. This has to be brought under control - quickly and quietly."

"But . . ."

"No buts about it! Get up there and see what it's going to take to get that man out of the park and this issue out of the press."

Armand knew when not to argue. "Yes, Minister, I'll leave presently."

Patrick lay looking at the motel room ceiling. The room, although new and modern, had a slight musty smell and even though it was a non-smoking environment, the taint of stale cigarettes lingered in the carpet and exuded from the walls and ceiling.

He watched the morning news, and decided to phone Eric, his sales manager. The conversation did not go well. Eric told him that if the other salesmen had to deliver the cars that he had sold, he would have to split the commissions. This was neither policy nor practice, but it was Eric's way of punishing Pat for not coming back when he was told. Pat could do nothing about it and he acquiesced.

Strangely, he was not as upset as he would have imagined. He didn't care about the commissions or Eric's feelings; he just wanted to get off the phone.

His thoughts continually returned to Suzette. He could picture her in his mind and the image was very pleasing, very soothing, but it also brought some discomfort. There was a feeling of profound isolation that burnt into him and brought images of his last lover - images that he could not escape.

He had lived with Wendy for many years and it always seemed that they would stay together, but in hindsight, he couldn't imagine how. Their relationship was more of a practical agreement than a coupling of two people deeply in love, and Wendy had been an ambitious woman with a constant eye on position and advantage. If Pat bought a new guitar, Wendy wanted to know what she was going to get. Nothing could be done unless Wendy got her share and everything was a negotiation.

She had pushed Pat to work toward sales manager and give up his band, but he had resisted, saying that he didn't want the additional responsibility. He didn't want to devote his life to the automotive industry and playing guitar in his small blues band was his only joy. She pushed and pushed until she got her way and he quit the band.

Eventually, when it appeared that he would never move up the food chain - that was Wendy's charming way of describing the climb through various levels of social status - she dumped him and moved in with the assistant sales manager in a large Ford dealership. Pat had been heart-broken at the time, but he was over her now. What remained was burning emptiness, a pointlessness that he tried to numb with alcohol and pills.

Suzette had been one of the few women, or girls, who had truly loved him, but the image of her brought back the image of Wendy; Wendy, pointing her finger and yelling; Wendy being contrite and condescending; Wendy offering sex as a payment, or a reward. He tried to focus on the image of Suzette. He tried to remember kissing her and feeling the genuine warmth and excitement of their desire.

When he had been with her yesterday, he had felt that same attraction, and a few times, he thought he saw the spark in her eyes, as well. Sometimes she had been flippant, distant, even cool, but then briefly, after the tingle of a touch, the warmth of a smile, the passion and surprise would be in her eyes. Had he been seeing what he wanted to see, or had she really felt something? He couldn't be sure.

He looked at his travel alarm. It was time to check out. He wasn't sure if he would stay in the north any longer, it would depend on today's meeting with Ken, but there was no need to remain in the hotel. Last night he had held his breath each time he heard footsteps in the hall, but no one ever knocked on his door tonight he would stay in Ken's cabin.

Suzette and her two co-workers were already eating when Ken arrived in the Country Style donut shop near the hotel. Feeling a little self-conscious about his weight, he ordered a soup and sand-wich, but he did not take any desert. With his lunch balanced on a little tray, he walked to Suzette's table and waited. Her hair was up in a loose bun, and her eyes seemed brilliant in the bright light of the shop.

"Have a seat," said Jaro, pointing to the one empty place at the moulded table, the spot across from Suzette.

Pat sat and nervously took his food off his tray. "Thanks."

"Morning Pat," said Suzette. Her voice sounded warm. "Did you have a good night?"

"Not too bad. You?"

"Lots of work. This story seems to be getting bigger than imagined."

"Yeah, you'd think no one cares what happens to a bunch of people from Northern Ontario."

Mike spoke. "The townspeople aren't the story; it's the way your friend made a fool of the police. That and the fact that Francine Roussel used to be the MPP."

Jaro looked at Pat. "Did you ever meet Roussel?"

Pat thought for a second. "I heard her name, but I doubt I ever met her. I don't know much about her other than what I've heard on the news."

"Didn't she ever come out to the town?" Mike asked.

Pat shrugged. "Maybe. But I don't remember. We were just kids." He looked at Suzette, but didn't meet her eyes. "You have to remember that we were only in our teens when we left the town. How many teenagers do you know that are interested in politics?"

Jaro looked over at Suzette as if he forgot that she had been a teenager in Kiosk as well. "Yeah, I guess not many."

"If Pat's uncle were still alive, he could have told us lots," Suzy added. "Pat's uncle was a real radical. He was always protest-ing and talking about the government."

Jaro looked at Suzy with raised eyebrows, as if to say, "So?"

Mike sipped his coffee and asked: "How hard is it to get to this spot where we're going to meet Campbell?"

Pat was taken aback. He hadn't really thought of taking all three to the train trestle. Of course, it was logical that the news reporter would take her camera crew, but it just hadn't crossed his mind. "It's quite a ways and I don't know if it's a good idea for all of us to go."

Now it was Jaro and Mike's turn to look shocked. "I thought this was all arranged." Suzy's expression showed that she did not have any knowledge of them not being welcome.

"Well, I said that it would be alright for Suzette to come, but if all of us go wandering up the rail line, we're bound to attract attention."

"Don't worry about that. We know how to be discrete."

Pat continued to protest. "It's just that . . ."

"Look!" Jaro said forcefully. "We stayed here another day, at our own expense, to do this shoot. I'm not going back empty-handed!"

Pat backed down immediately. "Okay, but we have to do it quietly. I don't want to give his position away."

"So where are we meeting him?"

"He's built another cabin in the park, but we decided it would be best to meet just outside. That way, we're less likely to be followed. Two miles out of town, the train tracks cross Bear Creek and there's a high trestle. The tracks are gone, but the trestle's still there and that's where we'll meet.

"So if we don't have to go into the park, why are you worried that we'll attract attention?"

"The trestle's on the other side of the Amable du Fond River. The only way to get there is to go to town and walk."

"Two miles!" Mike said. "Can we drive?"

Pat smiled and shook his head. "Don't think so."

They finished and walked out to the parking lot. The sun was high in the sky and the heat lifted off the black parking lot in waves. Pat looked at Suzette. "Would you like to come with me?" He steeled himself and was surprised when she agreed.

"We'll be right behind you," Mike said walking toward the Jeep.

The drive along Highway 17 was calm and pleasant. Suzy talked about her work and about the story. She distanced herself from the town when she talked, never referring to our feelings, but to the feelings of the townspeople - as if she hadn't been born and raised in Kiosk.

Pat was happy just to listen to her voice. Her French-Canadian accent had almost disappeared, but it was still evident with certain phrases. She didn't talk like a reporter; her voice had a soft lilt that was as sensual as it was pleasant.

As he drove, he was conscious of his belly. It was difficult to maintain a complimentary posture while driving a car and whenever he looked down at his belly, he reminded himself that he really needed to eat less and exercise more.

He occasionally took his eyes off the road and looked over at Suzette. A few strands of hair had fallen from the bun at the back of her head and now hung seductively. He could see them brushing against the soft downy hairs on her neck, the sunlight making them shine.

Her hand lay on top of her leg and he studied the long delicate fingers, the fine structure, the soft skin. He imagined her touch. He could almost feel her running her fingers over his face, across his forehead and into his hair. He closed his eyes for just a moment and the right wheels touched the gravel of the shoulder. Quickly, he opened his eyes and steered the car back on the road. "Sorry," he said quietly.

"That's okay," she said, looking as if she too had been wakened from a daydream.

Ken passed Wolf Lake. He intended to use the road until he was close to Bear Lake and then cross through the forest toward the trestle. The sound of an approaching vehicle caused him to walk into the trees. The wardens and police were too lazy to walk and they would announce their presence from a long distance with motor noise. He could easily avoid them.

He had photographed the warden driving back to Kiosk, apparently having given up the chase, and perhaps this was the same fellow coming back for another look. He found a spot in the trees and readied the camera. Pictures would put additional pressure on the authorities to take action, but they would also bring additional media attention to Kiosk.

As the truck passed, he saw that it was an old GMC 4x4. The rusty fenders banged against the supports and flopped like the wings on a bird. This certainly wasn't an MNR truck. After it passed, Ken walked back to the road, but he hadn't gone far when he heard the truck returning. It was going slower this time. He darted off to the other side and walked toward Wolf Lake.

The motor noise diminished and then quit, but it didn't sound as if the truck had passed. Ken listened . . . rustling leaves, twigs, branches. Someone was walking through the bush.

He scrabbled up a rocky outcropping and stood behind a large red pine. If someone was following him, he could run down the opposite side as they slowly climbed. An older man appeared at the side of the lake and Ken watched as he put his hands on his hips and surveyed the shore of the lake.

"Just what are you doing?" The man was not looking at him, but instead was turning right and left. He was rough looking, with a pockmarked complexion, long black hair and dirty jeans.

"Who are you?" Ken asked calmly as he stepped from behind the tree. The man looked up.

"None of your business."

Ken smiled. "But you know who I am?"

"I came here to tell you that I don't like what you said on TV."

"Oh? Well, I'm sorry to hear that."

"This is native land you're on and I want you to get out."

"If you talk to the MNR, they say it's their land."

"That's for now. Soon it's gonna be Indian Land. Now, you get out of here."

"For now, I have as much right as you to be here."

"You're a damned racist!"

Ken worked hard to suppress a smile. It was often the case that anyone opposing anything Native was a racist. He regretted mentioning the Natives in the one television interview, but he knew the damage was done as soon as the words had left his mouth. "I'm not a racist."

"Then why did you say that our people shouldn't have a claim to the land?"

"I never said that. I think that everyone has a right to belong to the land. I said that everyone believes that natives are connected to the land, so they should also believe that everyone is connected to the land." Ken glissaded down the rocks to the shore.

"Your people stole the land from my people."

"It has nothing to do with 'our people' and 'your people'; it's just about 'all people.' Everyone needs to be connected to the land, to their pasts."

"You took this land away from my fathers and mothers and now you just want to keep it."

Ken hated these arguments and it was the reason he avoided the entire Native issue. He again regretted his comments to that one camera crew. "You don't understand, I . . ."

"Just a dumb fucking Indian, eh?" The man jabbed himself in the chest and then started to advance on Ken. "You get out of here!" He tried to grab Ken's shirt, but Ken stepped out of the way and patted away his hand. This caused a streak of anger to cross the man's face. "This is my land, and you're getting out!" He jumped toward Ken again, and again Ken twisted and avoided contact.

The Indian's face blossomed in rage. He squinted and clenched his teeth as he came charging, arms flailing. He was determined to strike.

Ken danced to the side again, but then moved toward his attacker, and kicked him swiftly at the side of the knee. This destabilized the Indian who wobbled on his feet. Ken ducked under the blows, reached behind the man, grabbed his arm and spun him like a top into the air. With arms still flailing, the Indian splashed into the cold water. He got to his knees and then stood, water dripping from his hair, his shirt, his chin. He studied Ken for a moment, smiled and nodded. "You fight good, but you still leave. This is my lake."

"This is our lake," corrected Ken, "but I have no interest in staying here. My home was in Kiosk."

"You grew up in Kiosk, eh?"

"Yup. I did."

He reached out his hand and Ken grabbed it and helped him out of the lake. "My name's Pinneskum, Gary Pinneskum. I grew up here too."

Ken shook his hand. A distant memory flashed in his mind. "You know a man named Tabby?"

"Yeah, that was my dad."

"No kidding. I remember him. He lived not too far from here with Richard Rankin."

"He lived not too far from here with my whole family."

"Well, now I understand why you say it's your lake. Gee, I remember your dad. He was a neat guy." Ken scuffed at the ground. "Hey, how did you know where to find me anyway?"

"I saw you on the news and I know about your little camp." He pointed to the spot on the lake where Ken had his cache. "Then I found your tracks on the road. It wasn't too hard."

Ken felt slightly foolish. "Sorry about dumping you in the lake."

"Yeah, well, you were lucky that time. You won't be so lucky next time." Gary smiled again. "I'm glad the sun's shining. The water's cold." He shook his head and drops of water splashed on Ken. "What are you tryin' to prove out here, anyway? You think the government is going to let you live in Kiosk?"

"Your people have been fighting for land rights for years. I think it's time . . ." Ken paused for a moment, because he did not want to use the term 'my people'. Whom would the term 'my people' refer to? "The people of Kiosk should fight for their land rights."

"But that isn't gonna happen. What's gonna happen is that the government is gonna say there are no land rights and instead of giving them to your people, they're gonna take them away from mine."

"Why does it always have to be about your people?"

"Because we were here first."

Ken felt the joy of finding Tabby's son disappear. "This isn't a race, damn it! It doesn't matter who was here first! What does matter is that people were chased out of their homes and no one seems to notice."

"You really think that the government if going to give you your land back?"

"Well . . . I . . ."

"Exactly. They're not. So, all your little protest is going to do, is make people think about who should and should not be in a park. And they're gonna agree you shouldn't be here and they are gonna say that since you shouldn't be in here, the Natives shouldn't be in here either."

"Well . . ." Ken hesitated again. "Maybe they shouldn't. If this is supposed to be a place of no development, and no people are allowed to hunt and live here, then Natives shouldn't be allowed either. Why should there be one set of rules for one group of people and another set for a second?"

"Because your people . . ."

Ken angrily interrupted. "Ah, don't give me this again. I don't want to hear it. What happened here was wrong. The government abandoned hundreds of families; let them blow away like dust, just to satisfy the wants of some people who didn't live here. This country has become so complacent about family and land that this whole thing is being treated like a non-issue, but I intend to let people know what happened. And it's not just about an issue, it's about human beings." Ken narrowed his eyes and studied Gary for a moment. "If you want to stop me, you better be prepared for another dip in the lake."

Gary looked at him and shrugged. "It's not just me you're gonna fight."

Ken puzzled over this for a moment, but he knew he had to leave if he was going to make it to the trestle for the meeting. "I'm prepared," he said as he walked away.

Armand sighed deeply as he waited for the person on the other end of his cell-phone to stop talking. He had called in a favour at the Solicitor General's Office to pressure the OPP to bring a quick conclusion to Ken Campbell's protest. Officially, there was no link between the Federal Ministry of Indian and Northern Affairs and any provincial policing agencies, but there were always ambitious people somewhere looking for favours. It was just a matter of knowing who wanted what. The person on the phone had aspirations and they now wanted to share them with Armand. "Yes, yes," he said when there was a momentary lull in the conversation. "We'll get together sometime later and discuss this, but if you'll excuse me, the traffic is heavy and I don't want to stay on the cell too long."

He hung up the phone and tossed it onto the passenger seat

of his rental. He clicked on the radio and found the CBC hoping to hear the news. In a recent cabinet shuffle, Matthieu had been stripped of his post in the Ministry of Health. The Prime Minister hated opposition, but even so, this was a bizarre slap in the face for Matthieu. Some were rallying to support ex Minister of Health, but others, like rats on a sinking ship, were abandoning ship.

This would affect his strategy on the BAT tobacco probe, but it didn't matter because it might swing even more support to his boss. What was important now was to negate any negative publicity being created by these stupid people in Kiosk. Let Matthieu take the negative press; keep the positive for Roussel.

Pat came to a stop near the side road that led to his old house and waited for the Jeep. When it arrived, Suzy pushed the button to open her window and spoke to Jaro. "Go on to the parking lot. Pat and I are just going to have a look at the spot where his house used to be." Jaro started to protest, but she waved her hand impatiently. "We won't be long . . . It's just a personal thing."

Jaro pulled away and Pat turned onto the sandy path. He drove for a short distance and parked. As he climbed out of the car, he was careful to tuck his shirt into his pants and straighten his hair. He felt very self-conscious.

Suzette said she had been here already, but for some reason, he wanted to see it with her. It gave him a chance to be alone with her, outside of the car, and a chance to share a few memories, but there was something else. "Not much to see, is there?"

Suzette seemed reluctant to get out of the car and when she did, she walked over to a low growing shrub. She touched the serrated leaves. "No." She paused for a long while. "It's hard to imagine it's where we grew up."

They walked up the soft sandy path toward the school - or the spot where the school had stood - and Pat tried to picture it in his mind. It had not been an antiquated, one-room schoolhouse with a little bell and a box stove; it had been a large, modern, brick building, built in an 'H' with lots of windows. It didn't look much different from the schools that were still in use today, except it had been located in a beautiful town, near a lake, surrounded by majestic pines. There had been swings, playing fields, and even a base-ball diamond. The children who played here had breathed wonder-fully clean air, heard deep silence, saw brilliant stars, and found pleasure in the people around them. Now, it was only for tourists - birdwatchers. Now, only the backstop of the baseball diamond and worn path of the sliding hill remained.

"You remember sliding down there in the winter?" Suzy asked, following Pat's gaze.

"Sure do. We had some dandy snowball fights."

"Yeah, with the lake in the summer and the hills in the win-ter, it's amazing we got anything done at school."

Pat didn't reply. He was uncomfortable talking about school. He had not finished college and his grades had never been that good - not as good as they could have been. He looked at Suzette. Her dark hair, tied back, caught the sun and shone like pol-ished jade. One strand was blowing onto her cheek and he moved it back, tucking it behind her ear. His fingers brushed against the soft skin of her cheek and electricity moved through his fingertips, down through his hands and into his arms. It caused his breath to catch in his lungs.

He moved closer to her, looking at her, trying to grasp if she was feeling the same, but he couldn't be sure. A smile would appear for a second and then be replaced by indecision. Wariness? Perhaps anticipation? It was difficult to read, but it seemed that many things were going through her head - or more precisely, through her heart. She seemed confused, lost. He moved a little closer, hoping, pray-ing that she too would move closer, but at the moment, he was ready to draw her into his arms, she turned and moved away.

"Did I tell you that I saw Mr. Loeffler?" Suzy asked.

"Yes." Pat took two short breaths and turned in the opposite direction, afraid that his disappointment would show. "You remem-ber the night my uncle died? We were sliding and we went to his house soaking wet."

"I do. And you know what? Loeffler remembers too. He asked me if I ever read the book he gave me."

Pat didn't remember that Loeffler had given her a book, but he did remember that he had brought something with him that Suzy had given him many years ago. He also brought something for Ken.

"Strange how memory works," he commented.

"Yes." Suzy was silent for a moment and then added: "I feel like there's a memory watching me here."

"What?" Pat was nonplussed. "What do you mean?"

"I came here yesterday and I felt like I was being watched."

Pat looked around. He could see no one. "There's no one around now."

"Isn't there?" She turned and looked back toward where the majority of houses had stood. "I don't know."

Pat felt a shiver. The hairs on the back of his neck stood and the top of his head tingled. His feelings of romance disappeared. "It really bothers me to think this is going to be a new campground."

"What!"

"Didn't I tell you? That's how this whole thing started. A girl at the Ranger Station showed me the blueprint for a five-year-plan. They're going to put in a new campground here and another one over at the mill site. Then they're going to build and rent four replicas of the old Ranger Cabin."

"How come I haven't heard about this?"

Pat shrugged. "They're also going to build an office just over there," Pat pointed toward the main road, "for the MNR."

"All this after saying that buildings couldn't remain because this was a wilderness park!" Suzy started thinking about a story-line. 'Secret Five-Year MNR Plan Sparks Protest!' "We better get back. It's a long walk to the trestle."

Pat nodded and then led the way back to the car.

Armand drove onto the dusty road and was surprised by the lack of buildings. The town he had known as a child was gone, supplanted by open grassy fields, groups of shrubs, and trees. At the end of the road, he slowed to find a small group of police cruisers and vans and he pulled over to the shoulder.

The police had probably been on their way before he had made his phone call, but the extra push might help the situation reach a quicker resolve. He stepped out of his car and was confronted by a uniformed officer wearing standard soft body armour, but dressed in a grey rather than a blue uniform.

"This is area is closed to the public today, sir."

"It's okay, officer," he said. He fished in his pocket for a business card. "I'm with the Ministry of Northern Affairs and I just want to make sure that . . ."

The officer was distracted. He took the card, didn't look at it, and interrupted. "That's fine, but you'll have to move your car. We have a dog team operating here. If you wish, the Incident Commander is over at the MNR station. He can answer your questions."

Armand reluctantly climbed into his car, and drove through the dusty streets. The empty town had surprised him, but so did the crowd of people in the parking lot. It appeared that this tiny town was attracting more interest than he anticipated. He parked on the grass near the rail bed and locked his vehicle. As he walked toward the ranger station, he received greetings from people he did not remember - people he did not care to remember. He was the success story; they were the failures.

Suzy walked with Pat, Jaro and Mike along the old rail line. The slag grinded noisily underfoot and the smell of creosote hung heavily in the air. "Where we are right now," she said to Jaro and Mike, "is at the beginning of what used to be the mill." She motioned with her hand off to the left. "A spur line used to go into the kiln so they could pick up lumber, and everything from here to the lake was mill."

Jaro and Mike glanced at the open field and pine trees that stretched out toward the lake. They nodded. Jaro had given Mike the camera and was in a hurry.

"I used to come here to see my papa and it seemed so big. It's hard to imagine that it's all gone."

"Yeah, it must have been exciting," Jaro said sarcastically as he walked ahead with Mike.

"You remember the water tower?" Pat asked. Both Pat and Suzy stopped and looked up and to the left as if expecting to see the giant structure.

"Yeah. I wonder if it was as big as I remember it. It seemed huge, but we were a lot smaller then. Everything seemed bigger. I remember it stretching way into the sky. I was never able to climb to the top."

"No. It was big. It must have been six or seven-stories tall. Remember we used to dare other kids to climb it? We'd put together whatever change we had and then say we'd give the money to whoever climbed it."

"I remember that idiot . . . umm . . . Stefan . . . who climbed up over the walkway at the bottom of the tank and got right up onto the rounded top. You remember he was afraid to come down and some of the men had to go up with ropes?"

Pat laughed. "Yeah, but I think if I'd climbed up there, they would've needed a helicopter to get me down."

"I'll bet his dad gave him a beating." She laughed, but the laugh was shallow and short. A memory of her father and his quick hand flashed through her mind. After they had moved to Quebec, her father's temper had been short and he was quick to leave the marks of his fingers on her face.

Pat turned and looked at her. "There's something I want to show you," he said, digging in his pocket. He took out a small, black, oil-filled compass and held it out like a prize. "Do you remember this?"

She looked at the object for a moment and it suddenly came to her. The recognition was so powerful that it prevented her from touching the object. "Is that the one I . . ."

He nodded and smiled. "That's it."

Aside from Michelle, no one had ever cherished anything that she had given and the realisation that Patrick had kept this all these years, was stunning. She wanted to fly into his arms and hug him, but she was also cautious, wary. A tear grew in the corner of her eye, she could feel it swelling, pushing at her eyelid, but she fought it back. She turned toward Jaro and Mike, mustered control, wiped her face casually, and then turned back. In a controlled tone, she said: "You've kept that for all these years. Imagine that."

She could see the look of disappointment spread across his face. He dropped his hand and then returned the object to his pocket. She silently admonished herself for her reaction and willed herself to tell him how much the sentiment touched her, but the words would not leave her mouth. She was through with relationships and she was unwilling to show warmth.

Mike and Jaro were now some distance ahead and Pat started to walk. "We should get going."

She stood still for a moment and had to hurry to catch up. "You know Pat, a lot has happened since we knew each other as teenagers." As soon as the words left her mouth, she regretted them. This wasn't what she wanted to say.

"Yeah."

She walked quietly. Emotions surged through her like oil, making her movements sluggish and heavy, making her knees weak with the effort of walking. With each step, she fought to suppress the feelings that threatened to bring her to the ground. She tried to focus her thoughts on her job, on the tasks that she had to accomplish.

Off in the distance, Jaro and Mike where almost at the bridge, but a uniformed figure was hurrying to reach them. It was an OPP officer and although she couldn't hear the words well enough to understand what was being said, she could tell that the officer was going to prevent them from crossing the bridge. Jaro was showing his press credentials, but the officer was shaking his head. Suzy started to walk quickly, but Pat resisted. She stopped and turned to him. "Come on; let's see what's going on."

"No, you go on ahead. I'll wait here for the moment."

She wanted to drag him along, but she could sense his resistance. She walked away.

"We've got a dog working the area and we can't let you in," the young officer said. Rather than the traditional blue of the OPP, he was wearing a grey uniform.

"We're all the way from Barrie," whined Mike.

"That's too bad, but I can't help that, and I'll tell you this: That dog's name is Diablo, and he lives up to his name. You don't want to get in his path."

"When can we go in and do some filming?" Jaro asked.

"I wouldn't count on today. Depends on how soon they find the subject, but these searches usually take a long time."

"Can we film the dog?" Suzy asked.

"You'll have to speak to the incident commander. And you better do it quickly, because the handler is getting ready to leave."

"What happens if you find this guy?" Jaro asked.

"He'll be arrested and taken into custody."

"What if someone had an idea where he was? Could we arrange a special interview?"

The officer squinted as he studied Jaro. "You watch too much American television. If someone withholds information about the whereabouts of a fugitive, they would be charged."

"We heard that he was a few miles down the train line at an old trestle. That's where we were heading. We'd like to cover the arrest."

Suzy's jaw dropped. What had Jaro done?

"Talk to the Incident Commander. He's either back at the other bridge, or back at the ranger station."

"I'll do that." Jaro started walking through the brushy field that would lead to the other bridge. Mike followed closely.

"Thank you officer, I'll . . ." Suzy was interrupted by the officer sharply raising his hand. He spoke into a microphone connected to a two-way radio and relayed the information that he had just received. Suzy waved goodbye and turned toward Pat, whom she now saw had walked further away. What could she say to Pat?

"What was that all about?" he asked as she approached.

"They won't let us past. They've brought in a dog team and they're going to use it to search the woods for Kenny. They don't want any other people in the area."

Pat looked at her in surprise. "Damn! I'll bet Ken never thought of that. They know he's in the area because of the photographs he took of the police. I better go and warn him!"

Suzy put her hand on Pat's forearm. "You better not. They say that dog is dangerous. Anyway, they won't let you pass."

"I'll drive up the highway. I should have lots of time; they don't know which way to look. It'll be okay."

He smiled at her, appreciating her concern and Suzy felt very guilty. How could she tell him that Jaro gave away Ken's position? "I don't think . . ."

His smile broadened, but he turned on his heals. "Thanks, but I've got to go," he said as he quickly rushed back toward the ranger station and his car.

Suzy watched him go, knowing that she should call out to

him, but the sounds refused to leave her throat. He was a grown man; he could take care of himself. She turned and followed Jaro and Mike. If she didn't do the stand-up, Jaro would, and she couldn't let that happen.

Pat was perspiring by the time he reached his car. He unlocked the door, swung inside, and started the engine. The air-conditioner quickly replaced the muggy outside air. A group of vehicles blocked the road behind him and he leaned on his horn. Heads turned as he backed out of his parking space and spun his tires in the loose gravel.

Many years ago, there had been a small forest fire north of Kiosk and afterwards, blueberry bushes had grown in the ashes. As a child, he and his mom, singing Irish folk songs, had picked many baskets of berries among the blackened stumps. He remembered that in the distance, he had often seen the train trestle. It crossed Bear Creek on the other side of the Amable Du Fond River, and although it could not be reached without swimming the river, he thought that he could call loud enough so that someone on the bridge would hear.

The day was clear and warm and visibility was good, which would help him find the best place to turn, but it would also make it easier for the police to find Kenny. He had to hurry. Ken would probably not be watching for people on foot.

The road to the blueberry patch dropped down a steep decline into the open field of low-growing shrubs. It was no more than two tire tracks, rutted and rocky, and Pat had to drive carefully so that he would not hang up the undercarriage. It was murderously slow, but faster than he could manage on foot. Another few minutes would put him on the bank of the Amable du Fond.

Ken sat on the trestle dangling his feet in the air. Below him, Bear Creek flowed over rocks and through some reedy, marshy patches before it reached the Amable du Fond a few hundred yards downstream. The trees around the creek were not as tall as the trestle and Ken could see their tops. He found it interesting to see trees from this angle. They looked very small and fragile.

The soft breeze carried the scent of berries and cedar, of dried vegetation and cinder. The air was still and with the exception of the odd insect and bird, it was quiet. He lay back, looked up at the few white clouds that drifted lazily toward the southeast, and drank in the peacefulness.

He closed his eyes and felt his body drift like the clouds overhead. A buzzing fly circled, lost in the late summer's warmth, and a distant blue jay called, squawking and drawing attention to some important event. A light breeze crossed his bare skin and gently moved the hairs on his forearms. The jay continued to squawk off in the distance and Ken tried to focus on it - envision it. He suddenly sat up. The call was a warning; the bird was disturbed.

He focussed all of his attention on the rail line leading toward town. He could not see very far because the line curved to the right, but at the edge of his hearing, there was something, a scratching sound, constant, quick - the crunching of cinder under many hard boots. It was distant, but approaching.

Had Patrick brought people with him? He started to walk up the line, but then realised that he would be in plain view of whoever was approaching. Scrabbling down to the side of the cinder path, he crept forward, staying low, constantly looking ahead. Far into the curve, he saw the uniformed figures. One of them was holding a dog that was not barking, but straining to get up the road.

'Dogs! Shit!' He hadn't considered that. It angered him. This was no longer a game on equal footing; they were hunting him like an animal. He bobbed his head up again and saw them moving toward him. Turning, he dropped lower into the shrubs, away from the rail bed, and began to run back toward the trestle. He could easily outmanoeuvre the police in the bush, but could he outrun a dog? It was unlikely.

He was certain that a dog would have trouble tracking through water, but Bear Creek was short, less than a mile in length, and he didn't have a canoe on Bear Lake. Once he reached the lake, what would he do? He could go in the opposite direction, toward the Amable du Fond, and swim the river, but then he would be on the highway and the only place he could go to would be his cabin. The dogs would easily track him there and he would lose his most important cache. He would definitely not give away the position of his cabin.

When he was around the corner, he climbed back up on the rail bed and ran. He needed speed and distance, but he needed control. His minded started to churn as his feet danced over the wooden superstructure. He stopped in the middle of the high bridge, wiped his forehead, and rubbed his wet hands on the wooden ties, and the metal tracks. Then he backtracked. From a point about eight feet above the ground, he dropped and scrabbled down the steep incline to the creek. Hopefully the dog would get confused by the scent trail that stopped in the middle of the trestle. He curved to the east, as if he were going to run down the creek toward the Amable du Fond, and then entered the creek and turned west.

Churning his feet through the muddy bottom, he stuck to the middle of the stream. The water in places was up to his waist, making movement difficult, but he was worried about leaving any visible clues. He decided that, when he reached the lake, he would swim for a short distance and then put to shore in the least likely direction.

He reached a bridge that allowed a small bush road to cross the creek, and was trying to decide how to proceed when he heard the excited voices back at the trestle. The cops had reached it and were shouting. The dog still wasn't barking.

He looked back at the bridge. He didn't want to walk out of the water, but he had no choice, the bridge was very low and he couldn't get underneath. Dripping and feeling the heaviness of his clothes, he took four quick, but wet, steps across the road and jumped back into the river on the other side. His heart was beating so quickly in his chest that he felt dizzy. Would the dog scent him here? He had no way of knowing and all he could do was press on as quickly as possible.

Provincial Constable Bob McBride trotted along the rail bed behind the dog handler wishing he were somewhere else. He was burning hot and his soft body armour bounced murderously on his shoulders.

The dog, Diablo, definitely had a scent. He was straining at his chain, trying to pull away from the handler, but the handler held on tight. In the past, they let the dogs go, but a few years ago, in Gowganda, a small mining area to the north, two criminals had shot the pursuing dogs and almost escaped. Now, dogs and handlers stuck together.

McBride suffered from acrophobia, a fear he tried to keep to himself, and when he saw the trestle looming out in the distance, he felt his heart stop. Had the suspect run across the trestle? God, he hoped not.

Without hesitation, the dog ran straight out onto the high structure pulling the handler behind. McBride slowed almost to a stop, trying to muster the courage to walk out onto the open trestle.

The dog was half way across when it stopped. It turned right and left as McBride studied the steep incline. Surely the suspect couldn't have dropped from where the dog had stopped. It was at least a thirty-foot fall.

He saw one of the other officers looking over the side. Had the suspect committed suicide? His curiosity pulled him toward the trestle, but his fear wouldn't allow him to step onto the wooden ties. Not knowing what to do, he looked around again. Off to the right, he spotted movement.

It was a person and he or she was shouting. He couldn't make out the words - the running water and the footsteps of the other officers muffled the sound - and he put his hands to his ears to focus on the voice. He heard the words, "police" and "dogs". Someone was obviously talking to the suspect.

He called to the team and pointed to the figure in the distance. They couldn't see it, but it was the clue they had been waiting for. They ran back toward him as he keyed his radio and relayed the information back to the IC and then the entire team charged down the steep bank toward the creek. The dog seemed confused, but the team ran along the edge of the creek until they came to the much wider Amable du Fond.

An autumn wind blew the leaves across the empty rink, as Suzette sat waiting for Pat. She let a small handful of sand sift through her fingers and onto her right canvas shoe. The pile covered her toes and was forming a mound on each side. Pat was at Kenny's house and she could have met him there, but she wanted to see him privately. He said he would be here at four o'clock. He was late.

She rested her chin on her knee and looked down at the train tracks. A passenger train was slowly clicking toward North Bay. There were lots of people in the cars and she wondered if some might be leaving the town for the last time. The town was starting to empty.

Her parents were talking about moving. Her dad was collecting UIC (unemployment insurance), again, but soon that would run out and the family needed money. It had been more than two years since the mill fire and it looked like the town was doomed. The government would not allow the people to buy their homes and there was no employment in the town.

A new mill had been built in Rutherglen, but it was not as big as the Kiosk operation and it could not employ all of the workers. Some of the workers had taken jobs in Mattawa, others in Temiscaming and North Bay, but these places were too far away. Finding a job meant moving. Her papa was even talking about returning to Pointe Claire in Quebec. She had to convince him to stay, but she did not know how.

The worst thing was the lack of control. She could do nothing but give in to the wishes of her parents. Whenever she tried to talk about her feelings, her mother would get upset and go into one of her rages, while her father walked around silently with his hands in his pockets.

Some of the men had started to cut firewood, which they hoped they could sell in North Bay and Mattawa, and even though the work was hard and the money poor, they were doing something. Her father did nothing. He seemed to be sinking into himself. He was losing weight, and he had stopped washing and shaving. He smoked cigarette after cigarette and lived in a blue haze muttering 'maudit' time and time again.

Pat's parents, on the other hand, were more definite. They had already told Pat that they were moving, and of all places, to Toronto. It might as well have been another planet. Toronto was a very long way away. How would she ever see him?

This thought filled her with an empty dry pressure. It felt as if the autumn air was suddenly too thin and she was slowly suffocating. She needed to talk to Pat about it. She had to talk to him.

Pat had stopped treating her just like a friend and had started to see her as a girlfriend. They had held hands, gone for walks, and slowly learned to kiss. The best thing was that they had also remained friends. They could tell each other everything.

But it seemed to be coming to an end. For two years the town had remained optimistic, thinking they could win a legal battle with the government, but time and money were running out. Now, most people were talking about the rotten deal and the sneaky government as if it was all over.

Her parents were always either sad or angry. Tempers flashed quickly; unwarranted beatings were followed by tears. She had drawn closer to Pat as a way of dealing with the bitterness, the isolation.

Pat was going through the same thing. His parents were always angry and although Pat never complained, his eyes were red from time to time. She and Pat had accelerated their closeness with a kind of desperation. They talked to each other about what was going on and Pat had grandiose plans for the town. He said they should turn it into a tourist area and open up hunting and fishing camps all over the place - this way the tourists would be happy - but no one listened; everyone was moving away. The thought of losing all they had, caused her to cling more strongly to Patrick, but cling as she would, the forces that were destined to tear them apart seemed stronger.

She didn't know what she could do about the future, what she could control, but maybe Pat would help. Maybe he could think of a way to change the future. She could not allow fate to drive her and Pat and Kenny apart without a fight.

But why was he late? Surely, he knew she was waiting. The leaves of the hazel and alder rustled and the scent of sweet berries wafted across the dry grass. She considered wandering among the thorns off to the left, but did not feel like standing. She was not that hungry and she didn't really care to eat.

The train accelerated, moving further away and the clicking of the wheels became more rapid and quiet. The sound merged into the rustling leaves and slowly became indiscernible. An eerie silence remained. The breeze shifted and the leaves became still. Only the moaning of the wind through the small pines remained. Suzette took in two short breaths and felt her throat tighten. There had to be a way out of this.

"I don't know who's gonna go next," Kenny said. "But it doesn't much matter. It seems like everybody's pulling out." Kenny's inexpensive record player, which looked like a fat brief-case, was playing Billy Preston. The record was badly worn and the song was punctuated with the pop and crack of scratches in the vinyl.

Pat could tell Ken was upset and he figured it had something to do with him. He looked up at the fishing poster on the wall. "Yeah, the whole thing is pretty strange, huh?"

"Why couldn't they have just rebuilt the mill here?" Kenny whacked a rubber ball into his baseball glove. "They could have kept all the people."

"My dad says that the government sent someone in here to burn it down so they could get rid of everyone."

"I know. Your uncle said it too - before he died."

Pat knew Ken was angry, but he didn't like to talk about his uncle. He missed him. "Yeah, he didn't like what was goin' on."

"People have been talkin' about this stuff for years now and nothin' ever happens."

"But everyone knows the government was responsible for the mill fire."

"So, I don't get it," Ken said banging his hand down. "If everybody knows, how come they don't get arrested or something?"

"Are you nuts? It's the government! The cops can't do nothin'. Anyway, they probably don't even know . . . or care."

"Oh, they know. The water tank's empty, the power's turned off for the water pumps, everyone's sent home early, a line of box-cars is set on the tracks to stop the fire from spreading, and then the fire starts? How much more do they need to know?"

"Well, there's nothing we can do about it."

Kenny shrugged. "What I don't understand is why the men at the mill didn't do something. They could have built another mill . . . just like when they needed to fix the weir." Kenny dropped his glove on a chair.

"But the mill didn't want to. Some say it happened before in Fossmill - and in that place in Quebec. They wanted to burn the place down."

Kenny suddenly lost his temper and kicked his chair. "It's all bullshit, Patty! It's all bullshit!"

Pat looked at Ken with raised eyebrows. Kenny very rarely swore, but for the last weeks, he had been really tense. Ever since the lawyer had lost the case with the government, everyone had become more vocal. The whole town was angry.

Kenny opened the box on his dresser, took out the little stone crystal, and twirled it in his fingers. "I don't know where my folks want to go, but I heard 'em talk about Sudbury."

Pat grimaced. "Damn, Kenny, I hope not. That's an awful place. You'd hate it there. They've got big mines and no trees."

"Yeah, but what can I do? I'm not old enough to go and get my own place. I guess I gotta go. Anyway, what're you talking about? Sudbury wouldn't be as bad as Toronto."

Pat didn't respond. He knew Ken was upset about him leaving and this was certainly not a race to see who got to the worst city. "Yeah, you're right; maybe Sudbury might not be so bad. Hey," he said, changing the subject, "isn't that the crystal you said was magic?"

Kenny looked down at his fingers. "Yup."

"You still got it, eh?"

"Yup. Didn't do much good protecting the town."

"It's gonna take a lot more than a magic crystal to save this town."

"Yeah. I guess. So, when are you leavin' again?"

Pat was silent for a moment. "On the weekend."

"Man."

"Yeah, I know what you mean."

"Well, whatever happens, we're gonna stay friends, right?"

"Yeah, sure."

"It's gonna be strange when you're gone. I'm gonna miss ya."

Pat sat up and looked at the floor. "Me too, but I'll see ya sometimes. It's only Toronto. Maybe I can come up to Sudbury in the summer to see the mines or something." Pat suddenly felt very awkward.

"Yeah, my folks would let you stay . . . all summer, if you wanted."

Pat didn't answer and looked around the room. He knew that everything was coming to an end and there was little likelihood that he would ever go to Sudbury. It was time to leave and he didn't quite know how to say goodbye. He felt his throat tightening. He glanced at the white metal clock on the dresser. It was ticking loudly. "Is that thing right?" Kenny nodded. It was a quarter to five. He jumped up. "I gotta go."

Suzette walked away from the recreation centre, craning her neck, but could not yet see Pat. She looked at her watch. Only a few minutes had passed since the last time she looked. Her shoulders tightened and her neck felt stiff. She started to shake. These feelings were almost unbearable. A tear burned down her cheek and she wanted to cry, but she held it back.

Something made her turn and as she did, she saw Pat coming up the rise. He was hurrying, so she knew that he knew he was late. She felt relief, but a flash of anger came to the surface. "You're late!"

"Sorry," Pat said softly.

Suzette's anger melted immediately and she stood facing him, awkwardly, not quite knowing how to act. "That's okay. I'm just glad you made it." She leaned forward and hugged him. At first, there was a little reluctance, but it eased and Pat felt looser in her arms.

In the last twelve months, she and Pat had grown very close, but Pat was still self-conscious about other people and he was probably aware of the rec. centre not too far away. Suzette let him go, stepped back and took his hand. She led him up the hill, past the building, and to a small clearing facing the tracks. Here, they were shielded from view.

"Sorry, I'm late," Pat said again, "but I got tied up at Kenny's house. I ran here as fast as I could."

Suzette blinked a few times and smiled a very small smile. It was the sensitive expression of someone who felt things deeply, but was not generally expressive. She put her finger to Pat's lips, looked at the confusion in his eyes, and then leaned forward and kissed him. At first, it was hesitant, but in seconds, she felt his arms encircle her and his body close to hers. She could feel his chest pressing against her breasts and then the rest of his body moulding into hers. It was a very passionate embrace and her first urge was to push him away - it would be what her mother had taught her to do - but she held on.

Pat started to ease his grasp and she could tell that the kiss was coming to an end, but she did not want it to. She wanted to hold on; she was afraid to let go. Letting go, was the same as letting him go to Toronto. With great bravado, she opened her lips and let her tongue touch his. She felt the softness of him. She could feel the surprise and excitement grow in Pat and suddenly he held her tighter and responded. He pulled her closer. One of his hands slipped up her back and his fingers tangled in her hair.

The kiss, the embrace, felt too wonderful. She had never kissed a boy like this in her life. She could feel the heat between them, the desire. And it was not just a physical desire; there was a connection, a link. No one else was listening to her, communicating with her, but somehow there was a bond forming between her and Pat. She had felt it so many times now. She could talk to him, and he to her. And when they touched, there was a spark, a surge of electricity that passed between them. How could he go away now?

The thought of him leaving killed all the passion in the kiss and she stopped suddenly and pushed Pat back. "You can't go away." Her voice was close to cracking and her eyes were red. "You just can't." All of the feelings, which she had been trying to restrain earlier, flooded to the surface, and with a few short breaths, the tears began to flow down her cheeks.

"Suzette . . . I. . . ." Pat reached forward and touched her on the face, but she pushed back violently and turned away.

"No. I don't want. . . ."

Pat slipped his hands in his pockets and stood looking at the ground. He hesitated, leaned forward, leaned back and then waited silently.

"You can't go, Pat. You can't."

"I . . . I don't want to, but . . ."

Suzette turned back and looked at him as she wiped her cheek with her sleeve. She wanted him to hold her, to react differently. He was standing with his hands in his pockets. Damn, why didn't he hold her? This turmoil, this torture was too much. She was angry, sad, hot, lonely, and desperate, all at the same time. The idea of everyone leaving the town, of losing everyone, was too much to bear. She sniffled and then, very softly, said, "I love you."

Pat's hands left his pockets and he reached out to her, but it did not seem right. She stepped back. There was panic in his eyes, he was trying to reach out to her, but there was something wrong. What was it? She could see the tears forming in his eyes too, but something was still not right - and it would never be right. He tried to find words, but nothing would come to his lips - nothing sounded right. It was as if he were speaking in a foreign language. Suzette's breaths became larger and she stepped back again. Everything was wrong and it would never be right. She could not breathe; the air seemed rare; there was not enough oxygen. She had to flee. "I have to go," she said in a whisper and then turned and ran off toward the bridge and toward her home.

"Suzette, wait!" She heard Pat's voice call from behind, but he was not following. Her flight was alone and she did not turn her head as she continued down the road, arms flailing.

On Saturday morning, the car was packed and the house empty. It was happening. Although Pat was somewhat excited about moving to the city, he deeply regretted leaving his friends. He had talked to his parents about moving somewhere closer, but his mom had brothers in Toronto and they would give them a place to stay until the family got on its feet again.

Pat's mother and father were saying goodbye to the neighbours. Kenny stood with him in the driveway pounding a hard ball into an old baseball glove.

"I guess you won't be playing any baseball around here for a while," he said. "Not enough kids left for two teams."

"I don't care about the crummy team . . . never any good." Kenny looked down at the ground as he spoke. "So what're you gonna do in Toronto anyway?"

"I don't know." Pat shrugged. "They got baseball there, I suppose."

"Yeah, but playing in the street can't be as much fun." Kenny laughed.

"Well, my uncle says there's no blackflies."

"That's something, I guess."

Patrick looked down at the ground. His suddenly did not feel so excited about going to the city, but he wanted to make it sound better. "There's supposed to be parks, too. Uncle Frank says that they got this big park near the house and there's lotsa trees."

"I was thinking about that. You were never too good in the bush. Always thought you might get lost or something." Holding the baseball in his glove, he reached into his pocket, pulled out the crystal rock, and handed it to Pat. "I want you to take this . . . for good luck."

Patrick shrugged and took the crystal. "This is the one you said was magic, eh? The one you said protected you from the bear?"

"Yup."

"Don't you think you need it more than me? You're gonna go to Sudbury and they got bears around there."

"Not as much as here. I think that you got more things to worry about in Toronto than I do in Sudbury."

Patrick looked at the crystal and turned it in his fingers. It was milky at one end, but clear like glass at the other. Maybe it was magic. "You mean it?"

"Yup."

"Thanks. That means a lot to me." He slipped it in his pocket and then folded his arms.

Both boys were silent for a while. The adults were moving around them in an animated and agitated way. Pat's mom seemed very emotional. Patrick looked toward Suzette's house. He thought he saw something, but it was just a shadow. He looked away.

Kenny had followed his glance. "You never got a chance to say goodbye to Suzette?"

"Nah, she hasn't come out of the house for the last two days. I wanted to see her, but her mom got mad at me when I went to the house."

"She's a crazy lady, that's for sure."

Patrick chuckled as he thought of his last encounter with her. Her hair had been a mess, a cigarette hung off her lip like it had been glued in place and she spoke half in English and half in French. "Yeah, I wouldn't want to mess with her, that's for sure."

Kenny shook his head. "I'll talk to Suzette for you."

This idea troubled Patrick but he nodded. "Sure."

"They're just uptight about the move."

"Yeah."

"My folks say we'll be moving too, real soon."

"Sudbury," Patrick said, shaking his head.

Kenny nodded. "I'll write to you as soon as I know the address."

A gust of wind blew some of the sand up from the road and Kenny shielded his eyes. Pat's mom got into the front seat of the car and pulled the door closed. Two women continued to talk to her through the open window.

"Come on Pat," said his father. "Time to go."

Groups of people gathered around the car were all talking at once. Pat put his hand on the door handle and felt an incredible coldness in his chest. He had to say goodbye and climb into the back with his older brother, Evan, but he didn't want to leave.

"Come on squirt, let's move it," his brother added. Evan had kissed his girlfriend earlier and he was alone at the car.

Pat looked at Kenny and was unsure of what to say. Suddenly, Kenny took his hand and shook it like an adult. The handshake was awkward, but it was the best he could do. He returned the shake, but the rhythm was wrong. His hand went up as Kenny's went down.

Kenny let go. "Good Luck, Pat." Kenny's voice cracked slightly.

"Thanks. Good luck to you." Pat jumped into the back seat and looked at this dad. He was talking to someone through the open window and the car was not going to leave for a few moments. Patrick stretched out and pulled an envelope from his front pocket. He held it out to Kenny. "Can you give this to Suzette for me? It's just my address."

Kenny nodded.

Pat looked down at the compass that hung around his neck - the compass that Suzette had given him.

"See ya," said Kenny.

"Yeah, see ya." Kenny turned and started to walk away, his head down.

Patrick's dad finished his conversation, shook hands with a man outside the car, and put the transmission in gear with a grind. "Is everyone set?" he asked, but before anyone could answer, the car pulled away.

Suzette stood in the shadows next to her house. She saw the car on the road in front of Pat's house and she could see Pat getting into the back seat. He didn't look happy, but he didn't look that sad either. He was leaving and they hadn't even said goodbye. How could this happen? This was all wrong. Her mom had been angry with her for the way she was behaving and her brother just laughed at her calling her a brat. No one seemed to care about what she was feeling.

Kenny was standing beside the car saying goodbye, like she should be doing. With closed fists, she beat against her thighs. She felt tears run down her cheeks. The car began to move south, toward the lake, and she felt as if her heart were being ripped from her chest. "No, no!"

In a sudden burst, she took off after the car. It was only a half of a block away, but between her and the car was the congregation of people who had been saying goodbye. As she approached, a few faces turned and she pounded to a stop.

The car was turning right at the fire hydrant, and it would turn right again and then start north to the highway. She turned and ran the other way. She could intercept it as it went up the road, if she cut through a few backyards. She leapt over a picket fence and tore through the Bellehumeur's yard, running over the garden and flailing through the wispy asparagus plants. The land dipped and she misjudged. The ground was not where she expected it to be. She fell hard, landing awkwardly. Her right arm was tucked under her stomach and she had the wind knocked out of her.

Part of her wanted to jump back to her feet, but part of her wanted to stay where she was. Would someone come to help? Please! she cried to herself. Tears filled her eyes, blurring her vision as she gasped for breath. It was all so stupid, the way she had acted, the way things were going. She had to change things, to make them better.

From the road, she could hear the sound of crushed stone under the tires of a car and she pulled herself to her feet. She had to get to the road.

A thick hedge of lilacs stood in her way and she ran to the left looking for a break. She could see the car, just on the other side, and she knew it would be gone in seconds. This could not be happening. How could she let Pat go without even saying goodbye? Why had she been so stubborn? So foolish?

Even though she had run after the car, even though other people had seen her run, even with this last act of desperation, she was still going to miss him. Like one of the children standing on the train bridge and leaping into the water, she dove through the tangle of the hedge. The course, woody stems grabbed at her and she struggled like a swimmer swimming through the weeds. A sharp pain tore at her ankle, causing her to cry out, and she twisted angrily, trying to force her way through. Finally, she fell to the ground next to the road.

"Pat!" she called, her voice a mixture of desperation, sadness and resignation. The car growled towards the highway, its speed never altering. She had been too late. Had they seen her and ignored her, or had they not seen her at all? She could see nothing in the back window but luggage and bags. She couldn't even see Pat's head. He was gone.

The air left her lungs and she felt numbness begin to travel up her arms. She couldn't believe it had ended like this. Surely, she should have reached him at the last second; surely, they should have hugged each other and promised to write. Her face flushed brightly as she stood and she clenched her fists tightly at her side. "I hate you!" she cried, "I hate you!"

Lifting her hand to her warm cheek, she touched the blood that was there. Mr. Giroux was on the other side of the road, studying her curiously. It was too much. She had to get away. The feelings were overwhelming. She wanted to scream at Mr. Giroux. Why was he staring? Was he so oblivious to her feelings? She shrieked, turned and flung herself back through the lilacs. Her retreat was as speedy as her approach, but with each step, she felt the stabbing in her ankle and she pounded her foot, torturing herself with the pain.

She ran back through the Bellehumeur's garden, ripping up plants, trying to destroy it. She didn't care. As she crossed the fence, she stumbled again and rolled on her side. People were still outside and she felt they were all watching her. Shrieking again, she rolled to her feet and continued. Her brother was outside and she ran past him, past the church and through the schoolyard. She ran into the woods. "I hate you, I hate you," she cried to herself. When she felt she was alone, she fell to the ground and covered her face with her arms.

P at saw the figure up on the distant trestle. "Ken!" he shouted, "Get out of there! The police are coming! They have dogs!"

In the distance, he could see Ken raise his arms and put his hands to his face. "The police have dogs!" he shouted again.

There was a soft drumming sound and then there were many figures; it wasn't Ken, it had been a policeman. Did they have Ken already? He scanned the area but could not tell. The group of figures had disappeared and he stood for a moment until he realised they would have radios.

As he jogged back to his car, his panic grew. The police could radio an officer in Kiosk and have a cruiser stop him as he drove into town. He fumbled with his keys, his hands shaking, and started the car. In reverse gear, with the wheel turned, he hammered the accelerator. The front tires dug into the sandy soil and threw a large cloud of dust into the air as the undercarriage dragged and scraped across the uneven ground. He threw the car into drive, floored it, his front wheels bouncing under the heavy acceleration, and rocketed up the steep incline onto Highway 630. A northbound car was only metres away and it skidded to avoid a collision as Pat careened onto the opposite soft shoulder. The other driver leaned on his horn as he passed and the sound dropped in tone as the two cars just barely missed each other.

Pat sat frozen for a moment, holding tightly onto the wheel. Dust swirled and settled around his car. He shook his head, accelerated out of the dirt and reached the end of the pavement in just

over a minute. He decelerated quickly and drove into town, acting
nonchalant as he passed the OPP near the bridge. He prayed they
would not look at him. They didn't. Before his pulse had slowed, he
had his car parked and was out milling about with old Kiosk residents.

Suzette was standing near the lake interviewing someone
and he walked within hearing distance. She looked up at him, but
did not acknowledge his presence. Jaro was running the camera on
a tripod and Mike was standing off to the side.

"No, it's not really a protest," said the man being interviewed. "It's just one man camping in the park without a permit."

Patrick studied the man. His dark hair, long nose and a thin
face looked vaguely familiar, but there was something odd about
him. He stood out. He dressed casually, but he wore dress shoes,
pressed slacks, and a starched shirt. He certainly wasn't roughing it
in the bush.

"But many of the people who grew up in Kiosk have concerns."

"This is a provincial park, maintained for the good of all the
people. The people of Kiosk were amply compensated when they
sold their houses. There are no concerns."

"So, to what do you attribute this sudden interest in the
town?"

"Have you ever driven by an accident on a highway? There
is lots of interest in that as well, but that doesn't mean that the people driving by are interested in speeding or dangerous driving. It's
just natural human curiosity. I understand it will all be over soon.
The OPP are rounding up Campbell as we speak."

Suzy looked vaguely uncomfortable. "Thank you, Mr.
Gingras, for your comments."

Armand Gingras nodded and then looked at the camera
intently causing Jaro to turn off the machine. Armand was no
stranger to the tricks of camera crews. He looked back at Suzy and
then followed her gaze. "Ahhh," he said, straining his memory. "Pat
James?" Pat nodded. "Isn't this just wonderful? All three of you
reunited."

Jaro motioned to Suzy. "We should move over to the
bridge."

"Yes, maybe we all should," said Armand. "That way, we can see them bringing in Campbell and putting an end to this foolishness." Armand turned to Pat. "Thanks to Suzy and her news crew, the police knew where to find him. Apparently he was waiting up at the north trestle to give them an interview."

Pat looked at Suzette quickly, his eyes wide. "I didn't tell them," Suzy said softly.

"Whatever happened?" asked Armand. "You three used to stick together."

"I don't know what happened," Pat said, shaking his head.

Jaro packed up the tripod. "We should get going."

"I . . ." Suzy exhaled and walked toward Jaro. She stopped when Armand spoke again.

"It's for the best anyway. He would have gotten hurt running around out there in the bush. And no one's going to agree with him. This is a park for all people, not just for the likes of Ken Campbell."

"It's true," Suzette said. "Kenny isn't getting as much support as he deserves." A few people had gathered. Tension was heavy in the air.

"If we don't protect wilderness areas," said Armand, "keep them pure and free of industry and habitation, there will be nothing for future generations to see. There will be no way for these people to experience true wilderness. That's what Algonquin Park is all about. It's supposed to be a place where the people of the south can come and experience nature in the raw."

"And what about the people who lived here first?" Pat asked. "What about the families that were formed here? What about them! Who decided that the people who pollute the cities have the right to displace the lives of the people who were born on the land?" Pat waved his hand dismissively at Armand. "Aahh, You just don't understand."

"I do understand. We need to have areas for all people, not just for a few who want to enjoy the wilderness. This park is here for everyone and I don't think it's fair that you and a group of people should claim it for yourselves. I was born here. I can see the truth." His French-Canadian accent still showed on certain words. He had trouble with the word 'truth'.

"What are you talking about? We don't want to claim the

park! We lived here, this was our home; we just wanted to keep the land around our houses. The park is almost eight thousand square kilometres, and Kiosk is at the very top end! We only wanted the few kilometres around where we were born."

A crowd had gathered and Armand was grandstanding. "But don't you see? You want this piece, someone else wants that piece, and before you know it - poof - there's no more park. We mustn't allow that to happen." He pointed at Pat. "Sometimes you have to think of the greater good."

"You don't see it do you? You want to preserve a piece of park for the people of a country, but you're not concerned with preserving the life of the people. What good is a people's nature park, if the people have no sense of roots or belonging to the land?"

Armand laughed and turned to look at some of the bystanders. "I don't know what you're talking about, and I don't think you do either."

Pat felt frustrated. He couldn't make his point. "Did you know the MNR is building an office for itself and setting up cabins where the old mill used to be?"

"So?"

"It's ironic. They said that our families couldn't stay, because our houses destroyed the wilderness atmosphere, but when the MNR can make money by renting cabins, somehow, buildings are not so bad."

"As I understand it, the office and those cabins will be ecologically friendly." His tone turned nasty. "It's one thing to have a cabin for a quiet visitor, but it's another to have a group of houses with a bunch of drunks!"

There was a murmur in the crowd. Many of the people standing around listening were the people Armand had just called 'drunks'. "Ken told me they have other cabins in the park as well. They've been renting them for years. It's all about illusion. The government is not interested in protecting this area; they are interested in creating an illusion. They log the forests, allow natives to hunt the animals and they build cabins, but those of us who were born here - were part of the land - were forced to move. It stinks!"

Jaro, hand-holding the camera, was filming again. He stepped back a bit to be less obvious, but Armand caught the movement. "So you think the rest of North America should just go away and let you have the park! It doesn't work that way. When people live in the path of a proposed freeway, their land is expropriated for the greater good of the community. When a new hospital needs to be built, houses are purchased so that construction can start. We live in a society where we can't always be selfish about our own needs." Armand grinned widely. He felt he had really hit the mark for the camera.

"I told you, I'm not talking about the whole park, just the town. This stinking government made a decision to make this park almost eight thousand square kilometres in size and the fact that a town would be destroyed didn't matter. They could have easily made it sixty square kilometres smaller, but someone thought they knew what was better. There's always some asshole who thinks he or she knows what's better for everyone else. But it shows that the government doesn't give a shit for the needs of the people." Pat's face was red and his fists were squeezed tightly at his side. "I can't believe you're talking like this. Your parents lived here. They got screwed out of their land, too."

"My parents are both dead, but they got twice as much for their house as it was worth. I was lucky to get out of here. There was no employment, no proper education, just a dead town! And now, greedy, self-centred people like you want to hold onto some vision of your past and bring it all back - at a great cost to every-one else."

"You're full of shit!" He pushed Armand like a ten-year-old would push another in a school-yard fight.

"Back off!" Armand shouted. "Unless you want to face the police on assault charges. And I've got witnesses." He pointed at the television camera.

Pat was immediately cowed. He was angry, but the police frightened him. He didn't know how to respond and he stood star-ing at Armand.

"You better get up to the bridge," Armand said to Suzette. He knew the camera had been filming. "They've probably already got Ken Campbell under arrest."

Pat saw Armand fold his arms over his chest and study the crowd. He seemed to be evaluating something, judging the mood.

Jaro turned off the betacam and walked with Mike and Suzy toward the Jeep, and with each step, they walked a little faster. Pat turned and walked as well. He decided not to drive and he walked past the Jeep with his head down. Suzette looked over her shoulder, but he did not look up as he walked along the sandy road toward the town.

The Jeep went by and Pat saw Suzette looking out. Her expression was full of guilt as she put her hand to the window in a half-wave. He looked down at the ground, ignoring her. What a bitch, he thought.

Ken reached the beginning of Bear Lake, a small shallow bay, and smelled the spicy, rich smell of swamp. The sun burned warmly on his skin and a few flies lazily buzzed around his head. He looked at the water, it was clean and clear, but the little bay was thick with small floating bushes, and the lake-bottom was covered in deep, heavy mud. He could not walk through this without leaving obvious footprints and the water was too shallow to allow him to swim. He decided to leave the safety of the water and travel along the shore, following it south.

It was difficult moving over the sticks and rocks that littered the shore and he knew he couldn't move quickly enough to stay ahead of the police. Since he was now on land and since the dog could again track him, he decided to leave the lake. The police had kept the dog on a leash, and he could move much faster than an entire group of OPP officers. Using his arms to shield him from being scratched, he forced his way through the bushes and in a direction that would take him to the road and eventually back to Kioshkokwi Lake and his canoe.

The sun shone through the canopy of the needles and leaves, creating a mosaic pattern on the lower vegetation and forest floor. It was difficult to see clearly, to pick a path, and he stumbled. Large ferns covered the ground and hid the many rocks that littered the area. Speed would carry the possible penalty of a sprained ankle or a twisted knee.

He came into a section of pine and for a while was able to move quickly among the tall trees, but the pines gave way to spruce, which hung their branches right to the ground. He had to run a circuitous course through these trees and often the dead lower branches clawed at his arms.

He finally came to an animal trail, a path that animals had created as they moved through the bush, and although it did not go exactly in the direction he wanted, it was easier than stumbling through the ferns. He started to jog.

The terrain was increasing in elevation and as it did, the forest became less congested. The trees were taller and as his eyes were adjusted to the patterns of light, he stopped to listen to the sounds of the forest. Quaking aspen leaves rustled in the breeze, flies buzzed around his head and a wayward mosquito danced in the air, unsure about what to do with this giant human. A single chickadee whistled off in the distance, but there was no sound of anyone approaching.

He started to run again, pushing through low growing branches, jumping over fallen logs and avoiding rocks and puddles. He stepped on one log and it banged against a rock with a hollow echo. He stopped suddenly, thinking for a moment that someone was near by, but the sound did not repeat and he continued.

A spider web wrapped his face and he wiped it away as he followed the path near a section of damp ground. From the direction of the sun, he knew he was travelling too far to the west, but he would still eventually reach the road. And the road would take him most of the way to his canoe.

He found a pace that suited the terrain and did not keep him gasping for breath. Leaves and dead branches flashed by and the odd bird accompanied the rhythmic pounding of his feet. The forest stretched out in all directions, seemingly endless.

He slowed to a stop at a group of denser spruce and studied the brighter section ahead. It was the road. He stood silently listening - right, and then left. He could hear the faint rumbling of a motor far in the distance, but knowing that sound travelled for many miles, he pushed his way through the low growing vegetation, feeling the ferns wrap around his legs, and walked to the side of the road.

The surface was hard packed and would leave no footprints. He looked both ways, saw nothing threatening and walked out into the sunshine. The heat pulled at his skin and warmed him and he stopped to listen. Another chickadee called mournfully in the distance, but now other birds chirped back and forth, communicating with each other. The motor noise remained distant. He started a slow jog down the road.

He could feel the wind blowing across his face, across his arms, and it felt comforting. It had texture and substance and seemed more than just the movement of air. It was a caress.

He had broken a few small branches and flattened some leaves at the point where he needed to re-enter the forest to reach his canoe, but he thought he should have reached it by now. It was not a strong marking, because he didn't want anyone else to recognize it and he was beginning to wonder if he too, had missed it. If he passed it, he would be forced to backtrack, which would cost valuable time and might deliver him right to the dog team.

The distant motor noise began to change. It was still distant, but now it varied in pitch, whereas before it was only a low rumble. Someone was coming. He ran faster hoping to reach his trail before whatever was operating that motor reached him.

He arrived at a vaguely familiar curve, just as the sound of the motor behind him became sharper. Over his shoulder, he saw a vehicle on the outside edge of a curve. It was distant and he could barely make out the form of the driver, but it looked like an ATV. Running faster, he got around the corner and out of sight, but from the sound, the vehicle was gaining rapidly. A few paces later, he looked over his shoulder, his feet tangled, and he fell with a grunt. He rolled onto all fours and looked back. The vehicle, an eight-wheel-drive Argo, was back in view and it was coming fast. There was no point of hiding in the trees; in minutes, it would reach him and its driver had probably seen him.

Not too far up the road, he saw his mark, the broken branches and trampled leaves. He ripped through the dense foliage at the side of the road and into the forest. The motor noise was softer now, muffled by the leaves. He ran aggressively through the undergrowth. Branches grabbed at him, scratched him and again he stumbled and fell. The world rotated, brightness, shadow, brightness, shadow, brightness shadow. He landed on his back looking up at the trees and for a second could not get his lungs to work. No air would enter his body. He saw the small aspen leaves vibrating in the tree tops playing light games with the sun and then suddenly air rushed in. He rolled onto his hands and knees, felt a sharp pain in his shoulder, and pulled himself up onto his feet. He took a deep breath and sprinted up a hill.

He was sweating and out of breath. This was different than running for exercise. He couldn't keep his body working the way he wanted and his reflexes were poor. He needed to get better control. At the top of the hill, he slowed and caught his breath, the air coming in ragged bursts. The sound behind him changed, became less muffled and then raised in frequency. He turned to see the Argo punching through the forest.

He jumped down the opposite side of the hill, looking for a path with lots of congestion, but the forest was fairly open, the trees were tall and widely spaced. With eight, soft, knobby tires, which not only gave great traction, but worked as paddles, these vehicles could drive through a forest, over a swamp, and even through a lake. He ran hard, trying to gain distance. The Argo could outrun him on a road, but it had to drive around trees and obstacles in the forest, and if he could reach his canoe, he could easily beat it in the water.

The motor noise behind him was changing rapidly as the driver gunned the engine and moved over logs and rocks. Once he was in the water, he would be safe, but it would take him a few minutes to free his canoe from the shore and to get the motor attached and started.

Sweat was pouring down his sides, dampening his shirt, and he could feel the fabric of his jeans pulling at his legs. The heat was oppressive and the forest was closing in on him. He had to get control of his breathing, but there was too much to think of. Was the sound behind him getting louder? Should he go around that tree to the right or the left? Where was the lake?

The ground was littered with branches and sticks and he had to be careful with his footing, but he needed to look ahead to choose his direction. He forced himself to stay light on his feet, rapidly shifting from side to side, and although this reduced the risk of a sprained ankle, it cost him needed speed. The engine noise was louder and he could hear the voices of people inside the Argo.

He climbed over a small pile of rocks and panted hard, his

breath rasping as it left his lungs. His shirt had dried a little after his journey up the creek, but it was wet again with sweat. The wet clothes made him feel heavy and confined. Sweat burned in his eyes as it ran off his forehead and he tried to wipe his face with the back of his hand.

He saw his canoe in the distance. It was not too far away, but when he looked back, neither was the Argo. Judging the distance, he couldn't tell if he could make it in time, so he ran straight toward the lake and the rocky shore. If he was lucky, the Argo would follow him and have trouble navigating at the water's edge. They would either have to go out onto the water, which was slower, or move back off the shore and travel inland, which would cost them time.

He leapt over a fallen log and onto the rocky shore and then turned in the direction of his canoe. Some of the rocks were sun bleached and light grey, but some were dark and partially submerged. His foot found one of the darker rocks and he slipped on the slimy surface. He broke his fall with his hands, which stung viciously as they hit the hard ground. With his heart hammering in his chest, he pushed himself back to his feet and continued.

The waves were light, but they rolled against the rocks and washed-up driftwood making it difficult to see where it was safe to run. He was travelling much faster than he should, but the Argo had not been fooled by his manoeuvre. They had not gone as far as the shore and had turned to follow him through the forest.

The canoe was just ahead and he jumped over a group of small-leafed bushes and rolled almost crashing into his canoe. Working furiously, he ripped it into the water, threw the motor and paddle inside, and pushed away from shore.

The Argo was just feet away and it charged, indifferent to the damage the rocks and sharp driftwood might cause. The engine screamed as wheels left the ground and the machine jumped into the air. Ken dove into the canoe and plunged his paddle into the water. He paddled furiously. Water splashed in all directions.

Two officers, a woman and a man, were shouting at Ken to stop. Their words were garbled by the motor noise and the splashing water. He paddled a few times, swung the motor onto the boat, tightened the thumb-screws, and pulled the cord. The engine didn't catch and he fumbled around looking for the choke. Everything that should have been easy was now difficult. He looked right and left. Where was it? He found the little metal plunger and he pulled the cord again as he adjusted the air-fuel mixture. The engine bubbled and gurgled, but died out. The splashing of the Argo was close.

He swung around quickly, paddled twice more, but the Argo had almost reached him. The woman was reaching for his canoe. He ripped at the cord and his engine caught. He dropped to his knees and opened the throttle. The front of the canoe lifted and he moved away, but a moment later, the motor gurgled and stalled.

Like a surfer, he fell back on the wave he had been riding. He jumped around and pulled the cord again. Nothing. Then again and the engine started, but the Argo was right beside him. The woman could have grabbed his canoe if she leaned way out, but she missed the opportunity. Ken opened the throttle half way and curved away from the eight-wheel-boat.

As the motor warmed, he cut the choke and fed in more fuel. The distance between the two crafts increased. He took a deep slow breath. He was getting away.

Sunlight sparkled off the surface of the lake and the spray of water cooled his neck and face as he heard the sound of the OPP using their radio. He couldn't go back toward Kiosk, not this time, and he turned toward Gull Island.

Suzy leaned against the fender of the Jeep and watched Jaro trying to carry on a conversation with the police officer. The constable was annoyed, abrupt, and answered Jaro in short phrases and single-word replies. There was a mood of tension among the twenty or thirty people who were milling about waiting for information on the arrest and the officer did not want to be distracted.

Earlier the Incident Commander had blown them off, giving them a prepared statement about the situation being 'under control', but refusing to answer any questions. Now they could only wait for the police to bring out Campbell. There was no other way in or out of this section of park other than across these two bridges.

The afternoon sky contained some drifting cloud and the

hot summer sun was driving moisture down to the earth. The light breeze did little to stifle the heat. Suzy felt a drop of sweat run between her breasts and she ran her hand underneath her hair. The back of her neck was already damp and her hair was beginning to frizzle. The synthetic fabric of her pants-suit was beginning to smell with the heat. There was nowhere to freshen-up and the story might take hours to break. She decided to sit in the Jeep with the air-conditioning running.

Inside the vehicle, she looked at Pat standing a long distance away talking to a number of the old residents. He was keeping his distance from the police barricade, and from her.

She had not questioned Jaro about his revelation to the police. She knew it had less to do with police cooperation and more to do with desiring a quick end to the story, and she could understand his feelings. After all, she was anxious to get back to Michelle. They had the only camera crew on site and if the story got interesting, they would have an exclusive, but often, these stories dragged out for days and the public lost interest. Having the story break today would be best for them and for the station.

Perhaps, after the arrest, she and Pat could arrange to get together some time. He was definitely angry with her, but it would pass. She folded down the visor and looked at her makeup. She took out some lipstick and eyeliner and attempted to give herself a sharper line.

Pat stood on the rise above the road watching the two police guards at the barricade. He was talking to Tommy Racine and Lorraine Beckett, both former Kiosk residents, and his stomach churned as he listened to them discussing Ken's future.

He felt vaguely uncomfortable this close to the police. He too could be in trouble for his involvement and perhaps the officers on the trestle had seen him through binoculars. If he were arrested, he would be of no further help to Ken.

"I don't see the need for dogs," said Lorraine,

"I can," said Tommy. "It's the only way they'll ever catch him. If I remember right, he was a damned good bushman."

"The whole thing with the dogs reminds me of them old

movies about the southern States."

An older man, wearing grey pants, a short-sleeve white shirt and a tie, approached the group and immediately shook hands with Pat. "Patrick James. It's been a tong lime since we last saw each other." His odd accent jolted a distant memory.

Pat had to think for a moment and then it came to him, 'tong lime', was 'long time'. He shook his head. "Yes sir, Mr. Loeffler, it has."

"So you're all together again, eh?" The 'eh' sounded contrived, as if Loeffler was trying to sound Canadian. It didn't work. His accent was still noticeable, even if it was unidentifiable.

"Who do you mean?"

"Well, I had a good talk with Kenneth and I saw Suzette briefly . . . Now you're here . . . The three musketeers, re-united."

Pat smiled. "Yes sir." He looked over at Suzette sitting in the Jeep and his smile turned to a frown. Loeffler followed his glance.

Tommy and Lorraine said hello. Mr. Loeffler remembered them as well and greeted them as if they were fourteen instead of forty.

"This is quite an event," Loeffler said, looking at Pat. "I certainly hope that Kenneth is not badly treated."

"If they even catch him," Pat said under his breath.

Loeffler was encouraged by Pat's comment. "You think he'll get away? Now that would be a feat to be congratulated."

"I hope he gets away," Lorraine said.

"Those dogs are pretty good," Tom said sceptically. "I don't think he'll get away for long. Even though he knows the bush, the police brought in those vehicles that can go through water and over land."

"Terra-jets?"

"No, those ones with six or eight wheels."

"Argos."

"Yeah, that's it."

Pat was surprised. He had assumed he had been safe across the Amable du Fond, but an Argo could have easily crossed the river and run him down. He wondered what kind of threat they posed for Kenny's freedom.

"I thought an Argo was a football player," said Loeffler.

Tommy grinned at Pat.

"No sir, it's like a four-wheeler, but it has eight big tires. It's not as fast as a four-wheeler, but it can go just about anywhere. They're waterproof, so you can drive them over a lake. If the police are bringing in stuff like that, they must be pretty serious."

"The US fought a war in Vietnam. They had jet fighters and computers and they were beaten by a bunch of local peasants with very little hardware."

"But years later, the US used all that technology to fight the Gulf War. They brought that one to an end in a couple of days."

"But look at the global war on terrorism. That's not as easy as everyone thought either."

"Hey!" Lorraine laughed. "This is not a war we're talking about. We're talking about Kenny hiding in the forest."

"But look at the OPP down there," Tommy said, "in the military style uniforms with bullet-proof vests. They don't look like they're playing hide-and-seek."

Lorraine frowned. "I wonder what made him do it."

"I remember giving Kenneth a book by Thoreau. It was called Walden, but at the end, there was a piece on civil disobedience. Kenneth must have taken that part to heart."

Suzy had talked about the day Loeffler had given them books and Pat tried to remember the book Loeffler had given him, but he couldn't. He figured he hadn't read it. It had probably disappeared when they moved. Many things disappeared when they moved. He hoped the old man wouldn't ask, because he felt as guilty as a schoolboy who hadn't done his homework. "I don't think Ken is just following the words of some writer."

"I'd be surprised if Kenny did much readin'," Tommy said, "unless it was in a good hunting or fishing magazine."

"We are all moulded by what we read," Loeffler said. "Do you remember the book I gave you, Patrick?"

Pat felt foolish. "It was a long time ago, sir."

"You had a lot on your mind that day." He smiled warmly as if happy that he could remember everything so clearly. "It was the Social Contract by Rousseau."

Pat remembered the book, a little, blue, hardcover. He had read some of it, but it was very difficult and he had never finished it. He remembered that there were a couple of things that seemed relevant at the time, but he couldn't remember what they were now. He nodded. "I remember it now."

"If you can find it, you should take a look at it again. It might help you understand Kenneth a little better. Like I said, we are all moulded by what we read."

Pat and Lorraine both nodded, but Tommy had lost interest in the conversation. He was looking at the barricade.

"There's another writer, a Canadian," continued Mr. Loeffler, "who might help people understand what Ken is doing."

"Who's that?" Pat asked.

"Just about the time the mill burned, Margaret Atwood wrote a book called Survival. It's partially about how Canadians need to fight for their survival."

Pat turned his palms to Loeffler in a gesture that said, 'so?' Loeffler might have said the sky was blue.

"Yes," Loeffler said, continuing with his monologue. "She wrote about how victims of oppression could be placed into four levels. The first level is where people don't realise they are oppressed, and therefore do nothing about it. This was the way most of the townspeople thought years before the fire.

"The second level is where they realise they are oppressed, but figure it's a matter of fate and there's nothing they can do about it. In this position, anger is displaced - a father hits his son and, in turn, the boy hits his younger brother. This could be the position of most of the people of the town for the last two decades. Everyone had just surrendered.

"The third level is where people realise they are victims and refuse to accept it as inevitable. This is the position that Ken is in now. He's decided that he doesn't have to take it any longer and he is doing something about it.

"And the forth level is where people are no longer victims. Atwood called this 'the creative non-victim'. Hopefully, this is a position we will all find ourselves in as a result of Ken's protest."

"It almost seems unfair," Lorraine said. "Ken does all the work and we receive the benefit."

"By your very presence here, aren't you showing your support? And isn't that a form of protest?"

"I don't know. If the police told me I had to move, I would move. As much as I would like to be able to have my home back, I don't think anything will come of this, and I certainly would not be willing to go to jail."

Tommy tuned back into the conversation. He looked at Lorraine. "So why are you here?"

"Same reason as you. Curiosity. This is where I grew up and these," she spread her arms out, "are the people I knew as a child, but I wouldn't go to jail to make a point. I've got kids to feed."

Tommy looked down at the ground. "I took the day off work to come here."

"Would you go to jail, or leave if the police told you?"

Tommy grinned. "They can't tell us to move. We're not doing nothing illegal."

"That's a double negative, Thomas," Loeffler said. Tommy looked confused.

"What about you, Pat?" Lorraine asked. "Would you be willing to go to jail to fight for this?"

Pat thought for a moment. "It's . . . hard to say," he said. He wanted to tell her that he had already been chased by the police and that he was secretly meeting Ken in the bush, but he was also afraid of the implications. The more people who knew, the greater the likelihood of discovery. It was better, for now, to keep his involvement secret.

"Your old girlfriend, Suzette has been helping," said Tommy. "She's brought a whole news crew here."

"Yeah, but she also . . ." Pat stopped. He couldn't say that she had told the police where Ken was hiding unless he admitted that he knew as well. This would then reveal his involvement. "The news hasn't been especially favourable. They talk about that politician, Roussel and they talk about the police action, but they really don't give much support to what Ken is trying to do."

Loeffler put his hand on Pat's arm. "While she and the news people are here, the police can't do anything outrageous."

On the road below, one of the police officers was talking excitedly into his radio. He ran back to a parked cruiser and pulled it forward as the second OPP officer moved the barricade. With his siren on and lights flashing, he moved through the crowd of people and roared toward the ranger station.

Suzette was out of the car, walking to the remaining officer and the rest of the crowd surged forward. Pat followed Lorraine and Tommy, occasionally giving Mr. Loeffler a hand on the short, but steep, hill. In the distance, the team with the dog was coming into view and Pat stopped and shielded the sun from his eyes with his hand. He could see a group of officers, but Ken wasn't with them. "It looks as if they didn't get him."

Loeffler stopped. "Good!" he said. He shook his fist in front of him. "That's the spirit, Kenneth!" He continued down the hill alone.

Jaro already had the camera rolling as the police-car tore up the road in the direction of the ranger station. He followed Suzy to the barricade, hoping to get some footage of the police bringing in their fugitive.

Suzy approached the remaining officer. "Has there been a new development?" she asked, aware of the camera at her back.

"We need a boat out on the lake." The officer studied the crowd moving toward him. He waved Suzy away impatiently.

"Is Ken Campbell on the lake?"

The officer walked away, ignoring her question. He tried to look busy guarding the barricade.

"Has anyone been injured?" Suzy asked loudly.

The officer turned to her. "You'll just have to hold your questions for the Incident Commander." The Incident Commander was on the other side of the bridge, well out of contact.

"Well, can we go and speak with him?"

"No one is allowed in until the canine team is out. Sorry."

"So you're saying that we have to speak to someone we can't speak to."

The officer turned toward her, grinned, shrugged, and turned back toward the crowd.

About forty people had gathered, many of them old Kiosk residents, and they stood in groups of three or four. Armand Gingras was circulating from group to group talking to people and gathering information.

Suzy noticed a few people past the officer and following their gazes, she spotted the returning dog handler. The support team was following. She craned her neck, trying to see Ken, but he was not in view. "He got away didn't he?"

The officer looked at her again, anger in his eyes. "Look, lady, if you don't mind . . ." He turned his attention back to the crowd, but also looked over his shoulder as a result of the attention of the crowd of people.

Suzy looked again and was sure she was right. The dog team had failed. She turned to face Pat. He was standing part way down the hill, near the road, and he too was looking in the direction of the arriving police. Although it had cost her some exclusive footage, she was glad that Ken had not been captured. Perhaps Pat would not be as angry. As she watched him, she felt a funny pressure in her chest. Her cheeks flushed a little and she felt a tingle in her forearms and shoulders.

She admonished herself. Sure, she was attracted to him, but this wasn't the time or the place. Maybe they could trade addresses and meet at a later time, but now she had a story to finish, and a daughter who was waiting at home.

Poor Michelle, she thought. She hoped the babysitter was okay. Nickeyfortune might expect them to stay, but she was ready to leave. She knew that Jaro wouldn't resist. He disliked the north. There were too many bugs and no clubs or bars that interested him. The story was basically over and it was time to get back to Southern Ontario.

Armand Gingras walked toward the barricade. His dress shoes were dusty from the road. "I need to speak to your commander."

"You'll have to wait until the area is clear, sir."

"I have some information concerning the fugitive that may be of interest."

"I can relay it, sir. Go ahead."

"I'd rather not. If you prefer, I'll just stand here and wait. If the information is no longer timely . . . well . . . then, that won't be my fault."

"You're that fellow from the government, aren't you?"

Armand nodded, but looked about furtively. Suzy noticed

his reaction.

The officer shook his head. "Hang on a moment." He stepped back and spoke into his radio. The dog handler had reached his own Suburban and after a moment, the officer waved Armand through.

A few people looked at Armand, wondering what he was doing with the police, and he spoke as he walked past. "Can't allow Ken to get hurt . . . wouldn't be right . . ."

Suzy wasn't impressed. She watched him as he walked toward the knot of OPP that stood near where Kenny had once had his cabin, and she turned to Jaro. "Film that guy as long as you can."

"He's out of audio range."

"That's okay. Just film him talking to the police."

The Incident Commander, a short wiry man with a neat moustache and a tight leathery face, stood with his arms folded, half listening to Armand. The support team officers were moving around, passing on information and requesting orders.

"It's important that we don't let this turn into a Native Protest."

"And how would that happen? There's been no sign of active Natives in the area."

"Mr. Campbell is effectively making a land claim protest, but an Algonquin Indian Band is also claiming part of this land. The Ministry of Indian and Northern Affairs does not want to see these sensitive issues turned into an ugly protest."

"Well, that's not my concern. My concern is picking up a fugitive who has resisted arrest." An officer came and asked a question about the Argo team. The IC held up his hand. He was becoming annoyed with the presence of this government employee. "So, what information do you have for me?" he asked, his impatience showing.

"I grew up in this area and I know many of the residents. I knew Ken Campbell as a kid."

The IC rotated his hand in a gesture that implored Armand to get to the point.

"I've spoken with a number of people and they told me that Campbell spends a lot of time in the park, and is an avid hunter. They say he has a cabin in the bush somewhere and that he has firearms."

The IC rubbed his moustache and thought for a second. "Are you saying that he's armed?"

"I don't know that. But I am saying that he likely has firearms at his disposal."

"And where is this camp of his?" The IC turned to one of the younger officers. "Get me a topographic map of the area!"

Armand held up his hands. "I'm afraid I don't know where it is." He saw the look of disbelief in the IC's eyes. "You have to understand the kind of person Kenny is. When I knew him as a kid, he spent most of his time in the woods. He would go all through the park and would travel by himself for days. A lot of the old-timers hid caches all over the place and Kenny probably did this also."

The younger officer returned with the map, which he spread out on the hood of the Suburban. "Two people said that they thought his camp was on Bear Lake," Armand said, looking at the map. It took him a second. "It's called Boulter Lake on your map for some reason, but it's just outside of the park." He pointed to it. "But the point is, he could be anywhere. He knows this area well."

The IC was rubbing his moustache again, thinking. "Did anyone suggest other locations?"

"Sure . . . Green Lake, Manitou, Lauder. Kenny was always a bit of a loner. He is a bush man." Armand could see the look of consternation on the IC's face. "Look, I don't want to see the man hurt. I grew up with him. I just thought that if you knew what you were dealing with, you could bring this thing to an end before someone gets hurt."

The IC looked at Armand's business card. ". . . and before it becomes an embarrassment to the Ministry of Indian and Northern Affairs."

Armand worked hard to suppress a smile. "The politics of this country are both sensitive and complicated."'

"Thank you for the information, Mr. Gingras. How can I reach you if I need anything further?"

"My cell-phone number is on the card."

"Cell phones don't work here."

"I'm driving back south this afternoon. There's no reason to stay."

The IC slipped the card into his pocket. "All right. Have a safe trip."

Armand held out his hand, but the IC ignored it. Armand let it fall, turned, and walked back to the barricade.

Kioshkokwi Lake was ten kilometres, or six miles, long and it had three arms, one to the west, one to the south and one to the north-east. The town of Kiosk was located in the middle of the lake on the north shore, but at this point, the lake was only a kilometre wide. Ken had put his canoe in the water by Wolfe's Bay, the western arm of the lake, and he wanted to get to the east end, but he didn't dare pass Kiosk to do so. Instead, he powered his canoe into the southern arm, found a good hiding place and started to walk.

He had considered portaging the canoe, but he decided it would be too difficult, especially with the motor, and he felt it was wiser to keep the boat in the west section of the lake. Near the shore, he took a reading with his compass and then started into the bush. It was going to be a long walk.

He crossed two hills and two bush roads before he finally reached the old rail bed. He had a hidden camp not too far from here, but he decided against staying. He didn't dare cross the lake in the light of day and the sun was already close to the horizon. It would be safer to cross tonight than tomorrow. His hunger was gnawing at him and he walked back on the rail bed to find some berries. Most of the berries were finished, but he found a few blackberries and some elderberries. The blackberries were sweet, but the elderberries were tart and he picked a bit of each and ate them together.

As the sun dipped behind the trees, the air started to cool and a light mist swirled up from the water. The loons called hauntingly. Ken walked out onto the rail bed and surveyed the lake. There were no boats visible on the water.

The train tracks crossed the lake on a man-made land bridge

that Ken always thought of as a bit of an engineering marvel. Instead of building a wooden or metal bridge, the builders of the railway had used backfill to make a land bridge across the narrowest point in the lake. It was about a mile east of the town and it stretched for almost a half-mile through the water. Kioshkokwi Lake was very deep and it must have taken hundreds of thousands of loads of rock and gravel. He had often canoed along its edge and watched in fascination as the steep bank dropped rapidly into the dark depths. The land bridge was thirty feet wide at the top and Ken had often wondered how wide it was at the bottom.

The builders had put in a small section of traditional bridge to allow the water to flow from the east to the west and to allow boats access to both sides, and this bridge, referred to as the 'one-mile-bridge' was a favourite fishing spot. It was on the north side of the lake and it would be the most dangerous part of his crossing. It would be impossible for anyone to hide on the land bridge, but they could hide under the metal bridge. Since he was on foot, he would be easy prey for anyone waiting there. It would be a half-mile back across the land bridge and the police could easily chase him down with anything motorized. He decided to wait for a half-hour before crossing.

He was disappointed with how nervous he had become when being chased through the forest and he decided to do some of his stretch exercises and meditations. With the sky turning dark violet and red, he stood in the middle of the rail bed, breathed deeply and began to move - slowly at first and then more aggressively.

Feeling relaxed and much more in-focus, he started across the bridge. A small motor boat was in the water near the ranger station, but this was a mile and a half away and of no threat. He walked slowly occasionally looking up at the stars and breathing the evening air deeply into his lungs.

The northern lights were beginning to show on the distant horizon, which indicated a cool night, and he walked a little quicker. He was still a long distance away from his camp near Lauder Lake.

In the middle of the land bridge, he stopped and looked around. For many years, he had been aware of the energy found in a large forest, but standing here in the middle of the lake, he was reminded that it too had force. He could feel its presence. He closed his eyes, breathed deeply, feeling his interconnection to the life that teamed in the waters, and then opened his eyes and continued.

As he approached the metal bridge, he felt confident that he was alone. There was no light, no human noise, just water and stone. It was unlikely that the OPP would sit under a dark bridge waiting for him, especially since they had no idea where he was, and he walked across and reached the north shore.

A trail ran from the old lumber yard in Kiosk right up to Lauder Lake and Ken decided to cut through the bush, find the trail, and follow it. Navigating in the bush at night was fairly difficult, but if he followed true north, he guessed he would be okay.

There was little moonlight, the northern lights had not developed to anything more than a glow at the horizon, but his eyes had adjusted to the dark, and he was able to see well enough to navigate. He swung around the darker sections of balsam forest and stayed in the taller trees where more light hit the ground.

He crossed a swampy creek, which he remembered from his childhood, and then finally reached the trail. He was glad to be out of the dark forest, and he looked up to see that there were fewer stars. Invisible clouds drifted across the blackness. He turned north and started the long walk toward Lauder Lake.

The trail had not been used for some time. The weeds in the middle were waist-high and the sandy tire tracks were undisturbed. The sky was getting darker. It would soon be difficult to walk on the road.

A few wolves started to howl to his right and he smiled. He did not fear the wolves, but he knew the OPP would. The presence of wild animals afforded him additional security, because most urbanites were afraid of bears, wolves and moose. He respected them, but he did not hide from them.

The path was now just black and white. Objects could only be identified when they were silhouetted against the pale light at the horizon, and although he could walk all night, he knew he would have trouble locating the path that would take him to his camp. He decided to sleep for a few hours and continue in the morning light.

He picked a soft dry spot in the sand bank of the road and broke some branches from a white pine to use as bedding. He curled up on his side, used his backpack as a pillow and allowed his thoughts to drift. A small animal scrabbled up and down the trunk of a near-by red pine, and in the distance, the wolf howl was mournfully answered by a loon on the lake. Ken drifted off to sleep.

Michelle sat in the passenger seat of the mini-van with her arms folded and her body slumped. She had not been friendly since Suzy had picked her up at Marcotte's house and Suzy felt that it was punishment for being left for such a long time. "So, will you be glad to get back into your own bed?"

Michelle shrugged.

"You bet I will. I'm tired." Suzy had been on the road for too many hours today. They could have stayed in Kiosk for another night, but the story had fizzled. Most of the police packed up and left and the two constables that had remained were completely uncooperative. It was as if they had information that Ken Campbell had left the area, which he may have done, and they were remaining just as a precaution.

They had put together a few interviews, but there was nothing that would have worked as a story. After driving to North Bay, they checked out and decided to return to Barrie. Everyone had been ready to leave.

"Did you see the stories I did?"

"No."

"How come?"

"The other kids were watching things on T.V."

Suzy decided not to push the issue. "Well, it's nice to be home."

"Humm."

"Look, I'm sorry, I left you alone all that time, but I had to work on that story."

"You could have taken me with you."

"I didn't think it would take that long."

"Hummm."

The rest of the drive continued in silence. Suzy drove slowly and relaxed. She knew Michelle was tired, it was late, and the mood would be better in the morning. Back at home, the air was close and stale. She opened all the windows and the cool evening breeze gently lifted the curtains. She put Michelle to bed, took a quick shower and then relaxed on the cool cotton sheets of her bed. There was no temptation to turn on the television. The news could wait till tomorrow.

Looking up at the ceiling, bathed in the bluish light that came in through the window, her thoughts drifted to Patrick. She pictured him standing inches away in that field that had once been their Kiosk subdivision. He was looking at her with quiet eyes and then he leaned forward and kissed her softly. It was gentle at first, but as their bodies drew closer, he pulled her lips between his. She could imagine the texture, the warmth, the moisture.

Slowly she moved her fingertips across her breast, down her side and over her hips. Shivers travelled across her skin, down her spine. Her hand came to rest on the top of her leg and held tightly to the soft skin of her thigh. She imagined the sensations of Pat's touch, the texture of his skin.

She could feel herself in his arms and she could feel the softness and the hardness of him. She wrapped him in her arms, pulling him closer and drawing him into her, merging, melding. Her body was like soft wax, wrapping around him, encircling him. Their tongues were touching . . . probing. She could feel the soft warmth and the hard ridges of his body, and she floated with the sensation of pleasure, of tension, of drift.

She imagined looking into his eyes and she saw his face again. Suddenly, the vision was replaced by one of anger, the anger on Pat's face as he accused her of betraying Ken. He was full of hurt and was moving away from her. She sat up quickly and gasped for breath. The gentle peace of the romantic fantasy was destroyed and she was completely awake.

She dropped back on the bed and looked up at the moving silhouettes on the ceiling. They were blue, cold images and they scratched and clawed at the white plasterboard. A tear rolled out of her eye and slipped across the side of her face. Another followed.

She hadn't cried in years. Nothing had touched her. She had remained stoic in the face of divorce, deaths in the family, and even isolation, but then tears had come as she walked through Kiosk. And now, again, for no reason tears flowed down her cheeks. It felt as if a great weight had been placed on her chest, making it difficult to breathe. She turned over and cried into her pillow. She did not want Michelle to hear.

Pat felt uneasy. The cabin, lit by one oil lamp, was full of shadows. Outside, the forest was full of sound, sound that melded together, chirps, croaks, rustles, snaps. An army of soldiers could have approached and the noise would have been lost.

Ken had said that they would meet here if the other meeting place was compromised and this was definitely the case. But now he would wait without a reporter. He wouldn't even trust that woman from the Nugget.

He was tired and he needed to sleep, but he couldn't find peaceful release. The day had been so full of disturbing images. It had been bad enough that the police had chased him, and that Suzette had betrayed his and Ken's trust, but it was his own reaction that bothered him most. He had retreated from every confrontation. Instead of facing Suzette, he had walked away, and when Armand had provoked him and then threatened to call the police, he backed down. Now he was coming up with all the "I should have . . ." scenarios, but it was too late. Why was he always so afraid of everything?

There would be no sleep for a while and he decided to go for a walk. As he bent to tie his shoes, he could feel his belly in the way. His entire physical condition bothered him. He was out of breath so easily and he sweated with the least exertion. He kept promising himself that he would change, that he would eat better, exercise more, but he always fell back into his old ways. Coffee, sweets, junk food, alcohol, and then more junk food. Life was a foggy haze of abuse and lack of personal strength.

He walked outside, closed his eyes, and breathed in the cool night air. Remembering Ken standing by the lake, he made up some kung fu moves and danced about against the evening sky. He had no idea what he was doing, he was merely copying what he had seen in movies, but he grunted, chopped at invisible foes, almost fell, and then stopped. A feeling of gloom, like the darkness of the night, fell over him and he sighed deeply. "What kind of an idiot am

I?" he said to the forest around him. When was his life going to start? He was always talking about what he was going to do in the future, but when did the future start? Always tomorrow?

He rubbed his eyes and listened to the insect sounds in the forest. Each chirp had a place in time. And after it was gone, it was gone forever. Was his life like that? Would it be over before he was aware of its existence?

He strode into the cabin, cleared an area of the floor and did sit-ups for as long as he was able. It wasn't long. When these were finished, he turned over and started push-ups. In the morning, he would go for a run. It was time to change. After a twenty-minute workout, he lay back on the cot and closed his eyes. The sound of the forest filled his thoughts as he drifted away.

Ken slowly opened his eyes. There was very little light and he could not see much, but he had the sensation that he was not alone. Slowly, he raised his head. The forest was barely visible, the morning sun was still hours away, but grey light was leaking in from the east. When he spotted the form of the woman, he wasn't sure at first, what he was seeing, but then his eyes adjusted and she became clearer. His body jolted as if shocked with electricity.

The woman was old, short, and dressed in slacks and a number of shirts, one on top of another. Her bushy hair was tied back in a kerchief and her mouth moved even when she wasn't talking. She stood on the road staring at him. "Why are you sleeping there?" she asked. Her pronunciation was strange, unfamiliar.

"Who are you?"

"I'm Catherine. Who are you?"

"Ken," he said rubbing his eyes. The name Catherine was familiar. A mist drifted across the road making it hard to see. Wiping his eyes did not help. "Are you camping here?"

"We have a place. You the fellow the police is lookin' for?" She pronounced "police" as if it were "pleese".

Ken nodded and smiled. "You're not gonna tell them where I am, are you?"

She shook her head. "You plannin' to live here too?"

The question took Ken by surprise. What was he planning? "I guess I'll have to wait and see what happens. I grew up here. It used to be my home."

"I lived here all my life, too," said the woman.

Ken had hunted and canoed all through these woods but he didn't remember an old woman living anywhere near here. "And you have a cabin near by?"

"I got a place," she repeated. She waved her hand in the air and Ken noticed that three of her fingers were missing. The index finger was nothing but a stub, the second finger a little longer and the ring finger about half its length. The baby finger seemed untouched. With the angle of the cut, her hand looked more like a foot with toes.

"I have a cabin too."

The old woman nodded, but said nothing further.

The name 'Catherine' came back to him and he remembered Gary. He said he had a lot of siblings and his mother was named Catherine. Perhaps this was his mother or one of his older sisters. "You know a fellow named Gary? Or, old Tabobandung?"

"I know them."

"Are you Gary's mother?"

"We're all mothers and these boys are all sons."

Ken shook his head, as if to clear the cobwebs. "I don't think Gary is too happy about me being here.'

The old woman cackled and took a step away. "He is lost . . . just like you. Not many people find their way in the bush any-more."

Ken realised that he wasn't following the same conversation as the old woman. Was he lost? "Is Lauder Lake very far up the road?" He pointed.

The old woman smiled, turned, and started to walk away. "You'll find it . . . and your friend."

This bothered him. What did she know about his friend? Had she been to his cabin? "Do you know my place?"

"You just remember to keep away from the big bird over the waves. The water is your friend. It tell you how to go."

"What big bird?"

"You'll see, but don't get caught by the big bird."

"I don't understand."

The woman was already walking away. She dismissed him with a wave of her hand.

Ken was still tired and there was no point in following the woman to the south. He curled up in the pine branches, closed his eyes and fell asleep.

Ken awoke to the sound of a gentle rain and the buzzing of mosquitoes. The sky was a soft pastel grey and the forest a deep emerald green; the rain would fall for most of the day. He sat up, wiped the moisture from his face, and rose to his feet. His muscles protested with every movement. Sleeping out in the open was tolerable, but it had been easier when he had been younger. For the next couple of nights, he would seek shelter from the open sky.

He stood in the centre of the road, swatted at the mosquitoes that flew around his ears, and stretched, forcing the blood into his muscles. His wet clothes tugged against his skin as he moved and he started up the road, hoping to soon see signs of Lauder Lake and the road to his camp.

It was much further than he anticipated and as he walked, he thought about the old woman. Surely, if they had been that far from Lauder Lake, she had been in the park. There were a few cabins to the northwest of the lake, like his, which were outside, but where he had slept must have been park property. Even if she was native, it was surprising that she was allowed to live within the boundary. He had some topographical maps at his cabin and he would check it out when he arrived.

As he approached his cabin, the smell of breakfast wafted

through the trees. Eggs, toast and coffee - the aroma reached him and made his stomach tighten. He was hungry. The rain had turned into a light drizzle and through the mist he saw Pat standing in the door way.

"Good to see you," Pat said, placing his coffee cup on the outside grey wooden railing. He walked into the drizzle and shook Ken's hand. "I was getting worried."

Ken smiled. "Glad you stayed." He pointed at the coffee. "Any more of that."

"Sure! Come on in."

Pat broke two eggs into the frying pan on the white-gas stove. "How did you get away from the dog team?"

Ken described the encounter as he towelled himself dry and changed clothes. "They got closer to me than I ever thought they would."

"Well . . . that was my fault. I was going to bring Suzette out to see you at the trestle and she told the police where you were."

"Suzette's here?"

"You've already talked to her," Pat said grinning.

"I did?"

"She was the television reporter you spoke to when you had your cabin across the bridge."

"That was Suzette? She never said anything. I thought there was something . . . Shit . . . I didn't realise . . . and she told the police where I was?"

Pat looked down at the ground. "Yeah. Sorry."

"Well, I got away didn't I? Shit, I can't believe I didn't recognize her."

"It's been a long time. People change." He looked up. "But, yeah, you got away. They almost got me, too. I was across the river yelling at you when they hit the trestle. They had dogs, Argos, all sorts of stuff."

Ken took a long drink of coffee. "Did you get the things I asked for?"

"Yep. I even bought some other things." He showed Ken a little battery-operated television set. "I wanted to keep up on the news reports, but you don't have electricity. It's pretty fuzzy, but you can see the news."

"So how is the coverage?"

"Not too bad, but they've shifted their focus. They don't say much about who the land should belong to and they're trying to guess if the mill was deliberately burned and if there was any involvement of Francine Roussel, the Minister of Northern Affairs. They also talk about how foolish the police look."

Ken shook his head. "Well, I guess it's a start."

"But if the point is to make the people think about the injustice that was done here, it isn't working. No one's touching the issue of land rights, the fact that people grew up here had their homes taken away from them."

"That's because they don't even see it as an issue. What about the native rights? Anyone talking about that?"

"Some, but . . . you know . . . I'm a little uncomfortable with that. I don't think it's where we wanna go."

Ken turned and looked at Pat. "Why? Because it's uncomfortable?"

"Native people have a lot of support in the larger cities."

"People are people, Pat." Ken's tone was dismissive. "We all have certain needs and rights. It bugs the shit out of me that people are willing to admit that natives have a connection to the land, but they deny this connection for non-natives."

"I don't . . ." Pat faltered. The sizzling of the frying eggs filled the room.

Ken interrupted. "Consider this: Imagine that Kiosk had been an Indian village for fifty years, but in the 1970's, the government forced all the Indians out. Imagine that the natives came back and said they wanted their land returned. Don't you think they'd get support?"

"I guess."

"So people see the principle, but they're racially prejudiced. They're stupid. They believe that we can reduce prejudice in our society by having one set of rules for one race and another set of rules for another. Goddammit, the same rules and principals should apply to everyone."

Pat's face contorted. "That may be true, but I think you're getting off track."

"Aww, come on! Are you saying that, because you believe

it, or because you're afraid of conflict?"

Pat was silent for a moment. "Maybe a bit of both." He shovelled the eggs onto a plate for Ken. "When you called me about this protest, I was against it." He paused again and ran his hand through his hair. "No . . . not against it, just not too excited about the idea. I guess I've learned to be quiet as a way of not drawing attention to myself. But since I've been back here, I've changed. I think you're onto something and I'm even getting to the point where I want to help," he waived his hand at the supplies and the television he brought. "But I don't understand your anti-native sentiment. I don't like it."

"I love nature, Pat, and the damned Indians come here and destroy things."

"Whadya mean, destroy?"

"They don't have to follow hunting regulations and they go out in the park and kill all kinds of moose and deer."

"They have certain indigenous hunting rights."

"Bullshit!" Ken banged the table. "If they lived in an isolated community and hunted on foot with bows and arrows, then maybe there would be justification, but these guys come out from their houses in the city, in pickup trucks and four-wheelers, and kill animals with high-powered rifles. They don't even need the meat. They set up ice fishing lines all over the lake in the winter, draining the lakes of fish, and they kill whatever they want, whenever they want, wherever they want."

"So you're telling me that natives deliberately go into the park and kill moose for fun?"

"Damned right! I've seen it with my own eyes."

"There's always one or two bad apples in a bunch, but you can't tar everyone with the same brush. I'm sure there are bad non-native hunters. You've got to remember: Those hunting rights are part of treaties."

"Aahh, come on, Pat! Don't be so naive. Last year the damned Indians were allowed 350 moose in the park and they shot over 400." He paused and noted the surprise in Pat's face, "That's right! Over 400! In an area almost the same size, just to the north, non-natives were allotted fewer than ten! The damned Indians killed over 400 moose and they fish and hunt where we were born and raised, even though we're denied that same right!" Ken pointed at Pat. "That denial is nothing short of racism!"

"You're pretty bitter, aren't you?"

"It's just not fair. I was born here and I've been coming here all my life. I don't deny that there has to be some controls on hunting and fishing, but the damned Indians are killing off everything. I'm not even allowed to ride a bicycle in the park, but they drive through in brand new pickups, four-wheelers, powerboats. I'm not allowed to hunt and I have to follow every fishing regulation, but they hunt everywhere, and fish whenever they want. They gill net, trap, leave animals to rot in the bush. It's bullshit!"

Pat studied him for a while carefully weighing his words. "Remember that old guy who taught you about the bush? Richard?"

Ken nodded.

"He hung around with that Indian guy all the time. They were best of friends."

"That's because they were on equal footing," said Ken interrupting. "But the government changed all that with all their special rights. Richard and Tabby both lived by the same rules. Now, the Indians have special ones."

Pat smiled. "It sounds like you're jealous."

Ken exhaled and shook his head. "I just don't like what I see."

"Let me ask you this. If you could get an Indian band card, would you drive through the park in your pickup truck?"

A small smile appeared at the corners of Ken's mouth, but he did not answer.

"So you see; you are jealous."

"I don't see why we should be denied the same rights that are afforded to the Indians."

"So fight the denial, not the Indians. Fighting the Indians isn't going to get us anywhere. That's what we were originally talking about. The focus is wrong; we want people to focus on our land claim rights, not on who started the fire."

Ken remained silent as he ate his eggs. "You're right, I know that," he said finally. He leaned back and looked at Pat. "You know, we once lived the life that people say is worth protecting for Natives. When we lived in Kiosk, we were close to the land. It wasn't perfect, but it was more connected than anything we've experienced since. That's why we drift so much. There's something missing in our lives.

"Our grandparents and our parents hunted in Kiosk. They grew gardens, built their own houses and cut their own fuel. They swam in the lakes and rivers, picked berries in the forest, walked through the fields. They were a part of the world around them. And through them, we were connected - even if not completely - to the land.

"But then some other people from hundreds of miles away said that they knew what was best. They wrote the laws, they held the deeds, and they said that they had righteousness on their side. What they were doing, they said, was being done for the greater good. But, whatever their reasons, it was wrong. And it shows a set of values in our society that everyone just accepts."

"So that's what we have to change." Pat said.

"I'll tell you one thing that has to change: The belief that one group of people should have dominion over all things. It was that belief that made it seem perfectly acceptable to throw out the people of Kiosk and it's that belief that will, one day, destroy the fabric of this country!"

"Destroy the fabric of the country?" Pat held his hands in front of him.

Ken grinned and scratched the mosquito bites at his hairline. "Yeah . . . I guess I'm getting a little carried away. I've been thinking about this a lot."

"No, it's okay." Pat laughed. "I understand what you're trying to do and I really wanna help."

Ken nodded. "Good."

Pat leaned back. "One thing is true. Much of this is about image. The government wanted to give itself and image by handling the park situation in a certain way, and now you have to develop an image with the media."

"Go on."

"One thing the media seems to be interested in, is that the police are completely ineffective in the bush. Most people see this country as just a lot of open space, and you're showing that the police are not effective in that space. That's one thing that is keeping the press interested. What we have to do, is keep the press interested and push them to talk about the issue of people and land."

Ken laughed. "The first part won't be hard. The police have no skill in the bush."

"So? How can we do it?"

Ken emptied his backpack. The camera was still in a plastic bag. "I've got a few shots left and we'll take them around here. That's why I wanted the newspaper, so the date is confirmed for the photographs."

"If you take shots around here, isn't there a danger that someone will recognize the cabin?"

"I've got some Fabrene in the shed. We'll build a little structure that looks like a new cabin and we'll take shots of me sitting in it with the newspaper held up. No one will know where it is and they'll just assume it's in the park."

"And then?"

"You get them to someone and push for a little more editorial coverage on the original decision to close down the town. Talk about the town's committee, the multi-use land plan . . . all of that. That's the important part, Pat. You have to get them to focus on the people's connection to the land."

"They don't seem very interested."

"I suppose we have to grab their attention." Ken thought for a moment and then smiled widely. "Think you can get some of the press out here by four o'clock?"

Pat looked at his watch. "Yeah . . . probably. Why?"

"We'll turn up the heat. If they want to talk about Roussel and the how ineffective the police are, I'll give them all something to talk about."

"What?"

"I'll get on the other side of the lake and canoe toward Kiosk." Ken dug out some clothes and threw them in a pile. "I'll drag another canoe, and in it, I'll have an effigy of Francine Roussel. I'll push it toward town, set it on fire and let it burn in protest."

"Yeah, that should cause a bit of a ruckus." Pat's smile stretched ear to ear. "Hey, do you remember that night they burned an effigy of Ray Smith on his front lawn?"

"Of course. That's why this will be fitting. People will catch the significance."

Pat frowned. "But won't it be dangerous? The OPP will have a boat on the water."

"I'll only cross half the lake and I have a small motor. I'll watch the current, come in from the back, and let the canoe drift in. Even if the OPP have their boat in the water, they'll have to respond to the fire first . . . and my canoe's pretty fast."

Pat's expression showed that he not only liked the plan, but that he was enjoying the idea of participating in its execution. He walked to a little shelf and picked up something. "Before I forget, I have something for you." He handed Ken a small pointed crystal rock.

"Ah, thanks."

"You don't remember it, do you?"

Ken twirled it in his fingers. It didn't bring back any memories, and then he remembered the time Pat was leaving town. He had given him a little crystal that he found on the south side of the lake. "This is the . . ."

"The same one. I kept it all these years." He laughed. "And you know, it must have worked because in all these years I was never attacked by a bear." He laughed.

Ken looked at the rock. He had thought it was a tooth or an Indian arrowhead or something. Now it just looked like a piece of quartz. Still, it was amazing that Pat had kept it all these years. "You're a sentimental fellow, aren't you?"

"Well, you did say it was magic."

Ken laughed. "So now you want to give it back to me?"

"You're gonna need it if you're gonna start burning effigies out on the water."

"Thanks."

They set up the Fabrene hut, took some pictures and then Pat left the cabin with the film. Ken took his boat from the back shed and prepared to canoe through Lauder Lake and down the east arm of Kioshkokwi.

Suzy was wakened by a distant police siren that cut

through the clamminess of her small bedroom. She had left her bed-room window open just a crack and the glass pane was covered with moisture that had dripped down forming tiny rivulets in the early morning light. Outside she could hear tires-on-pavement, busses moving along the main street one block over, and a mourning dove cooing to greet the day. She sat up slowly, swung her feet to the carpeted floor and pulled her tangled hair out of her face.

Her mind slipped back to her thoughts of last night. It was strange to feel that drawn to a man. The concept of passion, of being driven to be with someone, had become almost foreign. Sex was a need that sometimes had to be fulfilled. And, in the last few years, that need had become less frequent.

Jean Guy had been a reasonable lover, but sex with him had been very routine. It was like exercising, and like exercising, she felt it might have been better without him being present. And afterwards, on most occasions, she wished they had separate bedrooms.

She couldn't remember the last time she had felt truly drawn to someone, wanting to be with them, wanting to connect with them. And she couldn't remember the last time she cried.

In the kitchen, she made coffee and called her daughter to join her for breakfast. Michelle left the television on, ran up the stairs, and gave her an unexpected hug. Suzy looked at her suspiciously, and Michelle just said, "What?"

They talked about Kiosk, about life in the north and even about Patrick and Kenny. Michelle paid close attention when the conversation turned to these two men and Suzy began to wonder if Michelle had heard her crying in the night. She didn't want to ask. There was no way to tell a young girl that it was too complicated to get involved with another man at this time. Michelle saw everything in terms of love and adventure and she didn't realise that practicality was often more important.

Carefully steering the conversation, Suzy got Michelle talking about her stay with the baby sitter and she was pleased to learn that it had not been as bad as she had feared. Michelle didn't say so, but it seemed she had enjoyed her time there.

After breakfast, Suzy went for a walk. There was no side-walk and she walked on the hard packed dirt beside the cracking pavement. Cars whizzed past, swirling her blouse and leaving the smell of sulphur in their wake.

It was a nice area, but not perfect. The bushes that lined the road were littered with discarded tins, plastic wrappers, and other garbage. Barrie was cleaner than Toronto or Montreal, but it certainly wasn't as nice as Kiosk, or even North Bay.

She walked by a small home that was busy with activity. A dozen people had gathered in the yard and were laughing, joking and eating. Some sat at a picnic table, others in folding chairs, and others stood with plates in their hands. Although surrounded by other homes, it was a world unto itself.

She smiled as she watched a little girl in a frilly dress running from adult to adult. She was the centre of attention and seemed so happy. Suzy frowned for a moment when she realised that Michelle no longer had the support of a family, and she suddenly missed the christenings, the family get-togethers.

Lionel, Michelle's father, had alienated them from their family. When her father lost his job at the furniture manufacturer, the same company where Lionel worked, Lionel shunned him. He spent time with his friends and didn't want Suzy's family coming for visits.

And now she was in another city, with no family, no companion and no one to support her - no one except Michelle. The walk lost its appeal and she turned back home.

As she entered the house, Michelle called from the living room. "Mom, one of your stories about Kiosk is on the news."

Suzy kicked off her shoes, walked quickly to the living room, and sat beside her daughter. She saw Jaro's shot of Armand talking to the police on the other side of the bridge.

A male announcer did a voice-over. "Although no one is certain what demands are being made by Kenneth Campbell, it is clear that the Ministry of Indian and Northern Affairs is interested in the situation. Armand Gingras, Senior Assistant for Francine Roussel, the controversial Liberal Cabinet Minister, eagerly followed the conflict, getting constant updates from the police. The OPP have, as yet, been unable to apprehend the protester."

Suzy jumped to her feet. "Holy shit! They're using our tape and getting someone else to do the story!" She looked at her daughter. "Sorry."

"It's okay mom," she groaned. "I've heard the word 'shit' before."

She closed her eyes for a second. "I've gotta go into work. Will you be all right for a while?"

"Sure."

Suzy changed, tore out of the house, and drove to the station. She walked into Nickeyfortune's office without knocking. Jaro was seated inside.

"Achh. So you made it in too." Nickeyfortune's accent was very pronounced.

"Damned right I did! If you wanted a voice-over on our story, why didn't you call me?"

"What? I'm supposed to review your footage, write your copy, tell you when to say it, and pay you as a news team! I don't think so, lassie. You two walked away from the story."

"But it was our footage," Suzy said.

"Jaro shot it! If it hadn't been for him, you'd have had nothing."

Suzy's face darkened. She wanted to say that she had told Jaro to shoot it, but she guessed that Jaro had already said the opposite. Getting into a fight in front of Nickeyfortune would not be productive. She looked at Jaro coldly. "At least we got it."

"At least I got it!" Jaro said.

Suzy's jaw dropped. "You piece of . . ." She stopped herself.

Nickeyfortune looked at Suzy expectantly. When she did not continue, he added: "And then you two dropped it off and went home to relax! I shouldn't have to tell you this, but this isn't a documentary; it's the bloody news! You do it right away, not when the creative urge hits!"

"I wanted to edit last night," Jaro looked at Suzy. "But someone had a kid to get home to."

Suzy closed her eyes, clenched her teeth, and said nothing. What was she doing here? Working with people who spent most of their time trying to find a way to sabotage her career? Trying to do something creative, which was only creative in the sense that it had to be done on time?

Jaro turned to Nickeyfortune. "In Suzy's defence, we had been there a long time."

Suzy bit her tongue. Not now, she thought.

Nickeyfortune was unimpressed; he studied Jaro. "And you should have stayed there longer. Did you even know that fellow was Francine Roussel's assistant?"

"Well, I . . ."

"I didn't think so," interrupted Nickeyfortune. "People don't care if some wilderness freak is running around in a park, but when a ministry official is involved - for whatever reason - then it becomes news. Roussel is a powerful figure and the fact that she was a Provincial Conservative and is now a Federal Liberal is embarrassing enough . . . but there's something more. If you would have talked to that guy, instead of just filming him from a distance, you might have got the key to the story."

"You can't expect us to know every government assistant on sight," Jaro said.

"Ask questions, for Christ's sake! Now that INAC is involved, the police are getting nasty! And I don't know why! Maybe there's something to this fire. Maybe the government was involved in torching that mill somehow. If they were, there could be hell to pay. We need to know."

Suzy dropped into a chair. "We'll go back if there's more to the story."

"Oh, there's more! The police have a search warrant for Campbell's home. If they even sniff a firearm, they'll send in a Tactical Response Team."

"Holy Shit! A TRU team?" Suzy looked down at the floor. Her mind raced. Ken would have guns. He was a hunter, even in his early teens. "We'll go back up."

"No need. I sent Kirk. I don't want Sudbury beating us to the punch again. We're almost the same distance away from the story and we're not going to let them get the lead. It's bloody embarrass-ing."

Suzy pictured Kirk. He was one of the old guys who usual-ly did the colour commentating for the sports desk. "But I know the people," she said.

Nickeyfortune exhaled sharply. "Didn't help you so far, did it?"

"Why didn't you let me know?" Jaro asked. "I would have

gone."

Nickeyfortune looked at a wall calendar. "The Autumn Artisan tour is coming up. Why don't you both get working on that? A good human interest piece there." Nickeyfortune smiled sarcastically.

Jaro stood quickly and walked out of the room. Suzy looked at Nickeyfortune and stood. "I don't know what your problem is, but I need to get back up to Kiosk. If they're bringing in a TRU team, people could get hurt. I'm gonna go."

"You're freelance. Do what you want." Nickeyfortune picked up the phone and flipped open his metal phone directory. He had no intention of letting the conversation continue. Suzy walked out and went straight to the exit.

On the drive home, she reached a decision. She couldn't leave things the way they were with Pat and she had to warn Ken about the dangers of a TRU team. She steeled herself for the unpleasant task of telling Michelle that she would be leaving again.

Before leaving for North Bay, Pat drove into Kiosk. He spoke to a few residents and told them that there would be an important statement at 4:00 P.M. If they could, he said, they should attend. Everyone wanted to know how Kenny was doing and what was going to happen, but Pat put them off, telling them to wait until four.

He used the payphone to call the North Bay newspaper and MCTV television. He told the newsrooms of both operations that Ken was giving a statement in Kiosk and then he left a message for Maggie Perrault. He said he would meet with her and give her another roll of film.

He had exercised before breakfast and his legs were stiff as he walked to the car, but he felt good. He drove to North Bay, picked up additional supplies, ate lunch, and then met with Maggie in the Mall Coffee Shop.

Dressed conservatively in a long skirt and matching jacket, she was excited about the film and she asked many questions. She listened intently as Pat talked about the philosophy of being connected to the land. He described how he and other residents felt when they returned to find their town, their past removed just like the mill after the fire.

"You know," said Maggie interrupting, "I'm really interested in that fire. There were hundreds of people sleeping in the town on that night, and if it had gotten out of control, many could have been killed. If someone actually set that fire, they might still be charged with criminal endangerment as well as arson. It's a pretty serious matter."

"There were a lot of weird coincidences on that night, but I think the injustice of taking away the homes of so many people is more important. Don't you think?"

Maggie hesitated. "I'm . . . I think that the people of Kiosk were treated unfairly, and I think there was - and is - a grave injustice, but if there were a case of attempted murder and arson and I had some really solid evidence . . . well, that would draw some attention to your cause. If there's some proof that links someone in business or the government with the fire, a fire that could have killed hundreds of people, that would break things wide open."

"If there ever was proof, it's long gone."

"Well, it would be irresponsible to make accusations without proof. Let me ask you this: "Who do you think started the fire?"

"Maybe it's best not to dwell on it. Maybe it's best to talk about the political injustice." Pat thought about the burning of the effigy of Francine Roussel. "You best bring a camera for Ken's statement." He grinned. "I think you'll be impressed."

"Why do you say that?"

"I can't tell you." He saw the protest in her eyes. "Really! But, be there. You won't be disappointed."

Maggie looked at her watch. "Alright," she said hesitantly, hoping he would add details. Pat remained silent. "I better get going then." She picked up the film. "I need to get this processed and then I need to get to Kiosk."

Pat stood and shook her hand. He didn't eat a donut or a chocolate bar and instead went to the grocery store to buy some healthful food before he returned to Kiosk. As he walked, he tried to decide what music he wanted to listen to. It was difficult. His tastes were changing.

***

Adrienne Denny, Gingras, White and Roussel sat in the conference room of the INAC office and Denny was again in control. This was difficult for Armand who was accustomed to being his own boss. He would normally not allow a reprimand from a mere press secretary, but because Roussel was present and angry, he had to sit and listen.

"In the noon news," Denny said, "they mentioned Madame Roussel's name eight times. And, they mentioned the Progressive Conservative Party eight times. Every time the two are mentioned together, we lose a little Liberal Party support."

"I thought, you knew this area . . . these people?" Roussel said looking at Armand.

Armand didn't respond.

"Why haven't the police been able to apprehend this Campbell fellow? Are they really such fools?" Without waiting for an answer, she continued. "Why didn't you talk to this fellow?"

"You have to understand the area. Campbell grew up there and he's gone back camping and fishing every year of his life. This is not a movie-set forest; the trees grow closely together. There are fallen-logs and branches everywhere; there are swamps, ponds, rocky cliffs; and, there are even iron ore deposits that screw up compasses. Unless you are an expert in the bush, it is easy to get lost. Campbell has the advantage. I would have loved to talk to Campbell, but I never got close. I grew up there, but I can't track a man through the bush."

"Didn't you say this area was logged?"

Armand smiled. "Yes, it's constantly logged, but not strip-cut. The logging companies leave seeders and they don't take the small poplar and balsam. Two years after a section's cut, it's so thick with saplings, it's impenetrable. There . . ."

Roussel interrupted. "Yes, yes, but there must be logging roads."

"Bush roads through the forest. But Campbell knows his way around without having to use them. There are thousands of square kilometres of lakes and forests."

"You said that Campbell got pictures out to the press. He

must be in contact with someone."

Armand thought about it for a moment. Suzette and Patrick, one of them could be the contact person. He played the scene back in his mind. Suzette had told the police about the meeting place on the trestle and Pat had been angry. Pat was the contact. He should have turned him over to the police. "I have an idea."

"Who?"

"Nobody important . . . just one of the old residents."

Denny smiled. "Well, then you better take care of the situation."

Armand's face flushed. Denny was an amateur trying to take advantage of this awkward situation. He would pay her back, but for now, he bit his tongue. He turned to Roussel. "I'll go back to Kiosk. I have some ideas."

"Good. Then, get to it."

Armand stood and was about to ask a last question, but before the first words left his mouth, Roussel cut him off. "Just go and take care of this situation." He was unaccustomed to being dismissed in this manner.

Gary Pinneskum drove his old truck into Kiosk and parked on the side of the road. It was the first time he had seen vehicles parked this far away from the ranger station. He had heard that Ken was going to give himself up and make a statement and he wanted to hear what he had to say. The press was still dancing around some native issues and he wanted to make sure that he was there, if needed.

The Algonquin land claims office didn't treat him with respect and he had no official authority, but he didn't care. He would speak his mind if necessary. Many native groups were only interested in developing natural resources, setting up businesses, and opening casinos. A small piece of parkland - land that had already been clear-cut - was of little interest. But this piece of land had been his home as a child. If the people from Kiosk had any right to the land, then he should too.

As he walked among the Kiosk residents, he kept his head down, but was still recognized. He had grown up in the bush and had little to do with Kiosk, but many Kiosk residents had moved to Mattawa after the fires in 1973, and he was known in Mattawa.

He spoke with one woman for a few minutes and then approached a group of Mattawa loggers who were talking about the fall moose hunt. When he drew near, they stopped talking. "Indian lovers," he muttered under his breath. He walked away. He found a quiet place to stand and resigned himself to wait for Ken's four-o'clock statement. He would do nothing till then.

He sat leaning against the large pine tree across from the outdoor bulletin board and watched the two television crews and the spectators milling around. All the camping spots were filled with tents and trailers and the parking lot was jammed with cars. Everyone was waiting for Ken to arrive.

Three police vehicles arrived, one towing an OPP boat and the other two filled with tactical officers. Gary stood and moved away. He did not like the cops.

Ken was soaked with sweat when he reached his canoe and motor. Earlier, he had canoed through Lauder Lake, portaged into Kioshkokwi, paddled along the eastern shore and then hid his canoe near the Mink Lake portage. He had then run through the forest for almost two miles. He was accustomed to cov- ering large distances in a day, but with the stress of the deadline and the waiting townspeople, he tired more quickly.

During his trip, the cloud cover had dissipated and the sun began to shine, but a breeze was making the lake choppy. Nervously, he paddled the canoe back toward the point across from the town, thankfully with the waves. It would have been much quicker to use the motor, but he was afraid of the noise, of attract- ing any unnecessary attention.

He pulled his canoe onto a sandy beach. Not too far away, a cottage owner had canoes locked in a boat house. He walked up a stony path and found the cottage empty - as it usually was - and using a large rock, he busted a lock and took one of the canoes.

The next job was to make his scarecrow. He had brought clothes and safety pins, but he needed stuffing material. He found some rags in the shed, but they were not enough and he gathered organic material, leaves, needles and moss.

It was difficult to make it look like a woman, especially with men's clothes, but he had two cardboard signs that would identify it as the effigy of Francine Roussel. Once set on fire, it would merely be a burning mass, and if the signs weren't visible, it would be up to Patrick to tell everyone whom the scarecrow represented.

He carried the canoe and the scarecrow down to the beach and studied the weather. Large cumulus clouds drifted across the blue sky and a light breeze blew across the water. The lake was full of angular waves that caught the sunlight and looked like thousands of glistening gems. The wind was blowing from the west, which was ideal, because it would carry the second canoe right to the shore of Kiosk as he fled back the way he came. He would be able to hide his canoe on the west arm of the lake and still have his Lauder Lake canoe on the east arm.

The two canoes gently banged against the rocks near the shore as he tied a line between them, and looking at his watch, he saw that it was already just after four. He was late. He climbed into his canoe, paddled away from the shore, and started the motor.

He looked back. The scarecrow was surprisingly realistic, sitting in the midship position. He had decided not to throw the gasoline until he was ready to start the fire. With the sun and the breeze, the gas would evaporate quickly. "Sorry, old girl," he said to the dummy as he steered the boat toward Kiosk.

A loud rumble shook the air and Ken scanned the horizon. The clouds to the northwest were dark and warned of a coming thunderstorm. The buildings and people across the lake were just visible and he throttled his engine up to full speed. He and Pat had agreed that no one should know where he was until the sound of the motor was on the lake.

He could imagine Pat getting everyone excited and he figured that, any minute, a large group would appear on the beach. He wished he could go a little faster. Although he was moving quickly in relation to the water around him, he didn't seem to be moving quickly toward the shore.

From his angle of approach, he couldn't see the dock at the ranger station, but he could see, the cement boat launch, the public beach and the small island, which was no longer an island but a peninsula since the drops had been removed from the weir on the river.

There were still no people gathered on the shore, and he could see them milling about, standing in groups, some near the campsites, and some in the parking lot. No one seemed to be paying attention to his approach.

Had Pat not returned to Kiosk? Had something happened to delay him? Ken was nervous about getting too close to the town, but his demonstration would be ineffective if no one knew he was here.

He turned and looked at his scarecrow. The head, a plastic garbage bag, was tilted backwards, but the figure still sat in the middle of the canoe. He turned back to the shore. Where were the people? At the end of the point, off to the left of the ranger station, he saw someone waving his arms in the air. Ken shielded the sun from his eyes and looked. It was Pat. What was he doing? He had stopped waving and he was now moving his arm forward and backward in a motion that implied, 'go back.'

He had travelled far enough to the west to see the dock and Pat's panicked motions were suddenly clear. He gasped as he throttled back, bringing his canoe almost to a stop. The second canoe drifted past him and then turned on its tether. Sitting at the dock was an OPP cabin cruiser.

For a moment, Ken was frozen. The blood left his face and he could feel a tingle in his hands and feet. He grabbed the tether rope, pulled the second canoe toward him, and reached for the bottle of gasoline. He tossed the yellow fluid over the scarecrow and then untied the tether.

He looked up and saw a few people moving toward the beach, but there was also activity on the OPP boat. Shit, shit! he thought. He pushed the canoe away, lit a gas-soaked cloth, and tossed it toward the scarecrow. He watched in horror as it missed, fell into the water, sished and flickered out. Smoke drifted up and coloured bands of unburned fuel spread across the water.

In the distance, he could hear the sound of hard boots on the deck of the cruiser. "Shit!" he said through clenched teeth.

***

The Honourable Francine Roussel gently replaced the handset in the cradle and placed her finger on her chin. This was getting out of hand. She picked up the handset again and called Adrienne Denny. "I need you back in my office," she said. "And bring White with you."
She hung up forcefully and leaned back in her chair.

It took only moments for White and Denny to arrive. She heard the receptionist saying something as they passed - most likely telling them that the last call had come from the Prime Minister.

"Sit down," she said as they walked in. "As you probably just heard, that was the Prime Minister. He too is concerned about the protest in Kiosk."

"Oh?" White looked surprised.

"You know that the Prime Minister was the Minister of Indian Affairs?" The two nodded. "Well, he was Minister from 1968 to 1974. That is the precise time that the first protest started and it's the precise time of the fire that burned the mill."

"But the INAC has nothing to do with a logging protest."

"It doesn't matter what is, it matters what people perceive. He's angry that Gingras was on-camera in the area, because he feels it ties this Ministry to the protest, and that leads ultimately to him."

"But Gingras is going to state that the Ministry is not involved in the protest." White said.

"We have to go further than that. I think we have to make Gingras' connection to the town public. We have to state that we did not want him in the area, and his attendance was a matter of his own, personal interest in the town."

White pursed his lips. "But we sent him. And the Ministry is not involved."

The corners of Denny's mouth turned up a little. "I can put together a statement saying that Gingras was asked not to go to the town and that he did so on his own volition."

"Why?" White said under his breath. "To hang him out to dry?"

Roussel interrupted. "There are more important issues at play here. The simple fact is that we can't let this situation spiral any farther out of control. The Prime Minister is concerned. The damned Alliance Party is getting ahead in the polls - something no one expected - and I've had two phone calls from Luegenhauser. Everyone wants this squashed and no one wants the INAC involved."

"Who called from Luegenhauser?" White asked, sitting up slightly.

Roussel regretted having mentioned the name. Luegenhauser was a large corporation that owned, among its vast empire, a number of logging companies in Northern Ontario. They had contributed to her campaigns over the years, but always at a corporate level. Corporate officers should not be calling Federal Ministers asking for favours. "It doesn't matter," she said impatiently.

"I just thought . . ."

"Look!" Roussel interrupted. "We have one-hundred and fifty lawyers working full time handling native lawsuits on residential schools. We have a battalion of lawyers handling land claims. Our resources are stretched and we don't need to increase our exposure to any other land claims - from anyone! Two years ago, the Prime Minister created a 'healing fund' of two-hundred-and-fifty million dollars; last year it was three-hundred-and-seventy million. This year it's close to a half billion. These damned protests have to stop!"

"But again, this has nothing to do with INAC. At best, it's a provincial matter."

"And again, it's about perception. I was a Provincial Member of Parliament and I'm now the Minister of Indian and Northern Affairs. The Prime Minister was the Minister of Indian Affairs, and this whole fiasco is taking place in what the people of this country think is the north."

"I suppose," White said. "But I just hate to hang Gingras like that. He's gonna make a statement on behalf of the Ministry and at the same time the Ministry is making a statement that he is acting without sanction. Talk about a quick end to a career."

Roussel shrugged. Denny waited for the silence to be filled and when it wasn't, she said that she would prepare the statement and get it out to the press. She asked if she should show it to

Roussel first, but Roussel shook her head.

It was early afternoon as Suzy cruised north on Highway 11. She had driven non-stop from Barrie, and all the way, she had analysed her feelings and motivations. She was aware that she was attracted to Patrick, but decided this was not her only motivation. She felt a special allegiance to Ken and Pat. They had shared a common past. They were like family and they deserved her support in their quest to restore some dignity to the people of Kiosk.

As her mini-van decelerated on the dusty road leading into town, she saw that many more people had arrived. Cars and trucks were parked everywhere and there was a stronger police presence.

She drove through the town and arrived at the ranger station. It was packed. The parking lot was jammed and she pulled her vehicle into the bushes by one of the campsites. Outside of the van, she was greeted by a few acquaintances. It was enjoyable to reminisce, but right now, she had to find Patrick and get a warning to Ken. This was no longer a playful protest. If the OPP brought in a TRU, and suspected that Ken had weapons, shots could be fired.

Three television crews were set up in various locations and she found Kirk near the dock. He was trying to interview an officer standing near a large OPP cabin cruiser. The officer was not interested.

"Hi, Kirk. What's up?"

Kirk looked surprised to see her. "What're you doing here?"

"I'm on my own clock. Don't worry; I'm not here to steal the story."

"Oh, that's right; you grew up here didn't you?"

"Yep. I know a lot of these people."

"Well, maybe you can help me get . . ."

Suzy anticipated his question. "Sure, I'll help you get the right people for some interviews, but in the mean time, I need to know what's going on."

"The word is that Ken Campbell is going to give a statement here at four o'clock." Kirk looked around. "I don't know where he's gonna be, but there's enough cops around here that if he shows his face, he's done like dinner."

Suzy smiled at the colloquialism and then looked at her watch. It was almost four o'clock. She pointed at the cabin cruiser. "Is this part of a TRU team?"

Kirk shook his head. "No, they brought that in from North Bay. I heard that Campbell outran them on water two times in a row. I guess they don't want to let that happen again."

"But there is a TRU team coming in?"

"Nickeyfortune said that they were going to Campbell's home. If they found evidence of weapons, they would send in a TRU, but they would have to bring them in from Barrie, Belleville or London. They probably wouldn't get here till late tonight."

Suzy nodded. "Thanks Kirk. I'll look around and see if I can dig up anything for you."

"Sure, Suzy, you do that. But remember, it's my story now."

"Yeah, Kirk, no problem."

Suzy walked through the parking lot and campgrounds looking for Pat. She couldn't spot him, but she did see Armand Gingras. He seemed to be interviewing people, asking questions and he too, moved from group to group acting more like a reporter than a representative of the INAC - or a one-time resident of Kiosk.

She saw many people she knew and she spoke to a few, but they seemed cool, distant, and she could not get them to talk. She wondered if they still thought of her as a reporter, someone on the outside looking in, and did not see her as a participant.

Near a camping trailer, she saw Armand Gingras talking to old Mr. Loeffler. Gingras seemed to be trying to get away and when Mrs. Degagne joined in the conversation, he made an escape.

A little further away, she saw an older man taking pictures of Armand. She wasn't sure, but it looked like Ray Smith, the one-time mill-manager who was so disliked. Strange that he should come back to town, she thought, because there would not be many who would welcome him.

She walked over to Mr. Loeffler and when there was a break in the conversation, asked if she could speak to him privately. He nodded and walked a few paces away from Mrs. Degagne.

"Have you seen Pat around?" Suzy asked.

"He's here, somewhere. Did you come to hear Ken's statement?"

"Well . . . yes and no. I actually wanted to talk to him. That's why I wanted to speak to Pat. I need to warn them about something."

Mr. Loeffler eyed her cautiously. "I think you may have trouble gaining his confidence."

Suzy hadn't really considered it previously, but she suddenly remembered that there was a lot of gossip in a small town. Some people may have talked about her news team revealing Ken's position. "You heard about that, did you?"

"I think everyone has. You haven't made yourself to be Laura Secord, have you?"

Suzy screwed up her face. "Pardon me?" It was often difficult to follow Mr. Loeffler's line of thought.

"What I mean to say is that they probably wouldn't trust any information you provide."

Suzy swallowed. Sadness as dense as mineral water filled her throat. "No, they probably wouldn't . . . I suppose . . . but I still want to talk to Patrick." She studied the crowd of people, looking for him. Did she want to talk to him to pass on useful information to Ken, or did she want to talk to him because of the childish fantasies that were playing though her head? She didn't know.

"One thing about the people in this town is that they generally stuck together. When you were a little girl and you hurt yourself, you could have gone into almost any house in town and received assistance. Doors were left unlocked and people took care of each other . . . they trusted each other. When people retired, they continued to be a part of the community and they weren't left to sit in an apartment." Mr. Loeffler pouted and scuffed at the ground.

"So you don't know where he is?"

Mr. Loeffler looked up, caught in some thought. He shook his head.

"I have to go find him, it's important."

"That's okay dear. You go ahead."

Suzy walked away, now aware that people were avoiding her. She looked right and left and caught the odd person looking away. They did think of her as a traitor. She stopped and looked in a circle and stared right into the camera of the old person she thought to be Ray Smith. She knitted her eyebrows, watched him turn away, and then continued to walk toward the beach.

The OPP cruiser was pulling away from the shore. Kirk's cameraman was filming the action and a lot of people were gathering on the shore. She ran a few steps and saw two canoes out in the middle of the lake. There was one person in each canoe.

Ken's hands started to shake and he felt nauseous and dizzy. He had to ignite the effigy, but it was too far away and he had no more burnable cloth to throw. With every second, he was drifting closer to the police. He turned the throttle hoping to reach the second canoe, but the water surged between them forcing it further away. It was drifting closer to Kiosk - toward the police.

The OPP cruiser's motor came to life. With his breath caught in his throat, he knew he would never reach the effigy in time. Should he turn and flee? Without the fire, his actions wouldn't make sense. He grabbed the pocket of his shirt and ripped, tearing a ragged gash in the front of his shirt. He wiped the patch in the little gas that remained, lit it, and threw it onto the scarecrow. The scarecrow ignited with a concussive thaarrrump.

He stared at the flames for a second, watching them dance up the scarecrow's form, and then reached back for the throttle. The canoe whipped around under heavy acceleration as the stern dug in and the bow lifted. He leaned forward for better trim and then looked over his shoulder. The scarecrow was burning and behind it, the OPP boat was approaching. He could see the water curling on each side of its bow as its motors droned.

His canoe was much further away from the sandy beach than he had intended, but he was closing the distance quickly. He adjusted his course and headed straight for the nearest land, praying that the OPP would be distracted by the burning canoe. He needed to get his canoe to safety. Beyond the sandy beach was a cove and a small river. It was barely big enough for a canoe and if he could reach it, the OPP would not be able to follow and he could take his canoe inland and hide it.

His knuckles were white on the throttle, but his motor was wide open and there was nothing he could do but aim for land. He glanced over his shoulder and saw that the OPP cruiser was much closer, cutting through the lake like a knife through butter. Slow down, he thought, slow down. With a sudden relief, he heard the cruiser's motors drop in frequency as the big boat slowed and circled the second canoe.

Ken looked ahead and studied the land. He lowered his body hoping the drop in wind resistance might give him some extra speed. His mouth was dry and he licked his lips, tasting the splash that was running down his face. The motor noise behind raised in pitch and he turned to see the cabin cruiser turning, ignoring the burning canoe and accelerating toward him. Behind the large boat, people had gathered on the shore to watch the chase unfold. If nothing else, he thought, he'd managed to attract attention.

He looked forward. The shore seemed impossibly distant. How was he going to escape? He had so little control; all he could do was sit in the boat and wait till it reached shore.

The sound of the motor behind him was louder and he could now hear the splash of water on their hull. They were close. Over his shoulder, he saw a man on the front deck holding a long pole with a loop of rope. Ken ducked to make himself a more difficult target even though the large boat was still a hundred metres away.

Thunder clapped above him and he looked up to see dark threatening clouds. Although the sky was flecked with blue, it was mostly cloud covered, and to the north, over the town, it was black. He looked down and saw the first rocks. The water was still deep, ten metres or so, but some of the rocks were large and closer to the surface. He was close to shore, but too far away from the river. There was little hope that enough time remained for him to swing around and reach its mouth before being overrun by the police, but he hoped his luck would change. He kept his little motor running at full throttle.

The sound of the motor behind him increased in pitch. The police were getting reckless in their desire to stop him from reaching the shore. Ken could do nothing but continue. He could now sense the presence of the boat; it was bearing down on him and in seconds, it would be on him.

Suddenly, there was a loud bang and the throttle was ripped out of his hands. His small motor screamed as he was thrown violently forward and the world turned upside down. He turned, climbed back to his knees, and saw the little motor out of the water, propeller pointing to the sky. It gurgled and dropped in rpm's. Behind him, the OPP boat was decelerating rapidly.

It took a second, but he realised that the tail of his motor had a submerged piece of wood and been thrown into the air. This lake was full of dead heads, submerged logs that had never reached the mill. Scrambling back to the stern, he jabbed at the release button and the propeller plunged back into the water. The cabin cruiser was right behind him, pushing water forward as it tried hard to decrease speed. They had seen his motor pop up and if there were obstacles close enough to the surface to hit the bottom of a canoe, the cabin cruiser would surely suffer damage.

He turned the throttle and although the motor revved, his speed did not increase. The sheer pin, he thought, when he hit the log, he had broken the sheer pin. There was another in the casing of the motor, but obviously, there was no time to install it. He pulled the motor back out of the water, jumped forward in the canoe and grabbed the paddle. If he paddled, he could stay in shallower water, and perhaps stay away from the big boat behind him.

The OPP swung away from the rocks and the shore and circled toward the sandy beach. If they beached their boat, they had him. He was paddling over the rocks, directly toward the beach, but they would be there before him. He had no choice; he paddled directly toward the rocky shore. His only chance of escape now was on land.

The sky flashed and a loud crack, like a gunshot, sliced through the air overhead. Ken instinctively ducked and as he lifted his head, his canoe lurched. The hull scraped loudly and then whipped around in a half circle. He was on the rocks. He grabbed his backpack, jumped into the water, and lost his footing on the green, algae-covered bottom. He fell and sharp pain detonated bright white in his brain as his arm and ribs smashed into the jagged rocks. Frantically, he pulled himself to all fours and scrabbled toward the shore. Blood mixed with the water that ran down his arm and across his fingers.

At the shore was a barrier to the land. Waves had underwashed the roots of trees creating a fence of tangled and twisted wood. He jumped from rock to rock until he found a break and then forced his way through the flaky trunk wood and onto the packed ground above. Through the trees, he could see OPP officers jumping off the boat, and into the water. They were already at the sandy beach.

Assembling all his strength, he picked a direction and started to run. Another crack of lightening split the sky over the trees. This one was sharp and hard and it vibrated his very bones.

The sky turned bright and then sizzled with electricity. A high-pitched crack whipped through the air. "Holy Shit!" someone cried on the stony beach. "They're shooting!" The crowd was agitated as it watched the chase on the far side of the lake.

Patrick walked back toward the boat ramp, near where the OPP cruiser had been docked, and looked for the camera crew. He was pretty sure that Ken had escaped - he had seen him get to shore and he knew he could outrun the police on land - but now he had to tell everyone what the scarecrow was all about. The canoe with the burning effigy was still drifting toward town, but it seemed to be lower in the water. It was probably sinking.

"It's an effigy of the old Member of Parliament, Francine Roussel!" Patrick pointed to the burning canoe.

A very old woman with a heavy French accent cackled: "Ahh, dat's what dat is!"

"Ha!" shouted a woman with a scarf wrapped around her head. She laughed loudly, the relief evident in her voice. Black smoke rose from the canoe, but the flames were dying. The canoe was taking on water.

"It's just like the scarecrow we burned at Ray Smith's house!" someone shouted.

"Burn you bastard!" laughed the woman in the scarf.

The tension disappeared and was replaced by jubilation. People were hooting and shouting. A CBC camera operator filmed the crowd and the well-dressed woman who had been standing on the shore walked toward the largest group. "Why would he burn Francine Roussel in effigy?" she asked, holding a microphone.

"Roussel was the MP when the town was closed," said an older man.

"Did Ms. Roussel spend much time . . ." Another loud crack ripped through the sky, interrupting the reporter. "Did Roussel visit the town when she was the Member of Parliament?"

"Why are they shooting?" someone asked.

"It's just the lightning," said the woman in the scarf.

Maggie Perrault, the North Bay Nugget reporter, moved closer to the group. She held out her small micro recorder.

Patrick saw Maggie and moved away to another group. He had to tell as many people as possible that the burning blob in the canoe was Francine Roussel, but he didn't want to compromise his own safety by becoming the centre of attention. He found Joanne and Howard Scoffield and Annette and Tirj Dupuis. The Scoffields remembered the burning of the Ray Smith effigy and they seemed pleased that Ken had used this symbol.

A lot of people were talking about the possibility of shots being fired, but Patrick was fairly certain that it was simply the echo of the thunder dancing back and forth between the lakes. He decided not to dispel the uneasiness, however, since fear of gunplay garnered additional attention.

Patrick walked over to Mr. Loeffler and he told him about the significance of the burning effigy. Mr. Loeffler smiled, "Civil disobedience," he said, holding up a finger. "That's what it's . . ." His words were interrupted by the sound of crunching gravel. Heads turned as four police vehicles sped into the parking lot. They stopped near the lake, forcing spectators out of the way. Officers in black uniforms poured out. Two men moved into the crowd, one looking for an ERT officer and the other looking for a park warden. They ignored the spectators and refused to answer questions.

"This is getting serious," Patrick said.

"I wonder if this is what Suzette wanted to tell you."

Pat swung his head to face the old man. "Suzette spoke to you?"

"Yes, she was looking for you. She said she had to warn you about something."

"More likely she wanted to pump me for information."

"Somehow, I don't think so." Mr. Loeffler scratched his chin and smiled. "You may have finished school, but that doesn't mean you still don't have a lot to learn."

Pat raised his eyebrows and then turned back to face the police. They were moving purposefully, moving people away, talking on radios. Nothing was done slowly. Soon most of the crowd was herded away from the bottom end of the parking lot.

Ken tripped over a half-buried root, fell to the ground, rolled and sprang to his feet. As he twisted, he saw the police some distance away. They were scrambling through the bush, trying to locate him, but they were running slowly, laden with equipment.

He slowed for a moment, but then decided it would be foolish to underestimate his pursuers. He had done that before and almost paid with capture. He darted ahead quickly, quietly, using the forest to his advantage, and then turned to study their approach. They were all going in different directions, unable to track him, and only one was actually on his trail. He could hear the other cops shouting, but the voices were growing distant. They were going the wrong way.

He led the single officer further away, wondering why this cop had not called out to the others. Was this guy actually tracking him or just searching through the forest.

When he came to a boggy section of ground, he jumped from clump to clump placing his feet where the vegetation would provide the most secure footfalls. The bog between these clumps looked deep and sticky.

Ken reached the opposite side and turned to see the cop trying to follow. Ken wasn't sure if the officer had seen him, but he had likely been following Ken's tracks. He had stopped however and seemed daunted by the bog. One foot was already sunk in mud up to the ankle.

He swung his backpack off his shoulders, grabbed his camera, and pointed at the officer. The flash illuminated the dark forest and the officer looked up. Immediately, he lost his footing, fell, and hit the ground with a splat. Ken lifted the camera and took another picture, this time of the tactical officer wallowing in the mud. If it turned out, it would be a front-page item for sure. He stuffed the camera back in the backpack and turned as he heard the crackle and static of police radios.

Two park wardens circulated among the crowd. One was the woman Pat had met on his first visit and the other was an older gentleman with a moustache. Pat overheard the woman saying that, in the interest of safety, they were being asked to leave. All camping permits were being refunded.

"Can they do this?" Pat asked.

"They can do whatever they want to - as long as we let them get away with it." Mr. Loeffler looked to the right and Patrick followed his gaze. Suzette was walking toward them.

"I guess she found you," Mr. Loeffler said.

Pat turned to face Suzette and noticed that she slowed her pace. When she reached them, Pat put his hands in his front pockets.

"I'm glad I finally found you," she said. She looked at Pat's face and seemed to hesitate. "I need to get a warning to Ken about this TRU team."

"Well, thanks for the warning, but as you can see, it's a little late." There was a sharp edge to Pat's voice.

Mr. Loeffler jumped into the conversation. "What's a TRU team?"

"It stands for Tactical Response Unit. There are three in Ontario and they don't fool around. The police that were here are called ERTs, which stands for Emergency Response Team. They handle the local emergencies, but the TRU teams are only called in when a situation escalates."

Mr. Loeffler rubbed his brow. "Why would they call them in, then? Surely, Ken is not a threat to anyone?"

Suzy looked at Pat. "That's what I wanted to tell you. Someone told them that Kenny has guns and the police got a search warrant for his place. If they found any guns, the TRU team will be more aggressive."

Patrick felt his stomach sink. Of course Kenny had guns,

lots of them. He remembered seeing them on the wall of his home. He had shotguns, 22's, a 30.06, and the Winchester 30.30. "He has guns . . . people said there were shots fired." He searched his memory. Had it been just the thunder, or had shots been fired? He looked up at the darkening sky.

"I think that was just thunder," Suzy said, "but it doesn't matter. If they found guns in Ken's home, this whole thing could get out of hand. We have to . . . you have to warn him."

"But Ken knows the bush. He can outrun anyone from a city."

"I've seen the TRU team in Barrie. These guys train hard. They run, they work out. These are not your average run-of-the-mill cops. Kenny's in trouble here and the worst thing is that he doesn't know it."

The female warden walked toward them. "Hi. I'm going to have to ask you to leave." She looked at a pad of paper and spoke in a rehearsed manner. "The police have requested that the area be cleared. We'll refund the cost of your camping permit."

Patrick was about to answer - to stall for time - but before he could get the first word out, Mr. Loeffler spoke. His tone was sharp; it was the way he might have spoken to a disrespectful student. "And what if we refuse to leave?"

The warden looked up, the surprise showing on her face. "Pardon me?"

Mr. Loeffler spoke louder and raised his hands. "I said! What if we refuse to leave?"

A few people turned, attracted by the volume of Mr. Loeffler's voice. "I'm sorry, sir, I'm just relaying what the police told me to say."

"Well, I have no intention of leaving! This is a public park! We paid for the camping permit! And you can't make us move!"

Some people moved toward their group. "Way to go, Mr. Loeffler!" shouted a middle-aged man in a baseball cap.

"The police just said . . ."

A chorus of 'boos' rose from the crowd. The warden held up her hands, turned and walked back toward the station. She had no intention of having another confrontation. Pat looked at Suzy. She shrugged and burst out laughing. It was hard to imagine Mr.

Loeffler as the rabble-rouser, but that was exactly what he was turning out to be. A group of three people descended on the other ranger and loudly proclaimed that they also weren't leaving.

The older warden gave up the quest as the crowd moved back toward the shore of the lake. The police got out of the way and left the crowd alone, but they moved to protect the dock. The large cabin cruiser was returning.

The muddied officer spoke into his radio. He peered into the bush, shook his head in disgust, and then got to his feet. Ken watched him and tried to imagine his thoughts. He was probably wondering if it had been lightning or if someone had taken his picture. His face twisted in concentration and he stood staring - trying to reach a decision. He peered into the woods, looking for Ken, but couldn't see him. The forest was dark and Ken stood quietly waiting. Another command burst out of his radio and he dusted off his arm, turned, and walked away.

Ken was certain that he could outrun the officers in the bush, but hadn't thought they would give up this quickly. What was happening? Cautiously, he moved back across the bog and then craned his neck. Were they all retreating? Should he follow them?

He heard some shouts from the shore and after a few moments, he heard the motor of the boat fire up. Unbelievably, they were retreating. Why? He walked to the north, scrabbled down a short incline and peered through the tangle of roots. He could see the large boat with the OPP insignia, moving back toward the town. His canoe was roped to the back and skimmed over the water like a Frisbee. The other canoe was near the far shore and no longer burned.

The sky was awash with greys and yellows, but no rain had fallen. Moisture hung heavily in the air. Across the lake, the shore glowed with many flashing lights and many people moved back and forth. It seemed that more police were present than when he had first brought his canoe into the middle of the lake, but it was difficult to be sure.

With the thick cloud cover, darkness would come quickly and he decided to work his way back to the canoe he had used this morning. It was a long trip back to his cabin, but it would be nice to spend the night in shelter, especially since rain seemed inevitable.

The police seemed curiously unconcerned by the protest of the townspeople. They ignored them and erected a few barricades near the dock and the ranger station. The press tried to bludgeon them with questions, but the officers, dressed in military-style gear, refused to answer. One officer, dressed in grey, said that a statement would be available later. He asked the press to clear the area, but they were not moving, not as long as the townspeople remained.

Ray Smith took a few more pictures and looked around at the crowd. Armand Gingras was walking toward the police. Smith recognized him and immediately snapped a few head-and-shoulders shots. An older man just a few feet away, looked at Gingras and then at him.

"Ray Smith?" he said loudly. "Is that you?"

Ray turned to look at the man. He was wearing baggy green pants and a green shirt - a farmer's uniform. He thought he recognized him as one of the saw filers, but he couldn't be sure. "Hello," he said weakly.

The green-shirted man turned to a group of people near by and spoke loudly. "Hey, everyone! It's Ray Smith. He finally came outside when he saw the scarecrow burning!" A few people looked at Smith and broke into laughter.

Smith dropped his camera and let it dangle on its neck strap. He turned and walked away angrily.

"Don't go, Smith," said a woman in her mid sixties. "The fire's gone out already." She cackled and this sparked more laughter from the crowd.

Smith walked to his Grand Marquis and slipped into its luxury. Its quiet, white leather interior was an immediate escape from the noisy rabble outside. He started the car and relaxed as the air-conditioning blew across his torso.

He regretted his visit. It had been foolish and he wished he hadn't been recognized. These people had never understood the need for progress . . . for profit. Most of them still lived in poverty in Mattawa, whereas he had a large home in an upper-class area in Southern Ontario. He had done very well for himself - cottages, boats, beautiful houses, and plentiful retirement funds. "Bastards!" he said, but when he looked up, he saw he was alone. No one had followed him; no one was watching.

He reached over and picked up the phone handset. The cord snaked across the console and into a large nylon case. It wasn't a very portable phone, but at least it worked in these outlying areas - not like those useless miniature sets that everyone carried. "It's done. I have the pictures." He listened for a while. "I'm leaving now."

He smiled and put the car into gear. No one noticed as he drove away.

If Patrick had been surprised by Mr. Loeffler's loud protest, he was even more surprised by his own voice on the phone. He called work from the outdoor payphone to tell them he would be away a few more days and Judith, the only female salesperson at the dealership, refused to pass on the message. Instead, she transferred the call to Eric.

At first, Patrick felt nervous, but when Eric started to threaten and berate, Patrick lost his temper. He said he was staying and there would be no further debate. If he had to lose his job, then, so be it. He then went on to say he was tired of being treated like a child. He knew his responsibilities, and this was important. He should be treated with more respect.

Faces turned as he yelled into the phone and this somehow felt good. He slammed the handset into its chrome cradle and walked away.

As he neared the Park Office, he heard voices inside. He heard Campbell's name and someone said: "He's surely armed and definitely a danger." Pat paused at the partially opened door to listen. The voice continued. "People's lives are at risk all because of one psychotic protester."

Pat pushed open the door and found Armand Gingras talking to an ERT officer. He put his hands on his hips and spoke using the same sort of language that Eric had used on the phone. "What the fuck are you saying?"

Gingras turned his head to the side. "Excuse me, this is a private conversation."

"This is a public building! And you're full of shit! Ken is not a threat to anyone! He hasn't done anything more dangerous than stand up to authority!" Pat pointed at Gingras. "It's people like you that create the danger!"

Gingras ignored Pat and faced the police officer. "This man is a friend of Ken Campbell and I think he is the one who has been getting the photos to the press. He knows where Campbell is hiding!"

"You're full of shit! I have no idea where Ken Campbell is hiding!" Pat moved closer. "But you're right, he is one of my friends and even if he wasn't, he's a good man; I wouldn't allow him to get hurt."

Gingras continued talking to the officer. "I think you should take this man into custody. He probably has information that you need to find your fugitive."

"I think you should take this man into custody!" Patrick took a step toward Gingras and jabbed his finger at him. "He's trying to escalate this into something dangerous! He's trying to get someone shot!"

Gingras batted away Pat's hand. "Achh," he groaned gutturally.

Pat flew at Gingras and grabbed him by the shirt. "Just what the fuck do you think you're doing, you little prick?"

Gingras hesitated for a moment, debating what course to take. Suddenly he brought up his hands and broke Pat's grasp, but in the upward movement, he hit Pat in the face. Pat reacted immediately. He cocked his right fist and threw a straight jab, hitting Gingras square in the jaw. Gingras bounced back against the wall and the OPP officer grabbed Pat by the arms. Gingras advanced as if he expected the officer to hold Pat while he hit him, but the officer anticipated the attack and spun Pat out of the way. He fell onto Gingras, pinning his arms against his sides. "You two better cool it! Right now!"

Pat walked to the door as the officer relaxed his hold on Gingras. "Don't believe what that little prick tells you. He liked to see people suffer when he was a kid, and I don't think he's changed."

Gingras hoarsely whispered a taunt, saying that Ken was going to be buried by the end of the day, but the officer interrupted, trying to diffuse the situation. Pat left the building and walked through the parking lot. He had to find Suzy.

He could feel the blood pulsing in his neck. He was so full of rage that the gravel under his feet irritated him. Past a small group of trees, he could see Suzette and Mr. Loeffler and the sight of her calmed him slightly. "You were right!" he said to Suzette. "This is getting out of hand. That little Gingras shithead is trying to convince the police that Ken is armed and dangerous."

"The fellow from the Ministry of Indian and Northern Affairs?"

Pat thought for a moment. "Yeah, that's right. He . . ." His words were interrupted by the sound of a helicopter. It swooped over the camping area, the rotor-wash twisting trees and bushes. "Holy Shit!"

Suzette looked at the helicopter flying out across the lake. Its lights flashed and reflected off the water and into the dark sky. "What's going on here? This is way too much attention for just a single protester."

Drizzle wept out of the clouds and a light rain began to fall. Pat looked up at the sky. The thunderheads were being replaced by a solid mass of grey sky and it appeared that, rather than a quick cloud burst, the rain would stay.

Suzette spoke again. "Is there any way to get in touch with Ken? I'm sure he doesn't know how dangerous this is becoming?"

Pat shook his head. "I doubt I'll see him till tomorrow."

"Come inside," Mr. Loeffler said. "This rain is going to be here for a while." He opened the door to his trailer and left it open for Suzette and Pat. Hesitantly, they followed him inside.

The trailer was old. It had a bed at one end, a fridge, stove, sink and bathroom in the middle, and a table with two benches at the other. The aged particle board had swollen in places and the fake veneer and vinyl coatings were bubbled and wavy. Mr.

Loeffler bade his guests to sit at the table and then filled a kettle with water. The propane stove lit with an audible pop.

"I know Kenny's good in the bush," Suzette said, "but so are the TRU teams. They're well trained and if they think that Kenny's armed, they won't take chances. We have to let him know what he's up against."

"I think I'll see him tomorrow. I'll let him know then."

A helicopter flew over the trailer, concussing the air with the beat of its rotors. Suzy looked up at the white vinyl ceiling. "I hope it's early enough. That chopper probably has infrared sensors."

"Well, there's nothing I can do about it. I have no way to contact him. Those small cell phones don't work here and we only meet by prearranged appointment."

Suzy crossed her legs and leaned back. "Shit, Pat, how did all this start?"

"I'm not really sure, but I understand what he's trying to do."

"I just hope he knows what he's doing."

"I was telling Patrick about something Margaret Atwood wrote," Mr. Loeffler said. "She published it just around the time that the mill burned and in it, she talked about how Canadians are often victims concerned with a struggle for survival. She wrote that we move from stage to stage of victimisation and perhaps Kenneth has moved from the stage where he thinks that his victimization is inalterable, to a stage where he thinks he has the power to make a change."

"I see," Suzette said patronizingly.

Loeffler bent and opened a cupboard. It was full of books. He grabbed a black paperback and began to flip through the pages. "Atwood wrote that a Position-Two victim is one who acknowledges that they are a victim, but explains this as an 'act of Fate, the Will of God, the dictates of Biology'. She writes: 'You can be resigned and long-suffering or you kick against the pricks and make a fuss; in the latter case your rebellion will be deemed foolish or evil, even by you, and you will expect to lose and be punished, for who can fight Fate or the Will of God, or Biology)'

"But in position three," Mr. Loeffler continued, assuming the role of lecturer, "she says that a person acknowledges the fact they are a victim, but refuses to accept the assumption that the role is inevitable." Loeffler flipped the page. "She says that in this position, you can identify the real cause of the oppression - you can channel your anger against this oppression constructively - and, you can make real decisions about how much you can change.

"I think this is where Kenneth is at present. He has realised the truth of the situation and he is acting on it. I don't think he is being foolish."

Suzy looked at Mr. Loeffler. "Yes . . . but the problem is that Kenny doesn't have all of the facts."

"Can any of us have all the facts?" Mr. Loeffler shook his head.

Suzy raised her eyebrows. "I understand that you think the protest is a good idea, but I'm worried."

Patrick studied her and saw the concern on her face. It seemed as if a river of emotion was washing through her and he suddenly found himself drawn to her.

Mr. Loeffler smiled at Suzette. "Yes, of course you are. But you see, perhaps you are still in Position Two and Kenneth is in Position Three. You see the protest as foolish, because you see the outcome as inevitable, whereas Kenneth now understands more than we do and is able to see what will, and what will not, work."

"But he doesn't know how dangerous these TRU teams are. He's thinking he has a bunch of urban cops chasing him through the bush, but in truth, he's being followed by some very dangerous, well-trained soldiers. And, these people think he's armed."

"Then it's up to us to also make a difference. We have to assist Kenneth."

Pat looked at Mr. Loeffler and then at Suzette. "Yes, that's what we have to do. Let's gather what information we can and then we'll meet with him."

Suzy nodded and Mr. Loeffler smiled widely. "That's the spirit!" He took the kettle off the stove and threw in two tea bags. "Let's have a cup of tea, and then Pat, you can explain what he's trying to accomplish."

12. The Forgotten

Ken was soaked and the cold attacked his joints in a cruel intimation of arthritis. He couldn't sleep and he rolled out from under the tree. Everything was wet, the ground, the grass, the leaves, but it had stopped raining - something he hadn't realised while lying under the dripping branches. He was many hours away from his cabin, but there was no point in trying to sleep, it was just too cold. He started to walk.

Earlier he had crossed the river between Mink and Little Mink lakes and tried to get to his canoe on the eastern part of the lake, but the helicopter had flown back and forth along the shore of the lake. This had forced him to travel further south. Then the rain had started. He had taken cover under a very tall spruce, which had sheltered him from the rain, but the cold damp air had funnelled through the forest grabbing him with icy fingers. It had rained for hours and eventually the water found its way through the spruce branches and onto the prickly ground beneath. Now there seemed to be no escape from the cold.

A fire would have been comforting, and with the sun down, the smoke would be invisible from Kiosk, but he couldn't chance the flames being spotted by the helicopter. If they had infrared sensors, the fire would be a beacon.

The clouds had partially dissipated. Stars appeared in bands in the moonless sky. He took his bearing and walked toward the railroad tracks. He could follow these to Kioshkokwi Lake and then find his canoe.

After a long walk through the wet foliage, he saw the rail bed. As he walked toward it, his clothing was snagged by the stalks of low growing vegetation. The forest was redolent with life - cedars, dogwoods, mosses - but the recent rain had hidden the sweet smell of blackberries, one of the last berries to ripen in the year. A thicket of blackberry canes stood between him and the rail line and he had to pick his way carefully through the heavily thorned stocks that could easily cut through human skin. As he walked, he ate a few of the berries, which increased his hunger. He stopped and greedily stuffed berry after berry into his mouth.

When he could eat no more, he climbed onto the elevated rail bed. It was good to be out of the wet and he stood and stretched on the broken slag path. His muscles protested and threatened to cramp, but he worked slowly, twisting and turning, feeling the tension depart. The cold covered him like a wet blanket, but with the exercise and stretch, its weight decreased.

He had a crick in his neck, which he figured came from the cold, and he worked his lower back trying to regain flexibility. He stretched his arms, his shoulders and finally his neck and the tension dissipated. As he moved, he allowed his thoughts to drift into the forest and the world around him . . . to think of nothing and then everything at once. His balance returned and he was able to stand on one foot, to stretch and turn.

He started to walk and after a while, he spotted Mink Lake. Mink was fairly far to the south and he realised it was going to take some time to reach his canoe, even following the rail line. There were a few cottages on Mink, and he considered breaking in for some food and warmth, but immediately rejected the idea. He would return to his own cabin.

Animals moved in the forest on both sides of the tracks, scurrying and rustling the underbrush. Far to the west, a wolf howled, its soft distant cry wafting over the trees like mist floating over a lake. Another wolf, further to the north, answered.

It took an hour to reach Kioshkokwi and when he did, his clothes were almost dry. He walked casually toward the lake, near the spot where he had hidden the canoe, and he was about to descend to the shore, when he heard a splash in the water. He was suddenly cautious. He froze and put his hand on a red pine tree, feeling the flaky bark under his skin.

He waited, listening. Another noise reached his ears. It was barely audible and it had a strange quality - the hollow sound of a stone being moved in water. He wondered if it was a racoon, looking for clams, but it was too quiet. Were the waves moving the stones?

He moved closer to the red pine, leaned against it, and listened intently. Everything was silent, but then he heard a quiet, but deep sniffle. Someone was on the shore. Slowly he moved away and crouched down.

He guessed what had happened. The passing helicopter had spotted his canoe and now the police were waiting for him. They probably had listening gear and night vision goggles. He knew his night-vision was almost as good as night-vision goggles, but not quite. The police - if they were police - would have the advantage.

As quietly as possible, he slipped away from the lake and deeper into the forest. Without the canoe, it was going to take much longer to reach his cabin and he swore under his breath. Walking around the lake was not much further than walking across the train tracks, but it would be much more difficult - especially at night. It was hard to use the compass, the stars were not out regularly and he would not be able to stay close to the lake.

He considered trying the bridge, but he would be easy prey for the police on the thousand metres of rail bed that cut across the lake. If they spotted him while he was in the middle, they could surround him in minutes and he would have no place to go. He had no choice, the police were getting smarter and he was losing options. Slowly, he started walking to the east, toward the top of the ridge that would take him around the lake. He would have to walk for most of the night.

Pat stopped in the small clearing just before Ken's cabin. There was enough room for two or three vehicles and Suzette pulled in behind him. He locked his car and watched her climb out of her van. Although it looked out of place in the bush, Suzette didn't. She had grace in the forest. This was uncommon in the women he knew.

"Is Kenny's place far?" she asked.

"Not too far, but you can't drive all the way and this is the best place to park." He started to offer her his hand and then felt foolish. She didn't need his help to walk through the bush. He turned awkwardly and pointed in the direction they would walk.

As he led the way, he occasionally looked back. Suzette was looking at the trees and the various birds and animals that scurried back and forth. She had no trouble walking through and around obstacles and there was a comfort, a balance, to her gait that made it nice to be with her. He remembered Wendy, Wendy-the-bitch. She would have complained about the walk, she would have complained about the obstacles on the path, and she would have complained about him for having brought her here. Not that he ever would have brought the bitch out into the wilderness. Leaving the city limits brought on a barrage of complaints similar to Moodie's Roughing it in the Bush. High-heels were awkward in the dirt and sand, but that was all Wendy wore.

She had pushed him all the time to become the Sales Manager, but his advancement was only tolerated if it would benefit her in some way. She did not believe in art, literature, or music. Music was the stuff that filled elevators and shopping centres. His music was a complete waste of time, money and effort, because it would never bring profit. She worked hard, and successfully, to break up his little rock-and-roll band, and he was sure that when his prize guitar, a Gibson Hummingbird, was damaged at a party, it had been her doing.

"Are we in the park?" Suzette asked.

"No, we're just north of the border. This is crown land."

"So, doesn't Kenny have to have permission to build a cabin here?"

"I don't know. Why do you ask?"

"Because if the police know he has a cabin here, they'll come looking, won't they?"

"Kenny told me about that. This is a hunt camp and he shares it with a couple of guys. He's the only one who uses it, but it isn't in his name, so it should be safe."

"If Mr. Loeffler gets some people to start protesting in the town, the OPP are going to intensify their efforts. They're going to try to bring this to a speedy end, so I hope you're right."

"It should be safe."

"Okay."

When they reached the cabin, Patrick unlocked the door and walked in first. He and Kenny had left a mess and even though it wasn't his place, he felt self-conscious. He walked ahead of Suzette and picked up stray articles of clothing. "Ken's going to be here very late tonight or tomorrow."

"You're not sure?"

Pat picked up a few dishes and piled them in a green plastic bowl. "Well, nothing about this protest has been too certain." He turned and looked at Suzette. Her hair was down and it danced at her shoulders.

She looked at him, hesitantly. "No, it hasn't been," she said softly and turned away.

"It would take three or four hours to get here from the south side of Kiosk. With the helicopter flying back and forth, it'll be a while."

"Yes."

"You must be hungry." He picked up a tin of mushroom soup.

She turned and walked toward him. "No. Not really."

He didn't know what to do, what to say. No words came to his mouth. He could feel his pulse beating in his neck and his breathing was shallow. He was almost afraid.

"Are you hungry?" she asked, reaching for the tin.

"No, not really."

She took the tin and placed it on the cupboard, and as she did, she brushed against him. He had followed her with his eyes, but the touch came as a surprise. It was electric. She noticed it too, and she inhaled sharply as she paused next to him.

A moment frozen. He looked into her eyes and saw her looking back into his. He could not have decided what to do next, because he was denied reason. For that one moment, time seemed to jump around. They were apart, together, apart again. Feelings flooded into his chest with such intensity, such life, that he was unable to understand what they were. There was no country, no town of Kiosk, no cabin; the years had not existed. He was not a product of his life, he was not Pat the salesman, or Pat the musician. He was simply here, lost in this moment looking into Suzette's eyes.

If he could have thought about it, he would have realised that he was about to kiss her, and perhaps he would have been worried how she might react. But none of that existed. That was in another dimension, another time. He was simply here, in this moment, and they were moving closer to each other.

Their lips met, softly at first, and the room began to swirl. The softness of her kiss was intoxicating and the moment of time stretched beyond the moment, but was still within it. Their bodies were close, but he moved his head away and opened his eyes. She too, looked at him. He could see the pleasure in her eyes and somehow he knew that, she too, could see the pleasure in his.

Their lips met again, this time with more urgency, more desire. His chest tingled and his stomach sank in his body as he felt the closeness of her. She was pulling at his lips, his tongue, trying to draw him inside of her, and her arms wrapped around him, her fingers entwining in his hair, drawing him closer.

Somehow, they were on the floor. He had no recollection of falling, of kneeling down, but there they were, wrapped up in each other, flowing, twisting. The movement was not frantic, but enveloping and their bodies moulded together, wrapped around each other. He rolled to the side and lifted her. She was light in his arms and he placed her gently on the small bed.

They kissed again, deeply, and her hands ran circles over his back, pulling him close. The kiss was no longer a kiss but a journey, like swimming along the shore of a warm ocean, sliding effortlessly into a new place, lost in the comforting foam.

She slid her hands to the front of his shirt, opening the buttons, and he lifted himself to make it easier. He looked into her eyes and could see that she too was lost in the sea of sensation. It was passion, connectedness, completely without thought.

He unbuttoned her blouse and his fingers played over her delicate skin. Then he kissed the softness of her neck, her chin, her cheek. She arched up and removed her blouse and they kissed again, feeling the closeness of muscle and skin - the life beneath the surface.

He kissed her neck again, and then moved slowly across her chest and her stomach. He undid the button at the top of her jeans and slid them down across her legs. Sitting at the bottom of the bed, he ran his hands up the side of her legs as he touched his lips to the soft skin above her knee.

He breathed in the natural scent of her and found it intoxicating. Like a wonderful drug, it caused his stomach to feel heavy, his body to feel light, and the entire room seemed to turn white. He was lost in a swirling, white world where the soft moans that came from his throat, left her mouth, where the rapid heartbeat in her chest caused his blood to heat his face, where it became difficult to tell where one person began and the other ended. His palms lightly traced circles on her sides and he kissed the warmth of her legs, feeling not only the warmth of her skin but the pleasure of the touch.

With each sensation that Suzy felt, he was drawn deeper into the abyss. He was driven to touch, to kiss, to hold. And, as she arched her back and vocalized her pleasure, he felt he would explode the confines of his own body.

As the moment eased, the muscles relaxed, a sense of profound calmness eased over them. He could sense it in Suzy as easily as he could sense it in himself. Effortlessly, he removed the rest of his clothing and then he was again looking down into her eyes. He did not see the colour, he did not see the size, he did not even see the emotion. He saw himself. He could look out of Suzy's eyes and see himself above her and somehow he knew that she could do the same.

Slowly, he began to slip inside of her. Her eyes widened for a moment, as did his, and then time seemed to turn back on itself. The movement was very slow and with it came a stream of sensations that piled on top of each other in an impossibly growing crescendo. Each moment seemed like it could not be exceeded, and then another piled on top to pale the moment before.

Suzy locked her hands behind his head and pulled his mouth toward hers. She opened her lips and pulled him deep inside of her. The sense of being connected and no longer alone grew and the pleasure was overtaken by the complete release of self. All sensations merged, burning, white, and the division of two people finally blurred and disappeared.

They moved about together, awash in new and wild sensa-tions. Their hands moved across each other's backs, their lips and tongues together and then suddenly the bright, hot white light inten-sified into a brilliant burst, first once, then a second time. The inten-sity lingered and then slowly relaxed as a profound calm returned.

Pat opened his eyes, looked down at Suzy and then closed his eyes again. It took him a moment to orientate himself. He re-opened his eyes and saw Suzy above him looking down. The first thing he noticed was the smile in her eyes. Then he saw the smile on her lips and he realised he was smiling too. She leaned down and kissed him lightly, and then stroked his face with her fingertips.

They lay together for a long time, not talking, lightly touch-ing each other, exploring the curves of each other's faces. "I don't know what to say," Pat said finally, smiling.

"Neither do I. And, that's okay."

Pat watched the way the light from the lamp illuminated the soft downy hair on Suzy's neck, making it glow red and gold. He drifted. The room was bathed in warmth and the afterglow washed over him like a warm summer's breeze.

Suzy moved to his side, breaking the connection between them and Patrick gasped. He felt suddenly cold, and she sensed this. She quickly wrapped her leg over his and draped her arm across his chest. She pulled herself close, maximizing the contact, skin to skin. Pat felt the soft warmth of her, and he relaxed and breathed in the spicy scent that wafted in the air, the scent that would be, from this second on, etched in his memory as a reminder of this moment.

Ken was losing confidence and he checked his com-pass frequently. The trees were small and close together and he couldn't walk in a straight line. He had never been lost for a very long time, but there had been many times when he had found him-self very far from where he expected to be. It was easy to get lost in this kind of forest. It had been cut within the last twenty years and although it was supposedly managed, it had been neglected and the after-growth was a thick tangle of aspen and balsam.

It was sad that this was considered a wilderness park, when in truth it was a poorly managed woodlot. Most of the cuts were called 'selective cuts', because seed trees were left standing, but afterwards, these forests were ignored. Small weed trees claimed the open areas and choked each other for decades. The worst growths were the thick balsams that knitted together in a tight weave of tiny stems. These forests stagnated for 50 years, and lumber companies found different, older stands rather than re-farming what they had already used.

The park was a wood lot with older trees around the lakes. It was like those old western towns that put great facades on their boxy frame buildings. It was all a matter of supporting a false image; keep the big trees close to the shore so that the canoeist and campers think that the forests are old-growth, but cut everything else and mismanage it beyond the view of the public.

Another stick poked into his face and his neck jerked painfully sideways. It would be nice to walk through a large old-growth forest - to have a clear line of sight, an unrestricted walk. This section of forest was torture.

He reached an old pine surrounded by a mat of needles and he stopped for a moment to rest. The forestry people would say that this tree had been left to seed the forest, but when he looked up, he saw the truth. Not more than ten feet above the ground, its trunk divided in two and then twisted. Because of its twisty and split growth, there were no saw logs in the tree and therefore it was of little value. It had been left because it was not commercially viable.

Ken leaned against the tree and rested. He should have reached the river that flowed from Lauder into Kioshkokwi Lake, but he knew his progress had been torturously slow. He looked at his compass again, trying to read it in the very dull light, and decided to travel more to the west. He didn't want to miss the river and wind up at Thomson Lake - or worse, somewhere between. Keeping on-course through a thick forest at night was very difficult, but there was still a lot of ground to cover. He pushed away from the tree.

Branches poked his skin, grabbed his clothes, and tangled into the laces of his shoes, but he continued. The darkness was pervasive. There was no moon; no northern lights, nothing to help, and he continued to move forward, hoping soon to reach the shore and gentler forest.

The forest around him was full of life. Bird wings fluttered in the dark, small rodents scurried invisibly on the ground, and larger animals called and cried in the distance. After many hours of walking, he felt a sudden sense of relief when he heard the splash and flutter of wings on water. A duck. He was near a lake.

Looking around, he saw that, even though the forest was still thick and congested, there were many larger trees. He was close. When he saw the black water sparkling beyond the trees, he felt a weight lifted from his heart. He followed the shore, circling around an aromatic swampy section, and then finally reached the mouth of the river.

He was tired, and tempted to curl up and sleep in the camping spot at the lake, but he was nervous about being discovered. He walked toward Lauder Lake on the portage-trail. These trails, maintained by the park, allowed canoeists to get from one lake to the next and they were heavily used and clearly marked. He would be easily spotted here.

His hunger no longer plagued him, but tiredness dulled his senses. He felt uncomfortable. The heat from his body had dried most of his upper clothing, but his underwear and socks still chaffed at his skin. His trip up the trail was painfully slow and it stretched on and on. Although he had used it often in the past, it seemed unfamiliar.

He became aware of the smell of fire and he walked more cautiously. Not too far ahead was a campsite with a fire that still glowed. The orange tent was dark, and there were no voices, but that did not guarantee that the campers were asleep. These might even have been people he knew, but he did not want to reveal his location to anyone. He turned and quietly walked down the trail.

When he had gone a reasonable distance, he walked into the woods, crossed the small, twisting river, and forced his way through the bush until he reached the trail that would eventually lead to his cabin. It was such a relief to get out of the bush and he stood on the trail and breathed deeply.

It was brighter here and he could see further into the distance. At first, he assumed that this was because he was out of the forest on the open trail, but he turned to see the faint glimmer of light at the horizon. The morning sun was coming.

He felt a sudden, deep and soul possessing fatigue wash over him. It wasn't much more than an hour's walk to his cabin, but he needed to recharge. There was no point in trying to sleep, but he knew how to rest. On a dry spot beneath a couple of twenty-year-old pines, he sat cross-legged, and concentrated on his breathing. He counted each breath and when he reached four, he started again at one. It took only a few moments for him to reach a state where he was able to relax as well as if he were asleep.

Suzy thought Pat was asleep, but as she sat up in bed, she felt his fingers gently run across her back. Turning, she caught his eye. His gaze was warm, contented. "I'm gonna get a glass of water," she said. "You want one?" He nodded.

She slipped into a large shirt she found on a shelf near the bed and then stretched luxuriously. The air was dry and heavy, but a cool breeze floated across the floor, tickling the hairs on her legs. She poured two glasses of water, drank one, which coated her lips and throat like honey, and then filled her glass again.

Pat rose, put on his shirt and walked to her. He took the second glass, sipping the water slowly, without ever breaking eye contact.

There was something in his eyes that made her feel strangely calm. It was indefinable, something from their youth that had attracted her so many years ago.

If she thought about it, thought about their situation, she knew she should be uncomfortable. She knew very little about the modern Patrick James and he knew very little about her, and yet she was not threatened or troubled in any way. Somehow, her desire for him had nothing to do with logic and intellect. There was something magnetic drawing them together, like a compass needle being drawn to the north.

She was about to say something when the words stuck in her throat. She looked deep into his eyes and had a sense of what Pat was feeling. A connection existed that was almost eerie. When they had made love, she had lost herself in him. Not in the sense that her identity was unimportant, but in the sense that she was able to connect to him and experience something outside herself.

He stepped forward to refill his glass and his leg brushed against hers. She could feel the strength, the warmth, but she could also feel the softness of her own skin. The skin on her arms prickled, a shiver ran down her spine, and her knees weakened. This was too intense and she had to lighten the mood. "So . . . Pat, are you married?" She grinned.

He looked at her. There was no trace of response. Time stretched forward as their eyes locked them together. "No," he said finally.

"How come?"

He closed his eyes for a second and then looked back into her eyes. "Well . . ."

She shook her head, indicating that she didn't want him to answer. This was a stupid conversation and she didn't know why she had brought it up. It was all idle chatter, noise. It was the kind of conversation people had when there was no connection, when worldly rules seemed tantamount. His status outside of this time was strangely unimportant. It belonged to another set of rules. What mattered was this moment in time. The entire evening was moving forward like that - a whole string of moments, each important in its own way, each independent of the next. They were perfect moments and to make them dependent on other places in time would diminish their beauty.

Slowly she raised her hand and undid the top button on his shirt. At the same moment, he reached up and undid a button on her shirt. When both shirts were open, Suzy ran her hands under Pat's arms and pulled him close to her. His lips found hers and their two bodies came together.

The close contact made her stomach sink and she felt dizzy. Pat's arms were around her, his elbows at her sides, and he supported her weight as if he knew that she was having trouble standing. The light from the single oil lamp seemed to grow dim and change colour. The room became redder, softer and it seemed to undulate slowly.

Holding him close, she moved her head back and looked

into his eyes. He followed her gaze. His eyes were soft and revealed his feelings. He too was lost in the moment. There was no after-thought and no pre-thought. He was simply here with her.

Surely, this was too good to be true. Her logical side fought with her, causing her to remain frozen, waiting for a surreptitious reaction, but none came. Pat was as lost in her as she was in him. He continued to stare, his eyes widening, the pupils dilating.

Through the soft skin of her leg, she could feel the warmth of his thigh. Balancing on one leg and leaning against the counter, she wrapped her other leg around him. A powerful urge to draw him closer, to surround him, overwhelmed her. She kissed him hard, drawing his tongue into her mouth. She pulled him closer, holding him tighter.

Suddenly she again needed to see the passion in his eyes. She withdrew her lips and moved one of her hands to the side of his face. Without a word, his gaze found hers and at that moment, she learned what it was like to fall into someone's eyes. She was com-pletely lost. With a sudden force, uncharacteristic for her, she pulled him back. Their mouths found each other as he slipped inside of her. A rush of warmth spread up through her stomach and into her chest. Her entire body tightened. She needed to envelop him, to surround him, to merge with him.

She no longer knew where she was . . . who she was . . . but the sensations began to soften. The waves continued to flow through her body, washing back and forth, but then a gradual feel-ing of weakness overtook her. She opened her eyes to see Patrick, eyes closed. His bottom lip was pulled slightly between his teeth and a tear had slipped down his cheek. This did not surprise her; it made perfect sense. He opened his eyes and she smiled slightly. There was no fear, no weakness, and no loss of self - just beautiful release.

A harsh voice broke through Ken's meditation. "Ha! How often am I gonna find you on this road?"

Ken opened his eyes. The silver light of morning sliced between the trees and twisted down through the mist to the road. He wasn't sure if he had slept or just been lost in a deep meditative state, but his thinking was somewhat foggy.

He got to his feet and looked at the old woman. She was waving a deformed hand that seemed more like a club than a human appendage. It was the same woman he had seen before. Was it one or two days ago? Time was muddled in his mind. "Catherine. Right?"

"Dat's right."

"You got a place near here?"

The old woman grinned and nodded again. She removed a bowl that hung from a cord around her neck. It was half full of blackberries. "You look hungry. You eat?"

"I need to get back to my cabin. I need rest more than I need food."

"Here, take some berries."

Ken shook his head, but she insisted, forcing her wooden bowl at him. He reached in, took a handful, and put them in his mouth. They were incredibly sweet and juicy.

"You hurt yourself," Catherine said, pointing at him.

Ken looked down at his arm. It was still red with blood and there was a dark gash below the rip in his shirt. "I fell . . . on the rocks."

The old woman reached into a bag and took out something that looked like a root and something else that looked like bark. "Here, you chew this. It's gonna help."

Ken protested, but the old woman was persistent. Ken had often taken herbal medicine and he was normally not afraid of it, but he was leery in this situation. Finally, he relented. The root had no taste, but the bark was bitter. He grimaced. "Willow?"

She nodded. "Eat more berries."

Ken took another handful.

"You sleeping there under the trees?"

"Just resting . . . that's all."

"You can rest pretty good for someone who's got so many people after 'em."

"Yeah . . . well . . ."

"And so many of 'em mad."

Ken's interest was piqued. He wondered what this woman knew. "Who's mad?"

"Lots of people. Why you trying to get everyone so mad?"

He thought for a moment. "I guess I want them to be mad so they will see the bad things that happened to the people of the town."

"What bad things?" The woman scratched her head with her deformed hand.

Ken rubbed his face. His skin felt rubbery. The exhaustion pulled at his muscles and he sat on the ground. "They took everyone's houses away. They took away their homes."

"You talkin' about them people lived in Kiosk?"

Ken nodded.

"But them people got new houses, didn't they?"

The question annoyed Ken. He didn't want to answer; he was over-tired and he wanted to get back to his cabin. "You of all people should understand."

The old woman cackled. "Why's dat?"

"You're Native aren't you?"

"I'm Catherine."

Ken took this as a 'yes'. "They took away your homes and made you move onto a reserve and your people are always fighting to get your land back."

The old woman sat on a fallen log. "You have much to learn. When the elders spoke about 'the people' they were not just speaking about Indian people, they were speaking about all people of the land. Some people understand the connection to the land, some people don't. It don't matter if they's Native people or not."

"Well . . . that's what I want. I want the people in power to understand that the people who lived here had a connection to the land and it was taken away."

Catherine looked at him patiently. "Connection to the land's not the same thing as owning a house. Lots of people own houses." Her tone seemed to change. The cackle disappeared and was replaced with a softer sound. "If you got a connection to the land, then you got that connection no matter where you are. That can't be taken."

"You don't understand."

She cackled again. "Maybe I don't."

"The people here were forced to leave and they had their

homes taken away."

"But they were given other homes. They could have kept their connection to the land."

"But you can't in a city. Everything's about money, about success, about getting ahead."

"You was just sittin' there . . . or maybe you was praying . . . and how much are you connected to the land?" She pointed to a tall pine. "You got big trees here, you got bushes, you got earth. You tell me how much you're connected." She paused and Ken didn't answer. "You gotta listen." She pointed her club hand at Ken. "Did you hear what they're telling ya to do?" When there was no reply, the woman laughed again. "No matter. Maybe they wasn't talkin' to you neither." She looked at him more seriously. "You got to learn that what you carry in your heart is yours. Nobody can take that away. You can't find it outside."

Ken looked down at the ground.

"Praying, meditating, seeking a vision, resting, thinking; they's all the same thing," continued the woman. "You know part of it. You know that there is more to life than what you can see, hear, touch, smell and taste. You've seen that far. But I don't know if you've found that connection. You talkin' about it, but are you sure you know it?"

Ken suddenly felt the tiredness return. He ate some more berries. "When my parents took me to Sudbury, I lost something." He reached down and picked up a handful of dirt and pine needles and let it sift between his fingers. "I felt at home here, but in Sudbury I was lost."

"Your family went with you?"

"My mom and dad . . . but they changed too. They lost something . . . my dad started drinking heavy, smacking me around."

The old woman smiled. "Are you sure it's the land you missed?"

Ken thought for a moment. "That's part of it, for sure." A thirst was beginning to grow and brushing the dirt from his hand, he ate more berries.

"A home is not the same as a cabin. Maybe you lost your connection to the land when you lost your home, but now you're fighting for a wood cabin and a piece of property."

A profound and mind-numbing sadness fell over him like a layer of heavy wet snow. She was right. Even if he got back his house, he would still be living in the same society. The same values would exist. Family was of little importance and just because he obtained a new wooden structure, that wouldn't change. He would be forced to live in a society where values were based solely on productivity and progress - where it is more important what-you-do, than who-you-are. "What should I do?"

The old woman sensed his sadness. "Sometimes it is the time to fight and sometimes it is time to leave." She looked up at the tree over his head and spoke softly. "Don't just listen to the trees; listen to the wind, to the birds, and the animals. You are searching from something you cannot find on your own. Listen. Even the water of the lake can help you."

"You said something about that before. You talked about the big bird and the waves. What did you mean?" Ken looked down at the bowl. It was empty.

The old woman took it away, but did not answer. "I see you was more hungry than you think," she said. "I need to go find more berries. You got lots to think about, but you be careful with those angry people. It's not smart to poke a stick in a bee's nest, even if you think you's gonna get the honey."

Ken watched the old woman walk to the south and he wondered again where she lived. It was strange that he had never seen her. He had spent a lot of time in these forests.

He looked around. He couldn't remember this spot. The forest was incredibly green. The moss, the undergrowth, the leaves on the trees, all looked as if they had been painted on glass and then back-lit. Vibrant verdant swirls moved around him as his body swayed.

He began to wonder about the root that he had chewed. He fell back and looked up at the tall trees above him. They stretched up to the sky and seemed to wave back and forth. The clouds moved crazily and wind moaned through the tops of the pines.

Suzette awoke feeling rested and sensed the heat of

the day seeping in through the walls of the cabin. She knew it was late. She sat up, dangled her legs off the narrow bunk and looked back at Pat sleeping against the wall. Outside, a gull cawed and then the sound returned, very distant.

In a half stretch, she ran her hands up her neck and across the back of her head. She luxuriated in her own touch, moving her shoulders, feeling her skin pull, and then bent to pick up her clothes. Her sense of touch was electric. She could sense the air as it flowed across her skin; feel the fabric of her clothing, feel the rippling of muscle under her skin. Her body was alive with sensation.

A calendar hung on the wall and the picture, a yellow and red sunset over a lake, made her imagine the warmth of a campfire. She looked at the date and thought about how quickly the summer had passed. Soon the children would be back to school. Her thoughts jumped to Michelle and she decided she wanted to call her. She wanted to tell her about . . . about . . . what? How she felt, how she was . . . in love?

She put her finger to her chin. Was she in love? That was a complicated question and she decided that at this moment, it wasn't important. She was alive. And she wanted to share her excitement with her daughter. It was silly, she thought, but she was closer to Michelle than to anyone else.

She picked up her watch and looked at the time. Michelle liked to sleep in, but she would be awake by now. She might go out for lunch and this would be a good time to call. Her small cellphone wouldn't work, but there was a payphone in Kiosk. She finished getting dressed and then sat on the bunk. "Pat," she said, gently rubbing his upper arm. "Pat, I'm going into town for a few minutes . . . to phone my . . . my daughter." She stopped. She remembered how many men shied away from women with children. Had she even told him about Michelle? Then she remembered talking about her so very long ago in the Chinese restaurant. Pat had listened with interest.

He turned to face her. "Sure," he said softly. "By the way, good morning."

"Morning," she said brushing the side of his face and then leaning down and giving him a kiss.

"Do you have to go?"

"I won't be long; I just have to make a call." Then she added: "If Ken comes back, keep him here till I get back, will you? I really want to see him."

"Alright. I'm sure he'll want to see you too."

"I'm worried about him. Now that the TRU team is here, this could get really dangerous."

Pat lifted himself up on one elbow. "I don't think you'll talk him out of this, though. I doubt he'll listen. He has his own ideas."

She smiled warmly and nodded. "I know. I just want to let him know what he's up against. I did a report on a TRU team in Barrie. I know a little about them." She bent down, kissed him again, and then stood. She felt a warmth tingle through her body. It was like veins had been opened and blood was finally able to flow properly. "I'll be back in a short while."

Roussel sat in the darkened coffee shop and picked at her bagel as White dug into his with the zeal of a person who has stopped worrying about his weight. "I can't believe how far out of hand this has gotten," she said.

White swallowed and then replied. "It was a mistake to release that statement about Gingras." He sipped his water. "All that did, was confirm that we thought we had something to hide."

"But to burn me in effigy . . ."

"Yeah, that was a shocker. I don't think Adrienne quite found the right tone for her release."

"God." Roussel shook her head in exasperation.

"I guess in her defence, it was difficult to anticipate."

Roussel lit a cigarette. "Stupid Bitch . . . It's her job to antic-ipate. She knew I was MPP for that area. She was supposed to break the link between the INAC and the protest. She puts out a release saying that I am in no way connected to the protest at the same time that the television stations are broadcasting pictures of me burning in effigy." She shook her head again. "Fuck! I can't believe it." She stubbed out her cigarette.

White was chewing and he nodded in agreement.

"So, now we have to figure out what to do next."

"I think the best thing, is to do nothing, say nothing, and apply a little silent pressure to the police to resolve the situation."

"We've already tried that. The police are useless."

White broke out laughing. "Did you see the pictures Campbell took of the cops following him? Makes them look like fools. I'll bet that burned their asses."

"I can't believe a whole squad of OPP can't catch one man."

"It's one thing to track a man in a city; it's another to track him in the bush."

"Will they ever catch him?"

"They've got a TRU team there now - that's one of their tactical units, like a SWAT team. They'll catch the guy; it'll be over soon. The entire situation centres on Ken Campbell; once he's arrested, it turns into a criminal case and all the people go home."

"Perhaps, but I still wonder if they can catch this fellow. Armand was pretty sure that the original OPP team would catch him.

"They'll catch him and within days of the arrest, public interest will evaporate."

"Is it over then? He might continue talking to the press after the arrest. There's a growing interest in the idea that Kiosk was deliberately burned."

"Doesn't matter. While he's out in the bush, he's a renegade spirit attracting interest; once he's arrested, he's merely a criminal. We need to have him arrested, and, if the police can't catch him, at the very least, we need to get the press to focus on the criminality rather than the protest."

"So, how do we do that?"

White took a drink of coffee and thought for a moment. "I'm not sure," he said finally, "but I can tell you this. Whatever happens, it can't come from the INAC in any way shape or form. If we say anything to anyone, it looks as if we are trying to deflect blame."

"What about Gingras saying . . ."

White put up his hand. "Armand has turned into a big liability. I always liked him and it's a shame, but his career with the INAC is over. The public is supporting Ken Campbell and Armand Gingras is on the other side. The public and the press view him as the bad guy, and at the same time, we've let it be known that he is

not acting on behalf of the government. He's completely out in the
cold. If you bring him back to the Ministry, you establish the tie
back to Kiosk. As much as I hate to say it, Armand has to go."

"But maybe he can be useful to us while he's in the town."

"He's a smart fellow. I think, after Denny's press release,
he'll not be too helpful."

Roussel said, "Leave that to me."

White chuckled. "These machinations are pretty
Machiavellian given the size of this protest."

"Yes, but it's not the protest that's important here, it's the
race for the leadership of the party."

"The non-race."

"Yes, the non-race."

Roussel drank her coffee and left, letting White take care of
the bill and tip. She straightened her hair as she walked to the elevator. Reporters were everywhere and although her staff would
never reveal her whereabouts, a surprise reporter was always a possibility.

Alone in her office, she picked up the phone and dialled.
The person who answered recognized her immediately and no
niceties were exchanged. She agreed with White's assessment - it
made sense - and she repeated the highlights to the person on the
phone. The INAC had to drop out of sight, it was necessary to
manipulate the press to focus on the criminal aspects of what was
going on in Kiosk, and all links to Armand Gingras needed to be
severed.

She hung up the phone, sat silently for a moment, and then
picked up a memo from the legal department. It was time to get on
with other business.

Ken's body twisted and turned in a torrent of rain
and noise. Lights flashed crazily reflecting off the crystalline drops
of water making it difficult to see. One moment the rain pelted him
on the back and then suddenly, it slapped him in the face causing
him to close his eyes. It didn't matter because it was impossible to
see anyway. The drops of rain were so big that they broke up the
light and hid the images around him.

He wasn't running, but he was moving quickly and he seemed to be restricted. He was moving away from something, then toward something, and then away again. He was moving faster and faster, but he was no further out of danger. His heartbeat was rapid and his breathing shallow. He could tell the end was near.

Whatever was chasing him - a giant bird? - was about to capture him. It was all over. Then suddenly he decided to quit. He would not fight anymore. It was over. He let go and for just a moment, everything stopped.

Suddenly he was in the water. He gasped with the cold and struggled, but then he felt the water pull at him. It surrounded him like a cacoon and left him enough room to breathe. For a brief moment, there was nothing, no sound, no rain, no light, just quiet, peaceful isolation. Then there came a sensation of movement, of being pulled away from danger.

He gave himself to the sensation. He was no longer in the water. He was comforted, being aided, and he gratefully accepted the aide.

The water disappeared and he was in a grassy field. He saw Pat at the edge, standing by the trees, and he called to him. His voice was weak and Pat didn't hear him, didn't see him. He fell back and looked up at the sky. The clouds were moving too quickly and then a black shape appeared, blotting out the light. Its presence was menacing, but then it moved away and disappeared. The danger was gone. Ken closed his eyes and slept.

Gary Pinneskum watched the woman on the phone. She no longer had that from-the-city appearance and it was obvious that she had camped somewhere in the area. He knew she was a friend of Pat and Ken's and he figured that she knew where to find them.

He watched her move around as she talked. She was animated and upbeat. She replaced the receiver, stood silently for a moment, and then returned to her van.

He walked toward his truck, but then changed his mind. Since he wanted to reach Ken and Ken was out in the bush, he decided to take his four-wheeler. He stayed a fair distance behind the van to avoid being spotted.

Gary figured that Ken was hiding somewhere to the north, but he wasn't sure where. He watched as the van pulled onto Highway 630 and within minutes, it was doing over 80 kilometres per hour, a speed he couldn't match on his old machine. He lost sight of it on one hill, but then saw it again just past the next bend. Each time he spotted it, it was a little further ahead and he knew that, eventually, he would lose it completely. He had just decided to give up when he saw the yellow turning signal blinking in the distance. He slowed and watched as the van turned off onto a narrow gravel road.

He approached cautiously, knowing he would be easily spotted, and pulled off on the shoulder, staying very close to the trees. When the van disappeared over a small ridge in the distance, he accelerated.

As he reached the top of the knoll, he spotted some movement ahead of the van, almost a quarter mile up the road, and he coasted to a stop. A group of policemen swarmed out and surrounded the van. He froze and then looked back. He was not being followed and when he looked ahead, he could see he had not yet been spotted.

The woman got out and spoke to one of the officers. She didn't seem surprised. Had she been expecting the police? It was difficult to tell. Why would she meet them way out here on a bush road north of the park? It didn't make sense.

He looked over his shoulder again. There was still no one following him. Had she phoned the police and arranged this meeting? There hadn't been time. He crossed his arms and thought for a moment. He may not know what was going on with the police, but Ken Campbell was likely somewhere up the road.

He studied the cops. They had paramilitary equipment and seemed ready for action. He kicked the toe lever, putting the machine into gear, and accelerated.

One of the officers saw his approach and blocked the way. Gary slowed to a stop, but left the machine in gear. "Get outta my way!"

"I'd like to see some identification please, sir."

Gary was not frightened even though these cops were

dressed to intimidate. "Fuck you!"

"Get off the bike, sir."

Gary stood up and fished out his wallet and his Indian Band Card. He showed it to the officer without handing it over. "I got Indian Status and you're not going to detain me."

"You'll have to turn around. This area is closed." The officer looked at the moulded plastic rifle case attached to the four-wheeler.

Gary looked back at the gun case, shrugged and dropped his wallet back in his pocket. "You can't tell me what to do. I don't recognize your authority." The police officer that had stopped him moved forward a step. Gary raised his voice. "Hey! Unless you want to have an entire Indian Band up here, don't fuck with me!"

Another officer turned away from the woman and walked to Gary. "This is for your own protection. There is a fugitive on the loose, and we can't . . ."

"Yeah, yeah," Gary said, interrupting the officer. He pushed the lever on the front of the bike into reverse and rolled the bike backwards and sideways to the road. The two officers turned back toward the woman, as Gary dropped the bike into forward. But instead of going back the way he came, he continued the way he had been originally travelling and he scooted by the officers. "I got status and I'm going this way!"

One of the officers grabbed at the back rack of the bike and actually caught hold of it, but wasn't strong enough to hang on. He fell to the ground and rolled in the dirt. Gary sped away toward Ken's cabin.

He crouched in a racing position to lower his wind resistance, but also to make him a smaller target if the cops started shooting. No shots were fired and he heard no vehicles behind him.

In minutes he reached the cabin, he jumped off the bike and ran to the door. "Campbell! You in there?" Gary shouted as he burst through the door. Patrick was inside cooking bacon on the small stove.

Patrick looked frightened and he held up his egg-turner as if it were a weapon. "Who are you?"

"There's no time. There's a woman in a van down the road with the police. They're armed and they're looking for Campbell.

Where is he?"

Pat hesitated. He looked around the room as if he might find the answer among the clutter. He cocked his head sideways. "The woman in the van has the police with her?"

"Yeah, I said that, and they're looking for Campbell. Where is he?"

Pat walked toward the front door and looked outside. "He isn't here yet, but he's coming."

"He's walking into an ambush. Can you reach him?"

Pat shook his head. "I know where he's coming from, though."

Gary could hear four-wheelers back in the bush. "Well, get on my bike. We're gonna warn him."

"Hang on." Pat darted back inside, and then ran around to a shed in the back. A machine started and its tires sprayed sand back into the shed as it burst out into the open. "Follow me!" Pat shouted.

Gary gunned his machine but had some trouble keeping up with the faster machine in front. Pat was headed toward Lauder Lake and Gary realised that this made sense. Lauder Lake was a great place to hide. Pat slowed and Gary coasted to a stop behind him. "So, where is he?"

"Before I say anything else, tell me who you are!"

Gary explained that he had grown up in the bush not far from here. Pat's expression became pained as he tried to remember. Gary then told Pat about his meeting with Ken on Wolf Lake. In the distance, an ATV engine revved and screamed. "Come on, man, we've gotta do this now. Those cops mean business."

Pat grimaced and rubbed his hands together. The ATV's were drawing closer.

"Come on!" Gary urged, "We don't have all day here."

"Ken had a canoe. He took it down through Lauder and into Kiosk. He burned an effigy of the old Member of Parliament."

"I know."

"He should be coming up here by canoe this morning."

Gary shook his head. "He couldn't have used the canoe without being spotted. He's probably on foot." Gary pointed to the southbound trail. "He'll probably use this trail. It goes close to the portage and then goes right back to the train tracks." Gary knew this area well.

The sound of the approaching ATV's increased. "Ken knows the bush; he might have canoed at night. You go down that way and I'll check up toward the lake."

Gary nodded and started down the trail. He knew he would have to go slow because Ken would probably hide at the sound of an approaching ATV. He sat forward on the machine watching the marks in the sand and started down the road as Pat took off in the other direction.

Pat accelerated quickly, the urgency of finding Ken driving him, but when he approached the lake, he came to the vacant cabin and a scene of total quiet. "Ken! Ken! Where are you?" His voice echoed back from the surrounding hills. "Ken! If you're here, answer me! This is important." The only sound was the quiet lapping of water on the shore.

He stepped out onto the floating dock. The lake was shaped like a giant 'C' and he could see most of the bottom end. No canoes were visible. "Ken! Ken! For christssakes answer me!" No reply.

In the distance, he could hear the police coming and he was trapped down at the shore. There was nowhere to go. The cabin was lost, Suzette was lost, Ken was lost and he was trapped. He felt the blood pounding in his neck and temples. "Shit, Shit!" he cried in anger. "Ken!" Still, there was no answer.

Returning to the four-wheeler, he spun around in a tight circle spewing sand onto the dried vegetation. He was facing the opposite direction and he made a decision. He pushed his thumb on the throttle, toed the machine from first, to second, to third, and then up to fourth gear.

Bouncing over the rough pathway, he saw the first ATV heading toward him. He eased off the throttle for a second, but then pushed forward, regaining speed. Stopped, he could not defend himself, but with speed, he had a chance.

He was flying toward the oncoming ATV at 30 km per hour and accelerating. The tension in his arms and back made his entire body feel like a wet knot drying in the sun. He pulled as far to the right as possible and, up ahead, he watched the armour-clad officer waving a hand in the air. It made no difference.

The officer stayed in the middle of the path, holding his course, trying to force Pat to yield, and Pat could see that there was not enough room. He could see the tension in the oncoming officer's body. Instead of slowing down, or trying to pull more to the right, Pat swerved out to the middle of the path. He opened the throttle wide and the Suzuki roared in protest. A direct, head-on collision was imminent, but the officer wasn't moving.

Pat could see the man's face. The determination was suddenly replaced by panic and the officer decelerated, mouth open and then veered right. Pat steered the opposite way, but the two vehicles brushed tires. The Suzuki's engine screamed as tires left the road and there was no further resistance. Then, as the tires hit, the machine jerked right and left and bounced crazily. When he managed to regain control, he looked over his shoulder and saw the OPP vehicle on its side, its wheels spinning in the air.

The fork in the road appeared just as two other ATVs came into view. He knew he was not going to pass both of them and he released the pressure at his thumb. His mind flashed through the options. He couldn't turn back, he couldn't go on, he had no choice; he dropped down a gear and turned onto the southbound trail.

The two ATVs anticipated him and accelerated hard trying to cut him off, but Pat reached the corner first, leaning way into the turn to stop the machine from tipping. Mud and water from a small puddle sprayed into the air, as the first of the two ATVs turned right behind him. Blue smoke, muddy water and the sound of screaming engines filled the air.

He toed the machine into third, fourth and then fifth gear. It was much too fast for the road and with each bump and each rock he could feel the Suzuki's tenuous grip on the road weakening.

The Suzuki was fast, but it was noisy and he couldn't hear if the machines behind him were close. He dared not look back for he knew he would lose control, but he could hear the various engines resonating through the forest. They were there. In the distance, he could see Gary standing beside his machine and then he saw another figure. It was Ken.

He eased off the gas and shot his head around. Both bikes

were close, maybe ten lengths back and gaining quickly. He looked forward and saw Ken getting onto Gary's bike. They were pulling away, but Gary's machine was slow. The police would definitely overtake them.

He was gaining quickly on Gary's machine and he knew the only way he could help them get away was to act as a barricade. "Get out of here!" Pat yelled. Gary's hand came up in response.

The police were right behind him. Now he could hear their machines and the voices of one of the officers. "Pull over!" Pat slowed down, weaving right and left to stop the two ATVs from passing him. Gary was pulling away.

Pat felt the sudden impact at the back of his vehicle and his thumb slipped off the gas. He slowed down quickly and felt another sharp impact. The ATV behind him was trying to run him off the road. He accelerated to get away from another hit, but slowed again to allow Gary more time.

He considered stopping, but the OPP would merely push him out of the way. He had to think of a way to block the road. He slowed down a great deal and allowed the police to ram him one more time. As the officer slowed, he hit the throttle, turned the handlebars sharply, and spun sideways. The vehicle lifted sideways on two wheels and Pat grabbed the overhead rack and forced the vehicle to tip over.

The wind was knocked out of him as he hit the ground and then his head smacked something hard. He tried to move, but the OPP ATV crashed into his bike, pushing him across the dirt. Again, he tried to scramble away, but he was unable to untangle himself from the handlebars, the seat and the canoe rack. He heard a loud noise and looking forward he saw an ATV fly through the air and then impact the trees.

He managed to get to his knees, but saw the cop behind him lunging through the air. He grabbed Pat, threw him to the ground and held him in a position that made it almost impossible to breathe. He looked down the road and saw Gary and Ken bumping away toward the misty horizon.

Ray Smith spread the pictures out on the table in his

motel room. After Ray had introduced himself as Mr. Smith, the forty-year-old man sitting across from him introduced himself, with a smirk, as Mr. Jones. He was wearing an expensive suit and seemed reluctant to touch anything. He also seemed disinterested in the pictures. "You didn't get close to Ken Campbell?" Mr. Jones asked.

"No. He never came into town." Smith moved a picture of the two canoes across the table. "This is as close as he got. He's the one in the front canoe."

Jones smirked again as he pointed to the figure in the second canoe. "And that's you, about to be burned in effigy."

Smith frowned. "No . . . it's a politician."

"But years ago, it was you?" Jones was displaying the extent of his background knowledge.

"Yes."

"Seems appropriate."

"I don't have to listen to this."

Jones shrugged.

"I'm going back down south," Smith said quickly.

"No. You're not. You'll do as you're told."

"This isn't my line of work. Surely you have people . . ."

Jones smashed his hand on the table. "No! This is your mess and you are going to clean it up. You profited from it, now you will handle it. Understand?"

Smith looked at the younger man and didn't know what to say. Normally he wouldn't allow someone to intimidate him like this, but he had to exercise caution. Jones was different from the people he had dealt with in the past.

Jones relaxed, looked at Smith patronizingly, and then looked at the pictures on the table. "Why did you take all these pictures? We don't care about most of these people."

"I didn't know who you were interested in." Smith turned a picture of Suzette. "This is the reporter who's been helping him." He showed another picture of Mr. Loeffler and Armand Gingras talking by the trailer. "This is a foolish old teacher and that political aide, Gingras."

"Yes, Madame Roussel's special assistant."

Smith didn't know and he shrugged. He turned another picture around. "This is Patty James. I'm pretty sure he's the one who's meeting with Campbell in the bush. He acts mighty strange and he got into a fight with Gingras in the ranger station."

Jones picked up a picture of Gary. "Who's this?"

"One of the Indians who lived outside of the area."

"For or against?"

"For, I think."

Jones thought for a moment. "What's the general mood?"

"I don't understand."

"There are a lot of people there. Do they support Campbell or not?"

"I didn't talk to many of them."

Jones grinned. "Oh, I forgot, burned in effigy. Right?"

"Fuck you."

Jones' expression turned dark and threatening. "I don't think so." He did not raise his voice, but his tone was such that Smith knew it would be unwise to say another word. Jones smiled again. "Surely you must have noticed the general mood. Are they supporting this foolish protest? Do these believe that the mill was torched?"

"Oh, they believe it. They don't admit it at first, but everyone there thinks there was funny business back in 1973."

Smith shook his head slowly. "Stupid, stupid, stupid. They have no idea what really happened. Never will. Do they really think that someone from the government, or the company that owned the mill, set that fire?"

"Yeah, they do and that's why we don't have to do anything. They'll never figure out what really happened and they'll just go on making stupid guesses."

"That's the problem. Campbell is awakening many suspicions. Maybe one day someone will stumble onto something that . . . You sit here for a moment. I'll be back."

"I . . . I . . ." Smith stood and took a step toward the door.

"Just stay put!" The command sounded like one Mr. Jones would give to a dog.

Smith sat at his table and thumbed through the pictures. So many faces that he recognized; so few friends. He just wanted to get back to his house, get away from all of this. He crossed his arms and slouched. The silence was as black as a midnight walk in the forest.

Jones was gone for no more than twenty minutes. He returned, went directly to the table, and after a few seconds, turned one of the pictures toward Smith. "It's time to do what we discussed."

Smith felt suddenly cold. His stomach sank and his legs felt numb. "This is ridiculous. I'm an old man. Get someone younger."

"Do you wish to get any older?" He pointed at a face in a picture. "This one. It's too bad, really. He was useful once. Check out of your room and leave now. What you need, you'll find in the trunk of your car. It's a shotgun. Stay off the phone and I'll call you and tell you the precise place and time. But you need to leave now." Jones smiled. "I'll meet you afterwards, and once it's done, then you can go back home."

"Look here, we're over-reacting. The whole protest is going to blow over. There's no need."

Jones studied Smith for a moment. "I don't have to explain anything to you, but just this once, I will. Years ago, it was necessary to burn the mill to get the relocation grants - to stop the stupid protest - but the fire could have got out of hand and people could have been killed. It was done for the benefit of everyone, but there was also a great deal of money involved. And the people who made that money have made a lot more money since. If it became public knowledge that a mill was burned in the town for the sake of money, some people wouldn't understand. We can't have some do-gooders poking around in the ashes so this whole thing has to be stopped - at any cost. You also made a lot of money, and because of that money, you have certain responsibilities. After all, you're the only one left from the town who knows what really happened."

He wanted to say no, but he couldn't. He knew the alternative. "I . . . I . . ."

"Look, years ago we ended a protest with a fire that could have killed many people, now we're ending another with the death of one man. Since the bombing of the World Trade centres, the government is quick to end any violent protest. Once this man goes down, the protest will come to an end." Jones pointed at Smith. "And that will end your involvement. Stay off the phone. I'll call you while you're on the road. Now, get going and check out."

"Can't you have someone else . . .?"

"Do you really want someone else involved in this?"

"I just can't. Can't you get another . . .?"

"No! No fuck-ups Mr. Smith! Get this done!" Smith started to protest again, but Jones closed his fists tightly and lightly hit the table. His demeanour changed suddenly and with a twinkle in his eyes, he said: "It's not as if you haven't done this before, is it?" Smith closed his eyes and exhaled as Jones continued. "It's a fifty minute drive. I'll call you. If you haven't heard from me, stop at the twin bridges on Highway 630. Lots of people stop there to look at the falls. Now, get going." Smith stood slowly and gathered the pictures. Jones brushed off his jacket, and walked out the door.

An Engine whined in the distance and Ken sat up immediately. His dizziness vanished as he crouched and saw an ATV moving toward him. Its engine was unusually loud and the chassis rattled and banged. He decided it was not a police vehicle.

He had a low-grade headache and his judgement was impaired. He tried to focus on the driver, but the face was too far away. His heart was beating and he stood with every muscle tense, trying to decide if he should run into the forest or move out onto the road. His head started to pound and he realised he was holding his breath.

The driver yelled his name. It was the Indian fellow, Gary. Ken walked to the road and the ATV skidded to a stop. Gary explained that the police, who were on their way, had nabbed Pat. He ordered Ken onto his bike and then he took off.

"We can't go this way! It'll either take us back to town or down to the train bridge. Either way we'll be right back out in the open!"

Gary looked over his shoulder. "We can't go back, either!"

"Turn here!" Ken grabbed Gary's shoulders as the bike turned down a narrow trail that wound through a tightly packed forest of balsam and aspen. Branches tugged at their clothing and scratched their faces.

The trail, which was probably used by hunters on the very

edge of the park, skirted past two small lakes and then opened up into a red-pine forest. Ken remembered it. It had been planted by the school children of Kiosk when he was a little boy. The trees were all in straight rows and the thick canopy kept the forest floor bare.

Gary sped through the trunks until he reached the top of a little hill. When they could see in all directions, he stopped and shut off the bike.

Ken's head was pounding. "What happened back at my cabin?" He pointed with his thumb to the north.

"Ssshhh." Gary was listening for the police.

"What happened?" Ken insisted.

"Cops raided it. They have that woman reporter and I'm pretty sure they have your friend too."

"How did the reporter get involved?"

Gary was about to answer when he turned toward the sound of an ATV far in the distance. He started the bike. "Where to?"

"Let's get across the Amable."

Gary smiled. "So we're goin' to my place." He clicked the bike in gear and took off down the hill.

Their engine noise bounced back from the passing trees as they sped between the flaky trunks of the red pines. The route was dangerous and surreal and it was difficult to judge distance and time. They finally reached the highway and Gary drove to a place where the river was fairly wide and shallow. The four-wheeler stalled as they walked it through the rocky river, but it restarted on the other side. In fifteen minutes, they reached Bear Lake.

Gary stepped off the bike in a weedy clearing that had once contained a logging camp and Gary's home. "This is where I grew up."

Ken's head was still pounding and he was slightly disoriented. He sat on the bike and looked around. "Not much left of your home either."

"Nope." Gary studied him and then put his hands on his hips. "So, what the fuck is this all about?"

"What? The protest?" His thoughts drifted as he thought about it. What was this all about? He shrugged.

"I gotta tell ya," Gary said, " I came to put a stop to your little protest, but then I saw the opposition . . . you've got the government, businessmen, and police commandos trying to fry you. After I saw all that, I didn't think they needed any help from me."

"Nice to be popular."

Gary snickered. "Yeah, but what are you trying to do? You've got everyone pissed off and you're not making any points in the press."

Gary reached inside his green coat, pulled out some folded pages of newspapers and handed them to Ken. One page contained an article describing the five-year-plan as if it was a good thing for the area and then went on to offer some sympathetic support for Ken and the people of Kiosk, but in the way someone would side with someone who had unwittingly erred in their ways. There was little mention of the ideas that had sparked the protest.

The writer referred to the troubled reaction at the Ministry of Indian and Northern Affairs, and to the continued logging in Algonquin Park - something that might anger the logging conglomerates - but rather than deal with the resident's connection to land, she devoted a large section of the article to the fire. Was it arson? She tried to remain neutral, stating that it was an old mill with lots of dried wood, but that circumstances still were suspicious.

There was no mention of Indian land claims and no mention of the resident's land claim. Toward the end of the article, she predicted that it would be over soon because the protest was small and insignificant - almost unimportant. She used the phrase, "a handful of supporters." Damn, he thought, a large percentage of the living townspeople had shown up. Ken shook his head.

A second article focused entirely only on two issues. The inability of the police to find the fugitive and the "claims" that had been made by the residents of Kiosk about the origin of the fire. This article speculated that one of the logging conglomerates might have had the most to gain in burning the mill, because they wanted to protect their timber stands throughout the park. Getting rid of the mill would be a method of controlling public opinion. But the writer also suggested that perhaps a disgruntled employee had lit the match. After all, if one resident was now willing to lead the police on a wild goose-chase through the park, couldn't another have been willing to burn the mill twenty-five years ago? Again, there was not a single word about the people's right to the land.

"You don't look pleased," said Gary seeing the anger on Ken's face.

"I was hoping the press would focus on other things. The fire isn't important."

"So what is important?"

"The people's connection to the land. Their right to live where they were born, where their parents were born."

"Ha! That should be easy! The press is real interested in those kinds of things. Makes great headlines! Just think of how they report all Native issues. Do they report on the connection that Native people have to the land, or do they only write about violent protest?"

Ken suddenly felt deflated. He looked at the lake. It was dark and grey and had a quality that suggested an approaching storm. 'Even the water in the lake can teach you something,' the old woman had said. Ken looked up at Gary. "I have to find a way to make those issues as interesting as the fire."

Gary laughed. "You can't fight a battle in the press when the people you're fighting pay the advertising bills. You're screwed before you start. You've got some big enemies, the government, the logging industry, tourism operators, big business." Gary looked at him seriously. "Somebody don't want the press talking about that fire and they're gonna shut you down. Why is everyone so interested in it, anyways?"

Ken turned his head. "I don't know. Lotsa people think it was set."

"So? That was over twenty-five years ago!"

"People could have been killed. Maybe someone's worried that the truth will come out."

Gary walked to the front of his four-wheeler and placed his hands on the handlebars. "I think the best thing you can do is turn yourself in. You gotta fight from the inside . . . there's some serious opposition out there and you ain't getting the press you want." Gary studied him again. "What you're doin is not gonna end good. You know that don't you?"

Ken did not reply.

"What's really going on here?"

Ken shrugged. "I don't know."

Gary turned. "So, you don't know what you know and you're pissing off a bunch of powerful people who control some other powerful people with guns. What do you want?"

Ken looked down. "I'm not sure anymore. I thought I wanted the land back . . . and I just wanted to make people aware of what happened . . ." His voice trailed off and he shrugged. "Look, I don't want to talk about this right now." Suddenly, he looked up at Gary and his eyes brightened. "Hey! Does your mother live out here somewhere?"

"My mother? No."

"I met this woman . . . Catherine . . . I thought maybe you were related."

"Why? Is she a wagon-burner?" he asked, baiting Ken by using one of the derogatory terms for 'Native Canadian'.

Ken smiled. "No . . . Well, yes . . . but that's not why. You used to live here and she said she had a cabin. She's fairly old . . . old enough to be your mother." He held up his hand, folding in three fingers. "She's got a deformed hand. Looks like someone hit it with an axe . . . she's missing the tips of three fingers."

Something passed over Gary's face and then disappeared. "My mother's dead. Has been for a long time and she didn't have no deformed hand."

"She's a smart woman." Ken swung a leg over and sat sideways on the bike. "She said it didn't matter if you were Indian or not; a connection to the land is a connection to the land. She said the problem was with the way we lived in our society, both the Indians and Whites."

"She's right."

Ken studied Gary carefully. "Didn't think I'd hear you say that?"

"Why?"

"I don't know. You seemed pretty big on 'my people' and 'your people'."

"Well, maybe we all fall into old habits of speech." Gary walked over to a large boulder and leaned against it. "I see the good, but I also see the greed and dishonesty of some natives, just like anyone else."

"Hmmm." Ken nodded.

Gary pursed his lips. "You know what happened in the 1970's? At the same time your mill was burning? The government took a bunch of Natives and brought them to the city to train them. They taught them the ways of business. They figured that if they brought a few Indians into the modern age, these Indians would go back and change the reserves.

"They showed them how to be successful businessmen, how to manipulate, deceive, and use people. They taught them that success was more important than people were, that family meant nothing compared to money. Money is God.

"They weren't just teaching them about tactics and manoeuvres; they taught them a different way of looking at the world. They taught them that by being ruthless, they could get ahead. There had always been a few Natives who were greedy, but now the government was saying that greed and ruthlessness were good things - the accepted way to live.

"And now, to everyone's surprised these same people are making land claims - going after wealth and power. How do you think they learned to set up gambling casinos, and tobacco smuggling operations? The government taught them."

"How do you know this?" Ken asked.

"Cause I was one of the ones who was sent. I spent a year in Toronto learning how to be a success in business. I came back up north, did it for a while, and I hated myself."

Ken nodded. Catherine had been right. It was more than just the land. What had happened to him had happened to Gary as well. He stepped off the bike and felt his legs turn rubbery. "Yeah, that's a common problem - hating oneself." He smiled broadly. "But sometimes you just gotta stop and say enough is enough."

Gary studied Ken for a moment. "You're over your head. You know that, don't you? What do you think you're gonna do next?"

Ken started to see what he had to do. It was time to bring this to an end, but he had to do this dramatically. He looked at Gary and realised that there were very few other people in the north with whom he could have this same conversation. Earlier, he had been railing the Indians, but he felt very comfortable with Gary. He smiled. "Right now I'm standing here listening to you."

Gary shook his head. He was annoyed by the evasive reply. "What've you got planned?"

"I can't tell you that."

"Why's that?"

"Cause it involves listening to some things . . . some things that I used to listen to as a boy, but some things I've forgotten to listen to over the last years."

13.　　　　　In the Wind

Ray Smith stopped at Gagne's, a large general store in the last town before he reached Highway 630, and fuelled his car. When it was over, he thought, he would go straight home, no stops. He was so tired.

As he waited for the young female attendant to return with his change - he had paid cash to avoid a paper trail - he looked at his phone lying on the seat. It hadn't rung yet and maybe it wouldn't; maybe they would call it off. Absentmindedly, he turned his attention to a piece of paper swirling around in the parking lot. It moved and danced, controlled by forces much greater than itself.

He considered going into to the store for some food, but changed his mind. He looked up at the sky, which was dark and heavy and then saw the girl returning with his change. He took the money, threw it on the seat, powered up his window, and drove away.

At the turn off of Highway 630, he stopped in the parking lot of an outfitters' store. Although he'd been told to wait at the waterfalls, he decided this might look suspicious. It was going to rain soon and how many people stood in the rain watching a water-fall?

He spotted two people on the store veranda. They were chatting casually and one of them glanced in his direction. He drove away, and a few minutes later, pulled off on the hard-packed ground between the two single-lane-bridges and sat quietly in the car.

As he powered down the window, the rausching sound of the waterfall flooded into the car. It was a calming sound, like white noise and he started to relax. He had just laid his wrists on the wheel and closed his eyes, when a sharp sound startled him. All his muscles tensed as the telephone wailed for a second time. He grabbed the handset. "Yes . . ." His body slumped in the seat. "Yes," he said again, this time sounding deflated. He replaced the handset, and looked at his watch. He didn't have much time. A gust of wind blew raindrops across the front of his car. They hit hard, like a handful of pebbles. He shook his head, as if this would clear the fogginess, and then drove away.

Pat sat in the back of a large police van. He had been there for a long time. The OPP interrogator although not threatening, was firm and persistent. Pat told him nothing. Pat's strength of will was not unbendable; he truly knew nothing. He didn't know where Ken's caches were, he didn't know where Ken was, and he didn't know what Ken planned to do next. "I told you, I just met him to pick up the films. He left them for me at his cabin." There was no point in disclosing their various pre-arranged meeting places.

"Mr. James, this entire situation is out of control. People could be hurt . . . Ken Campbell could be hurt."

"You think I don't know that?" Pat narrowed his eyes. "But I can't tell you what I don't know!" This had been going on for far too long and his patience with authority was wearing thin.

"Sometimes we don't know what we know. Now let's go back to the day . . ."

Pat interrupted. "Let me ask you something. Where's Suzette - the woman who was with me at the cabin?"

The interrogator studied him for a moment. "The woman who led us to your camp?"

"What do you mean, 'led you to my camp'? Where is she now?" Pat asked impatiently.

The officer shrugged and then opened his mouth. "I don't know exactly, but at least she was worried enough about Mr. Campbell's safety to do something."

Pat looked at the officer for a moment. There was no sly smile, no condescension, but he couldn't believe that Suzette had betrayed Ken. Yes, she was in television, and she had something to gain if the story ended, but there was more to her than that. "So you're trying to make me believe that she deliberately brought you up to the camp?"

"I wasn't there and that's not a concern. Everyone here is just interested in bringing this whole situation to a peaceful end."

The officer's convoluted reply was proof that he had something to hide. Pat jumped to his feet. "This interview is over! I don't know what you're interested in, but you're twisting the truth. I'm finished here!"

The interviewer tried to remain calm but his face turned red. "You're finished when I say you're finished!"

Pat moved away. "I'd like to talk to Suzette now."

"I need some more information."

"I don't know anything." Pat sat down, folded his arms across his chest and crossed his feet. The officer asked another question and Pat looked at him sourly. "I told you. I don't know anything."

The officer sighed, exasperated. He stood and walked to the door. "Wait here."

Pat exhaled sharply and muttered, "do I have a choice?"

The officer left him. He had done this a few times, talked for a while, left and then came back with more questions.

In the quiet van, he listened to sound of rain beating on the roof. The night was turning nasty. Ken was out there alone, and the opposition was growing.

His thoughts turned to Suzette. Perhaps with her media connections, she might be able to help in ways they hadn't thought of yet. She did seem to have a lot of influence. This thought troubled him, because it suddenly made him realise that he had little influence in anything. He was just a salesman. Nothing. After this was all over, how could he and Suzy find anything in common? He felt drawn to her, but was he like a moth drawn to the flame of a candle? Something felt so right, but the doubt was growing in his mind. He was a low-life salesman from King City and he was just going to get hurt. Maybe it was time to cut his losses.

           Smith's Grand Marquis sailed past Burbot Lake and then through the tiny town of Eau Claire. The rain came in sheets, pelting the front of the car, as the sky darkened to multiple shades of taupe and grey.

           He hated being in this situation. It was ridiculous - something out of the movies. Why should he do this? He stopped on a long curve and pulled over to the gravel shoulder. What would happen if he turned around? He knew the answer. Mr. Jones was dangerous, but not as dangerous as the people for whom he worked. They could get reports from the police, they could adjust someone's credit, and they could eradicate someone's assets. They did not work for, or with the government. They controlled it. Ultimately, they pulled all the strings, big and small.

           People like Jones were ruthless because it was the only way they could be. Results and secrecy were all that mattered. Would he be allowed to talk? Would he even have a chance to talk? He knew the answer. Slowly, he took his foot off the brake and allowed the car to continue south.

           It took fifteen minutes to reach the spot. He knew it well. It was a side road that led to the Amable du Fond river just north of the town. Many of the townspeople had gone here to pick blueberries. He slowed as he approached, but he drove past. A vehicle was parked just far enough off the highway to allow another to stop. Smith executed a three-point turn and stopped behind the parked car.

           He walked out into the rain. The driver, who was thankfully alone, opened the window. "Nasty weather," he said. It was Armand Gingras, the man that Mr. Jones had pointed at in the picture.

           "I have something for you. Come with me."

           "What is it?"

           "You'll have to come and get it. It's important." Smith turned and walked back toward his car.

"It's pouring rain," protested Gingras as he got out of the car.

Smith walked toward his trunk, checking for approaching traffic. It was hard to hear in the rain, but there were no lights in either direction. The road seemed clear. When he opened the trunk, the lid blocked his view of Gingras. At the same time he ferreted around in the trunk with his left hand, he leaned to the side. Gingras was walking toward him.

He looked back in the trunk and picked up the pump action twelve-gauge, which sat on top of a plastic carrying case. He did not know if there was a round in the receiver, but he stepped to the side of the car and pulled the trigger. Nothing happened.

Gingras looked at him in disbelief. He stood frozen. "What do you think . . .?"

Quickly, Smith pumped the gun once and fired. The explosion was muffled in the rain, but the hit was no less deadly. The round caught Gingras directly in the chest and he flew backward off his feet and bounced on the ground. He flailed for a second, managing to roll to his side, but after a few short spasms, he lay still on the ground.

The kick of the shotgun had torn the weapon out of Smith's hands and it clattered to the ground as Gingras did his death dance in the gravel. Smith turned, picked up the gun and pumped it again. For good measure, he fired at Gingras a second time, hitting him just a little lower than the first shot. This turned the body so it was again on its back staring at the sky. Steam rose from the wound that was almost black. Smith retrieved the one shell, walked back to the trunk and dropped the shell and shotgun inside. He slammed the trunk lid with a thump.

Without looking at the dying man, he drove away. He turned up the heat, but his hand protested in pain. He looked at his fingers, which were starting to swell. It had been a long time since he had fired a shotgun and he had not shouldered it properly. It was true, he had killed a man before, but it had been a long time ago.

He was surprised that Mr. Jones had known about that, but he shouldn't have been. These people knew everything. They had knowledge and power. They had known how to reach Gingras and how to motivate him to show up for a meeting. They had known where Ken Campbell was last seen by the police and they had set up the meeting so that the first suspicion would be that Campbell had shot Gingras. They knew how to do everything - how to purchase a dying corporation for a song and then do what was necessary to make huge financial gains - whatever was necessary.

The tires of his car sang on the cold-top surface of the highway as he passed the Catholic cemetery. He looked over at the purple flowers that grew between the grey stones and then turned his head to see the old Catholic church. It was gone, replaced by a pottery store.

The twin bridges were just ahead and he slowed his car as he came around the sharp corner. He pulled off on the strip of land between the two single-lane bridges and looked over at the car that was parked on the opposite side. A man jumped out with two cups in his hands and ran over to the passenger side of his car. It was Jones.

He handed one of the cups to Smith. "I know I don't need to ask, but is it done?" He took a sip from his cup.

Smith nodded as he put the cup in the cup holder. His hand shook and he almost spilled the contents. Jones helped him.

"Good. As I told you, I'll take the gun and get rid of it. You just drive home and forget all about these people. When the police find Gingras, they'll bring in Campbell immediately and that will be the end of this protest. Then, no more questions." He drank another sip of coffee and looked at Smith. "Have some."

"No thanks, I'm already as taut as a tight rope."

Jones picked up the cup and handed it to him. "I put in a little brandy. I don't want you to have a nervous breakdown on your drive home."

Smith started to protest, but relented. He could smell the brandy and he took a long sip, feeling the warmth burn down his throat. It felt good.

"If anyone should ask if you were here today, don't lie. Say that you drove down to see some of the old townspeople, but you turned back when it started to rain. You're old and your arthritis bothers you in the rain. Understand?"

The wipers flapped back and forth as Smith nodded and took another drink. He was unaccustomed to alcohol and he could feel its calming effect. Ever since he had been diagnosed with high blood pressure, he drank only on rare occasions.

"It's time to go. Drink up." Smith finished his coffee and Jones handed him a candy. "Here, have a mint. Don't want you smelling like brandy." Smith popped the mint into his mouth as Jones opened the glove-box to hit the trunk release button. The trunk sprung open and Jones picked up the empty coffee cups and got out. He disappeared behind the car for a moment, slammed the trunk lid, and then stood beside the vehicle with the gun case in his hands.

"Bye, bye," Jones said as he waved. "It was nice knowing you."

Smith put the car in gear and drove away. He hoped he would never see that man again; he just wanted to get home and soak in the Jacuzzi.

The Global crew had set up an awning, and although it offered protection from the rain, it was loose and snapped in the wind. Suzy stood underneath cradling a plastic mug of hot coffee. The police had released her after she had made a fuss about being a television reporter and accused them of trying to suppress information. Standing beside her was someone she had not expected to see, her sister Denise. Denise had heard about the protest on the news and had flown in from Alberta.

After the mill fire in 1973, Denise had finished high school in Mattawa and then found a job in Kirkland Lake. She divorced her first husband, married a miner and moved out west. Over the last decade, she had only returned home for funerals, but she and Suzy had traded Christmas and birthday cards.

Contact with the rest of the family had been similar. Their two brothers, Andre and Gilles had also moved to different parts of the country and although they still travelled to Quebec from time to time, contact was minimal. The family had dissolved.

"I can't believe you're here," Suzy said. The news crew was setting up lights and they were in the way. Denise led Suzy closer to the trailer.

"I know." Denise grabbed her arms. "It feels so strange to

see all these people. And you, you look so good!"

Suzy smiled, but when a police officer walked by, the lines of concern returned. She had not had an opportunity to speak with Pat and she worried what the police were telling him. Would they imply that she had deliberately led the police to Ken - for a second time? She had gone to town and the police had followed, an accident, and she hoped that Pat would have enough faith in her to realise this - especially after last night.

"Where's Michelle?" Denise asked, bringing her from her thoughts.

"Back in Barrie," she said. "This is no place for a young girl."

"Why's that? We grew up here."

Kirk interrupted. "Suzy, I'm going to shoot a commentary, but I'd like to get you on camera as well. Is that okay?"

Suzy nodded. Denise seemed impressed and moved out of the way. The camera operator came out of the van and set up a tripod. It took only minutes to check balances, clip on microphones and adjust levels.

With the bright lights burning under the tarp, a few people gathered. The interview started and as Suzy answered Kirk's questions, she started to think of her job in Barrie. Many people would see this and it would put her in the centre of the controversy, a situation that could either be good or bad for her career.

Kirk asked her about local support and Suzy answered in a very logical, non-emotional fashion. She tried to sound composed and formal. Kirk asked about the police intervention, and she described some of the TRU's standard training.

"I understand that you were instrumental in leading the police to Ken Campbell," Kirk stated.

Suzy felt her face flush. In truth, she had been an unwitting stooge. This was not very complimentary. What should she say? She stammered: "This is a very complicated situation and I was concerned for Ken's safety."

"Horseshit!" someone called from the crowd.

Suzy stumbled for words and tried to regain her train of thought. What was she doing? Admitting that she had done what she had not done? Admitting that she had deliberately brought the police to Ken's camp. She looked at the faces of the gathered crown and saw much disapproval. She saw Patrick and in shame, she turned back to the camera. "Well . . . I didn't actually want to bring the police . . ." A few people left and Suzy turned to see Pat walking into the rain. Her leg muscles tightened as she fought the urge to run after him. The camera was still rolling. She turned to Kirk and mumbled something about the need for research into the tragedy of the destruction of Kiosk. He thanked her for her comments and she stepped out of the glare of the lights. She could not see Pat and she stood in the drizzle allowing the water to run across her face.

Ken watched Gary eat from the can of beans. The idea that was swirling in his head made him feel strange and even though he had consumed nothing other than Catherine's berries, he could not bring himself to eat. "I have to leave soon."

"Is it time to call it quits?" Gary said, wiping the rain from his face. "If you don't, someone's gonna get hurt you know."

Ken smiled, but did not answer immediately. "So you think I should just go back and turn myself in?"

Gary shrugged. "It's time."

"If I did that, it would all be over. You read what it said in the papers. This is just a handful of people with a grudge. No one's taking it seriously."

"That's why you go back and make them take you seriously. You've made your point. You can do more later."

Ken looked down at the ground. "You're right. This thing has to come to an end for me, but not be me giving myself up. If I did that, everything would be over."

"They're not gonna let you run away. There's too many police involved. It's better to give yourself up. That way you'll still be in the press getting support."

"No, it's time to take myself out of the equation."

"What're you talking about?"

Ken shook his head. "It's not my time."

"Time, time time! What are you talking about?"

"I don't belong to this fight anymore. It's time for me to be somewhere elsc."

"So what are you planning to do? Run away? Go hide some-where? You go through all of this and now you simply disappcar?"

Ken's eyes widened. "I'm not running away! I have to draw the attention of the media so that they'll look into things. My friend, Pat, knows what to do. First I'll turn up the heat, but the rest of this battle is not mine."

"What the fuck are you talking about?"

"Look, the press is only focussing on the fire and it's not important. It doesn't matter if someone burned the mill or if it caught fire accidentally. What is important is whether the people of the town have a right to the land on which they grew up, to the land that bore their parents. But people aren't seeing that; they are only looking for sensationalism."

"That's what I'm talking about! Tell them what's important."

"Even if I do, I'll just be at the centre of a circus. You know as well as I do that they're never gonna let me live here in Kiosk. And even if they did, I'm not sure I'd want to."

Gary protested, but it was feeble. "They might . . ."

"Come on! That's bullshit and you know it! The only hope is to open people's eyes!"

"And you've done that. And you can keep on . . ."

"So where would I go from here? Live in some apartment house and fight for animal rights? Become an environmentalist and fight to preserve the wilderness?"

"What's wrong with that? Someone has to protect the envi-ronment?"

"I don't wanna live like that! It's not a matter of being kind to animals, being responsible in the forest - it's a matter of being a part of the forest."

Gary's tone became slightly aggressive. "So now you think you're some animal? You sound like a fucking Indian! What are you? Running Wolf? Dancing Bear?"

"No," Ken laughed and placed his hand on Gary's arm. "Not some animal, just an animal. That's the connection to the land , , , being a part of it. It's a matter of giving up dominion over the for-est and its creatures." He turned his face to the sky. "I need to feel the rain, not protect myself from it. I need to feel the heat of the sun, the touch of the wind. I don't want to live in some city championing some cause."

Gary pursed his lips and shook his head.

"No matter what I do from this point on, if I stay here, I wouldn't be happy." His voice became quieter. "I know one thing. I couldn't live in a jail."

Gary started to protest and Ken cut him off. "I know it wouldn't be for long and I know I would have support, but I still would hate the wait, locked up. And even if the government did allow us to rebuild here, I would be the central figure in some cause that I don't really feel apart of. I'm not interested in causes. I did this to make a statement and I have to do one final thing to put an exclamation point to the entire protest."

The distant concussion of a shotgun blast echoed through the forest. The two men looked at each other. Neither spoke. A second shot sounded. "Maybe it is time to run away," Gary said.

Ken sighed. "It's time to do something. You want a ride back to the highway?"

"Where are you going?"

"It's time to get out, but before I do, I gotta tell a couple of people in town . . . maybe talk to one reporter."

"So . . . I'll go with you."

"You'll just slow me down."

Gary grinned. "I don't think so, old man. What? Are you gonna make a statement to the press and you don't want to be associated with some drunken Indian?"

Ken started to protest, but Gary cut him off, laughing. "Just kidding. You gotta learn to take yourself less seriously. It's funny, you know. You even think of yourself as prejudiced against natives, and yet you're probably the least prejudice guy I know. It's not natives you dislike, it's the whole bullshit politics. You gotta learn to respect yourself."

"Thanks. I appreciate that."

Gary grinned, "But I don't mind getting off the bike before you get to town. There's gonna be a lot of television cameras there and that's something I don't want to get involved with. I'll help you get across the river, and walk from there. You can take the bike." Gary paused for a moment, raised his eyebrows and looked at Ken.

"You are going back into town, aren't you?"

Ken nodded quickly. "Sure."

Gary climbed back on the machine. "If I were you, I wouldn't go by the main road. Cut through the bush and drive into town from the east. That way, you won't run into the police before you get to the media and the townspeople." Gary started the machine and noise filled the forest clearing.

"That's the way I was going." Ken said with a strange grin. "Actually, that was already part of my plan." He paused. "I want you to take something." He reached in his pocket, felt the roll of film and the crystal rock, and handed the film to Gary. Just in case something happens, I want to make sure this gets out. There are some great shots of the cops . . . should cause a stir." Gary nodded and slipped it in his pocket. "Sell it to the press. They'll pay for the pictures for sure."

Ken put his hand back in his pocket and felt the crystal - the magic crystal that might protect him from attacks. He hoped its magic was still good. He was going to need it.

Pat walked down to the shore. Most people were in the camping ground seeking shelter, but he wanted to be by himself. Sadness weighed him down like the rain that was soaking through his clothes.

The night was black and the waves broke over the rocks and the concrete boat launch throwing water into the air. Pat wiped his face and looked into the distance. How often had he played on this shore? How much of his life was tied up here? It didn't matter; that was gone now.

What was the point anyway, he asked himself? In the next few days, Suzy would return to her life and he would return to his apartment and a job he hated. They might meet a few times, perhaps spend a few nights together, but their lives would be on such different paths and at such different speeds that they would not stay connected. Eventually, she would find some excuse to cancel a meeting, then another, and finally she would tell him that she had met someone else.

Was there any point in going through all of that? It would

make more sense to break it off now. Their entire relationship was based on a short protest. Once it was over, so was the only common connection that they shared.

What could he ever do to hold on to her? What did he have to offer her? Even if the ultimate happened and he was allowed to build a house in the town of Kiosk, would Suzy come and live with him? Would she become a reporter for the Kiosk tribune newspaper? No.

He shuddered, hunkered down and wrapped his arms around his legs, feeling the wind pull at his clothes. He thought of the black waters by the town dam. He was caught in them and the emptiness, the hollowness, threatened to pull him under. There were no solutions, no roads to redemption, just a swirling turbulence of blackness.

The worst part of the sadness was the imminent loss, the loss of Suzy and the loss of Ken; and then he suddenly realised, it was happening again. It was the same as all those years ago. He was in the back seat of his dad's car being taken away from everything he cared about. He saw Suzy standing by the rec. centre asking him not to go and he pushed away the image. Before it became any more painful, he decided that it was time to leave . . . again.

He stood and with hot tears in his eyes, he looked at the black sky. The rain was heavy and it was not going to let up. He walked back to the camp and found almost no one outside. Some people sat in their cars, while other crowded in their tents and trailers. Only the police and a few souls in yellow rain coats braved the wind and rain. The press had packed up their equipment and were sitting in their vehicles deciding if there was any reason to stay. A number of vehicles had already left. The exodus had already started.

Pat felt tired. The sadness had drained him. He looked around, trying to spot Suzette, but she wasn't around. It was awful to think of losing her again, but did he have a choice? Had there ever been a choice?

A Chevy pickup truck started to back out of a parking space and came to an abrupt stop. A tan coloured car sped behind it and stopped at the police barricade. A man jumped out of the car and, oblivious to the rain, ran toward one of the rain-suited police offi-

cers. He frantically waved his arms in the air and pointed to the
north. The police responded quickly and in less than a minute, the
first police vehicle tore out of the lot with siren blaring and lights
flashing.

Loeffler's camper trailer was crowded and the air
heavy and oppressive. Denise and Suzy sat across from each other
at the foldout table.

"So you met up with your old boyfriend and had a romp in
the hay," Denise said. "Imagine that!"

Suzy exhaled in exasperation. "There was more to it than
that." She saw Denise's smile and then continued. "It's complicated. I don't really understand it . . . and I don't think I want to."

Denise pouted and shook her head. "So you start a relationship with an old boy friend, and then just when it's getting good,
you give up? Suzette, you haven't changed."

Suzy looked at her sister sharply and then looked away.
"You know, it's always so complicated. The police just followed me
there and he thinks I brought them. I was actually phoning Michelle
to tell her about him."

"Yeah. So you go back, the police follow and arrest him,
and then you're too proud to talk to him."

"Why is it always the woman's job to come and make things
right? He could have trusted me a little more."

"Yeah. So then you do an interview on television that he
sees and when you're asked if you brought the police, you say you
did. Now he jumps to a conclusion. Imagine that!" Her voice oozed
with sarcasm. "I can't imagine why he would react that way!"

Suzy looked down at the table and shrugged. "Yeah . . .
you're right."

"A relationship isn't a gift. It's something you have to work
at. If you love the guy, then you have to go out of your way." Denise
looked Suzy in the eye. "Sounds like you at least care a bit. Don't
you?"

She was silent for a moment. "I started to feel this connection. It was really great, but I don't know if it's love."

"What do you mean by 'a connection'?"

Suzy leaned close. "When we were . . . um . . . close . . . it was special."

Denise flung her hands up and laughed. "Sounds to me like you have it bad."

Suzy pouted.

Denise lowered her voice and placed her hand over Suzy's. "No, I think I understand what you mean. It's like me coming back here. It just seems as if I never left. There's just . . . something special."

Suzy sat up. "There are some people you feel connected to and some you don't. Have you ever met someone that you just couldn't get along with no matter how hard you tried?" Denise nodded. "And then there are others who just seem to be on the same wave-length as you. It's this whole connection thing. Pat talked to me about it. At one time, there was a connection shared by all the people of Kiosk. Not anything out of the ordinary, just a large group of people who shared lives . . . stories . . . backgrounds."

Denise looked around the trailer. "You know, that's how it was here. All these people stuck together, but then they all left." She looked down at her hands. "I left too . . . for my own reasons . . . but if I could've, I would've come back. I've never found that connection you're talking about since I left here."

"Never?"

"I think I found it with my kids, but even that seems to be weakening. It's sad really. The way this country works is that everyone has to move to get a job."

"I listened to my ex talk about Quebec Separatism, I listened to Papa talking about how wonderful my ex was - even though he always threatened me - and I watched our entire family move away. I've moved more times than I care to think about and the only thing I have left in my life is Michelle."

Denise looked around at the faces in the trailer and nodded. "I know what you mean about moving around. Stefan's job moves us all over the place. I no sooner get to know people than it's time to pack up and move. For a long time, it was fun - see new places, meet new people - but now I'd like to have some real friends in my life."

Suzy sighed.

Denise turned her head quickly. "So you came into town to tell your daughter about this romance? That was pretty brave. How'd she react?"

"Not bad. She's just a kid, but she was okay with it. In fact, she even said that she just wanted me to be happy." Suzy felt warmth pass through her when she said this. Her daughter was a great person. Another thought ran through her mind that took her completely by surprise. For the first time in a decade, she considered the possibility of having another child, a sibling for Michelle. It was only last year that she had seriously considered having her tubes tied.

Denise saw the change in Suzy's expression and she looked at her curiously. "What?"

Suzy shook her head. "Nothing. I was just thinking about how nice it was to be among friends and family. Now I sort of wish that Michelle was here."

"You're not glad to get away?"

Suzy laughed. "Well, there's that. But I've been getting away from everyone for a long time." She looked back in the trailer and wished she could talk to Pat.

"You're thinking about him again, aren't you?"

"Who?"

"Pat."

Suzy smiled, but didn't answer.

"You know, you're gonna hafta make the effort."

"Excuse me," said Mr. Loeffler. "I wasn't purposely eavesdropping, but I am aware of the situation with you and Patrick."

Suzy looked up. Her eyes widened.

"Your sister is a smart woman. I think you have to make an effort to put things right."

"It's not that I don't want to, but I think it may be too late. Maybe it's better to walk away."

"'Tis better to have fought and lost, than never to have fought at all."

Suzy looked at Denise, lost for words.

"What I'm saying," said Loeffler, "is that that it will be a difficult thing to fight, but even so, worthwhile."

"He's right," Denise said. "It's really up to you."

Outside, the sound of sirens erupted and conversation ceased. Suzy stood and walked out the door of the trailer.

After they crossed the river, Gary drove across a small field, through some blueberry bushes and forced the ATV up the incline to the road. He climbed off the machine. "You take it from here."

Ken slid forward. "You sure you're gonna be okay?"

"Yeah." Something attracted Gary's attention and he looked down the road.

Ken followed his glance and saw the flashing lights of police vehicles, then he looked in the other direction. A car was abandoned at the side of the road. It didn't make sense at first and then he saw the body and remembered the shot. He turned again. The police vehicles were coming fast.

"Get outta here!" Gary shouted. "Now!"

Ken gunned the machine and lurched part of the way across the road. The engine backfired and stalled. Without power, it came to a quick stop.

"Come on! Go! Go! Go!"

Ken pulled at the choke and pressed the starter. The metallic whine was dry and raspy. He looked desperately at Gary who had moved to the middle of the road as a kind of roadblock. He readjusted the choke and tried again, once and then a second time. Nothing. His fingers shook as he grabbed at the choke and then reached for the button again. The engine ground, but not so dryly and then it caught.

Ken dropped into the seat, pushed the accelerator and felt the thrust as the machine lurched ahead. He knew there was no way the ATV could outrun the cruisers on the pavement and he had to get into the forest, but the ditches were just too deep and he couldn't take a chance. He flew past the abandoned car and looked back. The police truck had stopped, but the cruiser had not. The volume of the siren increased as the cruiser closed the distance between itself and the ATV.

Up ahead, he could see a bush road cutting into the forest, but it was too far away. He leaned forward and pushed hard on the throttle. A sudden jolt caused his machine to jump and swerve right and left. The cruiser had hit him and he was losing speed quickly. He jammed his thumb back on the throttle.

The wet pavement was slippery and Ken saw the cruiser's headlights swing back and forth. The car was fishtailling wildly behind him. Then the car's engine roared as the driver powered his way back to control. Ken knew the cruiser was about to hit him again and if he wound up in the ditch, it was over.

He drove off the pavement onto the gravel shoulder and the ATV bounced up and down on the rough terrain. He hoped this would cause the police to back off, but the tactic worked only for a few seconds. The cruiser pulled up beside him.

Lights flashed brightly as the car moved closer, ostensibly to force him off the highway, and then he reached the trail to the right. He turned hard, forcing the ATV onto two wheels, and then leaned to stop the machine from rolling. If he fell now, the police would be on him in seconds. He flattened his turn, barely missing the trees on the side of the trail, and tore up a hill into the woods.

The siren passed, the frequency changing as it did. He had a few seconds to power the machine up the rough road and the engine strained. He was gaining ground, but the siren returned. It was back behind him and growing louder. He looked over his shoulder and saw that the cruiser was trying to follow him up the rough bush road. He leaned forward and pushed the throttle all the way.

Behind him, he could hear the grinding of metal as the undercarriage of the cruiser ground over rocks. Finally, there was a loud bang and he turned to see steam rising from the hood of the car that was jammed into a tree. He relaxed a little as he felt the machine pull his weight up to the top of the hill. It wouldn't matter if the ATV broke down now. He might not outrun a cruiser, but he could definitely outrun one of these officers.

Fewer people were outside than Suzy had expected. The sirens had split the night air, attracting attention, but the rain had kept most people inside. Heads poked out of tents and swaths of yellow light spilled across the camping ground. As she walked toward the police vehicles, Suzy saw Patrick and a few other men. Pat's hands were at his sides and he was shouting. "What's going on!" he demanded.

"Just move along!" the officer shouted into the wind.

A few people surged forward and a second officer grabbed one of the townspeople by the arm. This provoked two loggers, who crowded the cops. A voice squealed over a loudspeaker. "Calm down! Calm down! No one's getting hurt!"

Movement ceased and in that split second, Suzy saw Patrick look in her direction. He was a distance away and his expression was difficult to read. There was a weak smile and then he squinted and turned away.

The conflict suddenly lost importance. Pat was giving up on her. She had seen it in his eyes. Whatever connection they had was waning. Why? Why would he give up on her so quickly?

She wanted to walk over to him and grab him by the arm - shake him - but something prevented her. Was it pride, anger, fear of rejection? She wasn't sure. Maybe it was time to go home. This wasn't her story, and maybe this wasn't her future.

One of the loggers shouted something in French and a police officer raised his baton. Townspeople moved toward the police and the drone of the rain was broken by the harsh metallic sound of a voice over a loud speaker. "Move back!" The crowd inched forward and the situation was ready to explode, but the OPP official who had been talking to the interrogator outside of the van, waved his hand at waist height, palm facing the ground, and the police moved back just a little. The townspeople halted and the tension dropped a little.

Suzy spotted Pat again. His face was twisted with anger as he yelled at the police. This was not the time for reconciliation. Maybe it was time to go home. She turned and walked toward her car.

The loudspeaker squeaked again. "We need you people to clear the area immediately!"

The cell phone in her purse rang. Francine Roussel fished it out and said hello. Very few people had this number and she was surprised to hear the voice of an official at Luegenhauser. "I just wanted to let you know that the police have found your senior aide, Armand Gingras, dead on the side of the road."

Roussel's jaw dropped. "What?"

"The police just found him."

"A traffic accident?"

"He was shot."

Roussel blinked, held the phone away, and thought for a moment. "How?"

"Details aren't yet available, but suspicion is that it was that protester, Ken Campbell. He and an Indian were seen in the area."

"Jeesus! I can't believe it." There was silence on the other end of the line. "Well, thank you for letting me know."

"Madame Roussel."

"Yes."

"I think it might be appropriate to put a little pressure on the police to bring this guy in."

She thought for a moment and then replied indignantly. "A Federal Cabinet Minister does not call a Provincial Police Force and apply pressure."

"Well then, perhaps a few discrete calls to the appropriate people are in order."

She was quiet for another moment. "Yes . . . well . . . thank you for your call."

"Au revoir."

She hung up the phone and placed it back in her bag. She picked up the desk phone and dialled.

The warm air from the dash vents blew onto Ray Smith's face, but would not dry the sweat that clung to his skin. He wiped his arm across his forehead for the sixth time. Tension was an awful thing, he thought, it tied his stomach in knots, made him sweat and caused his heart to beat fast. He would be glad to get home.

The large car sailed from lane to lane as he worked his way through another section of construction. There was a push to four-lane this single northbound highway and every year, a little more construction was completed. Concrete 'C' rails lined the temporary route that twisted back and forth, on what would one day be a four-lane highway.

He had a sudden urge to go to the bathroom and he cursed, because he knew there were no service stations for a long distance. A sharp pain hit his chest and he jerked forward. "Damn!" he cried, holding his chest. The pain radiated down his side and into his left arm and felt like the steel jaws of a vice grabbing him, squeezing the air out of his lungs.

Heart attack, he thought, Damned! In panic he tried to plan his next course of action, how to get out of this dangerous situation. He knew Jones had taken the gun, but had he taken the empty shell? He could barely move, but if he stopped and the police towed his vehicle, would they find the spent shell? Did he have enough strength to ditch the bullet and then drive on? A memory floated to the surface. Jones had said, "You're the only one left from the town who knows what happened." He shook his head, angry at his stupidity. It had never been about Armand. Killing Armand had only been a bonus. It was him they were after - the last person alive who knew what happened.

Another sharp pain stabbed through his chest and pushed at every muscle. Through clenched teeth, he cried out as his legs straightened and his right foot rammed the gas to the floor. The car lurched off the grooved pavement, rocked slightly as it ploughed over some fresh gravel and then imploded in a violent stop as it dug its way into the end of a 'C' rail. The front of the car folded like tissue paper and inside, even with the airbag, the violent grab of the seatbelt broke three of Smith's ribs. The rear of the car bounced back to the ground and Smith fell forward into the folds of the deflated air bag, his heart quiet in his chest.

In the trunk, the loaded, and recently fired, shotgun fell back onto the carpeted trunk floor. When the police found the car, they would call this an improperly stored firearm and it would start an investigation, but it would take a couple of days before any link was made to the shooting in Kiosk - more than enough time to end the protest with swift police action.

Watching the tall pines was disorientating. The wind

moved them like blades of grass and Ken had to keep his eyes on the ground ahead. As he wove among the trunks, the forest took on a surreal quality; it writhed and twisted around his passing machine, as if it were seeking a way to grab him.

The four-wheeler lurched over a rock and then came to a stop against a fallen log. He backed up and looked for another route. The wind howled and cried in the coarse needles of the pines and he felt a horripilation of dread travel down his neck and back. He gunned the machine, dirt flying up in a rooster tail, and skirted the fallen log.

The trunks of the pines were swaying crazily and the movement was mesmerizing. Why didn't they break? How could something so solid, move so much? He looked to the side for a moment and when he looked back, he was heading directly for a large red pine. He jammed the footbrake, turned sharply and bounced off the side. Skidding around in a circle, he came to a stop in the soft layer of needles.

After taking three deep breaths, he climbed off the machine and stood on the dark black earth that had been exposed by his skidding tires. He needed to regain control of his senses. The mental fogginess that had followed him since this morning was threatening to cause an accident. It was time to focus.

He closed his eyes for a moment and tried to slow his thoughts into a liquid line instead of the flashes that were going off in his brain. If he didn't gain control, he would not be able to do what he wanted to do. Standing with his feet apart and his hands at his side, he breathed deeply, drawing in the air, feeling it flow into his lungs and then into his blood. He took another breath and this time, as he exhaled, he raised his hands to shoulder height and then slowly lowered them, palms facing down. His right foot moved to the side and then he turned as his one hand pushed forward as the other moved down. He then stepped forward with his left foot as he reversed the position of his arms, his fingers splayed.

His mind drifted back to the police and the conflict, but he forced himself to remain focussed on the movement, on his breathing. He needed to become centred and the regimentation of a set of exercises was the best tool. He continued in his movements until he was isolated from everything and then, slowly, he allowed the world to seep back in.

Another image filled his head. It was dark water surging around him, enveloping him. Then flashing lights over his head. There was a feeling of danger and a feeling of safety. He breathed again and washed away the image, the sensations.

He felt stronger and he decided to return slowly to the moment. The words of the old woman echoed in his head. 'Praying, meditating, seeking a vision, resting, thinking; they's all the same thing. You know part of it. You know that there is more to life than what you can see, what you can hear, touch.' It was true. He had a connection to the forest, to the lakes and he could not give it up.

He walked over to a thick red pine and placed both hands on its bark. He could feel the movement of the tree - its flexibility, its life. He looked up. It moved against the dark sky filtering the driving torrent and turning it into simple rain. The tree was part of the forest, just as he too was now part of the forest.

It was time to bring this to an end. He walked back to the ATV, put it in gear, and drove across the soft forest floor. In twenty minutes, he reached the trail that would eventually take him to the campground. From there he would execute his plan.

Away from the protection of the canopy, he was again exposed to the full force of the weather. The wind drove the rain sideways and pushed the small plants to the ground. He could feel it pushing the moulded fibreglass body of the bike and he toed the machine into a lower gear. He was hungry, tired, and ready for all of this to come to an end.

The trail forked and Ken turned to the left, knowing this would take him to the upper end of the camping ground. When he reached the old rail bed, he would follow it back to the top of the parking lot and then put his plan into action. It would be fun to see the reaction of the press and the people.

This section of trail had obviously been out of use for years and it was overgrown. He forced the ATV over one and two-year-old trees, which bent under the weight of the machine, and powered his way forward. When he came to the raised rail bed, he dropped into second gear, climbed the embankment, and turned toward town. On the flat surface, which only a few years ago had contained railroad tracks, he stopped suddenly. He was staring at two men in full military gear pointing assault rifles. One of the men raised his weapon to his shoulder.

"Shit!" he said under his breath. He froze. The way back to town was blocked. What should he do? He could not get past these two, armed men.

He studied them quickly, looking for any advantage. Their faces were covered. There were no eyes, just coloured lenses, and without thinking, Ken slid his thumb upward and turned on the headlights. The men reacted, moving back. He hit the throttle as he pulled on the handlebars and the ATV spun around one-hundred-and-eighty degrees as the tires dug into the slag.

"Shit! Shit! Shit!" he swore as his machine tore away in the wrong direction. He had been so confident in his plan and now it was all going to hell. The air behind him erupted with sharp concussive burps and slag by his right leg exploded into fragments. Something hot stung his face and as his hand rose up in the air, his bike swerved back and forth. More shots exploded, and instinctively he ducked, but there was no more pain, no further impact.

The track veered toward the lake and he looked over his shoulder to see if he was out of the line of sight of the two men. His thoughts raced. Why had they fired? He looked over his shoulder and saw the plastic gun case attached to the ATV sticking up in the air like a flag. They had assumed he was armed. He buried himself into the seat and jammed his thumb against the throttle. He heard a loud thumping sound off to the right.

The storm was a violent force now and the cabin cruiser banged noisily against the dock in the angry waves of Kioshkokwi Lake. Only one officer was on board because it was unlikely the boat would leave the shore again tonight. Water ripped off the tips of the waves and slapped against the hull.

Details of the shooting on the highway had leaked and rumours were spreading. There was a collective concern about Ken's well-being and, since the flurry of police activity, many more people were back outside in the rain.

Suzy first heard about the shooting as she stood beside her car. She dropped down into the driver's seat and sat while a concerned woman stood above her with an umbrella. What was going on? It was all spiralling out of control.

Was it Ken on the road? This thought made her weak and dizzy. Then the woman said that the person had been found next to their car and Suzy realised it couldn't have been Ken. He didn't have a car. She told the woman this and the woman speculated that it may have just been an accident with one of the onlookers. With all these guns, and all these tempers around, accidents were bound to happen.

Yes, bad things were bound to happen, she thought to herself as the woman talked. She either had to leave, or she had to find a way to take the danger out of this situation. It was out of control and she couldn't leave. Not just for Ken's sake, not just for Pat's sake, but for hers.

As she walked back toward the police van, Suzy saw Pat shouting at a policewoman. His face was contorted and angry. She was surprised by his determination. He had shied away from conflict with authority figures when she had first met him and now he was aggressive and demanding. She decided to act as a buffer. She took his arm. "Pat," she said. "I need to talk to you."

He stopped, turned and looked at her. "Sure," his tone was softer. "But this isn't a great time."

Suzy stepped back. This was too complicated. She studied Pat and fought the urge to walk away. "No. We have to do this, now."

"What is it?" His tone was cold.

She paused for a moment, looking for something in his eyes. "I know how it looks . . . but I didn't betray you or Ken."

"Didn't you?"

"No!" Her nostrils flared.

Pat put his hand up. "I know you didn't bring the police to the camp. I figured they followed you."

"That's exactly what happened." Suzy tilted her head slightly. "I don't understand. Why are you acting so distant?"

"I saw your interview. When that old guy asked you if you had brought the police, you didn't say no, even though you had the chance."

"Well . . . I . . ."

"I understand," Pat said interrupting. "It's your job. You have responsibilities, but as I listened, I realised something. Who we are is now so defined by what we do that we can't escape it. Given the choice of either a media person or of a supporter of Ken, you chose the media person."

"I was being stupid." After she said this, she paused and then shook her head. "I was being incredibly stupid. I thought that important people were listening, but I didn't stop to think that some-one who is really important to me was listening."

Pat smiled. "Thank you for that. Really. But you know, the whole thing made me think that soon . . . very soon . . . this protest is going to be over and you're gonna go back to your job and I'm gonna go back to mine."

"So! What does that have to do with anything?"

"A lot. I'm not proud of who I've become. And I don't think there's really any place for me in the world of a television news per-sonality."

"That's horseshit! It really is! I think you're trying to make an excuse. There's something else, isn't there?"

Pat looked down at the ground. "No, nothing else."

Suzy exhaled forcefully, throwing the anger away. She touched Pat's arm lightly. "Pat," she said softly, "the important thing is, that I think I'm falling in love with you. And that's more impor-tant than anything."

Pat looked up quickly, catching her eyes. Suzy couldn't tell if it was the rain or the sadness, but his eyes swam in moisture. Suddenly, she was in his arms. Her lips met his and she could feel the warmth of his cheek on her face.

Everything disappeared, the rain, the other people, the police, the parking lot. The kiss, the contact was all that existed. But then, there was a loud, deep, staccato sound - the burst of an assault rifle. She moved away from Pat. There was a second burst.

Pat's eyes widened. "What was that?"

In the distance, they heard the deep beating sound of a rotor. "What's going on?" asked Suzy.

They both looked up as a helicopter flew overhead.

Jessica held the Astar in a hover at thirty-five metres

and danced its spotlight across the shiny black highway. It was only early evening, but the dark clouds were thick and visibility was poor. She watched as OPP officers moved busily around a body covered with a white tarp.

The wind and the rain were making the cyclic feel stiff in her hands and she considered the repercussions of turning back to North Bay. Ultimately, the safety of the helicopter was her responsibility, and it was her call, but the Incident Commander, the I.C., was a powerful officer and seemed determined to stop the suspect who was apparently on an ATV. Even though the wind was below 30 knots, sudden gusts could prove dangerous at low altitudes, but the I.C. was insisting that she try to track the suspect. She had found the disabled cruiser, but there had been no sign of the ATV. The suspect was obviously driving with his lights off and it would be necessary to hover just over the trees to find him. With the wind, poor light and the driving rain, it was just too dangerous.

She keyed the intercom and spoke to the two officers in the back of the chopper. "I think we're heading back. The weather's too unstable." The VHF radio crackled and another voice broke through the headset. It was the I.C. telling her that the suspect had been spotted heading toward the land bridge that crossed the lake. The suspect was to be prevented from crossing at all costs. The I.C. gave her coordinates.

She sighed and punched the coordinates into the GPS system, even though she didn't really need them. She knew the bridge. The AS350 had a range of 400 miles and she had flown over Kiosk before. She would be there in minutes, but she was troubled by the idea of putting down on a land bridge. If it were too dangerous, she would hover and call for additional instructions.

The chopper swooped across the water and Jessica spotted the bridge through the windscreen. It was a straight path of gravel and rock, about a kilometre long, crossing the lake from north to south. It was about fifteen-metres wide, which was more than wide enough, but there were telephone poles on the east side. Wind and wires, she thought, a dangerous combination.

She reached the middle of the bridge and turned to the north. She could see the light of the ATV as it bounced onto the bridge. 'He did have lights on,' she thought, and she dropped to 30

metres, turned on the spot, and moved slowly forward. The idea
was to intimidate the rider with loud noise and the bright light. She
only had to get him to turn back so that ground forces could arrest
him. She hit the avionics switch that turned on the loudhailer, and
ordered the man to stop.

The driver did not seem intimidated and the ATV never
slowed. It went right through the rotor wash and Jessica pulled
back, turned over the water, and flew to the middle of the bridge.
She would not use the helicopter as a barricade - even an ATV
could do serious damage to the bird - but she could drop one or two
officers in the path.

Normally she would have touched down facing the oncoming vehicle - that way she could watch him approach - but she did-
n't want her tail rotor too close to the lines. She decided to touch
down perpendicular to the oncoming vehicle and leave the tail
hanging over the water to the west.

As she descended, a gust of wind caused the chopper to
sway and one side of the gear hit the rocky surface. The chopper
bounced up and rocked and she had to fight the cyclic to regain
control. She looked down and to the side and saw she was out of
time. The officers seated behind her had thrown open their doors,
but it was too close. "Hang on!" she shouted, "We're going up!" She
would, under no circumstances risk a collision. She lifted up and
back as the ATV skirted around the front of the chopper and continued down the bridge.

As Kenny accelerated, he saw the helicopter
approaching from his right. It was headed to a spot in front of him
and he suddenly realised what it was going to do. It intended to
block his passage and the troops behind him would cut off his
escape. He would be trapped on the long land bridge over the lake.

The cold dark waves smashed into the rocks and water was
thrown up in the air. It was colder here than it was among the trees
but the darkness swirled around him like a blanket. He could not
turn off, could not turn back, so he had to push on.

The helicopter was ahead of him now, speeding toward him.
He was in a tunnel of electricity, its light blinding, and its noise

deafening. It was difficult to tell how far the helicopter was above the ground. Surely they wouldn't endanger his life, he thought. The rain was illuminated by the spotlight and turned into a silver swords driving toward him, glistening. He couldn't see where he was going and he knew if he swerved, he would careen off into the lake and likely drown. He was simply too far from shore.

He knew the lake was out there, a blackness of water that was both cold and deep. How many people had given their lives to Kioshkokwi, the Lake of Gulls? Could he survive the depths? Then suddenly he realised what he must now do. It was not his plan, but it had been handed to him.

The pounding noise was so loud that it reverberated in his body, but then suddenly, it whooshed overhead. Kenny found himself in the darkness again. He realised that he had decelerated and he pushed the throttle to regain speed. The helicopter was swinging around.

He stood on the pedals and looked into the distance. The south shore was still a long way away, but he could hear the sound of the water again. He could feel the wind, sense the clouds. The helicopter was off to his right, flying out over the water trying to circle in front of him, but it was not as threatening as it had been.

The helicopter was in front of him again, but this time it was not attacking as it had done earlier. Instead, it seemed to be landing. He couldn't let them land. He had to go faster. He had to pass the machine. If they landed, he was done. He jerked his body forward, throwing his weight, trying to squeeze every bit of speed out of the machine. "Come on! Come on!" he shouted into the wind.

It was difficult to see in the rain, but it looked like a door opened. Someone was going to get out. The thumb-operated gas lever bent as he pushed harder, but there was no more speed to be had. He sped straight toward the helicopter, using the same tactic that they had tried to use on him. He wanted them to think he was going to ram them. His bouncing light sparkled and shone on the helicopter's body as he approached.

He knew he had to veer around the bird, but he wanted to leave it till the last second. He had to prevent them from jumping out. Unexpectedly the bird wobbled side-to-side and Ken saw the huge disk of the rotors come closer to the ground. If they hit him, he realised, he would be sliced like a tomato in a powerful fan.

Holding his breath, he passed underneath for a second time and continued toward the south shore. There was electricity in the air, he could taste it, feel it prickling his skin, but as he entered the darkness on the other side, he could see what he had to do. He looked at the distance. It was closer, but it was still too far.

The helicopter was behind him now, its spotlight lighting the way. He listened. He could hear the water over the sound of his screaming engine, and the thump of the rotor. To his side he saw the whitecaps, churning and folding together like the froth of rapidly boiling water. He thought he heard a woman's voice call to him, but he dismissed this.

A shot exploded behind him and he jerked. The sound was oddly hollow as it emerged from the sound of the rotor wash, but he knew it represented great danger. He hadn't expected this. He did not think they would fire again. Every time he formulated a new plan, something happened to jeopardise it.

He looked quickly toward the end of the bridge, the south shore. How far was it? It was difficult to tell because the light from the helicopter's spot was illuminating the area just in front of him. If he was going to act, he would have to do so soon. He was running out of options.

Jessica gained altitude, turned and looked at the two officers in the back. They both had their doors open and did not know what to expect. She keyed the VHF radio for instructions. "It's no longer possible to block the suspect," she said into the microphone. She was already matching speed with the ATV when she heard the command to disable it and not let it cross the bridge.

Rain was being driven into the cabin. "What's up?" shouted the marksman on the right side of the chopper.

"Disable the vehicle!" she said, "Do not let it cross!" Quickly she shouted a warning into the loudhailer, but she knew she was wasting her time. The storm had become so violent that she doubted the man on the ATV would hear her.

The marksman placed one knee on the floor and pointed his weapon out the door. The helicopter jumped and the barrel of his gun went up and down in the air. "I can't shoot in this!" No one was listening. He shook his head as he wrapped the gun strap around his forearm.

Jessica moved the chopper lower and just to the left of the ATV. She tried to match its speed and keep the light on the suspect as she fought with the cyclic to hold everything steady. The wind and rain pounded the bird and telephone poles zipped by underneath. She knew if she were forced down, it would be over. "Take the shot!" she yelled. She just wanted to get some altitude and get out of here.

The first round popped and she saw it explode just behind the moving ATV. "Fuck!" she heard over the intercom. A gust of wind slammed the bird and the cyclic was pulled out of her hands. For a split-second, she felt as if she were in an elevator going down. "Shit!" she screamed. She grabbed control frantically, feeling the bird tilt, and her thoughts raced to the marksman near the open door. He better be strapped, she thought. There was another loud pop, but she was no longer looking out the window. The tail rotor roared in protest as the back of the machine whipped one way and then the other. She stabilized flight and looked back at the ATV. It was heading off on an angle toward the water. 'Christ,' she thought, 'had they shot the guy?' The ATV hit a ridge of dirt and then became airborne as it flew out over the lake. Out of the corner of her eye, she saw the man and the machine moving away from each other, but her sight was drawn to the lights of the machine. It hit the water and rolled end over end - red, white, red, white - then it hit a big wave and it stopped suddenly. The light became diffuse and foggy as the machine started to sink.

The voice of the officer in back burst through her headphones, distorted, angry. "Fuck! Fuck! Fuck!"

The helicopter was still moving toward the south shore and she turned away from the bridge and circled. "Suspect has been hit!" she said into her headset. "Repeat! Suspect has been hit!" The spotlight swept the surface. She saw the ATV between two waves, and then she lost it. She hovered, moving the spotlight frantically. The light was bad and the water looked black underneath the foamy whitecaps. Then she saw the driver trying to fight the waves.

"Drop a ladder!" she yelled and then tried to swing over the man in the water. He was gone. She swung around and found him again, but he disappeared in another swell of waves. She increased her elevation so that her spotlight would cover a larger area, but the rain was so heavy that it reflected the light like a thousand tiny mirrors.

"I think he's over to the right!" yelled one of the officers in the back.

The bird bounced right and left. "Time to get out of here!" she said into the intercom.

"Hang on!" shouted the shooter. "We gotta find him!"

Against her better judgement she hovered, feeling the wind fight with her for control. She didn't see the man in the water and she dropped further. She didn't know if she was hit by a wave, if the ladder was in the water, or the wind pulled through the open door, but suddenly the helicopter tilted a full 30 degrees. In seconds the rotor blades would hit the waves and the bird would crash.

Suddenly the bird dropped and its feet were in the water. Jessica's breath caught and her eyes widened. She pushed forward and for a microsecond, the engine was no match for the power of the wind and the suction of the water. Jessica looked sideways. The next wave would take them down and she worked her feet and hands frantically. With a jerk, they broke free and regained a few feet of altitude. If that happened again, she thought, she would slice the guy in the water with the rotors and bring down the bird. It was the first time in all her years of flying that she had panicked and she was not sure how she prevented the crash, but it was a sign that she should not be here. She looked down and saw the puddle of water at her feet.

She climbed to a hundred metres, feeling the tail rotor compete with the vicious gusts of wind. Autorotate, she thought. She was too high to see anything on the surface and she hovered trying to decide if she should drop down again. A rip of wind took the bird sideways and forced it down toward the water. She saw the rocky side of the bridge and remembered the wires. She fought the cyclic and then became disoriented as the bird swung around in a complete circle. The centrifugal force was so strong that it moved her off her seat.

She regained altitudes and searched the waves, but she was

too high. The spotlight caught the heavy rain and turned it into a silver shaft.

The lights of vehicles could be seen coming across the bridge and she could see the lights of an approaching boat. The bird dropped again and then twisted to the left. "Shit!" she said again trying to keep control. "We're going back!"

"No!" shouted the shooter in the back.

"A boat's coming in!" She could feel the wind tearing at the machine. It was well over 35 knots and it would be worse at higher altitudes. "And we'll be in the water, if we don't get out of here!" She was suddenly angry with herself for feeling the need to explain her actions. The safety of the machine was her responsibility. She took one last look, saw nothing and turned toward North Bay. As she flew over the shore, she reported to the I.C. that she was clearing the area. It was their show now.

Only a few people heard the automatic weapon fire, but those who did, started yelling into tents and trailers. People poured out into the driving rain. The helicopter focussed everyone's attention and within a couple of minutes, the shore was congested with people. The crowd watched as the helicopter flew with its spotlight along the one-mile bridge.

Two more police vehicles tore out of the campground and other emergency vehicles passed the parking lot on the old rail bed. Pat grabbed Suzy's hand and ran out to the point. Together they saw the light of the ATV drive under the hovering helicopter. The helicopter swung further back along the bridge.

A news crew hurriedly set up a betacam on the shore, as people ran back and forth craning their necks to see what was going on at the bridge. The helicopter had tried to put down, but was now back up in the air. In the distance, they could see the receding red taillight of the ATV.

Pat smiled because the ATV was ahead of the helicopter and it looked like it was going to get away. Then his heart stopped when he saw the two bright bursts in the air. Suddenly the red light of the ATV was replaced by white light as the bike flew off the bridge. The light changed to red, white, red, and white and then disappeared. He realised that the ATV had rolled end over end.

"Holy shit!" He was holding Suzy's hand way too tight. "They've shot him!" He looked at her face and saw the terror there. "Come on!" He let go of her hand and ran to the cabin cruiser. He grabbed the railing and yelled to the figure inside. "You've gotta get out there!"

A police officer came out on deck and looked at Pat. "Get away from the boat," he ordered.

"Get your fucking boat out on the water! My friend just went in!"

The officer seemed angered by Pat's tone and he jumped onto the shore aggressively as he shouted: "What did you say?"

Pat grabbed the heavy officer and pushed back toward the boat. "Don't fuck around! There's someone drowning in the water!"

The officer was picking himself up as two other officers ran past. "Let's go!" shouted one as his feet hit the deck. A third officer pushed Pat out of the way as she untied the lines.

The engine growled and the smell of fuel permeated the damp air. The boat gurgled for a moment and then dug deeply into the lake as it sped away toward the lights on the bridge.

Suzy and Pat stood exposed to the black rain, which drove sideways. The wind tore at their clothes as they watched lights flash and move in crazy patterns in the distance. The helicopter continued to circle, the boat bobbed and the lights from the land bridge moved back and forth. The intricate ballet of light and sound continued for a long time, but no-one thought of leaving.

It was difficult to tell if they had found Ken. There was so much rain that it obscured their vision, creating dancing swirling patterns of reds, whites and blues. Then, surprisingly, the helicopter turned off its spotlight and moved back toward the town, its strobe light growing in intensity as it approached. Was it giving up? Had they found Ken? The lights on the shore, and those on the boat, continued to sweep the water as the helicopter flew over their heads.

Rain washed down Suzy's hair and over her face. "Is he still in the water?"

"I don't know. I can't see."

The movement of people in front of bright headlights

caused the lights to appear to flash on and off. Everyone's attention was focussed on the blackness of the lake, but nothing seemed to be happening. The boat just bobbed around like a float on a fishing line.

The wind blew the rain sideways, stinging Pat's face. "What are they doing?" No one answered.

"What's happening?" asked an older woman, hair hanging in her eyes.

"Someone check with the police," Pat said.

A young man ran up to the shore. "I just came back from the bridge!" he said. "The police have it blocked and they wouldn't let anyone past!" His yellow rain slicker snapped in the wind like a flag.

"If they've shot him," said Mr. Laconteur, a retired mill mechanic. "We'll make 'em pay."

"Let's get out of this," Suzy said, taking his arm.

Pat resisted, but then looked at the waves hitting the shore. They slapped the rocks viciously. In the distance, he could see vehicles moving back off the bridge. He could do nothing from here; he could see nothing from here.

A large group of people had gathered at Loeffler's trailer. They were jammed inside, but more stood outside in the rain holding ponchos and plastic sheets over their heads. A young couple moved aside so that Pat and Suzy could get by.

A woman poured Suzy and Pat a cup of tea. Suzy sipped hers, but Pat leaned against the counter and put his down without drinking a sip. Water dripped from his hair onto the ground. Suzy tried to dry her hair with the damp towel and then she ran it over Pat's head. Pat seemed not to notice.

The young man with the yellow slicker burst into the doorway. "They say they can't find him," he said breathlessly. "They're still looking, but they can't find him."

Annette Dupuis, who had been sitting at the back of the trailer, near the large windows, looked out toward the lake. "Holy shit!" she said. "Those bastards! If they shot him and he's gone into the lake, the lake will take him forever."

The room became silent as everyone pondered this. "We don't even know if he went into the lake," said Mr. Loeffler finally.

Tirj, water still dripping from his hair, put down his beer and spoke. "I was trying to watch through my binoculars. Couldn't see much, but I saw a headlight spin off the bridge and hit the water."

"Did you see him after that?" Mr. Loeffler asked.

Tirj grimaced. "No, but I'm sure he hit the water." The room was silent and Tirj tried to be more positive. "My glasses were wet from the rain," he added. "Maybe I'm wrong."

No one spoke for a long while. The silence was only broken by the pounding rain on the roof of the trailer. It came in waves, pushed by the wind. Suzy drank her tea and wrapped her arm in Pat's. He held onto her tightly. She looked up and saw Denise at the back of the trailer. She saw Denise's eyes; they were warm.

A few hushed and quiet conversations were interrupted when Gary burst into the trailer. Everyone looked at the intruder. He was a mess. His old coat was dirty and wet and his long hair looked like coiled snakes on his face. "They told me I'd find you here," he said speaking to Pat.

Patrick took a minute to identify the man as the same fellow who had rescued Ken from the police near the cabin. His eyes lit up as he grabbed Gary's hand. "How are you? What happened on the trail? How's Ken?" His questions came quickly, with enthusiasm, as if he expected to hear good news.

"Slow down, there, fellow," Gary said.

Everyone in the trailer was staring, attentive.

"This is the guy who got Ken away from the police," Pat said. Faces lit up.

"I got him away once, but not the second time. I don't think things went well."

"What happened?" asked a woman who had been sitting quietly at the table.

Gary told everyone about the man who had been shot in the road, and how the police found him and Ken at the scene, how he had stayed behind while Ken tried to reach the northeast end of the town. "The police tried to hold me for questioning. The stupid bastards didn't even realise that they'd chased me earlier on the four-wheeler." Gary leaned closer to Pat and said: "It's a good thing I had my get-out-of-jail-free card."

Pat looked at Gary with a puzzled expression.

"You know," Gary said, "my Indian band card."

Pat's eyebrows raised and he was about to ask what Gary knew about the incident on the bridge, when Maggie Perrault put her head in the door. Water dripped from her face. "The police are saying that Kenny didn't survive the accident. They're searching the shore, but only as a formality." She looked down at the floor. "I'm sorry."

Gary looked at her and wiped his face with his hand. "Is that what they're calling it? An accident?"

"Those were their words," Maggie said.

"Well, I guess we have to put it in our words," Suzy said to Maggie.

"Jeesus Christ!" said Gary. "He's only protesting land rights and they execute him? What kind of justice is that?"

Tirj looked at his wife and noticed the tears. "We won't stop," he said. He banged his fist on the wall. "Those fucking bastards are gonna pay!"

Pat was surprised not only by the anger in Tirj's voice, but the way his face twisted with rage. Revenge was burning him from the inside. Then he looked at the other people in the trailer. Some had tears on their cheeks, some looked furtively from face to face, some were angry, and some were frightened, but all were touched in some way.

Mr. Loeffler seemed the most affected. He looked as if he felt guilty and Pat wondered if he felt responsible. One day he would have to read the books that Loeffler had given him and Ken so many years ago.

"Yeah, Tirj," Pat said finally. "We'll make them pay." He was silent for a moment. "But we won't do it here. If we're gonna make them pay, we have to fight different battles now. Outside is a police force that believes its actions are justified and correct, but they're not the ones who set the policy. I'm not afraid of them anymore, but we won't change that here by fighting with them. They're following the rules. If we want to accomplish anything, we have to change the rules. We have to change the way people think."

"We can't change nothing," said the quiet woman at the table. "Nobody gives a damn about us and we don't have any power."

Pat was silent for a moment and then he added: "We have one thing that we have all forgotten about. We have each other."

"It won't do us any good. We're nobody."

"Maybe by ourselves we're nobodies," Patrick said, "a car salesman, a logger, a clerk. But collectively we were a town, a community, and together we had a connection to this place that was stronger than most people even understand. We are just as important as anyone else and together, we are a force to be reckoned with."

Suzette took Patrick's hand and held it tightly.

Pat, Suzy and Michelle were ushered into the small living room. The air was cool, but dusty. The sunlight streaming through the picture window created a large band of gold through the middle of the room.

"It's good to see you again," Gary said. "I'm glad you came." He introduced his wife, Pierrette.

"Can I get you anything?" Pierrette said, holding out her own mug to show that she was referring to coffee or tea.

"Whatever you're having," Suzy said.

Pierrette nodded and walked into the kitchen.

Gary watched Michelle as she studied the various small sculptures that decorated the room. She gently touched a carved rock that had two feathers drilled into it. Although simple, it looked very much like a gull in flight.

"I've been making things like that all winter," Gary said. "You can pick them up. They won't break."

Michelle lifted a small intricate bone carving and turned it in her hand. "This is really nice."

"You like it?"

"Yes."

"Then it's yours. Please, take it as my gift."

"Thanks." Michelle held the sculpture gingerly and walked over to look at the buffalo head on the wall.

"One day, I'll explain the four points of the circle to you," he said.

Michelle nodded self-consciously.

Suzy explained that she and Pat were looking to buy some property between North Bay and Mattawa. They had been together since last fall and she had found a job with MCTV in North Bay. Pat had left his job in sales and was working for the Citizen's Action Group fighting for political reform. They both knew about Gary's work in Canadian human rights and were anxious to meet with him when he requested this meeting.

Pierrette returned with tea. Gary took his cup and studied Pat. Pat hadn't said much and seemed uncomfortable. "It's amazing, how much change Ken brought about with a truck load of two-by-fours and a couple of canoes."

Patrick nodded, but looked down at the floor without replying.

"A woman who thought she would be the next Prime Minister is out of politics, and the police still haven't got the egg off their faces."

Pat smiled. "And you're heading a committee on Canadian citizen rights. Five years ago, you probably would have laughed at the idea."

"I suppose so."

Pat didn't speak again. Gary continued. "You know who is really involved in all of this? That old teacher from Kiosk, Mr. Loeffler."

"I can believe that. I think he was always a bit of a rebel."

"Of course it didn't hurt that all of the former residents put their support behind the committee. I just hope we can count on your assistance when you move here."

Pat nodded.

Gary suddenly realised that Pat still hadn't come to terms with what had happened to Ken. He put his cup down and said suddenly, "Did I ever tell you about the woman with the deformed hand?"

"No," Suzy said.

"It's kind of interesting. When I ran into Ken in the bush, he told me that he met this old woman. He called her Catherine. It's not out of the question to meet an old person walking in the bush, but something Ken said really stuck in my mind. He said that this woman had three of her fingers chopped short, as if someone had hit her hand with an axe. When I got back to Mattawa, I talked to this old woman named Imaqua. She told me that old Amable Du Fond's mother was named Catherine and this Catherine was missing the tips of three fingers on one hand."

"And?"

"Amable was an Indian who lived on Lake Manitou back in the 1860's. The Amable du Fond River is named after him. His mother would have been a hundred years old by the 1890's. She would be long dead."

The room was silent. Then Michelle spoke. "So, she was a ghost?"

"I don't know . . . that's for sure . . . but it's pretty strange, eh?"

Michelle nodded.

"It's too bad that Ken didn't live to tell us more about this woman," Suzy said. Her voice cracked as she spoke.

"It's too bad he didn't see the results of his protest," added Pat.

"Yes," Gary said, looking down at the floor while exhaling loudly.

Pierrette entered the conversation. "Did anyone ever find out why Ray Smith shot that Gingras fellow?"

"No." Pat said, "It never came out. He died of a heart attack, but it was his shotgun that killed Gingras. Some people said it was because of the burning in effigy out on the water, but that had nothing to do with Armand. I've always thought there was more to it than that."

"And the police were cleared in Ken's shooting?" Pierrette asked.

"Yeah, another bugbear. The courts called it an accidental shooting."

"And they never found his body?" Her question seemed strange to Pat. It was as if she knew something but wasn't yet ready to reveal it.

Pat played along. "Kioshkokwi is a very deep lake and there are some nasty undercurrents. Other people have drowned in the lake and never came up."

Pierrette looked at Pat cautiously. "But don't bodies rise

after awhile?"

"There were thousands of logs floated across that lake and there are many at its bottom. Something could get lodged in . . ."

"There something you don't know," Gary said, interrupting his wife and Patrick. He looked at Suzy and then at Pat. "I'm going to tell you something that I haven't told anyone else," he looked at his wife, "with the exception of Pierrette. And I think it's best you don't tell anyone either." He paused for a moment. "As you know, I have an Indian Band card and it allows me to go all through Algonquin Park on my ATV." He drank a sip of tea. "Before the snow fell last winter," he continued, "I drove all through the park. I went up and down every road I could find, but it wasn't there. See, there was one thing that everyone seemed to forget."

"What?" Suzy said expectantly, her eyebrows knitted together.

"Ken's truck. The MNR had chased him into the park in his truck, but then they never found it. I looked everywhere around Manitou Lake, but never found a clue. Then, one day, I was on an old logging trail below Kioshkokwi Lake and I found some of the stuff that Ken must have had in his first cabin, but," he paused for a second, "no truck. I made some discrete inquiries and as far as I could tell the police or the MNR have never found it. But someone moved it."

"So, you're saying . . ." Pat stopped himself, as if mouthing the words might make them untrue.

"Ken talked to me about God's Lake. It's up on the border of Ontario and Manitoba. He said it was like Kiosk was many years ago. God's Lake . . . Manitou Lake? I don't know, but it's a possibility."

Eight years later, a young boy walked with his family across the land bridge on Lake Kioshkokwi. The slag was now covered in sand and the telephone poles were gone, but the rocky sides still dropped quickly into the deep blackness of the depths. The boy climbed down to the rocks, picked up a large stone, and tossed it into the water. He was pleased by the loud plop that it made.

"Kenny," his mom said. "Don't get too close to the edge. I don't want you to fall in."

"Sure, mom."

It was a beautiful day; crickets chirped, a few white clouds drifted across the blue sky, and the wind played gently with the surface of the lake. Kenny could taste the sweetness of the air on his lips. He loved being outdoors. His family lived in the country, but not out in the open like this. He loved Kiosk, with its deep forests and blue water and he wished he could live here.

He picked up a flat rock and looked at his dad, who had been unusually quiet all day. "I'll bet I can get more skips than you can," he said.

His dad scrabbled down to the edge of the water, selected a rock and nodded to Kenny.

Kenny looked up at his older sister. She smiled as she watched him. He turned and threw the rock. It skipped four or five times.

Kenny's Dad threw next, but his rock went too high. Instead of skipping, it plopped into the depths.

"I think you better practice a little," said Michelle.

Kenny looked at his sister. She was okay, even for a girl, thought Kenny. He turned to see the reaction on his father's face and was surprised to see that he was looking up into the sky. Kenny followed his gaze and saw that he was watching a lone seagull circling over the lake, looking down at the water.

"Lake of Gulls," his father said softly.

Kenny shrugged, walked a little further to find another flat stone - a good one for his dad - when something caught his eye. He knelt and picked it up. At first, he thought it was a tooth, but on closer inspection, he saw it was a crystal rock. It looked neat and felt good in his palm. He slipped it into his pocket and continued to explore the shore.

The End.

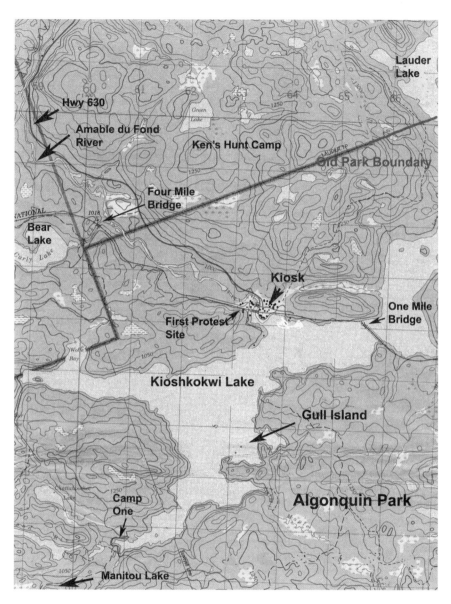

Northern Algonquin Park
the location of the ghost town of Kiosk, Ontario.